Moon Over Humboldt

A Novel By

Jim Hight

Black Rose Writing | Texas

First printing

ISBN: 978-1-68513-462-4
PUBLISHED BY BLACK ROSE WRITING
www.blackrosewriting.com

Printed in the United States of America
Suggested Retail Price (SRP) $23.95

Moon Over Humboldt is printed in Georgia Pro

*As a planet-friendly publisher, Black Rose Writing does its best to eliminate unnecessary waste to reduce paper usage and energy costs, while never compromising the reading experience. As a result, the final word count vs. page count may not meet common expectations.

PRAISE FOR
MOON OVER HUMBOLDT

"An emotional tale full of love, anger, regret, and the other things that make us human. The story brought me to tears."
–Brian Kaufman, author of *A Persistent Echo*

"A stunning heart-tugging debut—Hight paints a setting reminiscent of Richard Powers' *The Overstory* while weaving a tale of addiction as crushing as David Sheff's *Beautiful Boy!*"
–Cam Torrens, author of *False Summit*

"Jimbo, I used to like you, but now that you've managed to make me get all choked up and cry, I'm not so sure about that."
–Mike Hess, Humboldt County logger

"I've never read fiction about the 12 steps that didn't sound like bullshit. This is no bullshit—100% on the money."
–Aaron C., Bay Area teacher

"I was a forest defender for years in the Pacific Northwest. Jim Hight gets both the excitement and dysfunction of our movement right, and he depicts timber workers with grace and insight."
–Patrick Oliver, zoology and biology teacher, Pleasanton, California

"This is a beautiful book about how men love each other—and how they hurt and misunderstand each other. Bill and Jonah are both men we'd like to stereotype, yet Jim Hight does a magnificent job bringing them to life."
–Rachel Eve Moulton, novelist and short story writer, author of *The Insatiable Volt Sisters*

For Eugene Wilson

Moon
Over
Humboldt

Chapter 1

The rain had stopped, but the wind shook the tree canopy, and thick raindrops splashed on Jonah's head. In the light of his headlamp, he saw a muddy stream flowing across the road. It was too wide to jump, so he sloshed through it, feeling his shoes fill with water.

"Hold up," Buzzy yelled from behind. Jonah stopped and waited. Buzzy bent over and rested his hands on his knees, catching his breath. When he stood up, he asked, "How much farther?"

"Not sure," said Jonah, wiping snot from his face with a wet sleeve. "Where's Alder?"

"Dunno. Somewhere back there." They looked down the road. After a minute, a light appeared.

When Alder reached them, he said, "Had to take a shit." He looked at his watch. "A little after four. We better keep moving. No telling when those sons of bitches will show up."

"Any idea how far we got to go?" asked Buzzy.

"Mile, mile and a half. Why? You getting tired?"

Buzzy said, "Hell yeah. Aren't you?"

Alder shook his head and continued up the road.

On the map, their route had looked like an easy three-mile hike. But they hadn't factored in the rain, mud, lack of sleep, and the weight of their backpacks filled with climbing gear, water, and food.

•　　•　　•

Bill's alarm jolted him awake. He hit the snooze button and lay back down, trying to remember his dream about a late summer day by the river. Kenny and Denise played in the shallow water while Cheri read a book. Bill had sensed danger in the ice-cold river, and he argued with Cheri about letting the kids wade over their knees.

The alarm shrieked again, and Bill swung himself out of bed, walked to the bathroom and splashed water on his face.

He started the coffee machine, then opened the front door to feel the day. A light wind blew up from the gulch, and the rain had stopped. Too bad, he thought. Nearly Thanksgiving and the first big storm had only dropped a half-inch. Another dry winter would be murder for the fish.

Bill was drinking his second cup of decaf when he heard a truck idling out front. He put on his jacket and cap, grabbed his lunch and phone and walked out to the street.

"Hey, Bill. How are 'ya?" asked the driver, a burly man in his early thirties with a thick red beard.

"Not bad, Eric. You?"

"Great, man. Looking forward to wrapping up this job today. And getting paid."

"Yep, we should get 'er done today."

As they rode through the sleeping town of Eureka, dawn's first hint glimmered over the hills to the east. Soon, they left the houses and streetlights behind, and the road took them down through a dense grove of trees and into a wide valley. A half-moon hung above the fields and pastures.

"Too bad the rain didn't keep up longer," Bill said.

Eric scowled. "I wouldn't mind if it held off a few more weeks—keep the season going. Shit, it's a good thing we're done with all the falling up there and just got yarding and loading to do."

· · ·

Jonah's shoulders had gone numb from the backpack straps. He needed a rest, so he pointed his flashlight at the forest above the road bank, looking for a spot to shelter out of the rain. But the terrain was too dense with trees, ferns, and brambles.

In a few minutes, the road started to level off. Alder was in the lead, and Jonah heard him say, "I think we're here."

Jonah saw a landing where big yellow machines with massive tires squatted in the mud next to long pyramids of dead trees. The scene made him want to puke.

Buzzy arrived and leaned against a pile of logs. Jonah perched himself next to Buzzy—too tired to talk. Then Jonah noticed something odd about the logs they sat on—they were too thin to be old growth.

"What the fuck?" he heard Alder yell from the edge of the landing. He and Buzzy struggled over to Alder and followed his gaze down a steep slope. In the moonlight, they saw a landscape of fallen trees and limbs. "We're too late," Jonah said.

Alder's eyes narrowed. "Maybe not."

· · ·

While Eric slalomed up the muddy road, Bill held tight to the grab-handle and braced himself with his left hand against the dash. He considered asking him to slow down, but Eric loved speed and knew the road like his own backyard.

"Muddier than I thought it'd be after that paltry half-inch," said Bill.

"They keep it in good shape, though," Eric replied as he sped out of a corner. "Rock it every few years, keep the ditches and culverts clear. They got to—otherwise Fish and Game would be all up in their shit."

"Must've missed that one," Bill said. The truck headlights illuminated a brown stream crossing the road from the inboard ditch. Bill expected Eric to slow down, but instead, he sped up.

"Yee-haw!" Eric yelled as muddy water exploded onto the truck's windshield. His rear end fishtailed as the tires cleared the stream, and Eric eased off the accelerator to regain traction. "No charge for the roller coaster ride."

Thank God testosterone declines with age, Bill thought.

•   •   •

At first, Jonah thought Alder was joking. But then he saw him get out a knife. "No way, man," Jonah said urgently. "You know we don't do monkey wrenching."

"Who the fuck says?" Alder barked, fiddling with a hydraulic line on one of the machines.

"Uh, like, everybody in the group, man," countered Jonah. "You know that as well as I do."

Alder shook his head with disgust, gripped the line with his left hand and began sawing at it with his knife. "Gotta stop these motherfuckers somehow."

Jonah heard a truck engine. Then he saw headlights bounce around the landing. A truck was bearing down on them. Jonah ran for the hillside, feeling his backpack smash up and down on his back.

"You better run, you punk-ass bitches!" yelled a male voice.

Jonah scrambled over a maze of logs and slash down the clearcut slope, dimly aware that Alder was ahead and Buzzy just behind. His wet pants stuck to his legs, and pitch from the freshly cut timber pasted his fingers together. A bright light fell on them from above, and Jonah saw a man coming after them.

Alder veered away from the clearcut slope and into the forest. Jonah followed. After dodging trees and pushing through thorny shrubs for several minutes, they stopped to catch their breath. Jonah heard a bird singing in the dawn. From farther away, he heard angry voices.

"I think they've given up chasing us," he said.

"Probably," agreed Alder.

Buzzy had taken off his backpack and lay panting on the wet forest floor.

• • •

After calling 9-1-1, Bill put his phone away and examined the vandalized grapple with Eric and a truck driver named Ernie, who'd just arrived. Oily fluid dripped from a severed hydraulic line.

"Dumb-ass punks," said Eric. "This won't take long to fix."

Bill went to Eric's truck, got a bucket and placed it under the grapple to catch the oil. Ernie asked, "You got replacement lines here, or should one of us go into town?"

"I doubt we got one here, but I'll look." Bill walked around the site to find a toolbox or something that might contain spare parts. After a minute, he spotted a muddy backpack leaning against a pile of logs. He took it to show the others.

"Let's see what's in it," said Eric.

"Not sure, but I think that's evidence," said Bill. "We ought to wait for the sheriff's deputy to get here."

• • •

As the trio rested, their perilous situation became clear to Jonah. They'd planned for Alder to climb a tree at the edge of the logging site and set himself up in the canopy. Buzzy and Jonah would hike out before the loggers arrived, gather more troops and supplies, and return to support Alder. Their goal was to stop the chainsaws until the annual ban on logging during the wet season started.

But they hadn't thought through their exit strategy, Jonah realized. If they'd walked out by the road, they would have risked being spotted by loggers coming to work. And now, after Alder had disabled the loader, getting caught might mean taking a beating before the cops showed up to take them to jail.

He thought about when he'd first met Alder at a public hearing in Eureka. The company that owned this land was spinning lies about how clearcutting wouldn't hurt the frogs and the salmon nor cause flooding downstream. Jonah was disgusted and about to leave when Alder started chanting: "No More Clear Cuts! No More Clear Cuts!"

Jonah and other young activists stood and joined the chant.

At the front of the meeting hall, company reps and state officials fiddled with their laptops and papers. One got on the phone, probably calling the cops. Alder led the group outside, and they stood in the rain and chanted.

He'd seemed like a natural leader. But Jonah realized—too late—that the man was reckless and arrogant. Then he noticed that Alder's backpack wasn't nearby.

"Where's your pack, dude?"

Alder looked away. "Must've left it."

Jonah said nothing. He heard the distant squawk of a police scanner.

• • •

The responding deputy was Bill's friend, Steve. "Looks like the monkey-wrench gang paid you all a visit," he said as they shook hands.

"More like the Marx Brothers," said Bill. "Didn't do anything that we can't fix pretty quick. Just cut a hydraulic line. And they left this." Bill showed Steve the backpack.

Steve smiled. "Let's see what we got here." He took the backpack to his cruiser, set it down on the ground and opened the trunk. With the three men gathered around, he unpacked the contents: a coil of thick climbing rope, a nylon bag clinking with carabiners, a gallon jug of water, and two plastic bags full of nutrition bars.

"How many were there?" Steve asked.

"Three," said Bill.

"Looks like they were planning to do a tree-sit," said the deputy.

"Total fuck-ups," said Eric with contempt. "We were done cutting a couple days ago." Eric pointed at the crane-like yarder with cables running down the slope from its boom. "Today is supposed to be our last day yarding and loading."

Another log truck drove onto the site, with the crew boss behind the wheel. He had spare hydraulic lines in his cab, so within a half-hour, they'd fixed the loader and got to work.

•   •   •

In the lead, Alder strode easily through the thick forest without the burden of his backpack. Jonah's head buzzed with irritation at Alder—and at himself for not packing spare socks and a scarf for this long trek through the damp hills around Humboldt Bay.

They wandered into a narrow gully and were perched on a cliff above a dry creek bed when they agreed to take a break. As soon as Jonah had taken off his heavy pack and sat on the damp ground, he noticed the mid-morning sun streaming down through the canopy.

But instead of sitting, Alder walked to the cliff's edge and looked around. "I thought if we just kept the creek on our left, we'd end up at the road," he said. "But now we've lost the creek, and I think we're getting farther away from the road. We should head back up a ways and try to find the creek."

•   •   •

To make up for lost time, the loggers worked through lunch. In the yarder's small cab, Bill wolfed down a sandwich and apple between gulps of coffee while operating the controls. An OSHA inspector might disapprove, but after running yarders for a couple decades, Bill could work them in his sleep.

After eating, he took a break to pee. Then he stood behind the yarder, arched his back, and inhaled as he brought his arms up over his head. He exhaled and bent forward until his fingers dangled inches above his boots. Getting looser, he thought.

"You practicing for Madam Butterfly, Bill?" said the crew boss as he walked by with Eric.

"Yeah, see if you can find your balls while you're down there," added Eric.

Let them laugh, Bill thought. His dad had got so crippled by the time he retired that he had to use a grabber to pick up the newspaper. Logging would do that to you.

•   •   •

As the afternoon warmed up, Jonah stripped down to his T-shirt. That cooled him off, but exposed his bare arms to scrapes and scratches as he struggled through the dense forest. Alder was so far ahead that Jonah could barely see him. Behind him, he heard Buzzy plodding along.

Then Jonah heard a motor vehicle, which meant they were close to the road. In a few more minutes, he emerged from the forest, so tired he wanted to lie down and nap on the grass by the side of the road.

Buzzy emerged from the trees, looking even more spent than Jonah. "Just a little farther to the car," Jonah said. Buzzy smiled weakly, and they walked single file on the narrow shoulder.

Alder was leaning on Buzzy's old green Subaru, a smug grin on his face. "We pulled it off, fellas." He raised a fist. "Couldn't save those trees, but we threw a wrench into the machine. It'll cost them plenty to get that monster fixed."

Jonah was about to object when Buzzy said, "Damn straight." He bumped Alder's fist. "By any means necessary."

"No compromise in defense of Mother Earth," Alder said proudly.

They loaded their packs into the hatchback and began the drive back to town. Sitting in the back, Jonah felt confused and anxious. He agreed with the "no compromise" philosophy and thought it was a crime to slaughter ancient redwoods. But they should have discussed a Plan B after discovering the logging was all done. Instead, Alder took over. And after seeing the skinny logs piled on the landing, Jonah doubted the loggers had cut down any old-growth trees.

Thinking about the yellow log loader that Alder mangled, Jonah remembered another big yellow machine. He was sitting in the cab on his father's lap. His legs couldn't reach the foot pedals, but his dad let him play with the sticks and levers. "Vroom, vroom," said Daddy, bouncing Jonah on his thighs.

The building site was quiet and empty, but Jonah imagined he and his dad were piloting the excavator around the dirt and the concrete foundations. Daddy pointed ahead. "Okay, Jonah. We gotta dig up those big boulders right there. Think you can do it?"

"Pull out that joint, bro," Jonah heard Buzzy say to Alder. He glanced back at Jonah. "Sorry, man. I know you're trying to quit, but I really need to get high."

"It's cool, man," said Jonah, feeling far from cool. He hadn't smoked for three days and planned to stay off weed through Thanksgiving when he'd visit his mother and brother in the Bay Area.

Alder lit the joint, hit it and passed it to Buzzy. The pungent aroma filled Jonah with longing, and before he could stop himself, he put his hand forward. "I'll take a hit.

Buzzy hesitated, then passed the joint. Jonah filled his lungs and held the joint until he was ready for a second hit. As he handed it back, he felt the familiar warm pressure in his face. His thoughts sped up, and the landscape of pastures and forests outside his window brightened.

As they passed the crossroads marking the Arcata city limits, the farms and fields gave way to the college town Jonah had fallen in love with when he'd arrived from San José six months earlier. There were no six-lane roads and strip malls here. People decorated their homes with Buddhist prayer flags and planted their front yards with vegetable gardens. And it seemed like every VW camper van on the West Coast had gathered here for a convention in 1975 and never left.

They arrived at the town's central plaza, lush with damp grass. Parents chatted over their strollers, panhandlers held cardboard signs asking for money, clumps of young people lounged on blankets, beating drums and playing guitars, drinkers hid their bottles, and weed dealers tried to look casual.

Buzzy pulled up in front of a café. "Guess we'll have plenty to report at that meeting tomorrow."

"Damn straight," replied Alder.

Looking over his shoulder, Buzzy asked, "You want to get some food before we head up to camp?"

"Think I'm going to hang out here for a while." Jonah grabbed his pack and opened the door. "See you tonight."

Jonah felt cold, disoriented, and hungry as the sun sank behind a fog bank. If it were still fall harvest season, Jonah would have had enough cash to spend $15 or $20 on a hot dinner at a restaurant, then linger with a paperback or a magazine while his clothes dried on his skin. But now he was down to less than $150. So, he walked to the Co-op supermarket and bought bread, cheese, and a ripe avocado—and loaded up on free packets of salt, pepper, mayo, and mustard.

Back at the plaza, he made himself a sandwich and devoured it while listening to a man nearby singing Sublime's "What I Got" in a strong voice. Bar patrons gathered outside along Ninth Street and smoked cigarettes on the sidewalk. And on the corner, a young couple waved a sign at passing cars—"Stranded, need gas $."

Jonah usually loved this downtown Arcata scene, but he couldn't relax and enjoy himself because he was too upset by the botched forest action—the bad intel about old-growth trees being logged, Alder's arrogance, and Buzzy's support for what Alder had done.

•　　•　　•

When the logging crew knocked off for the day, Bill felt tired but satisfied with the day's work. Despite the vandalism, they'd pushed through and sent every last log to the mill.

After careening down the logging road, Eric steered toward the plaza—even though it wasn't on the way to the auto shop where Bill's truck was ready to be picked up. "Look at those lazy fucks," he said as he drove slowly by the busy grass quadrangle. "Why bother working when you can just beg money from the stupid liberals?"

"They work," said Bill, pointing at a couple on the corner holding a sign. "They had to find a marker and some cardboard, then write the sign. Probably took 'em half the day."

Eric laughed and banged on the dashboard. As he passed the panhandling couple, he yelled out the window, "Go back to Berkeley, you pussies!"

At the auto shop, Bill said, "Thanks for the ride," and shook Eric's hand. After he got out of the truck, Eric asked through the open window, "I don't suppose you've heard anything from Kenny?"

Bill's throat tightened. "Not since last spring."

Eric looked away and drummed his fingers on the steering wheel. "I heard something about him the other day. From Jerry, Ernie Miller's son."

Bill wanted to know, and he didn't want to know. "And?"

"Nothing good, sorry to say. He ran into Kenny at a meth dealer's house over on Green Street."

Thinking about Kenny was too painful, so Bill focused on the other character in this anecdote. "Yeah, I heard the Miller kid was into meth and booze. Weren't you working with him on that job up Maple Creek?"

Eric frowned. "Not all of us are so damned picky about what people do in their spare time. As long as he shows up on the job sober, I got no problem."

"It's your funeral. You remember what happened to old Skelly White?" With his right hand, Bill karate-chopped his left elbow. "Lost half his arm because his yarder driver was stoned."

"I ain't going to let Jerry run no yarder—even if I had one," Eric said. Then he added, "Want to go surf fishing sometime?"

"Kinda early, I think. Maybe in a few weeks."

Eric laughed. "Well, it's not like you're gonna catch anything."

Bill's mood lightened with the teasing. "Yeah. Be good to get the waders out early. Maybe up on the Klamath? Invite Jim for some eeling?"

"Definitely too early for that. Guess we'll see. Talk to you soon."

"Yep." Bill tapped on the roof and went to get his truck.

Chapter 2

Bill held a miniature logging truck, sanding the top of its cab. He blew off sawdust, held it up to the light, turned it over and spun the wheels. After setting it on the workbench, he attached two trailers loaded with sticks, and pushed it through a wide turn.

It was done—the tiny version of the 1958 Peterbilt that Bill's father had driven was ready for Bill's grandson.

He straightened up, put his palms on his lower back and slowly arched his torso to relieve his back pain. Bill looked at the truck again and thought about the day he started work for his dad's logging outfit.

Up at five, they were on the logging site by six-thirty. A crew member showed Bill the basics of choker setting, and then he was on his own, wrestling cables around enormous logs so they could be yarded up to the landing.

After a ten-hour day, Bill was exhausted and covered in pitch and dirt. Before heading to the shower, though, he and his dad had to clean and stow all the gear. Bill tried to rush the work, and his father said sternly, "I hope you don't think you're going to get away with doing a half-assed job because you're my son. You'll do this right, or you can get another job."

Bill had resented his father's insistence on keeping every tool clean and sharp, every cable wrapped. But Bill eventually became just as meticulous about his own tools.

Another memory of his son Kenny, about eleven, came to him. The boy had once again used Bill's tools without asking and left them scattered around the shop. He'd even nicked the edge of Bill's two-inch chisel, leaving Bill with a half-hour of grinding and honing to fix it.

Bill had tried to control his anger, to speak calmly to his son. But he could not. Kenny didn't cry, but his son's face twisted with shame, and his little shoulders hunched up toward his ears.

Bill's cell phone rang. It was his friend King. "Hey, King. What's up?"

"Hey Bill, how you doin'?"

"Doin' all right. You?"

"Good, good. Listen, you know not to spread the word about what those assholes did up Freshwater, right?" King was a consultant for the forest landowners whose property Bill had been working on.

"Sure. We don't want to put ideas in other people's heads."

"Right, right. I figured you knew. Just wanted to be sure. I know the Sheriff's office isn't going to issue a press release," King said with a chuckle. "The real reason I'm calling, though, is I may have a little job for you. This redwood on my ranch down in Shively has to come down. It's right next to the house. My last tenants freaked out every time there was a storm. So, I want to see if you can take it down before I rent the place again."

Bill thought for a moment. "I'm going down to Santa Rosa a few days before Thanksgiving to see Denise and Aaron. How about I check it out on the way and give you an estimate?"

"Sounds good, partner. And go easy on me with the price, okay?" said King with a whine. "In fact, I was wondering if you would do it for half the lumber. You know I got that new mini-mill."

Bill chuckled. "Might take a few bucks off for some choice all-heart, but I'll be charging cash." Bill didn't mind King's bargaining style, but he knew his friend would pay minimum wage to a diesel mechanic if he could get away with it. "I'll give you a fair price."

After they hung up, Bill opened a cupboard to inspect his climbing gear.

• • •

Jonah knew the meeting would be contentious, but hadn't expected anything like this.

"Man, what does 'no compromise' mean to you anyway?" Alder shouted, like he was speaking to a packed auditorium instead of a dozen activists sitting around a small living room. "We stopped those monsters in their tracks. What were you doing to save Mother Earth while we threw a wrench into the machine?"

Alder's target was Owl, a thin, red-bearded man who sat on a couch that slumped like a hammock. Owl sighed, leaned forward, and looked up at Alder. "Like I was saying, if you had checked with us, we could have told you that there was no old growth up there and that they'd be all done falling by this time of year. But most importantly, man, we don't do monkey wrenching."

Alder jabbed his finger at Owl. "Why the fuck not?"

Owl stood to face Alder. "That's just who we are." Jonah could see Owl's thin arms trembling, but the man's voice stayed calm. "We're committed to peaceful, non-violent civil disobedience, and that includes non-violence toward property and equipment. It's been that way since this movement got started in the nineties."

"And the rape of the forests just goes on," countered Alder.

Owl raised his hands plaintively. "You're right. Destructive logging continues. Now, CalTrans is trying to log Richardson Grove. But violence and vandalism don't help. We've got to win people over who've never been up in these woods—donors, newspaper writers, state legislators, members of Congress. And if word got out that we sabotaged equipment or endangered loggers, we'd lose support. That's what happened in the old days when people would spike the trees. Loggers got injured and the movement lost ground."

Alder spread his arms and opened his eyes wide. "Man, that is some weak bullshit! You're just gonna let the bulldozers destroy the forest while you wait for some new laws and shit."

"You're entitled to your opinion," said Owl, sitting back down. "But that's how we roll. If you can't go along with that, maybe this isn't the group for you."

"Damn right. Buncha pussies!" Alder yelled before slamming the door on the way out.

Jonah considered mentioning things that Alder had left out—like the fact that Alder had left his backpack when they fled, and how that meant the cops had it and might track Alder down. Nor did he mention that he'd tried to stop Alder while Buzzy egged him on. Buzzy sat on the floor, his eyes cast down at the dingy carpet.

The meeting wrapped up, and the group took a collection to buy dinner. Jonah volunteered to get the food and was thrilled to see Fawn—a cute woman who'd joined the group recently—jump up to join him.

On G Street, Jonah savored the warm fall afternoon and the stimulation of walking with Fawn. Six inches shorter than him, she had dark brown hair in raggedy dreadlocks, a pleasant smile and good energy. And under her baggy clothes, Jonah could see the outlines of her pert breasts and tight round ass.

Jonah searched mentally for something profound to say about the meeting. But the best he could come up with was, "Pretty intense back there."

"Alder got really aggro," she said.

"Yeah. He's an intense dude." That came out wrong—like he approved. "I'm not sure how good he is for the movement, though." That sounded better.

She frowned. "I can see his point, though." Fawn gestured to the tree-covered hills that rose from Arcata's eastern border. "I mean, what if they started logging the community forest? Would we just stand by and wait until the courts or some people in Sacramento decided to stop it?"

Jonah grasped for an answer. He believed in direct action but not vandalism. The movement had achieved huge victories with these tactics a decade or more ago. Activists had locked themselves to sawmill gates, bulldozers, and even the doors to a congressman's office. And the mainstream groups lobbied Sacramento and Washington legislators, and a bunch of old growth was saved. But Jonah couldn't articulate that thought to Fawn.

"Yeah, I see what you mean," Jonah said, wanting to avoid disagreement.

She hung her head. "Well, I'm new to this scene. Not sure what I'm talking about."

The store was quiet because most Humboldt State students had gone home for Thanksgiving. At the deli counter, Fawn and Jonah agreed on vegetarian items to order. Then they picked up bread and carrots.

When they arrived back at the apartment, a giant bong was going around. The notion of abstaining fluttered through Jonah's mind. He even visualized passing the bong on when it came to him—to keep his mind clear and his energy fresh. But as he and Fawn laid out the food on the kitchen counter, he knew he would get high.

They filled their plates and sat next to each other on the floor. "Where'd you grow up?" Jonah asked.

"Marin. Glad I got outta there. My parents say it used to be a great place back in the day, the birthplace of the Grateful Dead, artists living on houseboats. But now it's just traffic and super-expensive homes."

The bong came their way. Jonah hit it and passed it to Fawn. After she exhaled, she continued talking. She was warming up to him, he could tell. Yet, he struggled to follow her as she talked about painful childhood memories. "My parents were into all that hippie stuff, but it wasn't all groovy and fun for me and my sisters."

Jonah wanted to understand, ask a thoughtful question, and show he cared. And he wanted to tell her about his father. But his thoughts drifted. He heard himself repeating, "That sucks. ... Ah man, that sucks."

•   •   •

Driving home from Costco, Bill took the long way along Eureka's industrial waterfront to enjoy the views of the bay and the peninsula. With his window down, he breathed in the sea air and listened to the squawking gulls that followed a fishing boat.

This part of town made Bill nostalgic for the old days, when mills around the bay employed thousands. Freight trains rumbled through Eureka several times a week, groaning with loads of fir and redwood lumber. Cargo ships moored at the piers, taking on pulp and wood chips. And the timber industry supported truckers, rigging shops, forestry consultants, and engineering firms.

Commercial fishing had also been busy—salmon trollers, crabbers, long-line boats, and big-net trawlers used to crowd the fish processors' docks to unload. On many weekends, a holiday spirit would spread through Old Town as fishing crews and timber workers spent their cash in the bars and restaurants.

It hadn't all been good. During recessions, Bill's father had struggled to keep his men employed. "When the big cities get a cold, we get pneumonia," his father used to say. And the pulp mills on the peninsula used to pollute Eureka's air so badly that it stunk like an outhouse half the time. But in Bill's reckoning, the boom-and-bust cycles and the pollution were prices worth paying for jobs and prosperity.

As he passed a vacant lot where rusty train cars sat idle, he saw a man hunched over a bicycle. Another vagrant, he thought. Then he noticed that the man wore an orange-and-red Louisiana-Pacific jacket. Bill stopped his truck and lowered the window. "Hey, is that you, Petey?"

As he got a better look, Bill could see the cyclist was not Petey.

"Sorry," he said, putting his truck in gear. "Thought you were an old friend."

"Maybe you mistook me for my dad, Peter Taylor."

Bill parked, got out and went over to shake the hand of the man he now recognized as Petey's son. "Charlie, right?" he said, absorbing the shock of his mistake: this young man could not have been Petey, who was over seventy.

"Yeah."

"I've known your dad since I was younger than you are now. He was kind of a mentor to me."

"I remember you, Mr. Collins. From the old days."

Guilt surged in Bill as he thought about how long it had been since he'd called Petey. "How is your dad?"

"Not too good," Charlie said. "Lives down Santa Rosa in a care home."

"No shit. What happened?"

Charlie shrugged. "He got dementia. And after my mom died a couple years ago, we couldn't take care of him."

Bill remembered the memorial for Petey's wife. Had it really been two years?

Charlie was about five-ten and strongly built, with his father's chin. His clothes were worn and dirty, and the milk crate on his bike was full of tools and groceries. He seemed high or socially awkward. But he was Petey's son. "Can I help you out?" Bill asked. "Looks like you got a flat tire."

"More than that wrong with this old clunker."

"Well, I got plenty of room in the truck. Can I give you a lift?"

"Sure, thanks, man," said Charlie. "I live out in Fairhaven."

Bill opened the cargo box, pulled out a heavy trash bag and handed it to Charlie. "You can put your gear in here."

They loaded up and got in. Bill drove toward the bridge that went over the bay to the peninsula. Then he recalled the last time he'd seen Charlie—at least ten years before at the Draft Horse Millworks and Museum, a Hobbit-like village of old industrial buildings and boat sheds on Eureka's waterfront. The owners—a couple who were Bill's old friends—ran a school there for kids who couldn't make it at Eureka High.

Kenny went there for a while, and Bill remembered visiting for one of the school's open houses. Charlie was supervising Kenny, about 14, as he worked at a blacksmith forge. When Charlie stopped the boy to make a suggestion, Bill expected Kenny to recoil—like he'd done every time Bill tried to teach him something. But Kenny smiled, nodded, then continued tapping on a hot metal rod. Bill's heart seemed to swell with every *bing, bing* of Kenny's hammer on the anvil. It looked like his boy had finally found something constructive that he liked to do.

"I think you were at the Draft Horse, maybe ten years back, with my son, Kenny," Bill said to Charlie.

"I remember Kenny." Bill expected Charlie to say more. And he wanted to ask Charlie if he remembered that day at the blacksmith forge. But he didn't.

As they crossed the bridge over the bay, he asked the younger man, "So what are you up to? Working?"

Charlie was quiet as he gazed out the window at the dark choppy water. "I have a mental illness, schizophrenia." After a pause, he continued. "I lived with my parents until my mom died. If it weren't for my brother and his wife taking me in, I'd probably be living on these streets. Might even be dead."

They were at the west end of the bridge, and Charlie pointed at the dense spruce and alder forest that protected Humboldt

Bay from the ocean. "A homeless guy got killed right in there not six months ago. Some love-triangle bullshit."

"Yeah, I read about that."

The rain started up again as Bill turned south off the bridge. The dune forest gave way to an empty beach, and a gray sky hung low over the tumbling waves. "Sounds like you've had some rough times," Bill said, glancing at Charlie. "I'm awful sorry to hear about your dad."

"Yeah. Things kind of went downhill after Mom died."

"You get down to see your father much?"

"Nah."

Charlie's home was typical for Fairhaven, weathered and listing on its sandy foundations. But the metal roof was new, and a boat on a trailer was tightly wrapped with an orange tarp. After they'd unloaded the bike and Charlie's possessions, Charlie thanked Bill, then said, "I saw Kenny a month or so ago, over behind the mall, where they call Devil's Playground."

Bill felt a lariat tighten around his chest. He had wondered if Kenny lived in that notorious homeless camp. Both men were quiet until Bill said, "Kenny gave up on himself a long time ago. Those of us who love him have had to do the same. Don't you give up on yourself, Charlie."

Chapter 3

It was almost noon, and Arcata was still cold and damp under gray clouds. But Jonah and Buzzy were driving east toward the sun on Highway 299. Jonah could already see a ribbon of vivid blue sky over the mountains.

He passed the joint to Buzzy and gazed at the farmland beside the highway, where hay bales and white silage rounds were stacked beside a barn and black cows grazed in thick grass. "Damn, it's beautiful here," he said.

"Sure is. Glad we're getting out into the sun today. My armpits are growing mushrooms." He handed the joint back.

"That's enough for me."

"Me too, man." Jonah put the big roach in a plastic bag and stowed it in the glove compartment.

The road started climbing, and suddenly they were in the sun. Jonah rolled down his window and inhaled the pine-scented air. Then, he saw a hitchhiker on the side of the road. "Want to stop for him?"

"Sure." Buzzy pulled the car over onto the shoulder.

The man who got in the backseat was husky and brown-skinned, about thirty-five, with American Indian tattoos on his thick forearms. "Thanks, brothers," he said, reaching his hand up to shake theirs. "Name's Jim." The smell of hard liquor filled the car.

As Buzzy drove back onto the highway, Jim sniffed loudly and asked, "Any reefer left?"

Buzzy said, "Sure, man."

Jonah passed it to Jim with a lighter. "You toke up much as you want 'cause we just got high."

"Gladly, thanks!"

"Where you headed?" Jonah asked.

"Up to Hoopa," Jim squeaked, holding a lungful before exhaling. "See my aunties. How far you guys going?"

"Not sure," said Buzzy. "Just wanted to get away from the damp coast for a bit."

"I heard that. You can drop me anywhere," Jim said confidently. "I got so many friends and relatives up in the Valley I'll get another ride easy. Probably right to my aunties' door. You fellas ever been up to the valley?"

"Never even been to Willow Creek," said Jonah.

"I grew up in Weitchpec," Jim said. "It's where the Klamath and the Trinity meet, middle-a-nowhere, but beautiful like you can't believe." Jim said his father was Yurok and his mother Hupa. They'd moved to the coast when Jim was twelve, so he went to high school in Eureka. "But I still love my mountains."

Jim talked on, and Jonah lost the thread, but he liked the sound of the man's voice. Then he heard Jim say, "That's when I got into working in the woods."

"Cool, man," said Jonah, turning to Jim. "We work in the woods, too. We're forest defenders, working to stop clearcut logging and protect Mother Earth."

That shut Jim up for a second. Then he smiled broadly. "Man, I'm a logger. A chainsaw-massacrin', owl-killin' logger. I turn your Mother Earth into two-by-fours."

Jonah couldn't believe what he was hearing. Weren't Native Americans supposed to revere nature? Was this guy kidding? About being a logger? About being native?

"What do your aunties think about that?" Buzzy asked.

"Man, they don't mind a bit. It gives me and my cousins a way to make a living without growin' weed or cookin' meth. The tribe up there logs plenty. Even old growth."

"Seriously?" asked Jonah. "Old-growth redwood?"

Jim waved his hand dismissively. "Nah, mostly Doug-fir. Redwood don't grow that far from the coast."

"And they clearcut old-growth Doug-fir?" demanded Buzzy.

"It's complicated, man," Jim said. "I haven't done any logging up there, but I know they do some kind of modified clearcuts, leaving trees and berry bushes and bear grass so my aunties and other basket weavers can go out and harvest what they need." Jim paused to take a long drag on the roach. "But there ain't nothing wrong with good old-fashioned clearcutting." He leaned forward and pointed to the right. "Pull over up ahead, and I'll show you what I mean."

Buzzy drove onto an overlook. Jonah and Buzzy followed Jim as he walked to the edge of the pullout, where they could see a thickly forested, steep-sloped valley. "You see that recent clearcut, right?" Jim pointed across the valley at a gray-brown patch of earth just down from the ridgeline. To Jonah, it seemed like a monster from outer space had swooped down and destroyed acres of forest. "That looks like hell, right?"

Jonah and Buzzy nodded.

"Now, look all around over there. Every acre you see has been clearcut sometime in the last twenty, thirty, forty years." Jim leaned closer to Jonah and pointed at another spot on the distant mountainside. "You see that one bright green stand? Look close and you'll see the trees ain't as tall as the rest. That's a recent clearcut, maybe six or eight years old."

"The trees grow back," Jim said, dropping his arm. "The companies make sure they do 'cause that's their bread and butter. And us loggers will go in there again when they're ready to harvest. And we'll clearcut another patch so you can get lumber when you need it—in case maybe you want to live in an apartment or a house instead of the tent you're living in now."

Jim was grinning so widely that Jonah didn't take offense at the man assuming—correctly—that he and Buzzy lived in a tent. But he wasn't going to let Jim win the argument uncontested.

"Okay, okay," said Jonah, putting his hands up. "I see what you're saying. But that doesn't mean there aren't better ways to do logging. For one thing, the timber companies use a ton of herbicides to kill off the oaks and myrtles and other hardwoods that would grow back faster than the conifers—and that's bad for the frogs, the fish, and other creatures."

Buzzy nodded encouragement while Jim crossed his arms over his chest. "You know, in Europe, they've pretty much quit clearcutting and changed over to selective cutting," Jonah continued. "They still harvest plenty of timber, but they do it in a way that leaves a more natural forest, with a healthy understory and diverse age classes."

"Damn, college boy," said Jim, still smiling. He reached out and slapped Jonah on the shoulder so hard that he almost fell over. "I see you've read a few books. But you'll never convince an old treeslayer like me."

•   •   •

Bill sat at his kitchen table, talking with his daughter Denise on the phone. She was asking—again—how he was adjusting to the single life. "I miss your mother like crazy sometimes. But I'm getting used to it. Even trying online dating."

When Denise didn't respond, Bill understood that she didn't want to hear more about his attempts at dating. After a moment, she asked, "Do you ever regret breaking up?"

Bill breathed deeply before answering. "Not really. It hasn't been easy, and I worry about her sometimes, you know, with no man around the house. But all in all, I'm glad we split up. We were driving each other crazy over how to deal with Kenny."

Bill fidgeted with a saltshaker. "We used to worry ourselves sick about him. I don't know how many times we drove around looking for him down on the waterfront and all the sketchy parts of town."

"Really?" asked Denise. "She said you wouldn't do that when she asked you to."

Bill tried to calm his rising anger. "Well, I stopped after the counselor at the rehab told us to cut it out. He said not to have any contact with Kenny unless he was back in rehab or wanted help getting into one. And that's what I've learned from other parents who go to Al-Anon."

"What about when he was in Sober Challenge?"

"Sober Challenge? That Christian recovery outfit? Kenny never went there."

Denise was silent. Then she said with a sigh, "He did, Dad. Last summer. I guess I forgot you didn't know about that."

Bill felt his face get hot and his stomach tighten. He hadn't heard from his son since last Easter.

Denise broke the silence. "I know that must feel terrible, Dad, that Kenny didn't reach out to you. I told him to, and he said he would, but I guess he relapsed before he got to that point."

Bill flipped through mental images of the rehabs Kenny had tried. Singing Gardens, just off the highway in Southern Humboldt. Three Rivers up in Arcata. Then Sober Challenge right in Eureka's downtown, followed by another relapse. Bill's grief at hearing that Kenny had failed once again mingled with his shame at being kept out of the loop by his son—and his daughter. "Did Cheri know?"

"Yeah."

Bill put his hands to his face and mumbled, "Oh, shit, shit." He felt a tear move down his cheek. His whole family had conspired to keep this a secret until Denise let it slip. Did they all think he was bad for Kenny?

•   •   •

Jonah and Buzzy had made their campsite in the Arcata Community Forest about 25 yards from a main forest road. But they'd concealed it well enough to live there undetected for a month. Still, it was a mile walk from the nearest legal overnight parking spot, so when they finally arrived home at night, Jonah flopped down on his sleeping pad and closed his eyes. He perked up when he smelled weed. Buzzy passed him the pipe.

"Man, that dude was a trip, huh?" said Jonah. "It's so weird that a native guy would buy into that corporate BS about clearcutting. You think he's just brainwashed or what?"

"Yeah. Either that or he just goes along with it, 'cause that's how he makes his living."

Jonah exhaled and lay back down. "I don't think we'll ever convince people like him."

"That's right." Buzzy passed Jonah a forty-ounce beer. "Don't matter, though. There are tons of people like us who get it. And we're going to stop those motherfuckers."

"Damn right."

They finished the pipe. "Think I'm going to hit the hay."

"Me too," said Buzzy.

Jonah took off his boots and outerwear and snuggled into his bag.

He woke up needing to pee. He pulled on his jacket and boots, ducked under the tarp's edge, stepped carefully through the ferns, and walked uphill away from the campsite. When he'd finished peeing, he walked farther to see Bella, the redwood tree he had adopted. He patted her wet bark. "Don't worry, Bella. I'll protect your cousins out there."

Back in his bag, Jonah listened to the wind play in the canopy and watched the tarp ripple. Seeing Bella had made him think of his father.

Before he died, Jonah's dad had managed to stay sober many Saturday mornings in the summers so he could take Jonah and his brother Django for hikes in the mountains west of San José. "Daylight's burning, boys," he would say, when he woke them up.

He'd hurry them through breakfast, then bundle them into his truck, where the boys would promptly fall asleep until they arrived at the trailhead.

On one trip, their dad took them to a state park with ancient redwoods. Jonah remembered his father standing next to a tree as wide as their garage, and so tall that it disappeared in the misty sky. "More than a thousand years old," his father said as he caressed the shaggy bark. "Can you imagine, boys?"

Jonah could not imagine a thousand years, but the awe he heard in his father's voice and the passion he saw in his eyes felt like a talisman to the young boy.

Thinking about his dad made Jonah ache. He turned on his side and drew his legs up. He wanted to cry but couldn't. The forest night was so still that Jonah could hear his breath, and the wispy sound of the sleeping bag's fabric as his chest rose and fell.

Chapter 4

After finally falling asleep, Jonah dreamed he and Fawn were driving an old school bus up the coast. They stopped several times to pick people up. She was behind the wheel, and he passed around sandwiches and water to the growing band.

The road trip ended abruptly when Jonah woke up to pee. When he got back under the tarp, he felt his head spin, and thought about how much he wanted to stay off weed and beer for the day. He'd abstained off and on earlier in the fall, telling Buzzy and other friends that he wanted to get more done and take a stronger stand for Mother Earth. That was only partly true.

When Jonah first got high on marijuana and beer during the summer between eighth and ninth grade, he felt like he'd found what he was longing for—freedom from his perpetual shyness and anxiety. Soon, he began to organize his life around getting and consuming weed and alcohol—and keeping his new hobby a secret from his acutely perceptive mother.

Jonah managed to graduate from high school. Then, to keep his mother from kicking him out, he complied with her demands that he work and take at least one college course per semester. It was 2005, and the Bay Area economy was in high gear, so Jonah soon got a job clerking for the produce department of a natural food store—where he got high with co-workers on the loading dock.

When Jonah wasn't in class or at work, he spent his time much like he did in high school.

Then, his community college science teacher showed a video of loggers destroying old-growth redwood forests on California's North Coast. Jonah had imbibed his father's love for the redwoods, so he was outraged. He wished he could have talked to his dad about it, but his father was dead by then.

He met other young forest activists, and they dressed up like salmon and birds and paraded around the streets of San José. They took the bus to San Francisco or Berkeley a few times to join larger protests. They even carpooled to the capital once to demand the legislature stop all clearcutting. These protests seemed to accomplish nothing. So, Jonah decided to go north to confront logging directly.

When he told his friends he was going up to Humboldt to defend the forests with direct action, they cheered for him and planned a goodbye party. At the party, he got so high he floated above the scene, aware that he would miss them but not feeling anything. He joked about sending postcards and said they might read about his exploits online.

At home, his brother Django acted like Jonah was going on a long vacation—and Jonah went along with that. His mother quizzed him about his packing list and what to do with his mail. But as she handed him $200 and hugged him, he felt her trembling, and that moved something in him. But he kept acting casual, detached.

A raven cawed nearby and woke Buzzy. When he saw Jonah was up, he asked, "The fuck time is it, man?"

"About eight, I think. Not sure. My phone's dead."

Buzzy rose on his elbows. Raindrops pattered the tarp over their heads. "Shit, more rain."

"Nah, I think it's just the wind. But there's more rain coming." Jonah reached up to touch the stoutly rigged tarp. "She'll hold up fine, though."

As soon as Buzzy returned from peeing, they got ready to walk to town. Then, they heard a low whistle. Alder squeezed under the tarp. He bumped Buzzy's fist and nodded at Jonah.

"We were about to head into town," said Buzzy. "Coffee and breakfast."

"And a warm place to shit," added Jonah.

"Yeah, me too. Just wanted to drop by and let you sample some of this dank bud I scored last night." Alder pulled a baggy from his coat pocket.

"Time to wake and bake," Buzzy said, rubbing his hands with glee.

Jonah felt excitement and panic rise in his chest. As Alder filled the pipe, he said, "Dudes, the sun is barely up. How the fuck are we going to get anything done today if we get baked so early?"

The words sounded ridiculous to Jonah, and the two men ignored him. His mouth watered, and he settled back to wait for the pipe. Alder hit it and passed it to Buzzy. Smoke filled the space, and Jonah was about to reach for the pipe when a gust of wind swept through the ravine. On an impulse, he rose to his knees.

"Gotta bolt, man," he said and took off.

For several minutes, Jonah considered running back up to the campsite and snagging a couple of hits. He wanted to get high. And he wanted to stay clean until he could attend his first Marijuana Anonymous meeting that night. Maybe that would help him stay off weed at least through Thanksgiving when he'd visit his mom and Django.

Jonah crossed a bridge over a creek and noticed something white sticking out of the ferns below. He climbed down the bank and discovered a mound of trash.

"What the fuck!" He fished a plastic bag from the mess and began stuffing it with burrito wrappers, old socks, and chip bags.

When he'd filled the bag, Jonah washed the slime off his fingers and clambered back up to the trail. He soon emerged from the forest into a large grassy meadow palisaded by tall redwoods and firs. Jonah deposited the trash in a can.

Leaving the forest, he felt uplifted by the view of Arcata's tidy grid of downtown streets and its plaza surrounded by ornate buildings. The pastures beyond the town were painted with silvery creeks and sloughs, dotted with cows and old barns. Beyond the pastures, a dark tree line marked the dune forest that held back the ocean. Jonah could even see a patch of blue sea.

Looking south, Jonah saw the bay at low tide, and beyond the bay sat Eureka, the county's biggest town and a mystery to Jonah. The few times he'd been there, he'd seen downtown streets crowded with homeless people who wandered by cheap motels, tattoo parlors, and office buildings. The town seemed hostile and rough.

•   •   •

On Eureka's waterfront boardwalk, the sun was breaking through and lighting up the boats crowding the marina and the thick woods behind it. Bill and King stepped to the railing for a better view. In the mudflats exposed by the low tide, they saw a white egret peering intently into the shallow water.

"She's hoping for a good breakfast," said King. "Which I'm about ready for, too."

"Let's go as far as the library," said Bill, pointing down the waterfront at a modern timber-frame structure. "Gotta get in my miles."

"You and your miles," grumbled King. Shorter than Bill by a few inches and older by five years, King limped slightly from a broken leg that didn't heal properly after a rodeo accident.

They passed men sprawled on cardboard and sleeping bags. "Got any papers?" one asked. King and Bill ignored him and walked on.

"Think he meant toilet paper or rolling paper?" King joked.

Bill barked a quick chuckle and tried to think of a new subject before King launched his usual tirade.

Too late. "I tell you, Bill, the tweakers and junkies and mental cases are ruining this town. You hear about those girls they pulled out of Devil's Playground?"

"Saw something in the paper."

King told Bill what he'd heard from his friends who were cops: After an anonymous 9-1-1 call about a rape in progress, Eureka police officers and county sheriff deputies went from tent to tent until they found two teen girls with two adult men. "The girls were stoned out of their minds." King sounded more excited than upset. "The guys tried to tell the cops they found the girls like that, and they were trying to help them. But their bullshit stories fell apart soon as the cops separated everybody."

"Glad they got those girls outta there and nailed those bastards," said Bill.

"Yeah, but the assholes got out. Lack of evidence," King fumed. "To put them away, the DA is gonna need strong testimony. But the girls were whacked out on heroin. And as usual, nobody else down there saw or heard anything." King's tone shifted from cynical to distressed. "Makes me think about my own granddaughters. You just never know."

Bill struggled to keep his voice steady. "Yeah, I know what you mean," he said, concealing his turmoil about Kenny, who'd recently been living in Devil's Playground, according to Charlie.

•   •   •

Jonah bought a bagel, peanut butter and a coffee at the Co-op, then headed for the plaza. As he started making a sandwich, he smelled pot smoke. He stuffed his food into his backpack and walked a few blocks to sit on the wall of a house with a vast spreading walnut tree and owners who didn't object to travelers perching on their wall.

After breakfast, Jonah wandered over to the Arcata Environmental Center for a meeting about how to stop Caltrans from logging the Richardson Grove on Highway 101 near Mendocino County. He opened the flyer-covered door and saw Mike Doyle, the center's director, sitting at the reception desk.

"Hey there, Jonah," said Doyle, a very large man with a long salt-and-pepper beard. "If you're here for that meeting, I just heard it was canceled."

"Oh damn." Jonah sat in a chair opposite Doyle. He liked the big man, even though he thought the AEC spent too much time writing letters and filing lawsuits, and not enough time blockading forest roads or organizing tree sits.

"How's Jonah?" Doyle asked.

Jonah began to say something cheerful and upbeat. But something about Doyle inspired him to confide, "Well, I'm kind of struggling at the moment, trying to quit smoking weed."

Doyle's big eyebrows rose. "Really? Is it a problem for you?"

"Yeah. I can't seem to get anything done when I get high." As the familiar words left his mouth, Jonah felt compelled to share more. "And I think I'm missing out on—don't know what to call it, exactly—you know, some kind of deeper connection with people."

Doyle nodded, and Jonah saw sympathy in his eyes. "Have you tried limiting it, say, to weekends? That's what I do, plus the occasional weekday nightcap."

"I've tried that, and it just doesn't work for me." Jonah leaned forward, forearms on his thighs. He looked at the corner of the desk, then at Doyle. "If there's weed around, I just gotta have some. When there's none around, I'll drink more. Then I'll get some weed or run into someone who's got some. You know how it is up here."

"Right," said Doyle.

"I'm going to try Marijuana Anonymous—my first meeting is tonight."

"Good for you."

Raindrops pelted the center's large front window. "Rain's starting up again."

"Yep, and we sure need it badly," said Doyle. He gathered some papers into a briefcase and stood up. "Gotta go to a meeting. You're welcome to stay here out of the rain for a while if you want."

Jonah nodded and smiled. "Okay if I charge my phone?"

"Sure."

•   •   •

Bill seated himself at a booth while King went to the men's room. He looked at the cars driving by and the businesses and apartments across the street and noticed a sign advertising "24-hour bail bonds." He thought about the last time he'd bailed Kenny out. What had it been: Two years? Three?

King came to the table. They ordered coffee and studied the menus. "Don't know why you bother," said King, pointing to the menu in Bill's hands. "Since it's my turn to pay, you know you'll get the steak and eggs."

"I was thinking about getting lunch to go, too," deadpanned Bill. King huffed mock offense, then the server came with their coffees. Bill ordered the steak and eggs—"and a bowl of oatmeal to keep the doctor happy."

After a moment, King asked, "So, how's the single life, Bill? Are you doing any dating? Meeting any fetching ladies who'll let you park your truck on their lawn?"

Bill sipped his coffee. "I'm trying the online thing, but hardly anyone seems interested in an old logger."

"Course not," said King. "Do you have to say what you do for work on those things?"

"Most people do. Some put their hobbies. Mostly, the gals on there write things like, 'I'm living my best life and looking for a partner to share it with.'"

"Is that what you're looking for?"

Bill saw genuine interest in King's face. He glanced around the restaurant, thinking how to answer. "I don't know. Kind of. I mean, maybe, eventually. Not right away. Just getting used to being single after all those years with Cheri."

King nodded. "You need to grow one of those beards like the millennials. Oh wait, I guess a gray rug would make you look even older."

Bill chuckled. The teasing felt good.

Bill briefly considered telling King about Angela. From the photos on her dating profile, Bill guessed she was about ten years younger than him—and gorgeous, with long black hair, a bright smile, expressive eyes, and a shapely body.

After chatting on the site, she gave him her phone number. That was three weeks ago, and they'd talked a half-dozen times since, getting more honest and intimate than Bill had expected. He'd told her about Kenny and his breakup with Cheri. She'd told him about growing up in Mexico City, and how she left her family and came to the United States for a relationship that didn't work out.

When Bill asked her to meet for coffee, she declined, saying she wanted to talk more first. Sometimes, Bill took this as a sign that she considered him a serious prospect. At other times, he guessed she was keeping him on the shelf while she dated other guys.

After the server brought their food, King asked, "So, what did you think of that list of speakers for the logging show?"

"I'm not crazy about any of them," said Bill, a forkful of eggs hovering over his plate. "That guy from Western Lands Council will just bitch about laws we can't do anything about. And those other two are politicians who don't know a clearcut from a haircut."

King frowned. "Well, who do you suggest?"

"What about Phil Nadelbaum?"

"Nadelbaum?" King scoffed. "Everyone knows his story. The broke logger who hauled some rusty machine out of the bushes and learned how to make fancy trim for the Victorians down in San Francisco."

"He knows the industry's history inside out, and he's a good storyteller. Plus, he and his wife have really made a go of that Draft Horse museum and school. They got tough kids into blacksmithing and letterpress printing and whatnot. And their place is a tourist draw."

King leaned back. "I give them credit for what they've got going. But this'll be an audience of people trying to make money in the industry today, not reminisce about what it was like fifty or a hundred years ago."

Bill knew he was rolling a log uphill, but he tried one more push. "We got all these technical seminars, and the gear makers will be there showing off their big machines, bragging about how many jobs they can eliminate. So why not somebody from our industry with a positive story—making it the old-fashioned way?"

King thought for a moment. "Okay, I'll run it by the committee."

After eating silently for a couple of minutes, Bill told King what he'd heard from Charlie—that their old friend Petey was down in Santa Rosa in a memory care home.

"Man, that's ... that's awful," said King, setting down his coffee cup. "What the hell is his family doing leaving him down there like that?"

"Ain't much family left. You remember his wife died a couple years back."

"I remember her funeral."

"His son Charlie has mental health problems. Lives with his younger brother out on the peninsula. But the brother's busy with a job and kids."

The men were silent for a moment. Then King said, "You remember back in '78?"

"The giant redwood peanut. It's still up there on the side of the highway in Orick."

King sat back and smiled. "Petey and old Hank Walcott spent about a week carving that thing with chainsaws." Shaking his head, he added, "I can't believe we thought that was a good idea, mocking the president just because he'd been a peanut farmer."

"I was still in high school," said Bill, "but my dad went."

King sipped his coffee and looked out the window at the traffic. "That convoy to DC was something. And it was Petey that kept us all together, making everyone drive fifty so the log trucks could keep up. Making sure the politicians didn't hog all the glory when we had our news conferences along the way."

"In DC, the Teamsters and Carpenters unions escorted us to the capitol," said King. "And that's about all the welcome we got. I remember Petey trying to talk to some big-shot TV anchorman about why we didn't want the national park to expand. The guy just said, 'I'm an environmentalist, the hell with you.' That's been the story ever since."

•　　•　　•

Jonah hung around downtown Arcata all afternoon, trying to stay dry while keeping away from the plaza to avoid friends who might have tempted him with weed. He went to Tony's café and made a small coffee last for forty-five minutes. During a lull in the rain, he wandered over to the railroad tracks, sat on some lumber, and ate another cheese sandwich for supper.

As he was finishing, his mother called. "Hi, Mom." He tried to sound perky.

"Hi, honey. I just want to know what time your bus will get into the city on Wednesday so I can pick you up."

"Not sure yet." He didn't want to tell her he planned to save money by hitchhiking. "But I'll be there. How about if I let you know tomorrow?"

Jonah waited for her to whine, but she sounded content and happy instead. "Okay, just let me know. I'm really looking forward to your visit."

"Me too."

The afternoon dragged. By five-thirty, the rain and wind picked up, and the clouds were so low and thick that it seemed like night had come early. Jonah sheltered in the alcove of a church and waited for the MA meeting to start.

•   •   •

Bill parked and walked to the church. Near the door, he saw a young man with muddy clothes and a dirty backpack standing in the alcove. Bill avoided eye contact.

He pulled open the big yellow door and heard men and women chatting and chairs scuffing on the wooden floor. After taking a seat, Bill saw his friend John smiling at him. Bill smiled back.

John wore his usual outfit: a tweed jacket over a V-neck sweater and a dress shirt. When Bill first saw him at an Al-Anon meeting, he'd pegged him for a Humboldt State professor—someone he'd have little in common with. After several more meetings, Bill learned his guess about John's profession was correct. But he'd stopped caring what John did for a living after learning that John was also a father struggling to cope with his adult son's addiction.

Then Bill saw the young man who'd been standing outside enter and sit against the wall.

The chairperson started reading. "We welcome you to Al-Anon and hope you will find in this fellowship the help and friendship we have been privileged to enjoy."

The young man grabbed his backpack and left. Bill thought about following him outside to talk to him. He knew Al-Anon could seem strange to people coming for the first time—all the references to God and prayer, the chanted responses when people introduced themselves. At his first meeting, Bill had almost bolted in frustration. But he managed to stay, and by the end, he felt encouraged enough to try again. That had been about three months ago, and now he was a regular.

The readings continued, and a basket was passed for contributions. People took turns speaking while the rest listened. After a while, John, the professor, spoke up. "I always thought it was my fault. I'd been too strict with him, or I hadn't been strict enough. I gave in too easy when he wanted some videogame, or I didn't give him enough help with his homework.

"When I came here, I started to learn that his addiction was not our fault." John leaned his head toward his wife, who sat and knitted beside him. "It just happened." He looked at Bill. "I've learned that I could have been the best father who ever walked on God's green earth, and he still could have turned out the way he did."

After the closing prayer, Bill approached John and stuck out his hand. John gripped Bill's hand and said, "How're you doing, Bill?"

"Not too good. Talked to my daughter yesterday and found out my son went into rehab last summer. He didn't make it more than a week, and he never even called me." Bill rubbed his eyes. "I keep thinking, you know, like you were saying, what did I do wrong?"

"Come here," John said, drawing Bill into a hug.

Bill wasn't used to hugging guys, but he accepted John's hug. When they pulled apart, John asked, "You going to join us for coffee?"

"Gotta get packed for my trip down south." That was true. It was also true that Bill didn't want to smile and make conversation with John and a bunch of folks, as nice as they were. "Next time."

"Well, give me a call anytime, Bill."

"Will do. Thanks."

Outside, the rain had picked up. Bill pulled his cap down and walked quickly to his pickup.

•   •   •

Jonah sat on his backpack, protected by an awning from the rain. He had two options for a dry night: the floor of Owl's apartment or his campsite, a two-mile walk uphill. In either place, his friends would be smoking pot and probably drinking.

He saw an old guy from the meeting hustle across the sidewalk to a brown Ford pickup. The man opened the cab door and swung himself onto the seat. As he was shutting the door, he caught Jonah's eye. He hesitated, then said loud enough for Jonah to hear over the rain, "Hey, you okay?"

Jonah shrugged.

The guy got out and came over. "Saw you in the meeting. Are you new to Al-Anon?"

"I was looking for a different meeting."

"AA?"

"MA," said Jonah, putting his thumb and index finger to his lips.

"Oh, yeah, I think that's on Friday nights." The man paused. "Can I give you a lift somewhere?"

Jonah considered. "Not sure where I'd go. I can't go home right now."

The man hesitated, then said, "Well, I'm going to stop at a coffee shop on my way home. You want to join me for a cup of coffee? Get outta this rain for a little while?"

That was the last thing on Jonah's mind, but it sounded better than his other options. "Yeah, I guess."

"Let's go."

Jonah got into the passenger seat, and Bill extended his hand, "I'm Bill."

"Jonah. Thanks, man. Appreciate this."

"No problem."

When they pulled to the curb in front of Tony's, Bill said, "My favorite place."

"Mine too."

They hustled across the wet sidewalk to the door. Inside, they hung their wet jackets on their chair backs and sat down.

"This is on me," Bill told Jonah. "And you gotta try the apple pie."

"Uh, thanks."

The waitress came, and they both ordered apple pie and coffee. "Decaf for me," said Bill.

Jonah noticed that his coat had shed a small puddle, so he used a napkin to wipe up the water. "Man, does it rain like this all winter up here?" he asked Bill.

"Usually wraps up by May. Where you from?"

"Down San José. My first winter here."

"Yeah, we get a lot more than down there. We need it, though," said Bill, pushing his hat back. "We're way behind for this time of year."

"Bet you've seen some big storms, huh?"

"I remember one time, the creek behind our house flooded so bad we couldn't get out. I had to stay home from work, kids couldn't go to school."

"Wow," said Jonah. "What was that like?"

"It was actually kinda fun. The power was out, and it rained to beat hell. But we had candles and plenty of food and firewood. We sat around playing that card game that kids like."

"Uno?"

"Yeah," Bill said with a fond chuckle. "Uno."

Bill gazed over Jonah's shoulder and continued. "The thing was, we had this cat, Felix. Real original name, huh? We didn't know where she was at. My kids were worried sick."

The waitress brought their apple pie and coffee. They thanked her and dug in. The pie was delicious, not too sweet, the apples a little crunchy, rich with butter and cinnamon. "Man, this is good," said Jonah.

"Best in town," Bill agreed.

"So, what about the cat?" Jonah asked.

"Oh yeah." Bill put down his fork and took a sip of coffee. "In the morning, the storm had played out, but the yard was a lake. We heard Felix meowing like crazy, and we could see she was stuck on the roof of our shed. She would've been all right till the water went down, but my kids were worried she'd starve or drown. So, I went out to get her."

"Water was up to my knees by the time I got to the shed. At first, she wouldn't come to me, but I'd brought a little bit of tuna fish, so I got her to come over." Jonah could see Bill was getting emotional at this memory. "I'll never forget how happy Kenny and Denise looked when I brought that cat in the door."

"That's cool. My dad might have done something like that, too. He was a good guy ... when he wasn't drunk."

"Dad had a drinking problem?" asked Bill, taking a big bite of pie.

"Yeah. Sometimes, he and my mom would fight. Couple times the cops came."

"Is your dad still around?"

Jonah wished he hadn't mentioned his father. "He died."

"Oh, sorry to hear that." Bill was quiet a moment, then asked, "How long ago was that?"

"Coming up on nine years."

Another pause. "How 'bout your mom?"

Jonah laughed. "She didn't drink, but in some ways, she's worse than my dad was. He was at least fun sometimes, but she's always pissed off."

"Does she know where you are now?" asked Bill. "Have you talked to her lately?"

"Yeah, and I'm going down to see her and my little brother for Thanksgiving." Jonah wanted to say he was excited about seeing his family—but he was not.

"I'm sorry with all the questions," Bill said, leaning back. "It's just that, like I told you, I'm a dad. My son Kenny is about your age. Haven't seen or heard from him since last spring. He's strung out on meth. That's how come I go to Al-Anon."

"Shit, that's rough. I had a friend in high school who got hooked on that."

Then Bill asked, "How you getting to the Bay Area?"

"Hitch as far as I can, then maybe take a bus from Santa Rosa or San Rafael. My mom'll pick me up in the city."

Jonah could tell Bill was considering something. Just as the silence became uncomfortable, Bill said, "I could give you a ride to Santa Rosa early tomorrow morning. I'm going down to see my daughter and grandson."

"No shit? That'd be great."

Then, Jonah saw Buzzy enter and stand in the takeout line. He hoped his friend wouldn't notice him. "Where do you want me to meet you?"

"How about on the plaza?" said Bill. "Can you be there by six?"

Before Jonah could answer, Buzzy came to the table. "Hey, bro. I wondered when I'd see you again, the way you bolted this morning. You want a ride back up to the forest?"

"I don't know," Jonah said, thinking about how to introduce Bill.

Buzzy saved him the trouble. "Hey man, I'm Buzzy."

Bill shook Buzzy's hand, then, with an edge to his voice, he said, "So, you fellas live up in the forest? I hope you're not like those knuckleheads that light fires in the stumps and leave trash around."

"No way, man," said Jonah, offended. "We're about taking care of Mother Earth."

"She's our home," said Buzzy. "We try to protect her."

Bill sighed. "Well, some of your comrades tore up our loader a few days back. I hope you're not involved in that kind of thing."

Jonah felt panicked, but Buzzy acted nonchalant despite Bill's accusation. "We believe in nonviolent direct action," he said. Then he added, "to stop clearcut logging."

"What, you never go the lumber yard?" asked Bill, the edge in his voice sharpening.

Jonah softened his tone as he said, "We know people need lumber, but there are more sustainable ways to do logging. There's this forest I heard about down in Mendocino..."

Bill cut him off. "All right, hold up. I know you and the college professors are the experts on harvesting timber, and you know so much more than us, who've been doing it for generations. But when you need some two-by-fours or some cardboard to make a sign for spare change, do you ever think that maybe we know a thing or two that you don't?"

The three men were silent long enough for Jonah to hear a woman in the next booth say to her child, "You need to eat your carrots before you have any more French fries, sweetie."

Then Buzzy said, "Gotta head out, man. My burger's gettin' cold. You coming?"

"Yeah." Jonah felt bad leaving during an argument after Bill had been so kind to him. But he didn't know what else to do.

"Thanks for the ride and the food." He stood up and grabbed his wet jacket.

"You got it. Take care of yourself out there." Bill sounded friendly again, and they shook hands.

When Jonah buckled into Buzzy's Subaru, he realized that in leaving so hastily, he'd lost his chance for a ride in the morning.

They arrived at their campsite drenched from the rain, so they peeled off their wet clothes and got into their sleeping bags.

"That was cool you were hanging out with that logger," said Buzzy. "That's the second one we talked to in a couple days. I think a lot of them really know there's better ways to do logging. They just go along with clearcutting because that's what the corporations want."

"We actually didn't talk much about all that." Jonah watched the tarp twitch in the wind.

"What did you talk about?"

Jonah felt a deep and unexplainable sense of loss. "We just talked. About the rain and stuff. He told me a story about rescuing his kids' cat during a bad flood."

Buzzy laughed with scorn. "Seriously, man? Did you tell him about all the ground squirrels and voles and other critters that need rescuing from loggers like him?"

Jonah was suddenly filled with the urge to get high. He sat up and asked, "You got any weed?"

"Yeah. But you sure you want to get high, man?"

"Hell yeah."

As soon as Jonah hit the pipe, his whole body felt light and floaty, and his mood soared. Buzzy passed him a bottle of strong ale. For a few minutes, Jonah enjoyed a pleasant buzz. Then, the familiar remorse over having broken his promise to himself—again—came over Jonah. Seeking relief from the despair, he asked Buzzy to refill the pipe.

Chapter 5

"So, you just walked out on him when he was at work, huh?" Bill sat on the couch in his living room, but he was mentally with Angela on a sidewalk under a scalding summer sun in Fresno. "I mean, did you pack a suitcase?"

"I left with only a little backpack and the money I'd been hiding from him," Angela told him.

"And you came up here, what, on the bus?"

"A bus and train to Santa Rosa, where my sister picked me up."

"That took guts to just take off like that."

"Si, pero ... Yes, but me moría con ese pendejo."

Bill smiled. He knew what pendejo meant, and he could guess the rest. He liked it when she slipped into Spanish because it meant she was excited about something—and relaxed enough with him to show it.

He visualized her in the apartment she shared with her sister. Was she still wearing her uniform from the restaurant? He imagined sitting next to her and felt himself get hard.

"How's your work going?" she asked.

That ended Bill's fantasy and dampened his mood. "Got one custom tree job lined up, but the commercial logging season is pretty much over 'cause of the rain."

"Well, at least you'll get some time off."

"Yeah, I just wish the bank would give me some time off my mortgage." He instantly regretted saying that. Financial security was no doubt on Angela's criteria list for a romantic partner. "How's your work going?"

"It's good. Busier since the students got back from their break. And the cold weather makes people hungrier, so they order more." She told him about one party of students that drank four pitchers of margaritas and left a five percent tip.

"Cheap kids," Bill said, suppressing a yawn.

Angela was a night owl. Twice she'd called Bill—wired from work, eager to talk—after he was in bed. He'd stayed awake to talk with her, but tonight he had some packing left to do and an early departure planned. "Well, I'm enjoying this, Angela, but I better get going."

"I hope you have a great trip, Bill." Then she added, "I was thinking it'd be nice to meet for coffee after Thanksgiving."

Bill's heart thrummed, and he felt like a kid who'd been picked first for the softball team. "Fantastic!" he exclaimed. "I mean, yes, that'd be great."

They made their arrangements and said goodnight. Bill felt so good that he hummed as he finished packing. He opened his toiletry bag and put in his new sleep medication. And in case Denise wanted to go out to dinner, he folded up a dress shirt and tucked it neatly into the suitcase.

After stripping to his underwear, Bill climbed into bed. He listened to the rain and the wind, then he fantasized about Angela. They'd meet at the mall's food court, and she would look sexier in person than on the screen. At first, she'd be shy. Then she'd warm up, laughing at his jokes. They'd talk for a while, then he'd suggest a walk on the waterfront. After walking for a few minutes, she'd gaze at him in a way that let him know she wanted him.

The phone ringtone jolted Bill from his sexy thoughts. It was Denise. "Hi, sweetie."

"Hi, Dad. How are you?"

"I'm good. Done packing. Really looking forward to seeing you and the kiddo."

"Great. Us too. Hey, I was hoping you could run to Arcata in the morning to pick up some clothes from Jennie. She'll leave them on her porch in a trash bag."

"Sure. What's her address?"

"Can I text it to you?"

"I'd rather just write it, honey. I still don't have the texting thing down."

"Dad, it's easy. When you're down here, I'll show you."

•   •   •

Before dawn, Jonah woke abruptly. He put on dry clothes, tugged on his boots and stumbled away from the shelter to pee. It seemed like the rain had stopped, but under the dense forest canopy, drops fell, and the air was thick with moisture.

When Jonah got back under the tarp, he couldn't see much, but he touched his backpack and the trash bag containing his wet, dirty clothes. Along with his sleeping bag and pad, these were all his possessions.

Leave now, he thought. The early start couldn't hurt, and he'd be away from the campsite before Buzzy awoke—and away from Arcata before he encountered any temptations to get high. He quickly packed up his gear, then grabbed paper and pen from an outer pocket of his backpack. "Going south. See you when I get back," he wrote, leaving the note under a rock where his bag had been.

•   •   •

Bill awoke before his alarm and listened for the rain. It had stopped like the weather service predicted—better for his drive south on 101. He lingered under the comforter and thought about his chat with that bedraggled kid last night. Too bad he was a dumb-ass environmentalist, and probably a good thing they hadn't worked out their plans to drive together. Bill didn't want to argue for 250 miles.

Still, the kid was trying to quit weed, which softened Bill's attitude toward him. Kenny had tried to get clean from meth many times. Bill thought about the last time he'd seen his son.

It was a bright spring morning—just before Easter. Kenny appeared at their door wearing clean clothes and looking like he'd showered recently. Best of all, his son had that bouncy energy in his body and a sparkly joy in his eyes.

Cheri dragged him into the kitchen and insisted he have a sandwich with his coffee even though it was only about 10:30 AM. "Oh, it's so good to see you, Kenny," she said, gazing at him with love. "You look like you're doing better."

"I'm doing great," said Kenny, spooning sugar into his coffee. "I'm over at Three Rivers rehab on a 30-day program."

"What's it like?" asked Cheri. "Do they feed you okay? Do you have much privacy?"

"The food's terrible, and there's no privacy. I share a room with three other guys. Pretty much everyone there knows your business. But the counselors are cool." Kenny seemed proud and happy. "I'm going to do it this time. No more meth for me."

"We're so proud of you," said Cheri, looking at Bill.

Bill had heard talk like that before from Kenny, always followed by crushing disappointments. So, he did not share his wife's enthusiasm. He mumbled something and held Kenny's gaze for only a second. Bill could tell Kenny wanted his approval and his blessing. He wanted to hug Kenny and tell him how much he loved him, how scared he'd been for him. But Bill kept quiet.

Before he left, Kenny told them the rehab offered family counseling.

So, the next morning, Cheri called to schedule an appointment. The counselor told her that Kenny had taken off before the morning wake-up.

Cheri began crying. Bill took the phone. "I'm sorry, but this happens a lot," said the counselor. "Addicts relapse. The only thing you can do is take care of yourselves. Don't give him money or let him in the house if he comes around. Tell him you'll help him get back here or into another rehab. Period. And check out Al-Anon if you haven't already."

Cheri yelled at Bill after he refused to drive around town to look for Kenny like he'd done so many times before.

Bill shook off the memory. Daylight was burning. He ate a quick breakfast and hit the road.

•   •   •

Jonah walked along a forest road until he reached a paved street at the edge of town. He walked carefully downhill, stepping across ribbons of slippery forest duff that the rain had washed onto the sidewalks.

•   •   •

On his drive to Arcata, Bill remembered what happened the week after Kenny's visit. He and Cheri had just pulled onto the highway when they saw Kenny and a woman hitchhiking.

"It's Kenny!" Cheri shouted. "Stop, Bill!"

Bill started to pull over, then gunned it back onto the highway.

"Bill, what are you doing?" she asked. "That was Kenny!"

"Cheri, we know he's using. If we pick him up, he'll just ask for money."

"I don't care, goddammit," she yelled, twisting frantically to keep an eye on Kenny. "Pull over at the next exit and drive back there."

"I'm not going to do it, Cheri. I love the boy, too, and I want him to get well. But the counselor said...."

"Goddamn you, Bill," she yelled with an intensity of rage he'd never heard before. "Pull the truck over right here. I'm going to walk back there and see my son!"

"I'll pull over at the next exit, and you can have the truck."

Later, Cheri told him that Kenny and the girl were gone. Bill and Cheri separated soon after.

Bill still had doubts about that moment on the highway. Was it right to drive by his son? Should he have stopped? And since then, whenever he saw a hitchhiker, he couldn't help himself from peering closely to see if it was his son.

After picking up the clothes from Denise's friend, Bill drove toward the highway. On the on-ramp, he saw a young man about Kenny's age standing with his thumb out. He slowed down and recognized Jonah from the night before. Bill pulled over, and Jonah ran to the door. He opened it and broke into a grin.

"Unbelievable," said Bill. "Looks like we're riding together after all."

"Yeah. Looks like it. Thanks."

Bill pointed at Jonah's backpack. "Throw your stuff behind the seat and let's go."

On the highway, the pre-dawn light showed flooded fields and tidal sloughs to the east.

Jonah leaned forward. "Man, that is a lot of water."

"Yep," said Bill.

The sky was mostly clear, with a few clouds sliding north. Suddenly, a bright slice of sunlight cut over the mountains and illuminated the eucalyptus trees that bordered the highway.

"Wow," Jonah said.

"Does wonders for the attitude, huh?" Bill said. "Seeing the sky clear after a storm."

Jonah picked up the wooden toy truck from the dashboard and spun the wheels.

"Made that for my little grandson, Aaron."

Jonah looked at Bill, seeming impressed. "Wow, nice work, very realistic."

They drove into Eureka on Fourth Street. "By the way," said Bill. "I have to make a detour to check out a job on the way down."

"I don't think that will interfere with my schedule." They chuckled.

South of Fortuna, they crossed the Eel River, a brown torrent that inundated the alder and willow groves on its banks and tossed big logs like bath toys on its fast-moving surface. "That's amazing," Jonah said. "When I came up here in the spring, that was barely a trickle."

"The Eel's got four main forks, and the whole watershed is over 3,000 square miles—third largest river basin in the state. From all the rain we've had these past few days, I think it's going to keep rising for another 12 to 24 hours, but it probably won't flood except for down near the mouth at high tide."

"How do you know all that?"

"Weather service and a couple local radio stations. Plus, I've been watching these rivers my whole life," Bill said. "Got to. A flooded creek, a washout, or a landslide can keep you from making it to work or leave you stranded out in the hills. Few years back, the whole county was cut off from the outside world—east, north and south—for about 48 hours. Grocery stores started to run out of food."

"Damn," said Jonah. "Nature bats last, huh?"

"Damn right. And that's something people seem to forget about in the cities. Forget about it up here and it can cost you bad."

They drove in silence for a while. Bill noticed Jonah fidgeting. Then he heard him say, "I don't mean to bring up a sensitive subject, but since you know the rivers and streams so well, what do you think about the impacts of clearcutting?"

Bill felt his anger rise but thought he heard genuine curiosity in Jonah's voice. So he took a deep breath, then said, "It's true that too much clearcutting too fast in one watershed can be bad for the fish. It can cause flooding. But thanks to all your logging regulations, that doesn't happen much anymore."

"So some of the regulations aren't so bad?"

Bill chuckled grimly. "All right, Socrates. I'll give you that one. Even though most timber harvest rules don't make any damned sense, some of the old-time logging practices were bad for the streams and the fish. But you know what's really bad for the fish? The pot growers."

"Seriously?" Jonah asked. "Why?"

"They're expanding like crazy, sucking all the water out of the streams that salmon spawn in. All to irrigate their pot farms."

"That does sound pretty bad," said Jonah.

"It is."

They crossed another bridge, then some industrial buildings loomed into view on the right. Jonah stared at them while Bill looked straight ahead.

The complex of sawmills and planing mills lay utterly still. No steam billowed from the roof vents; no logging trucks lined up to deliver their loads; no beetle-shaped Le Tourneaus wrestled logs off the trucks; no forklifts shuttled freshly milled boards to the drying stacks.

The events that had idled this industrial powerhouse, formerly the Northwest Lumber Company, had unfolded years ago. In the mid-1980s, a junk bond investor bought the company and cranked up logging and lumber production. Bill's friends who worked there were pleased with the overtime. They bought new trucks, boats, and hunting rifles.

Then activists discovered a small forest of old-growth redwood on company land. They named it Headwaters and spread the word that chainsaws and bulldozers threatened the grove. Protesters came up from the Bay Area, threw themselves in front of logging trucks and chained their bodies to sawmill gates. Others set up treehouses or played cat-and-mouse on the ground, daring loggers to topple a tree on them. One activist died that way.

Environmental groups raised money to save the redwoods, and liberal legislators and the Clinton White House got involved. Eventually, the investor made a deal to sell the old-growth grove to the government. And soon after that, the company went bankrupt—an outcome the environmentalists had predicted.

As the mill complex receded in Bill's mirror, he thought about his friends who'd worked there. Bob French went to Washington, where the industry was still strong. Old Frank Schmidt and his sons started their own trucking outfit. Others signed on with logging contractors or other sawmills, but too many had to settle for jobs in service industries that paid half as much as their old jobs had.

Bill knew the bankruptcy wasn't entirely the environmentalists' fault. Many of his friends knew it, too. But they rarely admitted it. Bill remembered Petey saying, "I know that son of a bitch is logging too damned fast, just like the enviro-nuts say. But I'll be damned if I ever admit that to those fuckers!"

Bill glanced at Jonah, who watched the forests and pastures speed by. He was grateful Jonah had not spoken up or asked about the shuttered mill. He must know the stories, Bill thought.

When they'd passed the last roadside town and were deep in the fir and redwood forest, Bill asked Jonah, "You looking forward to seeing your family?"

The young man stared out the window. "My brother, yeah. My mom, not so much."

Bill wanted to ask more but didn't want to be nosy. He turned off at Avenue of the Giants. "Job site's down this way."

They entered a valley where pastures and farms spread out to the hills in the east. Turning left through an open gate, Bill saw King's one-story ranch house and the redwood King had mentioned. About 100 feet tall, it grew right next to the house.

"You can stay here if you want or come with me," he said to Jonah. "But I'm going to say hi to my buddy who's here milling some lumber, and he doesn't really like, you know, people like you. He won't ride you too bad since you're with me, but he'll say something."

"How long you gonna be?"

"Twenty or thirty minutes."

"I'll come along."

Over the thrumming roar of the Eel River, Bill could hear the mini-mill's gasoline engine. He led the way along a gravel road. To the north, a farmer on a tractor pulled a disc harrow through brown stubble. To the south, a score of black and brown steers lowered their heads to the thick grass. Ahead were tree-covered foothills; beyond them, silhouettes of ridges and peaks dissolved into the clouds.

Alongside the road, young redwoods grew as straight as utility poles. King had planted them about twenty years before, and Bill thought that in another five or ten years, they'd be ready to cut, yielding about five hundred board feet on average, maybe $1,000 per stem if the market was good.

Bill saw Eric pushing a big bandsaw through a squared-up fir log. Eric nodded, and after finishing the cut, he stopped the engine.

"You get a look at that redwood?" Eric asked.

"Yeah. Going to measure it, but I figure me and Jim can do it in a day."

"King wants to pay you with lumber. He's hyped up to use his new toy here," Eric said.

"Yeah, so he said. But I don't need a bunch of un-planed redwood. I'm trying to pay for the house I got, not build one."

Eric chuckled. "Fuckin' King. He likes everyone to bend over without even a damned kiss. Then he 'spects you to be grateful."

"This is Jonah. I'm giving him a ride to Santa Rosa."

"Hey," Eric said, shaking Jonah's hand. "What's with the bum disguise? I know times are tough, but are you too broke to go to the laundromat?"

Jonah paused, then said, "I am pretty low on funds right now, but I've got a call in to my accountant to see about selling some stocks."

Eric and Bill laughed, and Bill felt pleased with Jonah's retort—the kid didn't act like a pussy.

"Listen, I gotta get back to work," Eric said.

"Okay. We'll see ya," Bill said.

Eric and Bill shook hands. Then Eric reached into his wallet, pulled out a five and offered it to Jonah with a sly grin. "Here. This oughta be enough for a couple loads."

"Man, I guess it's been a while since you've been to the laundromat," Jonah said, grinning. "I'd need at least twenty." Eric pocketed the five with a laugh.

Jonah helped Bill measure the tree. Then Bill got in the truck and was about to turn the key when he saw Jonah standing by the door, arching his back.

"I'll just be a minute," Jonah said. "Gotta stretch." He hinged forward from his waist and stretched his hands to the ground.

Wish I had that flexibility, Bill thought. "You do yoga?" he asked.

"Yeah, learned it in high school."

"Good stuff. I started taking classes a while back, feeling better."

"Nice."

Bill pulled out his phone. "Gonna let my daughter know about when I'll get there." He was about to dial Denise when he said to

Jonah, "Hey, maybe you can show me how to text with this thing. My daughter's been bugging me to learn."

"Sure." Jonah took the phone. "You have to push the keys one, two or three times to get the letter you want," he explained. "Like say you want to write 'hi,' you push the four twice and wait until the 'H' pops up. Then you tap four again three times to get 'I'."

"Really?"

"Yeah. Either that or get a new phone with a little keyboard."

"Let me see if I can do this."

Bill slowly tapped out: "hi denise be there about 3 love you dad."

"Now what?"

"Just hit that green button."

"There it goes. Thanks, partner. My first text." Soon, they were back on the highway, following the South Fork of the Eel.

Chapter 6

Through his window, Jonah admired the forest growing thick and dense from the ridges down into the ravines. On the peaks, he saw cantilevered cliffs and spiraling rock formations. Bright green upland prairies spread across south-facing slopes like lush carpets. And every few miles, Jonah got a good glimpse of the river.

Jonah also scanned for evidence of industrial logging. He didn't see any. Jonah knew clearcutting was plain wrong. The drunk Native American they'd picked up was an appealing character, but no expert witness. And Bill's attitude puzzled him. He was a logger, yes. But he also seemed to know a lot about the woods and rivers and ecosystems.

Jonah took a deep breath and asked, "So, do you really think clearcutting is the best way to do logging?"

Jonah could see Bill's jaw grinding. "It's true that when you see a new clearcut from the road, it looks like hell," Bill said with a calmness that surprised Jonah. "But the trees grow back, and in thirty or forty years, they're ready to be harvested again."

Bill continued. "Some of these stands up here have gone through two or three rotations. In Germany, they've been clearcutting and replanting the same forests for three hundred years."

Jonah was getting stirred up. "I've read about logging in Germany. They've started changing their practices because they recognized the long-term damage that clearcutting was doing. They're doing more all-aged management."

Jonah saw Bill tighten his grip on the steering wheel and shake his head. Like a lecturer, Bill said, "The name of the game in the timber industry is to produce as much wood per acre as we can. For redwood and fir, that means clearcutting because those trees grow back best in full sun. And trees grow straighter with more useable timber than trees that grow under selective cutting that you and your friends are so fond of."

"It still doesn't seem right." Jonah's passion was rising despite his intention to stay calm. "I mean, what about all the erosion? And the herbicides they use after they replant? And where are the birds and the rodents and other creatures supposed to live until the trees grow back?"

"What about us two-legged critters?" Bill pointed with an open hand at the forest they were passing. "These woods used to be full of logging crews. When I was your age, any kid could get a good-paying job at the mills or in the woods. But the environmentalists and the regulators are on us so tight now we can hardly cut anything."

"I'm not against logging. I know we need lumber. But there's got to be better ways to do logging that leave the forests intact for the wildlife."

Bill took his hand off the steering wheel and made a fist. "So, you think I'm just out there killing animals with my chainsaw, huh!?" he shouted. "Us dumb-ass loggers who've been taking care of these forests for generations should just change our ways and do it how you think we should?"

Jonah felt the truck shudder. A thumping noise filled the cab, and Bill struggled to steer. "Must be a blowout," he said. "Gotta find a place to pull over."

They were on a winding two-lane section of the highway with no shoulder. Bill slowed and kept as far to the right as he could, but as they approached a tight curve, Jonah realized they could get rear-ended at any moment.

"Stop for a sec, and I'll get out to warn other drivers," he said urgently.

Bill looked at him, then at the rearview mirror. He nodded and stopped. Jonah leaped out and ran back to where the road had a tiny shoulder. Within seconds, a black SUV came screaming down the highway. Jonah waved his arms and pointed down the road. As he passed, Jonah screamed, "Slow down!"

The driver braked hard before he hit the curve.

An RV came lumbering through the trees, followed by a semi-tanker fuel truck. Both drivers responded to Jonah's signal. Then, a brown Dodge pickup slowed and stopped. "Need help?" yelled the driver out the open window.

"We had a blowout," Jonah yelled. "My friend's down the road trying to find a place to pull over."

The driver, who wore a cowboy hat and smoked a cigar, looked in his rearview mirror, then back at Jonah. "How 'bout if I drive you to meet him? I'll go slow with my flashers on."

Jonah hopped in. "Thanks, man. He's probably just up ahead."

As the truck started moving, a blue coupe zoomed up on its tail. "Sorry, pal," said the driver to his rearview mirror. "You're just going to have to wait."

In about a quarter-mile, Bill's pickup truck came into sight, parked in a turnout. Jonah got out.

"You need any more help, a ride to the next town or something?" the driver asked.

Bill said, "Thanks, partner, but I think we can manage." Jonah saw that Bill had already gotten out the jack and tools. With a smoky salute, the cowboy drove off.

"Good thinking back there. I was down to the rim by the time I found this pullout."

Jonah grinned. "No problem."

Bill lowered the spare from under the truck and freed it from the cable. Then he said with disgust, "Damn thing is flat." He stood up and kicked the tire. "That's what I get for not checking it 'fore I took off."

"Shit happens," said Jonah, shrugging his shoulders.

Bill got out his phone. "No service."

Jonah tried to joke: "Well, at least it's not raining."

Bill didn't respond.

"There's a tire shop in Laytonville, right?" Jonah asked.

"Yep. And a tow company, but if we can't call 'em…"

"Let's take the tire, hitch a ride into town and get it fixed. Drivers will see we're broke down, and they'll know from the tire that we're just going to next town."

"Hitchhike, huh? Haven't done that in years. Why not?"

As Jonah predicted, they got a ride soon.

The tire shop wasn't busy, and they had Bill's tire size in stock. "Shouldn't take more than a half-hour," said the owner.

Jonah went for a walk by himself. The adrenaline spike from the blowout had eased, and now his feelings about Bill's angry outburst surfaced. He felt like he was about seven years old, and a memory swam up from his childhood.

It was early evening. His mom was in the kitchen while he and Django watched cartoons in the living room. He heard a car in the driveway and knew Daddy was home. Django, about four, got up and ran to the door. Their dad came in, buoyant and happy. "How are my boys?"

He was tall and slender, with blue-gray eyes and a toothy smile. He bent over to grab Django and hoisted him up almost to the ceiling. After putting Django down, he tousled Jonah's hair. Then he sniffed the air, made a face, and said comically, "Smells like spaghetti again."

His dad walked into the kitchen and said something to his mother that Jonah didn't understand. Then Jonah heard his mother's angry voice. "Maybe we could afford steak once in a while if you didn't drink up half your paycheck!"

"Dammit," his father yelled. "I work ten hours a day and deserve to relax with my buddies."

The shouting grew louder. Jonah grabbed Django and hauled him behind the couch to hide. Then he heard dishes shattering.

•   •   •

Bill sat on a stool at the counter. As he watched Jonah walk down the road, Bill regretted losing his cool like that; he was glad they had another hundred or so miles to Santa Rosa. That would give him time to apologize.

On the wall above a coffee pot, old postcards showed the early days of logging: trucks and flatbed rail cars hauled logs twelve feet thick, axmen stood proudly on a stump as wide as a dance floor. One postcard showed a 1960s-era yarder on a snowy landing site, anchored with cables. It reminded Bill of the used yarder he and Petey bought when they had their own logging outfit.

Kenny was nineteen when they'd hired him—and he lasted less than a day.

Bill remembered watching Kenny struggle to set the choker cable around a turn of fir logs. When he finally got it done, he flashed a smile and thumbs-up at Bill, who blew the whistle. Petey—in the yarder cab—lifted the logs. In the next second, one of the logs fell and nearly hit Kenny.

Panic gripped Bill's chest as he peered down the slope, looking for Kenny amid the tumble of logs. When he saw that Kenny hadn't been hurt, Bill's fear turned to anger. "Get your head outta yer ass before you get yourself killed!" he yelled.

When Kenny caught his breath, he yelled something back at Bill. Then Bill yelled something. Then Kenny threw his metal hat into the slash, walked up the slope, and disappeared down the forest road.

For years, Bill had stored that memory in a compartment labeled *Kenny couldn't handle his emotions because he was using drugs*. But since going to Al-Anon, Bill had gradually come to see that he had his own anger problems. Blowing up at Jonah just now was unnecessary—and immature.

Bill sank his face into his hands, his elbows resting on the counter. Had he lived his whole adult life without knowing this about himself? It frightened him how much he was still a mystery to himself. And he feared he would never get a chance to repair the damage he'd done to Kenny.

The bell on the shop door rang, and Jonah came in. He smiled weakly at Bill, who smiled back and mulled over some words of apology but couldn't come up with the right ones. Instead, he pointed at the coffee. "Get you a free cuppa?"

Jonah made a face. "I'll pass. Probably been there all morning."

The shop owner came in, rolling the wheel with its new tire. He offered them a ride back to Bill's rig.

Chapter 7

"You want to stop for a bite or anything?" Bill asked as they passed through the little town of Hopland.

Jonah was craving a good coffee but also wanted to save money. "Nah, I'm good," he said. "Don't mind stopping if you want to, though."

"No need," Bill replied.

Then Bill startled Jonah by asking, "So, how come you're worried about seeing your mom?"

Jonah resented the intrusion, yet he heard real interest in Bill's voice. He shrugged and looked out the window. "I've always felt intimidated by her. Still do. Seems like she's always judging me for not going to college or getting the kind of job she thinks I should get." He quickly added, "I know it's a parent's job to teach their kids responsibility and stuff. But she always gives me this feeling that I can never measure up."

Bill was quiet for a beat, then said, "I'm starting to know more about that, thinking about how I might have been that kind of parent with my own son." Bill kept his eyes on the road, and Jonah searched fruitlessly for something to say in response.

They'd left redwood country and were driving through the vineyards, farms, and hills of Sonoma County—green and lush from the fall rains. Billboards appeared at closer intervals, and they began hitting traffic. "Holiday travel," said Bill.

Soon, they approached Santa Rosa, the first real city south of Eureka. They'd been quiet for a while as if tacitly agreeing that they'd traveled far enough into each other's inner worlds.

"Where do you want me to drop you off in Santa Rosa?" asked Bill.

Jonah knew he could catch a bus to San Francisco—but his mom wasn't expecting him until tomorrow. She'd come get him, but that would mean battling rush-hour traffic to and from the city after her long workday. With a notion of hobo camping in Santa Rosa, he said, "How about that old downtown area?"

"Railroad District? Sure."

The rain had started again when Bill pulled to the curb. "Your mom picking you up?" he asked.

"I think so," said Jonah, leaving out the details. "Gonna call her now."

Bill reached into his jacket pocket and handed Jonah a business card. "Get in touch when you're back up north. Maybe we can go for coffee."

Jonah pocketed the card and extended his hand. "Thanks, Bill," he said quietly. "I really appreciate it. I mean the ride and everything."

"And listen," said Bill, looking serious. "Don't give up on your recovery. Make that your first priority. You can do it."

"Okay." Jonah closed the door and watched the truck disappear around a corner.

The sidewalks were busy with people clutching bags and hustling between stores in the rain. Jonah pulled out his phone. When he reached his mom's voicemail, he invented an itinerary. "Hey, Mom. I'm on my way down to Santa Rosa. Gonna stay with some friends. Could you pick me up in the railroad district tomorrow morning or meet me in the city later?"

At the railroad depot, he saw three young travelers sitting under the awning. He didn't recognize them, but their backpacks, dirty clothes, and sprawling postures were familiar.

He walked up, and they immediately accepted him. They said they'd also just come from Humboldt. Jonah sat with them, and they traded stories about trimming in the backcountry and avoiding the cops while camping in Arcata.

Later, Jonah followed them to a dry place under a bridge over Santa Rosa Creek. As soon as they sloughed off their backpacks, one broke out a pipe, and another unscrewed the top of a wine bottle. Jonah walked away to pee, and with his back to the group, he watched the creek roar and tumble with fresh rain. The wind jerked the willows around like manic dancers.

Jonah knew he should leave, but he couldn't find the willpower. He zipped up and walked back to the group. Putting a smile on his face, he sat down and waited for the pipe and the bottle.

•   •   •

Bill's heart flipped when he saw his eight-year-old grandson Aaron pedaling his bike on the driveway. When the boy spotted Bill's truck stopping at the curb, he hopped off the bike and ran to him. "Grandpa, you made it!"

"Hey there, buddy!" replied Bill, squatting down to take Aaron in his arms.

At the door, his daughter's brown eyes and wide smile filled Bill with joy. They wrapped each other in a hug.

After Bill put his gear in the guest room, he brought out Aaron's truck. The boy was ecstatic. "Grandpa, it's so cool!"

"Glad you like it, buddy," he said, rubbing Aaron's head.

Denise had made a beef roast with steamed broccoli and potatoes, and she'd already set the table. Accustomed as he was to eating dinner early, Bill was hungry. "Anything I can help with?"

"Nope," said Denise. "Everything's ready. Let's sit down and eat."

When seated, she asked Bill, "Do you want to lead grace, Dad?" Bill felt his shoulders stiffen. Cheri had taught the kids to say grace at special meals, but Bill had grown up without religion and had only gone along with the ritual to keep peace with his wife. Seeing Aaron looking at him expectantly, Bill rallied.

"Uh, okay, honey, it has been a long time. Let's see. Lord, we thank you for this food and for this time together as a family. We ask your blessings on our friends and our family. Amen."

"Especially Kenny," added Denise quietly.

"Where is Uncle Kenny?" asked Aaron.

Bill's appetite left, and neither he nor Denise responded for a moment. Then, Bill said, "Your Uncle Kenny isn't well. If he were, he'd be here with us."

"What's wrong with him? Is his leg broken?"

"Aaron's friend Kyle broke his leg," said Denise.

Bill gathered his thoughts. "He has a kind of ... illness in his mind," he said to Aaron. "Something went wrong in his brain, and right now, he can't do a lot of the things he used to do, not even things he'd really like to do. Like visit you and your mommy."

"When will he get better?"

Denise said, "We don't know, Sweetie. All we can do is pray for him. And think good thoughts about him."

They fell to eating silently. Then Bill nearly choked when Denise asked Aaron, "What do you remember about your Uncle Kenny?"

"I remember camping. By a river. It was really fun."

"That was at Tish Tang Campground, up in the Hoopa Valley." Bill struggled to hold his grief in.

"Yeah," said Denise. "That was a really good time. Grandma was there, too."

"Grandma's coming for Thanksgiving!" Aaron said. He turned to Bill. "You'll be here for Thanksgiving, right?"

"Sweetie, you remember what I told you," Denise interjected. "Your grandpa will be with us through Thanksgiving morning, then your Grandma is going to come later that day."

"It'll be like two Thanksgivings!" said Aaron brightly. Bill was pleased Aaron could find a bright side to his grandparents' divorce.

After they put Aaron to bed, Bill and Denise sat in the living room, drinking hot cider. Bill wanted to ask about her work and social life, but he knew they'd have to talk about Kenny.

Denise cleared her throat. "How are you doing after, you know, I told you about Kenny going into rehab last summer?"

Bill shook his head. "I don't feel too good about it, especially him relapsing again. But I guess I have to accept it."

Bill didn't add that he was also trying to swallow a hard nugget of truth about himself and his relationship with his son: Kenny had stayed in touch with Cheri and Denise when he went into rehab because they'd always shown him unconditional love. Bill had not.

Love for his son was always in Bill's heart, burning like a thick madrone piece at the back of a wood stove. But after seeing the boy killing himself, watching him clean up, and then relapsing, that fire was down to embers.

•   •   •

Jonah was awakened early by trucks driving over the bridge. He felt sick with remorse for getting high after he'd left Arcata so hastily to avoid temptation. He checked his phone and saw his mom had left a voicemail. "Jonah dear, I'm so glad you're almost here. I'll pick you up at that café across from the old depot in Santa Rosa about 9:30."

One of the other travelers stirred, and Jonah knew he had to leave before the wake-and-bake started. He rolled up his bag and pad, slung his pack, and headed to the café.

•   •   •

Bill and Denise sat at the kitchen table. She drank a smoothie and looked at her phone while he ate fried eggs and a bowl of oatmeal and read the paper. Bill appreciated the comfortable silence with his daughter.

After rinsing her cup at the sink, Denise asked, "You want to make Aaron's breakfast, then take him to school and pick him up at 2:45?"

"That sounds great," he said, putting down the paper. "In between, I'll go visit Petey."

"Your old friend and business partner? Is he down here now?"

"I just heard recently from his son, Charlie. Petey's in a care home. Dementia."

Denise sat back down. "Oh wow. I can't believe it. He used to be so—what's the word—such a big bright spirit."

"He lived large. Taught me how to climb and top trees and so much else. And he worked his ass off, owned a couple houses. It's hard for me to understand why his family can't take care of him back home."

"How's Charlie doing? I remember him being so fun when we were kids." She sat back in her chair and smiled. "I had a crush on him for a while."

Bill shook his head. "Just hanging on, it seems. Guess he's got a mental illness. Lives with his older brother."

"Well, that might explain why they can't care for him up in Humboldt."

"Yeah. Guess you're right."

Before Denise left, she woke Aaron. Bill was washing the dishes when his sleepy-eyed grandson appeared in the kitchen holding his stuffed boa constrictor. "Good morning, kiddo. What would you like for breakfast?"

Aaron smiled. "Pancakes!"

"Hmm. It's been a while since Grandpa has made pancakes." Bill pondered what to do. "How about French toast?"

"With cinnamon?"

"You bet!"

•   •   •

Jonah got a small coffee and sat in the café. Everyone else was watching a screen or reading a book or magazine. He thought about grabbing the free weekly newspaper but was too keyed up. He watched the door and soon saw his mom enter. She lit up when she saw him. They hugged, and she held on for an uncomfortably long time. Then she pulled back, held him by the elbows and looked into his eyes.

"Jonah, Jonah, Jonah," she said. "Oh my God, I'm so happy to see you."

"I'm happy to see you too, Mom," he said, surprised by the intensity of her greeting.

As soon as they got on the highway, his mother asked, "So, how's life in Humboldt County?"

"Good. I love it up there." Looking at the strip malls, motels, apartment buildings, and auto dealerships that crowded Highway 101, Jonah already felt stressed. "It's so much more chill and peaceful than down here. How's Django?"

Her voice quivered as she said in a monotone, "Your brother is doing okay. But his problems are getting worse."

Jonah's face and neck burned with guilt. He'd known about Django's bipolar disorder before he'd left for Humboldt. "Is he taking his meds?"

"Well, he just started a new one, so we'll see." Jonah heard sadness in her voice. "The last one worked for about a year and a half. Then the old pattern started again. You remember. When he's up, he feels on top of the world, like he can do anything. And he won't stop talking. Then the downs come, and he can barely drag himself out of bed. I hope this new med works." She smiled and added, "But the really great thing is that we've both been reborn in Christ."

"No kidding?" Jonah managed to say as he swallowed his shock. "Well, uh, good for you."

As they drove over the Golden Gate Bridge, Jonah checked the time on his phone. Because of the holiday traffic, it had taken them an hour to get this far. It would be another hour to San José, a long time to be in the car with his mom.

"So, how are you supporting yourself?" she asked.

He couldn't think of a way to sugar-coat it. "I made a bunch of money trimming weed in the fall. And I live in the forest, so there's no rent. I just pay for food, basically."

Bracing for her judgment, Jonah was surprised when she said mildly, "Well, as long as you're safe. We hear some terrible stories about that industry on the news."

"Almost all the growers are really mellow and fair," he said, happy that he could relieve her fears. "If they cheat their workers or try to hit on the girls too hard, word gets around, and people won't work for them."

As they entered his old neighborhood in San José, Jonah felt disgusted by the big houses with their lawns, green with water taken from rivers far to the north. And his anxiety about the next couple of days mounted. Holidays had been times of high drama in his family: his dad getting drunk, his mom reacting with the silent treatment or a screaming fit. His father was gone, but his mother could still find many reasons to freak out.

Django met him at the door, and he felt a rush of affection. "Big bro," Django said as he hugged Jonah.

He'd grown taller and leaner in just six months. "How are you, Django? It's good to see you."

"Pretty good, man. How's the north country treating you?"

Jonah let out a long breath. "Wow, so much to tell. I don't know where to begin."

His mom suggested Jonah settle into the guest room and take a shower. "I'll put a load of laundry in for you," she added, and Jonah gratefully handed her his bag of dirty wet clothes.

Later, while their mom prepared lunch, the brothers sat at the kitchen counter, and Jonah told them about his life in Humboldt County.

"You live in the forest?" Django asked with excitement.

"Yeah. It's pretty nice. My buddy and I found the perfect spot and rigged up a tight shelter that keeps us dry even in the heavy rains we get up there."

"How do you cook or shower?" asked his mom.

"Or do a number two?" asked Django.

"Once in a while, we dig a hole, but mostly we go to town, use the public restrooms," Jonah explained. "We get showers at friends' apartments or the town pool."

"Do you have a job?" Django asked.

"Uh, sort of," Jonah replied. "I worked on a weed farm during harvest season. Still got a little of that cash left."

"Whoa," said Django. "I guess that's sort of legal now, huh? With the medical marijuana."

"It's complicated. But I'm not going to do that next season because ... I, uh, I quit smoking pot."

His mother put down her knife. Jonah saw her eyes shine as she said, "Good for you, Jonah, good for you."

"Is it hard?" asked Django.

"Damned hard." Jonah held back from revealing that he'd gotten high the night before.

"You should come to church and talk to Pastor Mike," Django said with excitement. "Man has he got it goin' on. You can feel the good vibes coming off him. And he's got a ton of experience channeling the Lord's grace to heal people with addictions."

Jonah was about to say he was more drawn to Eastern spirituality or Native American practices, but Django plowed ahead. "One time, this dude came in, obviously drunk, smelling real bad. We all noticed him. When Pastor Mike got to the part of the service where he asks people who want to be saved to come down front, he walked right up to the dude."

Django stood and mimed the pastor, putting his hands on the drunk's shoulders. "At first, the guy looked really angry, like he's going to punch the pastor. But pretty soon, he started crying. Then Pastor Mike guides him up front. They kneel together, and the pastor tells us all to gather around."

Django paused for dramatic effect. "That same dude has been coming every Sunday morning and every Wednesday night, and he looks sober to me. Don't you think so, Mom?"

"Yes," she said. "That was a miracle of faith. Now it's time for lunch."

Jonah's mom led grace, then they dug into her trademark sandwiches: curry tuna on toasted sourdough with a green salad on the side. "Yum, Mom, this is great," Jonah said between bites.

"Ditto," Django said, reaching for another sandwich.

When they finished, Jonah helped his mother clean up the kitchen. "How long do you think you'll stay?" she asked as she loaded the dishwasher.

"I think I'll take off the day after Thanksgiving."

"So soon?"

"Yeah. I know it's a short visit, but Humboldt is home now." The truth was that Jonah didn't think he could stand more than 48 hours under his mother's roof in suburban Babylon.

"I understand, sweetie. Maybe you can come back for Christmas."

"Yeah, that sounds great," Jonah lied.

•   •   •

It was an ordinary suburban house with a sign in front that said, *Just for You Care Home.* Bill parked, walked up the wheelchair ramp and rang the doorbell. After a moment, a young man with thick black glasses opened the door. "Can I help you?"

"I'm here to visit Petey Taylor."

"That's great!" he exclaimed with a smile. "Mr. Taylor just had lunch, and I'm sure he'd love a visitor." Bill followed him through a dining area smelling of fried meat and ammonia. "His room is just ahead on the right."

The door was open, but Bill knocked anyway. He heard a feeble voice say, "Hello?"

Bill entered and saw the man who'd taught him how to climb and top 150-foot trees lying in a narrow bed surrounded by white walls that bore no trace of Petey's life: no John Wayne posters, no sixteen-point buck, no photos of African safaris or his kids with their football teams. The room wasn't even private. Another man lay in a bed by the window.

"Hey, Petey," Bill said, stepping toward the bed. "How're you doing?"

"I know you, don't I?" asked Petey, smiling.

Bill thought he was joking. "Of course, you know me." But Petey didn't seem to. "It's Bill. Bill Collins."

Petey frowned and shook his head. "How do we know each other?"

"Do you mind if I get a chair and sit down?"

Petey nodded. Bill walked into the dining area and grabbed a metal folding chair.

For the next 30 minutes, Bill talked about every subject he could think of to awaken Petey's memory. "When you weren't yelling at us, you were a pretty decent crew boss. You kept me from killing myself a few times."

"That's nice," said Petey, smiling vacantly.

Bill told stories about their lives as fathers, how Petey worried about his sons racing at the drag strip, how proud he was that they had the balls to rip up the asphalt. He mentioned hunting and fishing trips they'd taken together. He even asked Petey about his old family stories.

"Remember how your dad brought you to Humboldt from Oregon? How he was so appalled at the logging methods in

California? How he laughed at anybody who thought the Doug-fir trade would ever amount to anything? How he never liked to admit that you and your wife were smart to go in partners on that old ranch up Larrabee Creek, with all that fir timber?"

Petey kept nodding, smiling, and saying, "Do tell?" and "Oh my, we did that?"

Bill ran out of stories and wanted to leave. Petey didn't mind. "About time for my nap, anyway," he said. Then Petey stuck out his hand, and Bill saw a flash of the old commanding presence. "Nice of you to visit. Do come again." Bill said he would.

Bill drove in a daze through Santa Rosa's busy streets. Why hadn't he kept in touch with Petey? And how could a man like Petey end up living in a place like that?

He even thought about calling Cheri, the only person in Bill's life who had known Petey like Bill had. A wave of sadness swept through Bill, so strong that he almost pulled over to give himself time to cry. But he was due at Aaron's school.

When he pulled up at the school, the sight of Aaron running toward his truck snapped Bill from his mournful reverie.

"Grandpa!" the boy yelled as he opened the door. "Look what I made!" He thrust a rectangle of construction paper at Bill. "Do you see me and Mommy?" Aaron pointed helpfully at stick figures drawn with markers. "And here's you in your truck, come to visit. See, it's a Ford."

"By Golly, that is me," said Bill, squinting at the drawing.

"And here's Uncle Kenny." Aaron pointed to a piece of silver paper. "See, he's in a hospital bed, but he's getting better."

Bill swallowed his pain. "Well, look at that, Aaron. Aren't you a little Picasso."

"Pi-what?"

"Picasso. He was a famous Spanish artist."

"Neat-o. What are we going to do now?"

"Well, do you want to go buy your mom a Christmas gift?"

"Oh boy, yes. Can we go to the mall and get a hot chocolate at Strawbucks?"

"You bet, kiddo."

After shopping, Bill drove to a park, where Aaron ran to the swing set and leaped onto a seat. Bill marveled at his grandson's graceful movements, how he leaned back, stretched his legs out on the upswing, then curled into a tight ball for the downswing. But he wanted more than his own momentum for the ride. "Push me, Grandpa! Push me!"

They got home around four. Bill made them a snack, and they settled on the couch to watch a Disney movie—and promptly fell asleep. Denise woke them gently. She didn't have a dinner planned, so they ordered pizza and then watched the rest of the Disney movie.

When Aaron went to bed, Bill told Denise he would also turn in. "Big day, seeing Petey, running around with Aaron."

"How was Petey?"

"Pretty bad. I'll tell you more about it tomorrow." They hugged and said goodnight.

When he got to his room, Bill pulled out his phone and dialed his Al-Anon friend John.

"Hey, Bill. I'm glad to hear from you! How are you?"

"Well, I'm kind of having a hard time and wondered if we could talk a bit."

"Absolutely," John said. "What's going on?"

"You remember I told you how I learned that Kenny went into rehab, never called me, and then relapsed again."

"Uh-huh," said John with an encouraging tone.

"Well, it's hitting me harder now that I'm visiting my daughter and grandson. And then I went to visit a good old friend, a guy I've known like thirty years but lost track of in the last year or so." Bill found it hard to talk, but he managed to describe Petey's state of mind and his living conditions. "It was like he was just gone, a phantom, nobody home. And stuck in that place after how hard he worked his whole life."

John took a deep breath and asked Bill, "And how are you feeling?"

"I'm feeling... I feel like I'm a failure as a friend and a dad. How bad of a dad do you have to be for your son not to get in touch when he's trying to get clean? I mean, didn't he think I'd be happy to hear that and that I'd want to support him and stuff?"

"And what else are you feeling, Bill?"

Bill chuckled bitterly. "I guess I'm feeling sad. And ashamed. Ashamed that Kenny didn't think he could confide in me. Sad that he relapsed again. And sad about old Petey."

They were both quiet for a couple of seconds. Then John said, "You've lost a lot, Bill. You've lost your son to addiction. You've lost your friend to dementia. It's normal to feel sad. And the shame can be healthy, too, if we use it to change and not just beat ourselves up."

"Okay, but what do I do about Kenny?" asked Bill, choking up. "I mean, he was in rehab, and he didn't contact me."

"Bill, it's not for us to determine if our loved ones get into recovery or how they act when they do. This is real powerlessness, and it's tough to take. Of course, there's one thing you *can* do. It probably won't help Kenny, but it could help you."

"I know, goddammit—pray. Al-Anon's solution to every damn thing. I don't believe in God, though. You know that. What am I supposed to pray to? The Goddamned moon?"

After a second, John laughed pleasantly. "Hmmm, that's not a bad idea. Maybe you should try that."

Bill sighed, exasperated. "I just pulled that out of the air, John. I don't believe the moon has any power to help me."

"It's interesting that you mentioned it, though. You're a fisherman, so you know about tides and the phases of the moon.

Maybe you've just hit on something that could be your higher power."

John continued, "I mean if the moon can make the oceans rise and fall, she might be able to give you a little comfort," he said. "I think the human body is something like ninety-five percent water."

Bill surprised himself by saying, "Maybe I just will try that." He'd only meant to humor John, but as the words came out of his mouth, he warmed to the idea.

"Do it right now, Bill. Get down on your knees, tell the moon your troubles, and ask it for help. Let me know how it works, okay? And remember that you're loved by me and a bunch of other folks in the program."

"Okay. Thanks and have a good night."

Bill had promised to pray to please John. But now, he felt an urge to do it. He sank to his knees, put his face on the carpet and started praying to the moon. He felt a strange and pleasant sensation ripple from his lower abdomen to his chest. It was almost too much to take. After about thirty seconds, he sat up, feeling a little better.

Chapter 8

It was difficult to pry himself away from Denise and Aaron on Thanksgiving morning. But Bill wanted to leave the way clear for Cheri, as they'd agreed. So, he packed up and got ready to go right after breakfast. He hugged Denise and Aaron, then got in his truck and hit the road—watching them in his rearview mirror as they stood under Denise's big umbrella and waved. The visit had left him feeling raw and torn up but also comforted. Aaron's exuberant affection warmed his heart, and just being around Denise felt good.

As Bill drove onto the highway, he scanned the on-ramp, looking for Kenny. Or Jonah. Nobody was there, so he eased onto the highway, made his way to the left lane, and set the cruise control to seventy-five.

•   •   •

A hundred miles south in San José, Thanksgiving morning arrived with a clear sky. Jonah entered his mother's kitchen and saw her working a spatula under a giant pancake. Sausage and bacon steamed on the kitchen table next to a big glass pitcher of orange juice.

When she saw him, she put the spatula down and opened her arms. "Happy Thanksgiving, honey. I'm so glad you're here."

"Me too, Mom," he said, hugging her tightly.

Jonah poured himself a coffee and sat at the counter. "So, are you expecting the whole neighborhood for breakfast?"

She laughed. "I know. I'm making twice as much as we need, but I can't help it."

Django came in then, dragging his feet on the carpet. Jonah was alarmed at his brother's stuporous energy. He could see his mother was too, but she said brightly, "Good morning, sunshine."

"Mornin'," Django mumbled. He slumped on the couch, picked up the TV remote and flipped through channels.

"Were you up late playing video games, honey?" she asked. Django nodded. "You know what the doctors said about that, dear. Getting a good sleep is important to manage your mood swings."

"I know, Mom."

Jonah and his mother labored through breakfast to keep the conversation going while Django withdrew further. Jonah wished his mother would let him be depressed, but she kept at him. When they'd finished eating, she asked, "Have you taken your medications?"

"No."

She grabbed her plate, stood up, and said with a hot blaze of anger, "Honestly—on Thanksgiving Day!"

And then Jonah was a kid again, panicked and terrified as he watched his mom get worked up.

"I've had it," she said, flinging crumbs from her plate as she pointed it at Django. "If you don't cheer up, you're going to completely ruin Thanksgiving." Django pulled his head down like a turtle.

She stomped into the kitchen and put her plate in the sink with a clatter. "After all my work to make this day special." Without a word, Django got up and walked to his room.

Jonah wanted to comfort his mother—and he wanted to get away from her. After sitting silently for a moment, he said, "It's not like he's doing it on purpose, Mom. Maybe you should just let him be for a while."

"Easy for you to say, Mr. Hobo." His mother's face reddened, and she held her clenched fists against her thighs. "You have no idea how hard I work to keep things together here, to keep your brother from falling to pieces."

Jonah stood up. His heart was about to burst from his chest, and he felt desperate to escape. He noticed the liquor cabinet standing where it had always been, and he remembered how, as a teen, he would fill an empty soda bottle with small amounts of booze from several bottles, then sneak out and get plastered with friends. He went to the cabinet and picked up a bottle. Then he heard his mother moan. She was hugging her abdomen, leaning against the kitchen counter, crying.

On instinct, Jonah went to her and put his hands on her shoulders. She was shaking. He drew her into a hug. She kept crying, and he felt tears rising in his eyes. After a time, he pulled away and touched her face. "You're right," he said softly. "I had no idea. No idea of the burden you've been carrying with Django."

She nodded and smiled weakly. Jonah followed her to the couch, where she reached for a box of facial tissues, blew her nose, and wiped her face. He sat next to her. She handed him the box, and they chuckled as he wiped his face.

"Look at us two," she said.

Jonah could only nod and smile. His abdomen churned—his compassion on seeing his mother collapse with sadness competed with anxiety: what was going on here?

Jonah's mother stretched her arms up and yawned luxuriously. "Do you remember how your dad and I used to fight?" she asked.

The conversation was plunging into territory he'd never explored with his mother. Jonah felt tense—and intrigued.

"I remember you guys fighting a lot."

She swallowed and went on. "It was always about the same thing: his drinking." She wiped her face with a fresh tissue. "When we first got married, it wasn't too bad. Every two weeks, on payday, he'd go to the bar and drink with his buddies from work. Then he'd come home.

"But it got much worse in a few years. He got a DUI. We started fighting more. He got another DUI and lost his license. I begged him to quit. And I started hiding his alcohol, even pouring it out." She paused. "And, of course, you remember how he died."

The living room spun, and Jonah felt he was losing his balance. He gripped the arm of the couch and tried to steady himself. His mother looked at him fondly. Did she know what was going on inside him? She touched his cheek with her hand and said, "Addiction runs in your genes, Jonah." She nodded her head toward the liquor cabinet. "I couldn't stand for you to end up like your father. I just couldn't stand it. I worried myself sick when you were a teenager, living your secret life. And I'm so happy to hear you're quitting."

He was tempted to tell her how difficult it was for him to stay abstinent. But he held back, afraid to scare or disappoint her.

"Shall we make some more coffee?" she asked.

He said yes and followed her into the kitchen. With their coffees, they sat at the kitchen table.

"I don't think you ever knew how important church was to me growing up," she said. "Especially my youth group."

"No, I don't remember you ever talking about that."

"I loved that youth group, and I loved my pastor. We went on these great trips, and it felt like we were one big family." Jonah heard longing in her voice. "But your dad was very anti-religious. So, when we got together, I just stopped going to church."

In the last year, with Django struggling, she felt the need for something to believe in and a group to belong to, she told Jonah. "A friend took me to her evangelical church. It was weird at first.

I grew up Methodist. Services were very orderly, and when the pastor spoke, we just listened. But at that service"—she thrust her arms in the air—"people were so filled with the Holy Spirit they couldn't sit still."

"It took me a few weeks to get used to it, but I came to really like it. The Biblical messages were comforting and inspiring. And pretty soon, I started to feel the love of Jesus." She placed both her hands over her heart. "I was born again."

• • •

After Cloverdale, the rain slackened, and Bill relaxed into the Redwood Highway's curves and grades. He'd been driving this road for some forty years—decades in which pear orchards had become vineyards, mills had shut down, and the cannabis industry, still mostly illegal, was having a growth spurt. Huge garden supply stores could be seen along the highway, surrounded by endless pallets of bagged compost and fertilizer.

In Willits, where Highway 101 became the town's Main Street, Bill stopped at the Chevron Station for gas, a piss, and a six-dollar steak burrito.

Two and a half hours later, he crossed the Elk River Slough just south of Eureka. The tide was up. As he drove farther into town, he saw more and more ragged-looking people on the sidewalks. At the stoplight by the shopping mall, beggars were posted on both sides, holding cardboard signs. He wondered where Kenny was.

• • •

Kenny figured he had at most a half-hour before the manager kicked him out. His five dollars had bought him two beef tacos, a Thanksgiving meal he devoured in a few minutes. He looked out at the gas station islands from his table. Drivers pulled their collars and hats tight against the windswept rain as they pumped their gas.

If it were the middle of the night, Kenny could stay for as long as he was willing to listen to the graveyard shift guy talk about sports and his step-kids. But it was early afternoon, and despite being a holiday, the place was busy. Someone would want his table soon.

Kenny had no clue what to do with himself until the evening meeting. Nor did he know where he was going to spend the night. Probably at the mission. He wouldn't be welcome in the nearby community of addicts and junkies—not after what he'd done. Maybe they'd figured it out, maybe they hadn't, but he wouldn't take a chance finding out.

Kenny overheard a female server greet a customer warmly, "Hey, how are you?"

"Better, now I get to see you," the customer said.

"Aw. You made my day. Anything special for Thanksgiving or your usual: beef burrito, no guacamole, no onions?"

"Just the usual."

"Sour cream?"

"No, I'll pass. I'm sour enough, according to my wife," he said, eliciting a chuckle from the server.

Hearing them talk, Kenny thought about his mother and father, his sister, and his little nephew. He wanted to call them, but he was worried that his recovery wouldn't stick and he'd disappoint them again.

Kenny glanced at the other diners. Would anyone leave some food behind? And would he be able to grab it after they left?

•　　•　　•

Jonah tried to enjoy his mother's openness for the rest of Thanksgiving Day, but he also stayed alert, ready for her to erupt again. Django had come out, and the two brothers played video games on the couch while their mother worked on a pie in the kitchen, humming a familiar tune.

After eating their large meal and cleaning up, they watched their traditional Thanksgiving movie, *It's a Wonderful Life*. And this time, George Bailey's nightmare about a world made rougher and less kind by his absence touched Jonah deeply. Would he be able to stay clean and sober and give more of himself to his family and friends?

In bed, Jonah replayed the day's events. His mom did seem reborn. And he wished he'd taken her cue and talked about the night his dad died. Maybe tomorrow before he took off.

In the morning, Django was up and out early for his job at Starbucks. Jonah's mother made breakfast—and a couple of tuna sandwiches for the road.

"And here's some money, just in case." She handed him three hundred dollars.

"Wow, thanks. You sure?"

"You'd be surprised how much a legal secretary makes," she said with a smile and a touch of pride.

They drove to the San Francisco bus station, saying little. When they got off the highway and navigated the streets jammed with Black Friday traffic, she said, "You know, I'd be happy to loan you the money for a deposit on an apartment."

Jonah felt a deep pang of gratitude. His mother had his back. But he didn't want to rent an apartment. "Thanks, Mom, but I plan to keep living in the forest or maybe set up a tent on a friend's property. I want to save up so I can hitch to British Columbia next summer to see those old-growth forests before they're cut down, maybe help out with the protests."

"Well, that's very idealistic of you," she said harshly. "But I think you'll find it takes a lot of hard work to make it in this world."

Jonah thought about defending his choices, but he kept quiet.

"I mean, what about college?" his mother continued.

"I don't know."

As they approached the bus station, Jonah said, "You can just drop me off in front."

"I want to get out and hug you."

On the curb, she hugged him fiercely. "I'm sorry for nagging you about college and your lifestyle. I know it's what you need to do, at least for now. Just know that I love you, Jonah."

"I love you too, Mom."

"Call as often as you can. Please."

"I will."

Jonah got his ticket and then walked to the bus. He chose the front seat opposite the driver to enjoy the view of the bay and Golden Gate Bridge. But as soon as the bus pulled out, the city streets faded, and Jonah thought about his mother. She wasn't made of iron. She suffered. And she had needs and longings. With heat rising to his face, Jonah realized how much he meant to his mother, how much she loved him and wanted to spend time with him.

He recalled yesterday morning, the house filled with smells of pancakes, bacon, and strong coffee—and the expression on her face. She radiated joy just having him under her roof.

Was he wrong to go back to Humboldt? He could help her with Django. They could do things as a family. And was she right about college? Arcata buzzed with bright college students passionately learning about environmental sciences and alternative energy. He'd attended lectures by professors who'd blown him away with their knowledge of forest ecosystems. With knowledge like that, Jonah could be a better advocate for Mother Nature.

The rain picked up, and the windshield wipers slapped the water off the big window. The bus was rolling onto the bridge now, but fog and rain obscured the view.

Jonah awoke to the driver announcing, "Willits. twenty-minute stop."

The rain had stopped, but the wind whistled through the bare trees in front of the McDonalds. Jonah pulled his collar up and walked north on the highway. In a few minutes, he saw the town's iconic sign—*Willits: Gateway to the Redwoods.*

As glad as he was to be back in the coastal forests, Jonah felt anxious about returning to Arcata. He knew that as soon as he got off the bus, he would be tempted to get high by friends with bud, weed dealers on the plaza, and the alluring odors wafting from the grow houses.

Jonah looked at the mountains to the west, and they reminded him of the pot farm where he'd worked last summer. It was neatly terraced out a steep slope, with hoop houses and well-built cabins and sheds. The crew had included other young travelers like him—fast but clumsy with the scissors—and two old ladies who trimmed slower but beat the youngsters with efficiency.

A family feeling developed among the group, and they shared meals and rides to town. On their time off, they lounged around a swimming hole on the creek. Jonah had even had a lover for a time—gorgeous Jeronica.

The grower was the first armed hippie Jonah had ever encountered. He watched the trimmers carefully for pilfering. But he was a decent, friendly guy who made them dinner twice a week. And when the season ended, he sent Jonah off with a stack of money and a large baggie of bud trim. Jonah and his Arcata friends had stayed stoned for weeks on that stash.

Back on the bus, Jonah realized that to stay clean, he would have to avoid Arcata—at least for a while. All his belongings were in his pack, so he didn't need to go to his forest campsite. But where would he go? Eureka was the obvious choice, but it was a foreign land to him, with hardcore homeless and white-drug users prowling the streets.

But Jonah was confident that he wouldn't run into any friends there who'd offer to get him high on weed.

Chapter 9

The bus rolled into Eureka in the late afternoon. The rain had let up, but a damp ocean wind tore across the town. Jonah walked to a nearby supermarket. After buying some bagels and cheese, he sat at a table and made a sandwich. A steady flow of customers walked by—none giving Jonah and his backpack a second glance. Then, another traveler sat near him and began eating bread and hummus.

"Hey, man, how're ya doin'?" Jonah asked.

"Okay, you?"

"Good. Just got back from down south." The other man nodded as he dipped a slice of bread in the hummus. He was older, maybe fifty, his face red, and his lips chapped.

Jonah asked, "Say, you know a good place to camp or spend the night around here?"

"I'm going to the mission."

"What's that?"

"Rescue mission. A bed and breakfast for us broke hobos. Run by a Christian outfit."

"I got no problem with Christians. Where is it?"

The man pointed. "Just around the corner there. I'll show you when I'm done eating."

Jonah was surprised by the rescue mission's bright, clean appearance. A wiry man behind the reception desk assured him his backpack would be secure in the large closet by the entryway; then he directed Jonah to the showers.

The dormitory was a large room covered with sleeping mats and blankets. Jonah had expected bunk beds, but after camping for months on nothing but a sleeping bag and a thin air mattress, the thick foam pad was luxurious. He fell asleep instantly.

• • •

In bed with his laptop, Bill hovered the cursor over a folder Cheri had labeled *Kids*. Aaron's memories of Kenny had made Bill want to revisit that era. At the same time, he dreaded stirring up painful memories. His longing won, and he double-clicked the folder, then another folder labeled *Tish Tang*.

Kenny was sitting on a camp chair, his feet in the river, his strong muscular chest exposed to the sun. It had been hell to get Kenny to come that weekend. He was nineteen—a high school dropout, smoking pot, drinking, and trying to avoid his father. But Kenny's mother and sister prevailed on him to attend.

Kenny had met his nephew before but hadn't spent much time with him. Bill remembered his grandson following Kenny around like a puppy. And Kenny—for a few short hours—broke out of his teenage shell and played with the boy. One photo showed Kenny and Aaron holding hands, knee-deep in the river. In another, Kenny had Aaron on his lap while the younger boy roasted a marshmallow.

"Why, dear God, why?" said Bill to the empty room. He closed the laptop and curled into a ball. "What did I do wrong? Where are you, my boy?"

• • •

After a breakfast of hamburger mix on white bread and weak coffee, Jonah walked to the market to buy a decent coffee. Then, having nowhere else to go, he wandered back to the mission. The sun was cresting the mountains to the east, and he stood across from the mission in the sunlight, leaning against a chain-link fence and sipping his coffee. Dozens of other men and some women were hanging about—some in an outdoor shelter, others standing in small groups on the sidewalks.

Jonah noticed an older man across the street talking to two guys he recognized from breakfast. He was leaning forward and gesturing enthusiastically with a corncob pipe. The men shook their heads and moved on. Jonah figured the older man was a preacher. Then the fellow looked at Jonah, crossed the street, and said to him with a disarming smile, "You look like you've been traveling rough."

"You might say that. Slept here last night."

The man nodded and leaned against the fence next to Jonah. "I know that routine. Slept in missions from here to Vermont. Some even let me in when I was blind drunk." He extended his hand. "I'm Manny."

"Jonah," he said, surprised by Manny's firm grip. Even with his thin gray hair, wrinkled forehead, and pouchy cheeks, he had a youthful energy. "You still drink?"

"Shit, no! I'd have been dead and buried long ago if I hadn't quit." Manny tapped the ashes out of his pipe. "Been sober more than thirty years."

"How'd you do it?"

"AA." Manny pulled a pouch from his shirt pocket to fill the pipe.

"I wish they had AA for stoners," said Jonah. "I don't drink much, but I go crazy for pot, and it totally fucks me up."

"Well, who says you can't go to AA to quit pot?" Manny asked, lighting his pipe.

"Never thought of that."

Manny puffed his pipe, then said, "Listen, do you have a desire to quit drinking? Even a tiny bit?"

"Well, yeah. I mean, pot's my main problem, but I usually drink when I smoke. And if there's no pot, I'll just drink."

"And you want to quit both—the pot and the drinking?"

"Yeah." Jonah wondered where the old man was headed with this. "I don't think I could keep drinking and stay off pot."

"Okay, then. You qualify," said Manny, beaming. "There's only one requirement for membership in AA, and that's the desire to stop drinking. What are you doing tonight?"

"I'll have to call my secretary to see." Jonah grinned.

Manny laughed and squeezed Jonah's tricep. "I like you, kid. Sleeping in the mission, but you still got your sense of humor. So, where can I pick you up for the six o'clock AA meeting?"

Jonah wasn't sure he'd go, but he thought he might. "How about right here?"

"See you here at 5:40, then. Deal?"

"Deal." They shook hands and parted.

Jonah spent an hour strolling along Eureka's waterfront, pleasantly surprised by the beauty of the bay and islands. He watched a family of white-beaked coots patrol a sheltered inlet.

But when he arrived at a spot where he could see across the bay to Arcata—Humboldt State's white buildings popping out from the forested hills—he was seized with yearning. He'd be there in an hour if he took the bus or hitched. He'd go to the plaza, see friends, text Buzzy, and spend the night in his forest home enjoying nature's sounds and scents instead of the odors and snores of men just off the street.

He fantasized sharing a fat bowl with Buzzy, savoring the smell of the dank, pitchy resin and the acrid smoke. Then would come that feeling of pleasant detachment from the worries and challenges of life.

"Fuck this," he said aloud, then walked quickly south. Soon, he was on Fourth Street, its three lanes busy with morning traffic. Then he hit Broadway, which was even uglier up close than through a car window. A light patter of rain began, and

Jonah headed for the shopping mall to get another coffee, sit a while, and stay dry.

•   •   •

It was dark when Jonah got back to the mission. A couple dozen men stood outside, waiting to enter. Jonah nodded at guys he recognized from breakfast. Then he saw Manny across the street waving at him from the driver's seat of a blue minivan.

"How was the rest of your day?" Manny asked when he got in. "Did you meet any winsome lasses eager to follow you to your lair in the forest?"

Jonah grinned and said, "No, but I watched people at the mall for a while."

"Any alcohol or mari-ha-ha?"

"Nope."

"Good for you."

"Nice van," said Jonah as they got rolling.

"The sobriety sled," Manny said with a giggle. "Bringing gifts like you to AA meetings, whether they've been naughty or nice." Now Jonah laughed with Manny.

They pulled into a church parking lot, and after cutting the engine, Manny said, "Like I told ya, there's no problem using AA to quit weed as long as you also want to quit drinking." He pointed at the building, where Jonah saw people walking to a lighted side door. "God knows most of us used a lot more than alcohol. But it's easier for the uptight deacons in there if you just use the magic word 'alcoholic' or 'addict-alcoholic' when you introduce yourself—that is, if you decide to share."

"Okay. Not sure what you're talking about, but I'll figure it out."

Manny chuckled. "Don't worry, just stick with me." He led Jonah to a spot outside the door, lit his pipe, and introduced Jonah to the other smokers. Too nervous to go in alone, Jonah endured the smoke while Manny and the others yelled greetings at everyone who came to the door. Finally, he tapped the ashes from his pipe and said, "Let's go."

The room had poor lighting and smelled like mildew. "I'm speaking tonight, so I'll sit up front," Manny told Jonah. "You sit anywhere you like."

Jonah found a seat in the back row and surveyed the crowd: about forty people, mostly white, mixed in age. One woman used a walker and had an oxygen tube to her nose. In a back row, a half-dozen young men with buzzcuts and tattoos looked at their phones or stared into space.

Manny sat at the front table with a gray-bearded man who wore a bandana and a denim vest covered with biker patches. The biker looked at his watch, then said loudly, "Hi, I'm Bob, an alcoholic."

"Hi, Bob," chanted everyone except Jonah. Bob read a welcome statement, then a man sitting near Jonah read a text that sounded odd and old fashioned: "Constitutionally incapable... A manner of living which demands rigorous honesty... With all the earnestness at our command..."

When Jonah heard the phrase, "Turn our will and our lives over to the care of God as we understood Him," he almost got up to leave. He glanced at Manny—who was looking directly at him, nodding, and smiling encouragement. Jonah stayed in his seat.

When the readings were over, Bob introduced Manny.

"I grew up in a small town in Nebraska," Manny said. "In high school, I was too small to make the football team and too clueless to get a girl to go out with me. I didn't fit in. I knew it, and it felt like crap.

"One afternoon, I was playing touch football with some older boys. And after the game, one of them handed me a beer. I didn't want to look like a punk, so I drank it." Manny leaned back and opened his arms. "All of a sudden, my boring little life in that boring little farm town was transformed. My worries drifted away, and life seemed full of possibility. After that, getting drunk was pretty much all that mattered to me."

Manny described hopping freight cars around the West. He worked on farms and in factories, usually getting fired for drinking within a few months. Finally, he settled down with a wife and had a couple kids—only to abandon them and begin traveling again, getting into fights and spending nights in jail.

"In one of those jails, two AA members came in to run a meeting," he said. "I had nothing better to do, so I went. At first, I thought they were peddling some religion. But I could tell they were sober, and pretty happy about it. One of them handed me a card with a list of meetings. When I got out, I went to one, then another, and another. Within a couple weeks, I understood I was an alcoholic with a disease."

After the meeting, Manny took Jonah to the all-night Denny's on Fifth Street. AA members from the meeting had already taken over a section, but Manny steered Jonah to a secluded booth.

They ordered coffee, then Manny asked, "So, how long has it been since you got high?"

"Oh man, I wish I could say a week or a month, but it's only been since the day before Thanksgiving."

Manny nodded. "So, what did you think of the meeting?"

Jonah fiddled with the zipper on his jacket. "I liked it. Mostly. I really dug your story. And what other people said, too. Lots of honesty. I didn't feel comfortable with all that God stuff."

"Right now," said Manny, jabbing his forefinger into the table, "you don't have to worry about that." He looked at his watch, then back and Jonah. "The only thing you need to worry about is staying clean and sober for the rest of today. And when you wake up in the morning, that'll be your only job for tomorrow—staying off the drink and the drugs for one day. And going to at least one meeting."

Jonah slumped back in his seat. "I don't know if I can do it. Where I live, in Arcata, everyone I know gets high every day. I'm sure there are meetings in Arcata, but still."

"Well, I've got a proposition for you," Manny said, leaning against the booth's back cushion. "My wife Karen and I have a little cabin we rent to fellow travelers on the road to recovery. It's empty at the moment. I talked to Karen this afternoon about you, and she said if I thought you were okay, you'd be welcome to move in."

Jonah could hardly believe this was happening. Could he really stay in Eureka, go to meetings like tonight's, and avoid the Arcata scene until he felt strong enough?

"The place ain't much, just four walls and a roof," Manny continued. "There's a little electric heater but no running water or toilet. You'd share our facilities. And there are some rules."

Jonah's hope dimmed as he thought about his finances. "Manny, I don't have money for rent. I've got like three hundred to my name and no job."

"The rent is two-fifty a month, payable in cash or labor at ten dollars an hour. We got three-quarters of an acre, and there's always plenty I need help with—trimming hedges, chopping firewood, mowing the lawn, fixing fences."

"Man, that sounds great."

"Now the rules: you stay sober and go to meetings, or you're out. And whatever happens, you move out after six months. Our little place is like a halfway house—a place to help you get halfway through your first year of sobriety. Then we'll want to open it up for another newcomer."

"That all sounds really good."

"Do you accept?"

"It's a deal," said Jonah, shaking Manny's hand.

They drove to Manny's home at Eureka's southern edge, where suburban neighborhoods gave way to the forest. Jonah met Karen, a large woman of medium height with gray hair and kind eyes. They sat at the kitchen table and reviewed the rules once more. Karen stressed the six-month limit. "You can always come back and visit."

"If you're not sick and tired of us," joked Manny. "And speaking of tired, it's time for me to hit the hay. I'll show you to your suite."

"Maybe Jonah wants to take a shower first," said Karen.

"Yes, that'd be nice," said Jonah.

Karen showed him the bathroom and the linen closet with clean towels. Then Manny said, "Let me show you the place, then you can come back in and take that shower."

Karen hugged Jonah. "I think God put you in Manny's path this morning for a reason, Jonah. I think He's got a plan for all three of us to have some good times together."

"I hope you're right," Jonah said. He followed Manny out the door, along a gravel path under redwood and spruce trees to a cabin lit with a ribbon of LEDs. Manny opened the door, turned on the light—one bare bulb in the ceiling—and stood aside. Jonah saw a foam mattress on a wooden platform and a space heater plugged into the wall. To Jonah, it seemed luxurious.

Manny handed Jonah a set of keys. "One for this place; one for the house. You want to hit the 8 AM meeting with me?"

"Yes, absolutely."

"Okay, coffee's on by 6:30, breakfast around 7."

"Good night, Manny," said Jonah, tearing up. "Thank you so much," he said, reaching out to hug him.

After showering, Jonah went to bed and drifted off to frogs croaking and raindrops dripping from the trees onto his metal roof.

Chapter 10

On a Saturday morning, three weeks before Christmas, Bill sat at a table in the food court at Eureka's shopping mall. He shifted his gaze between the two entrances, watching for Angela. Nervous as a buck in mating season, he told himself, "It's just date, just a date, just a date." That didn't help.

He'd chosen a table away from the foot traffic because he didn't want to be seen by friends who might come over and chat—and gossip later about seeing Bill on a date with a young Latina.

When Angela walked in, Bill had to steady himself as he stood to wave at her. She wore tight blue jeans and a black jacket over a silky teal blouse that displayed the tops of her breasts. Coral earrings dangled under her long black hair.

"Hello, Bill. Finally, we meet." She put her small hand in his.

"Yeah, it's good to meet you in person," he said awkwardly. "Can I get you a coffee?"

"Sure. How about a small latte?"

"Coming right up."

Waiting in line, Bill glanced back at her. She sat forward on her seat, doing something with her phone. Then she looked up, caught his eye, and smiled. Was this really happening? Was this young, beautiful woman interested in him? Her profile didn't say her age, but Bill guessed mid-40s—more than a decade younger than him.

As he waited for their coffees, other questions stirred him: What about their cultural differences? What would her family expect of him? Would he have to learn Spanish?

But when Bill placed their coffees on the table and sat down, he had only one question on his mind. "So, Angela," he said nervously. "Now that we finally meet, I guess I need to ask you something."

She wove her fingers together, rested her chin on them, and looked at him attentively.

"We've been getting to know each other pretty good, and I feel like we're already friends, but ..." He groped for the words. "I guess I wonder why you're interested in an old logger like me."

Angela covered her mouth with her hands and opened her eyes wide. "Oh wow, Bill. That's a very direct question."

"Yeah, I know."

She sipped her coffee, looked away, then put the cup down and settled her light brown eyes on his. Bill's heart pounded. "I don't want to hurt your feelings, Bill, but it seems like maybe you're assuming too much," she said. "I like you, and I feel comfortable talking to you. But it's way too soon to say what's going to happen between us."

Bill wanted to get up from the table and flee from his embarrassment. And at the same time, he felt relieved from the expectations he'd built up. "Yeah, I guess I was getting ahead of myself," he said with a laugh. "Let's just take it one date at a time."

She laughed. "Good idea!"

They sat quietly, and Bill searched his brain for something to say. Finally, Angela said with a frown, "I don't think I've told you yet about our problems with my niece Angelica." Bill leaned forward. "Last night, she didn't come home till one AM."

Bill nodded and waited for her to continue. "Angelica used to be the best girl. She was the first one dressed and ready for mass on Sunday mornings. She always did her chores. And she loved babysitting her two brothers. Now, we don't dare leave her alone with them."

Angela looked around at the other tables, then back at Bill. "We know she's been smoking pot, drinking, and hanging around with gang members. She denies it, but we know it's true."

Bill remembered how Kenny started doing the same things when he was fourteen or fifteen. But Bill didn't want to scare her by mentioning that. Trying to sound sympathetic, he said, "The teen years are tough. I went a little crazy as a teen myself."

He could see that didn't help. "You and your sisters could try Al-Anon. I get a lot out of that program."

She looked confused. "But we don't have problems with drinking. Just a little beer or wine sometimes. And no drugs."

"Oh, I'm not talking about Alcoholics Anonymous, but Al-Anon. It's a twelve-step program for people like you and me. With family members who are—who have problems with drugs and alcohol."

She brightened. "You think we might learn how to help Angelica?"

There it was again—the same hope Bill had brought to his first Al-Anon meeting, that Al-Anon would teach him how to help Kenny. "It's really for the people who have addicts or problem drinkers in their family," Bill said. Angela's face registered disappointment. "We learn how to set healthy boundaries, to focus on our own well-being whether our loved one is sober or not."

Bill could tell she didn't get it. He looked outside and saw the clouds had thinned, and the wind had picked up. "God, I can't believe I'm saying this kind of stuff. If my logging buddies could hear me, they'd think I'd gone nuts."

"Don't worry about them. It sounds like Al-Anon really helps you, and that's what matters."

After a pause, Bill said, "So, how are your parents?"

She looked wistful. "Oh, they're good. But I miss them so much, especially my mom."

"Are you going down there for Christmas?"

"Unfortunately, no. They came up here last year to see us, but it's very expensive and difficult for them. I haven't been down to see them since I moved here."

"Wow," said Bill, imagining how hard it would be to move to another country and not see Denise and Aaron regularly. "That sounds really hard. Is it too expensive?"

"No, I've got the money, but I have some visa problems."

Bill nodded and left the subject at that.

He felt light and happy when they walked out of the mall into the bright mid-morning sun—such a change from the rain and gray skies. The cars in the parking lot sparkled, and mist drifted off dark green cypresses and pines across Broadway.

"Gonna be a great day," he said.

"Yes, beautiful. I wish I didn't have to work."

"Well, yeah, that kinda sucks. Maybe you can get out for a walk after the lunch rush."

"We'll see." She stopped at the curb, faced Bill, and held out her hand. "It was very nice to meet you in person, Bill."

He took her hand and tried not to sound too eager saying, "Yeah, it was great. I hope we can do it again soon."

She held onto his hand and smiled. "Me too. Until then, as we say in my country, cuídate bien, which means take care of yourself."

"You quee-da-tay too, Angela."

She gave him a big smile and turned to walk to her car.

•   •   •

Jonah followed Manny around the lumber yard pushing a metal cart. The yard was near the bay, and a stiff northwest wind whipped across the gravel lot and through the open sheds. Jonah stopped to zip his jacket tighter.

A young yard worker approached them. "Can I help 'ya?"

"Just pondering the age-old question of the fence builder," Manny said. "Redwood or cedar."

"Cedar's cheaper," said the yard worker.

"And just as sturdy. Unless I can find some all-heart redwood with tight knots. That stuff will outlast us all."

"Not much of that here, but you're welcome to look." The yard man pointed at the stacks.

Manny began pulling boards and handing the rejects to Jonah. After going through a dozen, he held one up and proclaimed, "Our first keeper."

"What are you looking for?" Jonah asked.

Manny picked up one of the rejects and pointed to some big knots. "Boards with loose knots like these won't last long in our climate." Then he pointed to a split at the end of another board. "This one's already checking."

"Checking?"

Manny chuckled. "Lumber jargon for splitting."

After ten minutes, they had about fifteen good cedar boards on the cart. "Why don't you re-stack the culls while I start picking through the redwood?" Manny said.

By the time Jonah rejoined Manny, he'd selected a half-dozen good boards and rejected about four times as many. "Almost impossible to get good redwood anymore," he said sadly.

Jonah picked up a board with red and blond tints. "What's wrong with this one?"

Manny pointed at the blond material. "This is sapwood. It grows on the outer edges of the tree and will rot away in a few wet winters. Only the red heartwood will last."

"Is any of this old growth?" Jonah asked, replacing the board on the stack.

"Definitely not. You can't get old growth unless it has been salvaged from a demolished building or an old fence—or pulled from underneath a river."

As they drove out of the crowded parking lot, Manny asked, "You ever worked on a fence before?"

Jonah chuckled wryly. "Once, with my dad. But he had strange ideas. Wanted to use only rocks around the posts, no concrete."

"That must've been hard to make 'em plumb."

"What's plumb?"

"Straight up and down."

"Oh yeah, there were maybe a couple posts that were plumb. It wasn't long before the whole thing started leaning."

Jonah looked out the window at a cemetery on a hill overlooking Broadway. "He made it fun, though. My dad knew how to make work fun."

"How'd he do that?"

"He'd joke around, pretend we were working on some rich lady's place. He'd talk to my mom in an English accent, call her *m'Lady* and stuff like that. She played along with it. Cracked up my little brother and me."

"You ever hear from him?"

Jonah looked at his hands and sighed. "He's dead. Died when I was a teenager."

•　　•　　•

"You're dating a Mexican?" asked Eric. Bill's young friend grinned at him like a clown through his red beard.

"If I knew you were going to be a prick about it, I wouldn't have said anything."

"Sorry, man," said Eric, still grinning. "I got nothing against Mexicans. Just didn't picture you hooking up with one."

"Me neither," said Bill, calming down. They were standing on the Eureka Elks Lodge patio, waiting for their steaks to come off the grill. "And ... and look, we're just dating, not, you know ...."

"Oh right." Eric nudged Bill with his elbow. "Just be careful of her older brothers. Those dudes really look out for their families. Might want to ask you about your intentions for their sister."

"Well, if you ever meet her, I trust you'll avoid that subject altogether," said Bill, grinning.

"Me?" Eric looked incredulous. "The soul of discretion."

"What's there to be discrete about?" boomed a voice behind them. It was King.

"Bill here has finally found a lady."

"What!? Do tell! Let's hear some details." King crossed his arms and tilted his ear toward Bill. "Ain't often us old married guys get to hear about young love."

Trapped, Bill said, "Look, we're just dating, okay?"

"Anybody we know?" persisted King.

To Bill's relief, the grill cook shouted their numbers. He and Eric got their steaks, then walked along the buffet line. Bill piled on the grilled veggies and salad and skipped the potatoes. Courting Angela had given him a fresh incentive to lose weight.

When Bill opened the glass door to the lodge, he heard a cascade of voices roaring like a creek after a storm. He and Eric walked by crowded tables, nodding at a few people they knew. At one table, a woman shrieked with laughter, and Bill thought it was too early to be so drunk.

They sat down with two men. One was Deputy Steve, who'd responded to the vandalism on Bill and Eric's logging job, and the other was Jim, a powerfully built, dark-skinned man with Indian tattoos on his arms.

Bill noticed Jim's puffy cheek and purple eye socket. "What the hell happened to you?"

"Does it still look bad?" Jim touched the skin under his eye and winced. "I haven't looked in the mirror for the last couple days. On purpose."

Eric asked, "You get into it with one of your cousins again?"

"Two of them."

Bill expected Jim to joke about how bad the other guys looked, but Jim kept quiet.

King joined them, and Bill launched into negotiations about the tree job to distract his nosy friend from asking about Bill's romantic life. "I checked out that tree, and I think Jim and I can take it down in a day," he said. "So, I'm figuring a grand, even."

King pretended to gag on his beer. "I was thinking six, including bucking up the slash." Then he added with a benevolent smile, "Gonna get Eric here to mill up the stem with my mini-mill, so I'll throw in a hundred feet of two-by-six, mostly heartwood."

Jim made a face of exaggerated disgust. "Cheap bastard."

Eric pointed his fork at King. "Like I said. He'll fuck ya' in the ass without even a kiss and 'spect you to be grateful."

Bill put on a sour face, but he didn't mind bargaining. It was part of the game.

Then Eric said, "You guys hear about that immigration raid over at the flower farm?"

"Heard they caught a buncha wetbacks," said Jim. "Good riddance, what I say."

"I heard they even rounded up some supervisors," said King. "That didn't make the newspaper," he added cynically.

Steve said, "Yeah, I heard that too."

Eric asked Steve, "Were you guys in on the raid?"

"Nah. The feds let us know, and we had a couple units there for backup. But they handled it on their own."

"It don't seem right to me," said Eric, leaning forward. "I mean, yeah, they broke the law. But they're just workin' people, doing damn hard jobs. Would you go and work over there?

Stooping over all day, planting and picking flowers for ten or twelve bucks an hour?"

"I did work there," said Jim with a snarl. "Right after high school. Hardest job I ever had. Stuck it out for a couple months, then moved on to something easier: planting fir saplings up and down Weaver Ridge." The men laughed.

"Right," said Eric. "So, who the fuck is gonna work there for longer than a couple months, besides, you know, illegals?"

Jim leaned toward Eric. "I don't give a fuck. This is our country, and if they want to come here, they can get in line and cross legal."

Eric looked at Steve. "What do you think?"

Steve shook his head. "I agree it's a sad thing, but what are you going to do? They knew the rules when they crossed the border illegally—or came on a tourist visa and decided to stay and work with phony papers."

"How about seven?" asked King.

Bill replied, "You can get some kid to buck up the slash, and we'll do the tree for nine, plus a hundred feet of that redwood, all heart."

King nodded and said, "Eight hundred."

"Eight-fifty, plus a twelve-pack of Jim's favorite beer."

Jim waved his hand. "Not for me, man. I'm sober now. Almost a week."

"No kidding?" Bill said with delight. "That's great." Drink had been Jim's Achilles' heel for as long as Bill had known him.

"Good for you, man," said Eric, bumping Jim's fist. "Ain't ready to give it up myself, but I ... I think it's good you quit."

"Yeah," said Jim. He looked around the table at the other men. "I think everyone who knows me would agree. Even my tweaker cousins. That beef with them was kind of the straw that broke the drunk Indian's back."

Bill and Steve nodded with encouragement. Then Bill said to King. "Well, now that Jim's sober, I think our rates just went up."

"Are you kidding?" rejoined King. "If he's not drunk, how're you going to get him to stand at the end of a rope with a three-hundred-pound limb bearing down on him?" The men laughed so loud that Bill wondered if they were making too much noise, even for the Eureka Elks' Lodge.

Chapter 11

Kenny put the last bit of pizza in his mouth, then stuffed his hands deep into his jacket pockets. He stood under an awning outside the Winco supermarket, sheltering from the rain.

In his pocket, he felt the business card of Jerry Watson, the big black man who had walked up to him at the seven AM meeting and said, "I'm your new temporary sponsor. When can you come over?"

Kenny had heard Jerry speak at several meetings. He liked the older man's humor and honesty. And from what Jerry had shared about his drinking history—his ruined marriages, estranged kids, and DUIs—Kenny didn't worry that Jerry would judge him for being a homeless meth addict.

But Kenny had been living feral so long that he couldn't remember what it was like to visit a non-addict at their home. He'd burned through his family and normie friends years ago. And addicts had two simple rules for social visits: share your drugs if you have enough to share, and if you don't, stay away, or go score some. And when you only had enough for yourself, there was no point in knocking on someone's door or approaching their tent.

Kenny saw four addicts he knew leave the market. He wondered if they were holding. Then he recognized one of the guys he'd called the cops on. He turned to walk in the opposite direction.

Twenty minutes later, he arrived at a mobile home park and found Jerry's single-wide trailer. He knocked, and a voice boomed from inside, "Yeah! It's open."

Kenny entered a hot, stuffy, cramped living room. Jerry looked up from an easy chair, cradling a box of colorful business cards in his lap. "Welcome." He stuck out his extra-large hand and smiled so wide his eyes nearly squeezed shut. Kenny shook his hand and managed a weak smile.

"Take a seat—if you can find one."

"Can I put my coat somewhere?"

Jerry pointed to a coat rack by the door. Kenny hung his coat, then sat on the couch between boxes and stacks of business cards.

"So, how are you, my young friend?" asked Jerry, sitting back and fixing Kenny with a thousand-watt gaze.

"Okay, I guess."

"Staying clean and sober?"

"About two weeks so far."

"Congra-dju-fuckin-lations, mah man! You've done the hardest part."

Kenny allowed himself a moment to enjoy Jerry's approval. But his mind raced with questions: how to find a place to live, what to do for work, when to contact his parents.

Jerry asked him, "So how are you going to stay sober?"

Kenny shrugged.

"Mmmrrrraaaahhhh!" Jerry bellowed like a game show buzzer. "Wrong answer."

"What do you think I should do?"

"I've got some ideas, but first, I want to hear what you think." Jerry looked at his watch. "It's now 10:15 AM. What will you do to make sure you hit the sheets tonight without taking a drink or a drug?"

Kenny chuckled. "Well, there ain't going to be any sheets, just a damp sleeping bag in my tent over yonder." He waved his hand toward the gulch a half-mile away. "That is if my shit hasn't been stolen."

Jerry looked at Kenny with such intensity that Kenny had to look away. When he looked back, he saw tears in Jerry's eyes. Jerry removed his glasses, rubbed his eyes, and sniffed. "I've been there, my brother. I've been there."

"You lived on the streets, too?"

Jerry nodded. "There'll be time for me to tell you my stories. But now I want to hear more about you."

Kenny sighed and looked around. He picked up a tray of laminated business cards. "What the heck are these, anyway?"

"This is my business, Love Without Limits," Jerry said proudly. "I find sayings and poems that inspire me, and I put them on these little wallet cards and bookmarks. Then I sell them to gift shops and recovery stores all over the country."

"No shit. You make a living at it?"

Jerry laughed. "Let's just say it supplements my social security. But, back to you. Tell me about you. What inspired you to try to get clean and sober?"

Kenny took a long, deep breath. "You know that transient camp back behind the mall? They call it Devil's Playground?" Jerry nodded, and Kenny went on. "I'd been staying back there off and on for months, living in a tent, begging and stealing to get by." Kenny felt his neck and chest get warm. "I was a mess."

"Maybe you've heard how crank makes you super-horny. Anyway, lots of casual sex going on. Some women, and even some men, would do blowjobs for twenty or thirty bucks. Then one day, these two high school girls showed up, strung out and desperate for smack." Kenny described how two men convinced the girls to suck their dicks in exchange for heroin. "I was right nearby and could hear the guys whooping it up in their tent. After a while, the girls stumbled out and walked away."

"A few days later, though, they came back. Only this time, the guys had different plans. I'd heard them talking, saying that if the girls came back, they would turn them out, you know, get them high, rape them, then pimp them out for as long as they could get away with it."

Jerry shook his head. "What happened?"

"When I heard what they had in mind, I thought about joining in. They were cute young things. I was horny as hell and tired of doin' hacked-up tweaker gals." He paused and exhaled heavily.

"What happened then?"

Kenny looked up. "I had some kind of … you know … moment of clarity or whatever. I thought about my sister when she was their age."

"What did you do?"

"Packed up my stuff, walked to the Chevron station, and asked the clerk to call the cops."

Jerry put the box of cards aside, leaned forward on his elbows and looked sternly at Kenny. "I admire what you did," he said softly. "But let's not forget what you almost did." He pinched his thumb and forefinger together. "You came this close to raping those girls. That would have scarred them for life—and you."

Jerry continued. "I'm guessing the old you, the real you, would have never considered doing something like that. Am I right?"

Kenny nodded his head.

"Those other addicts made the wrong choice. I pray they're paying the consequences, and those girls are getting the help they need," Jerry said. "But something led you to make a different choice. I think it was the Grace of God."

"But I don't believe in God."

"Well, it looks like He or She believes in you."

Chapter 12

The bay sparkled with sunlight, and white caps churned in the wind. A flock of geese flew overhead, and Freshwater Creek was full to its banks, the pastures bright with moisture.

Bill was driving to meet Angela at the Arcata Marsh for their second date, and he felt so good he started singing a favorite Montgomery Gentry song:

"I'm slowing it down and I'm lookin' around and I'm lovin' this town and I'm doin' all right. Ain't worried 'bout nothing except for the man I wanna be."

He couldn't remember the next line, but he knew the chorus: *"And it'd sure be nice if you'd roll with me."*

After their first date, he and Angela had talked on the phone two or three times. He was happy when she suggested they meet again—and at the marsh, one of his favorite spots.

Bill parked and walked to the shore. The tide was ebbing, and shorebirds pecked for food along the margins of the water. Most were greater yellowlegs, scanning the shallow waters, pecking their long beaks down for food. Nearer to shore, compact least sandpipers worked the exposed mudflats.

Bill saw Angela's green Toyota Highlander maneuvering into a parking spot. As she got out and smiled at him, he felt his face get hot and his lower belly tingle.

"How are you, Bill?" she asked, shaking his hand.

"Great. And you?"

"Muy bien. Enjoying my day off, and happy we could get together."

Her smile was like the sunrise. "Yeah, me too," he said, and they started walking around the lake.

A flock of starlings swooped across the mudflats, abruptly switching directions several times. "It's amazing how they can turn like that all at once," said Angela. "I love that."

"It is amazing," said Bill, feeling the wonder. "It's like they have one mind."

"God's creation is just so—in Spanish, we say maravilloso."

"Mehr-ah-VO-so?"

"Mah-rah-vee-YO-so," said Angela, sounding out each syllable.

"Merry vee uh, Merah vee ..." Bill stammered.

"Let's try bonito."

"I remember that one 'cause some guys I worked with liked to talk about their wives and girlfriends on the drive back to town."

"They probably said bonita since they were talking about ladies."

"Yeah, that's right. Bow-NEE-tah." Bill chuckled. "Like you. Muy bonita."

Angela smiled shyly and looked out at the bay. Then, like the starlings, they started walking together in the same instant.

When they came to a bench, she said, "Shall we sit down a while?"

"Sure." Noticing the seat was wet, he wiped his canvas jacket sleeve across the surface for her.

They sat without talking for a minute, then she said, "This is so different from where I grew up. We have beautiful parks and plazas in Mexico City, but nothing like this unless you drive three or four hours."

"I haven't spent much time in big cities. Visited San Francisco, of course. Been to Portland and Sacramento a few times." He paused and hoped she'd fill in the gap. But she kept quiet. "Is Mexico City much like San Francisco?"

She looked thoughtful. "In some ways, yes. Most of the central districts were designed by the Mexican president Porfirio Diaz to look like Paris. There are elegant neighborhoods with beautiful houses. And where I live, Roma, is one of the most beautiful."

"You miss your family a lot?"

"Yes." She took a tissue from her purse and wiped her eyes. "At least we have a video chat every Sunday, though. I talk to my mom, my dad, and my two nieces—my sister Lupita's daughters, who are living there for the school year. And some cousins, aunts and uncles are always around for a big Sunday dinner. I can almost smell the homemade tortillas."

"Don't think I've ever had homemade tortillas."

"Maybe I'll make them for you sometime." Then she looked back at the water. "I miss other things, too. Like cumbia dancing at the big parties and in the clubs." She looked back at Bill. "Don't you find Eureka a little boring sometimes?"

Bill didn't know how to answer. He had too many hobbies, friends, Al-Anon meetings, woodworking, and home renovation projects to be bored. But younger people often complained about how Eureka rolled up its sidewalks at eight PM. Angela's lament made him think of their age difference. "Honestly, it doesn't bother me. I'm a country boy at heart and stay pretty busy with projects and stuff."

She nodded and looked back at the water.

•   •   •

Jonah had immersed himself in Eureka AA for two weeks, attending two or three meetings a day. No one had objected to him using the program to quit cannabis. Instead, they welcomed him with warmth, affection, and three-word mantras: "Keep coming back"—"Go to meetings"—"Just don't drink."

When he first heard the phrase, "Get a sponsor," Jonah wondered if there were some commercial side of AA that had escaped his notice. But he soon learned that a sponsor was a mentor who agreed to talk and meet regularly with a newcomer. Jonah assumed Manny was his sponsor, and the older man seemed to think so too.

But there was one AA principle that Jonah could not swallow: that members must turn their will and their lives over to God to stay sober.

"I know Christianity helps a lot of people," he said to Manny when they were having coffee at Denny's. "Like my mom and my brother. They've found a church that really works for them. My mom seems like a different person since she was born again, as she calls it. But I could never believe in a supernatural deity who walked on water."

Manny laughed and stroked his stubbly chin. "You're not alone. The most important part of that third step for you to remember is the ending, 'as we understood Him.' And it doesn't have to be a 'Him.'"

Jonah had indeed clung to this phrase to reassure himself that AA wasn't a Christian cult. "It wouldn't matter if it said to turn your will and your life over to Goddess or Brahma or the Creator. I'm not a 'supreme being' kind of guy."

Manny's smile widened, and Jonah could tell he was enjoying this. "Your higher power can be any damn thing you want. One gal in AA gal made that actress, Betty White, her higher power."

"Seriously?" Jonah tried to decipher Manny's enigmatic grin.

"Yep. You'll probably hear her talk about it at a meeting sometime. She says she was in a video store one night when she started thinking about getting a bottle. She knew she needed a higher power, but, like you, she was an agnostic or whatever. And so, she closed her eyes and told herself the first thing she saw when she opened them would become her higher power. And when she opened her eyes, she saw a poster for that old series Golden Girls. And old Betty White has helped this gal stay sober ever since." Manny folded his arms in bemused triumph.

Jonah liked the story but doubted such a tactic would work for him.

Manny continued. "Listen, I'm a Christian through and through. I'm a deacon at the Methodist church. I run a Christian men's group over at the Rescue Mission where we met." He pointed toward the waterfront. "But when it comes to spirituality in AA, I support anything that helps people stay clean and sober. Anything."

Jonah relaxed. "I'm drawn to Native American spirituality. I want to learn more about it. And Eastern religions, especially Buddhism."

Manny's eyes glowed, and he put his palms together and bowed comically. "Hallelujah! Praise Buddha!" He laughed at his performance, then added, "That sounds perfect for you. I look forward to hearing more about it. Maybe I'll even learn to cross my legs and chant 'Om.'"

Manny also recommended a chapter in AA's Big Book called We Agnostics. And that's what Jonah sat reading on Manny and Karen's couch. He was surprised to read that about half of AA's original members were atheists or agnostics who found they needed more than a "code of morals or a better philosophy of life ... to overcome alcoholism."

Jonah understood that. He had been storing up reasons to quit weed and beer for years. Getting high stole his time and energy, kept him from connecting with people—like Fawn, the cute woman he'd met at the activist meeting whose childhood stories were lost on Jonah because he was stoned.

But even with ample reasons to quit, Jonah couldn't stay clean and sober. "Lack of power was our dilemma," the book said. That sounded exactly right. "We had to find a power by which we could live, and it had to be a Power greater than ourselves."

"We did not need to consider another's conception of God. Our own conception, however inadequate, was sufficient."

This sounded perfect. But then, the text took a bewildering turn. It described atheists and agnostics as people who thought "life originated out of nothing, means nothing, and proceeds nowhere." Non-believers, the book stated, considered "human intelligence ... the last word, the alpha and the omega, the beginning and end of all."

Jonah closed the book in disgust. He had never met an atheist or agnostic who believed what the book said they did. For his part, Jonah considered human beings to be a part of a vast web of life, one species among millions in a mysterious universe, not some "alpha and omega."

The front door opened, and Manny entered followed by a fit middle-aged man wearing paint-stained clothes. "Hey, Jonah. This is DYE-vid," Manny said, mimicking an English accent. "He's from Aus-TRAWL-ee-ah."

"New Zealand, actually," said David.

Jonah and David shook hands. Manny put the kettle on, and they all sat around the kitchen table.

"New Zealand, huh? What's that like?" asked Jonah.

"Fucking unbelievable, mate." David's face lit up. "Like nowhere you've ever seen. Ancient forests you can hike in for days. Rivers like you wouldn't believe."

"Wow. Sounds kind of like here."

David considered that. "It is a bit like here."

Manny brought their tea. Surmising that the two men had planned on a private chat, Jonah stood to leave. "Great to meet you, man."

"You too, bro." David stood to shake Jonah's hand. "Listen, I'm taking a hike up to the Headwaters Reserve tomorrow. You want to join me? Weather's supposed to be decent."

Jonah had been wanting to see the Headwaters. "Yeah, absolutely."

David looked at Manny, who shook his head. "Have at it, you two. Don't think I could keep up."

David said to Jonah, "Pick you up here at seven?"

"Wow, that's early, but sure, why not."

"Bring a lunch and some water."

• • •

David arrived promptly at seven AM in his beat-up green Subaru Outback. The mist hung thick over Eureka as they drove, but the eastern sky was brightening. At the trailhead, Jonah strapped on his daypack, and David got two walking sticks out of the hatchback. "You have an injury?" Jonah asked.

"What, you mean these?" David said, holding up the sticks. "Nah, mate. My dad got me my first pair when I was a kid. You get more power on the hills. And they come in handy when you're crossing creeks or coming down a steep patch. Plus, you never know when you'll run into a mountain lion." David raised a stick in each hand, pumped his fists, and roared so loudly that the sound echoed in the trees.

"That'd scare away a whole pride," Jonah said with a nervous chuckle.

David set a fast pace, but Jonah had no trouble keeping up. The paved road went through a dense forest of alder, myrtle, and spruce. Occasionally, they glimpsed a creek flowing strong and full.

After about forty-five minutes, they reached a trail and started climbing. Half an hour later, they arrived at the old-growth reserve. They were alone except for a raven cawing at them from the canopy.

Jonah noticed a surreal glow to the landscape, at once brighter and more diffuse than what he was used to in a forest.

When he looked up, he understood: the old-growth canopy—maybe a hundred-fifty feet above the ground—refracted the sunlight. With no understory of young trees or shrubs, the light beamed down to the forest floor unimpeded, giving a magical quality to the terrain.

"Man, isn't this amazing?" remarked David. "Why would anyone want to fuck up this kind of experience by drinking or doing drugs?"

"Or coming in with bulldozers and chainsaws," said Jonah.

David responded with a shrug. "I'm glad they saved this old growth, but I've got no problem with logging. Lumber doesn't grow at lumber yards, you know."

"Yeah, but, I mean, clearcutting is just plain wrong."

"Maybe," said David. "It sure doesn't look good, but I've heard foresters say it's the most efficient way to produce timber in this coastal climate."

Jonah didn't want to spoil their hike with an argument. "I don't buy it," he rejoined simply.

On the drive home, Jonah told David how he came to live behind Manny and Karen's place. "It was amazing how I met Manny. It was almost enough to make me believe there is a God looking out for me."

David looked closely at Jonah. "So, what are you atheist, agnostic, pagan?"

"All of the above, I guess." Jonah paused to think about what he wanted to say next, and he noticed that David didn't interject but gave him space. "I've started looking for a spiritual practice or higher power. I mean, they say that a real addict or alcoholic needs spirituality. And I believe that."

"That's the second step, my brother. 'Came to believe that a power greater than ourselves could restore us to sanity.' That was an easy one for me. But that Third Step is a motherfucker."

"I know!" Jonah agreed. "Turn my will and my life over? That actually sounds kind of insane. Even if I get to define my own version of God."

"Tell me about it, mate."

David told Jonah he was remodeling a rental house in Arcata. "It's a beautiful house with good bones from the 1950s, but it needs a lot of work. I'll be on it for a few months, be lucky to finish by May, when she wants it ready to rent. I'm looking for a helper. You ever do any building work?"

• • •

It hadn't rained for a few days, but the lawn was still too wet to mow. So, Bill vacuumed his bedroom and living room and swept and mopped the kitchen and bathroom floors. He took out the recycling, then entered his shop. He opened the wood stove and stirred the charred logs with a metal rod. He blew on the embers, then stuffed in some newspaper and kindling.

Sitting on a stool by the stove, he looked at the old-growth redwood boards he'd stuffed in the rafters and stacked against a wall. The boards were dull gray on the surface, but once planed and sanded, they'd reveal beautiful redwood with grain so fine that you'd need a magnifying glass to count the lines, wood so durable it had once been used to make water tanks and pipes. You couldn't find it in lumber yards—only at specialty dealers who'd salvaged it from demolition projects, as Bill had, or hauled long-submerged logs out of a creek or river bottom.

Bill had been gathering this stash for a couple of decades, and he felt responsible for using it wisely. A few years back, he'd purchased a plan for Adirondack chairs and calculated that he could make about forty chairs. He would have earned about five grand.

But he'd decided he wanted to do something more creative, more personal. He'd considered making something for Kenny—

maybe a model of the Dodge Charger they'd worked on with another family before Kenny went off the deep end. Then he'd give it to him when—if—his son ever got sober and came back into Bill's life.

Now he was thinking about carving a heart or something for Angela. But as he envisioned handing it to her, he realized that would not be a good move.

Bill wanted Angela with a longing so feverish that he had trouble sleeping. But Angela had yet to show Bill that she wanted to be anything more than a friend.

No, he told himself: Angela Garcia from Mexico City would not be wooed with a heart carved from old-growth redwood.

Chapter 13

David's remodeling project was in Arcata, and Jonah only accepted the job offer after David assured him that the home wasn't near the plaza. "It's on the other side of town, mate," David said when he dropped Jonah off after the hike. "But what's the big deal? I love the plaza."

"I do, too, man, but going there makes me want to get high. That's where I used to hang with all my stoner friends. And when I first got to town and didn't know anybody, that's where I went to score."

"I get it," said David. "It'd be like me going to one of my favorite pubs."

"Exactly."

But the next morning, when Jonah looked across the bay from the highway and saw the deep green forest where he used to live, he felt such intense longing that he considered telling David to drop him off at the plaza.

When David turned off at the first Arcata exit, the fantasy eased and Jonah breathed deep with relief. They parked in front of a one-story red and yellow house. David pointed to a bucket of tools for Jonah to carry in. Inside, David put on a white jumpsuit that covered him from ankles to head.

"Forgot to tell you to buy some coveralls," he said, then shrugged.

Jonah followed David to a back bedroom, then down through a trapdoor in the closet. They dropped into a crawlspace so low that Jonah had to kneel on the damp dirt. Torn insulation and spider webs hung from the floor joists, and old tarps littered the ground.

"Welcome to paradise, mate!" said David with a grin.

"Yeah. Pretty gnarly down here."

"Well, not to worry. We should only be down here for a month, six weeks max." David kept a straight face for a second, then broke into a laugh. "Just foolin', mate. We'll be done down here in a couple days."

"What exactly are we doing?"

"I'm going to start taking out the old screens on the vents while you clear away all this plastic and crap. Start by using the shop vac to suck up any standing water on the tarps."

Jonah crawled to the edge of the basement with the vacuum. He turned it on and pushed the hose into a puddle that floated on a tarp. The tarp material instantly clogged the hose. He tried dipping the hose in sideways, but that sucked up only a trickle. So, he placed two fingers like a screen over the end of the hose. That worked.

It took Jonah about ninety minutes to vacuum the water and collect the plastic sheeting. Then, David handed him a trowel and a bucket. "Go around and scoop up as much mud as you can."

When lunchtime finally came, David broke out a sandwich, apple, and a Thermos of coffee. Jonah had no lunch, so David offered him his car keys. "You better get some food in you. But we only take a half hour, so I don't think you'll have time to get that gear, too."

Jonah was filthy from head to foot, his knees and elbows caked with mud, spider webs in his hair. "I'll get that stuff tonight. Should I give you the receipts so you can reimburse me?"

David looked hard at Jonah. "It doesn't work that way in the trades, mate. You got to bring your own gloves, coveralls, knee pads, tool belt, utility knife, and other basic stuff. I'll write you a list before we knock off. I could advance your pay if you're broke."

This was unwelcome news, but Jonah managed to keep the displeasure out of his voice as he said, "Well, okay. That'd be good."

After lunch, they returned to the crawlspace, and David explained what they'd do next. First, they would install a perforated drainpipe at the downslope perimeter, cover it with gravel and connect it to a sump pump. Then they'd smooth the ground so it sloped with an even grade toward the pipe, filling in any low spots with sand. "Finally, we'll lay down some thick ten-mil plastic to keep the ground dry." David pointed to the sub-floor above them, "Then we'll install a new vapor barrier and insulation under the sub-floor."

"I think I get it," said Jonah.

"We're starting from the ground up," David said, folding his arms and looking intently at Jonah. "We don't want to make her house all fancy on the surface but leave this funky crawlspace to fester."

Jonah used a short-handled spade to dig the trench for the drain. He kneeled where he could, but in tight places, he had to lie on his side and use the trowel to shovel out a few ounces at a time. When the tub was full, he hauled it outside to dump it in a corner of the garden.

They quit for the day at four-thirty. David drove Jonah to the hardware store and gave him sixty dollars and a list of gear to buy.

At home, Manny and Karen were out, so Jonah took off his clothes in the laundry room, stuffed them in the washer, added some detergent, turned it on, then walked to the shower in his underpants.

After showering, he scampered to his cabin with a towel around his waist and collapsed on his bed.

An hour later, he woke up, feeling like he'd taken a beating. He dressed, dragged himself to the house, put his clothes in the dryer and microwaved a frozen burrito. Sitting at the kitchen table, Jonah noticed blisters on both palms. His lower back screamed with pain.

Jonah had thought he was in good shape. Now, he wasn't sure if he could make it through another day on that job. After he finished the burrito, he brushed his teeth and staggered back to bed.

Chapter 14

Bill pulled into the driveway of a single-story 1960s house, gray with turquoise trim. Perched above a gulch, the house was surrounded by redwoods and shrouded in morning mist. While he waited for Jim, who would hear his truck idling, Bill noticed the yard was immaculate except for some toys on the lawn. What a change, he thought, from the last time he'd been here: the blackberries had been out of control, and old appliances had littered the yard.

Jim came out the door, then turned back and said, "Okay, Ma. See you tonight." He bounded over to the truck and got in. "Morning Bill," he said with a huge smile. "My mom says hi."

"How's she doing?"

"Pretty good. Got that diabetes under control."

"And how about you?"

"Man, I am loving my sobriety."

"Good to hear. How long has it been?"

"Just three weeks, man. Can't believe how good I feel. And all it took was to put the damn plug in the jug."

As Bill drove, he could not help contrasting Jim's dramatic turnaround with Kenny's perpetual relapses. "You going to meetings?"

"Fuck yeah, like ten a week," Jim replied. "And the men's recovery sweat lodge every Friday. That's the shit."

"Always wanted to try a sweat lodge."

"You should, man. Any Friday you want."

Bill hesitated, then asked, "Do you guys get, you know, naked?"

Jim laughed. "Fuck no, man. We're Indians, not hippies."

Bill drove south and slowed for the slick pavement where the road wound down into a gully. At the top of the next hill, they passed the Elks Lodge, then turned and saw the bay under the early morning sun.

"Clearing up nice," said Bill.

"Yup."

After a few minutes on the highway, Jim asked, "So, what's going on with your son?"

Bill sighed and looked out his window. "I wish I knew. Haven't laid eyes on him since Easter. Couple weeks back, I heard that he'd been behind the mall."

"Devil's Playground. Glad I never ended up there." After a beat of silence, Jim asked, "You want to pray for him with me?"

Bill wanted to say no—or even "hell no." But he glanced at Jim and saw how earnest he looked. "Sure, let's do that."

"Heavenly Father," Jim said. "We know you see all your children and love us no matter what. We ask that you give special attention to Bill's son Kenny. Let him know that his family still loves him and will welcome him back when he's ready. We ask these blessings in the name of Jesus Christ our Lord."

"Thank you," Bill said softly.

After the highway crested Table Bluff, Bill saw that the lower Eel River had spread across pastures, surrounding barns and farmhouses. "Man, look at that," said Jim. "What do those folks do when it's like this? How do they milk their cows?"

"They've seen worse, and they'll get through it."

After a few minutes, Bill asked, "If you don't mind me asking, what made you decide to get sober?"

"You know my Uncle Jackie, right?"

"Since I was a kid." Bill pictured the tough young man who'd fought half of the other boys in Blue Lake when they were growing up.

"And you know how he has been sober for, like, thirty years and how much he helps other people?"

"Sure."

They were in the forest now, tall trees crowding the highway. "Uncle Jackie always knew I was an alcoholic, but he never said anything about it. Never. Not till I brought it up a couple weeks ago when I saw him at the elder's dinner."

"What'd you say?"

"We were watching the dancers in all their regalia, the headgear, the beads, everything. Man, it was beautiful. But as usual, I'd shown up drunk off my ass, and I was in my own little world. Plus, I was still hurting from that fight with my cousins."

Jim was holding back tears. Bill had never seen his friend like this. After taking a few deep breaths, he continued. "I looked at my Uncle Jackie. He was watching the dancers and seemed so happy, his smile coming up from deep inside. And I just knew right then, I wanted that. I wanted to feel what he felt."

Bill pulled onto the dirt road that led to King's place, and Jim continued. "I said, 'Uncle Jackie, can I go to a meeting with you?' He looked at me and said, 'I'll pick you up at 5:15 tonight.'"

"That's all it took?"

"That was the start," said Jim. "First few days were hell, but after a week or so, it started getting better. Then, it was like the healthy part of me had woke up after being dead to the world since I was a teenager. Now, that part is in charge. As long as I keep feeding him and don't feed the other one, I'll be good."

"That's great to hear. I dearly hope Kenny can get there someday."

Bill felt Jim's powerful grip on his arm. "I have faith that he will."

Bill parked in front of King's rental house, and when he opened the door, he heard the river roaring like a freight train.

The two men unloaded their gear. Then Bill started putting on his spike boots and harness.

"Still not going to let me climb, huh?" asked Jim. "You know I done it plenty of times on commercial jobs."

"It's not that I don't trust your skills, but you're better at the ground work than me, especially at my age."

Jim nodded, then he started inspecting the ropes and lanyards.

"Already did that after the last job," Bill told him.

Jim shrugged his shoulders. "Don't hurt to double-check."

Bill looked around at King's spread, its rich flat terraces of soil formed by sediment that had washed down with the river over millions of years. King's grandparents used to farm this land, growing everything from tomatoes to green beans. They ran cattle and even milked dairy cows. After King and his wife took it over, they started selling grass-fed beef to the health-food stores. Now they rented the house to tenants and leased twenty acres to an organic farmer who'd put in dwarf apple trees and raised row crops. And King still ran his little timber operation.

When Jim had finished checking the climbing gear, they looked up at the tree. "We'll have to take off most of those limbs, then top her," Bill said.

Jim nodded. "Lower those big limbs, then zip the rest, right?"

"Yep. Might as well get to it."

Jim grabbed a yellow pole that had a slingshot at the top. He put a small, weighted bag in the slingshot's pouch, squatted on one knee, pulled the elastic taught, aimed, then let it go. The bag shot up into the canopy, trailing a thin cord from a bucket. It passed over a thick branch, then got stuck. Jim jerked the end of the line until the bag dropped to the ground. Then, the two men used the cord to haul up a safety rope.

Bill bellied up to the tree, wrapped his lanyard around the trunk, dug in the gaffs on his boots, leaned back against the lanyard, and began climbing. A small chainsaw and other gear swung from his harness.

When he reached the lowest branches, Bill glanced down and saw that Jim had secured the braking device to the trunk. Bill's heart sped up as he released one end of the lanyard and grabbed branches to climb higher. After climbing about ten feet, he secured another rope to a thick limb, then climbed back to his original spot, re-attached the lanyard, and breathed the relief of again having three points of contact with the tree: boots, lanyard, safety rope.

After strapping the lowest limb, Bill fired up the saw. In a few seconds, the big branch came free and descended slowly, controlled by Jim.

They cut and lowered a half-dozen more large limbs this way. "We can speedline the rest," hollered Bill.

"Hang on a minute," Jim said. He was untying the strap from the last limb.

The morning sun twinkled through the canopy, and Bill listened to the river and birds. Then he looked up and saw the moon: waning gibbous, he thought, and laughed out loud.

"What's so funny?" Jim yelled from below.

"Too much to explain," Bill answered.

That night at his daughter's house, Bill had tried John's crazy idea—praying to the moon—and felt some respite from his grief and guilt over Kenny and Petey. Since then, he had paid attention to the moon, keeping track of its phases and following online discussions among hunters about whether bucks were more likely to roam a few days before the full moon. And a few times—when deeply distressed by thoughts of Kenny—he had prayed again to the moon. It felt weird but also comforting.

"Ready," yelled Jim. Bill looked down at Jim standing about fifty yards from the tree, gripping the line. He started the saw, cut a limb free and watched it hurtle down the line toward Jim, who let go at the right instant. The limb settled a few steps from where he stood.

They worked like this for two hours. When Bill was almost out of straps and carabiners, he yelled, "Time for lunch."

"The fuck are you doin', man?" Jim asked.

"Downward dog," Bill grunted, straining to hold his arms straight and his hips high.

"What the hell is that?"

Bill lowered his body to the ground, then used his arms to bend his torso up. "My PT recommended yoga, and damned if it doesn't help."

"Whatever," said Jim, taking an enormous bite of his sandwich.

After completing another sun salutation, Bill plopped into a deck chair, poured himself some decaf from his thermos, and tucked into his ham and cheese.

Jim asked, "So are you going to Al-Anon meetings?"

"Yeah." Bill took a sip of coffee. "Since the summer."

"Does it help much?"

Bill's first thought was that Kenny was still lost in his addiction—dead for all Bill knew—so no, it didn't help. Then he smiled at himself, still thinking first about Kenny when Al-Anon was for him. "Kind of."

"How so?"

"Hard to describe. I went there at first thinking I'd get help for Kenny. But that's not the way it works."

As Bill sought words to explain, Jim interjected, "You know my uncle Jackie goes there. Says he needs it to stay sane with so many drunks and addicts in his family."

Bill chuckled. "Yeah, I know. I see him now and then. Wasn't going to say anything because, well, it's anonymous."

"Oops," said Jim with an impish grin. "I'm sure he don't mind. Dude is famous for being in recovery."

"Used to be famous for being a wild-ass drunk, worse than you."

"I've heard the stories. Guess he barely made it out of Blue Lake alive."

"He was older than me, but I knew him by reputation." Bill thought about stopping there, but he went on. "Times were different back then. When Jackie was coming up in Blue Lake, some white people expected an Indian to step off the sidewalk to let them pass."

Jim's eyes went dull. "Yeah, I heard about that."

"By the time Jackie was eighteen or nineteen," Bill continued, "he wouldn't put up with it. He'd just walk straight on and make the white people step out of his way. Got into a few fights, but he didn't back off. Least that's what I heard."

"Heard about that, too," said Jim.

Wanting to lighten the conversation, Bill said, "Now the Indians could buy and sell Blue Lake five times over with their casino. I guess nobody expects you to step off the sidewalk now."

"You'd be surprised." Jim gazed into the woods. "A lot of white people still don't like Indians."

"That's too bad," Bill said, feeling awkward because he knew it was true. Even some of his friends held onto prejudices against Indians.

Jim stayed quiet. Finally, Bill said, "I heard Jackie say a while back that he started going into Pelican Bay State Prison."

"Damn right!" Jim said, beaming. "They even let him lead sweat lodges for the Indians in there. Can you imagine a buncha lifers and gang-bangers sittin' on the ground praying and chanting to the Great Spirit?"

Bill geared up, then climbed slowly to where he'd stopped before lunch, about seventy feet up. This high in the canopy, the limbs were only a couple of inches thick, but they still had to zip them clear of the house and the outbuildings below.

After cutting a half-dozen limbs, Bill prepared to move higher. He began to change the rigging, then a stiff breeze swept the canopy. Bill felt dizzy. He steadied himself, then looked up to pick out where to move the rigging to. Another gust pushed the treetop harder, and Bill felt so dizzy he almost puked. He gripped a nearby limb and saw himself falling to his death. Or would he just be paralyzed? Who'd take care of him?

"Goddammit!" he yelled and hit the tree with his gloved hand.

"You okay?" Jim hollered.

"Yeah," yelled Bill, trying to collect himself. "Comin' down." Bill looked at the new boots and chaps that had set him back five hundred. He wondered if he could sell them for three.

When Bill hit the ground, Jim clasped his shoulder and looked at him with concern. "You okay, man?"

"Got dizzy, and it wouldn't go away," he said. "I guess it's your turn to climb, partner. I'll see if I can manage the zipline."

"You were up there a long time," Jim said with a consoling tone. "It's good to share the high work."

"Yep."

Jim put on the harness and spikes, and Bill helped him load the other gear. Then Jim asked Bill if he thought they'd need the brake when he topped the tree. "Not unless the wind gets a lot stronger."

"Roger that," said Jim.

When the first limb flew down the zipline toward Bill, he dropped the rope early and had to jog halfway to the tree to undo the strap and free the line. On the next try, his timing improved, and the limb dropped 10 feet in front of him. He managed to put the rest in about the same spot.

Bill watched as Jim prepared to top the tree. Bill had done it a hundred times, but he still got nervous. He'd never seen Jim top a tree, and he was anxious for him. If something went wrong, it could kick back and injure or even kill him.

Jim made a straight cut from the front. Then, he made a forty-five-degree bottom cut up toward the first cut. A small wedge fell to the ground. He turned off the saw and worked his way to the back of the tree. He fired up the saw again and disappeared in the sawdust. Then he idled the saw, let it drop to his side and pushed. The ten-foot top tilted forward, broke off clean, and fell straight down. Jim let out a whoop, and Bill yelled, "Yeah, baby!"

Jim came down while Bill fetched his big saw. For ten minutes, Bill worked the chainsaw into the tree trunk. Then Jim took over. After a few minutes, Jim put down the saw and began pounding wedges into the back cut with a sledgehammer. After a few taps on the third wedge, Jim stepped back. The tree's bare top started leaning.

"Timber!" yelled Jim.

It landed right where they'd planned.

•　　•　　•

Bill didn't get home until about seven PM. He was dog-tired and barely had the energy to shower and eat before falling into bed. He thought he'd go out like a light, but anxious thoughts kept him awake. What if he couldn't climb anymore? He was fifty-nine, with six years until Medicare and seven or eight until full Social Security. After his divorce, he'd probably have house payments the rest of his life.

He got up and brought his laptop to bed to look at porn. He checked his email first and saw a message from Angela. "Hi Bill, I hope everything went good with your big tree job today. Would you like to meet my sisters Friday before we go to dinner? They've been asking about you. Call me. Abrazos, Angela."

With his mood lifted by this invitation, he picked up his phone and called her.

"Hi, Bill. How are you?" she said brightly.

"I'm totally beat. The job was really tough. In fact... well, I'll tell you about it Friday. But I just wanted to say, yeah, I'd love to meet your sisters. What time?"

"How about five-thirty at our apartment? It's 1921 J Street, right near the high school."

"You bet. See you then."

"Good night, Bill. Sleep well."

"You too." He hung up, feeling less alone and scared.

Chapter 15

Late the next afternoon, Bill stood in front of his bedroom mirror, debating with himself what shirt to wear. He liked the teal plaid better than one with blue and white checks, but his belly stuck out when he tucked it in, and he thought it looked sloppy untucked.

He was also considering whether to wear his bolo tie. Its black leather cord, silver tips, and turquoise clasp looked great with either shirt. But would wearing it make him look too eager to impress the sisters? He'd never worn the bolo, which Cheri had helped him pick out at a store in Santa Rosa.

Thinking of Cheri, Bill was gripped by a tremor of weakness and fear. He sat down on his bed. Life without her, after twenty-five years together, sometimes seemed impossible. It was over with Cheri. He knew this, yet his heart was still catching up.

He wondered what Cheri would say about his outfit. She'd always been so blunt. He could hear her now: "Too fancy," or "Makes you look fat." Thinking about this made him laugh.

"You're on your own now, old-timer," he said to his reflection. Then he left the house with the plaid shirt on—tucked in and accented with the bolo tie.

Angela opened the door wearing a tight orange and black dress. "Come in, Bill," she said, extending her hand. "Nice bolo."

Standing in a tidy living room were Angela's two sisters—one of whom Bill recognized from her restaurant.

"These are my sisters, Lupita and Pamela," Angela said.

"It's great to meet you," said Pamela. "Angela has said so many nice things about you."

"Well, I hope you won't be disappointed by the real me," said Bill awkwardly.

"Would you like a beer or glass of wine?" asked Lupita, moving to the kitchen.

"Just some water would be great." Bill sat down and looked around. Bright Mexican blankets draped the couch and covered a TV. Above the sofa hung three paintings in a whimsical style that showed village scenes Bill assumed were in Mexico. Lupita handed Bill a glass of water, and Angela passed him cheese and crackers.

Pamela asked Bill about his daughter and grandson. "They're well and happy," Bill said, "Just wish they lived closer." He turned to Lupita, "Angela told me you have three kids."

"My twin boys are eight," she said happily. "They're across the street at the youth center right now."

"I took my kids there for years," said Bill. "Good place."

"And my daughter Angelica is in high school. She should be home soon."

After a brief silence, Bill addressed Pamela, "And your kids? Angela said they're in Mexico City."

"That's right." She smiled and crossed her legs. "Spending the school year with our parents. They're having a great time, but I miss them."

The front door opened, and a teen girl came in. She wore a black Eureka Loggers hoodie over torn jeans. She looked surprised to see Bill. "Please say hello to our guest, Mija," Lupita told her. "This is Angela's friend, Bill."

Bill stood, and Angelica offered her hand. "Pleased to meet you," she said, glancing briefly at Bill's face. Her eyes were red, and she smelled like cigarettes. Bill pointed at her shirt. "Went to the Arcata game the other night. Loggers are really strong this year."

Angelica looked confused, then said, "Oh yeah, yeah. Lots of my friends were there. They said it was exciting." She looked pleadingly at Lupita. "Okay if I go to my room?"

"Yes, Mija. We'll eat in an hour, and before that, we'll go over your homework." The girl rolled her eyes as she walked away.

Bill looked at Angela, and she nodded for them to go. They all stood up.

"It was so nice to meet you," said Pamela. "I hope we'll see you again soon."

"Have fun, you two," said Lupita, adding with a giggle, "Don't stay out too late."

"I'll have her home by midnight." Bill grinned, and they all laughed playfully.

$$\bullet \quad \bullet \quad \bullet$$

Jonah hopped on his bike and pedaled toward Eureka's Henderson Center for an AA meeting. Winter solstice was approaching, so the sun had already set, but there was still a glow on the western horizon. As Jonah pedaled, he felt his stiff back and knees loosening up.

He arrived early and went to a café on the corner. As he waited in line, a young woman glided up behind him, smelling of sweet shampoo. Jonah glanced at her and felt his breath quicken. She was about five feet four with a voluptuous figure, smooth pale skin, and long black hair. She held an infant on her hip.

In a casual tone, she said to him, "I always wonder why there's still a line for coffee this late in the day."

"Yeah, like, are we all vampires?" Jonah said. As she laughed, Jonah tractor-beamed his gaze on her face while using his peripheral vision to take in her black Mickey Mouse sweatshirt and shapely breasts. To distract himself, he looked at the baby—

a boy, judging from his Spiderman sweatshirt. "How old's your little boy?"

"Four months and growing like crazy," she said. "He's great but a real handful for a single mom. I haven't got a full night's sleep since he was born."

"What's his name?"

"Oliver."

"Hello, Oliver." Jonah smiled and waved at the infant. Oliver smiled back and clapped his hands.

"He likes you." She offered him her free hand and said, "I'm Paige."

"Jonah," he said, savoring her soft skin.

Oliver squirmed and whimpered, and then Paige said, "Would you mind getting his pacifier out of my bag? It's in the zipper pocket."

The skin behind Jonah's ears tingled as he brushed her hair aside to unzip the bag. He had not been with a woman for months, and with no weed or alcohol dulling his senses, he felt more sexually alive than ever. The sensations rising in him were so intense that he looked away from her as he handed her the pacifier.

"Here you go."

"Thank you."

A clerk signaled to Jonah that it was his turn to order. Jonah got his coffee and went to the creamer station—where he regretted not offering to buy Paige and Oliver's drinks. As he poured in some half-and-half, he glanced at Paige, settling Oliver in a child's seat and waiting for her order. Jonah imagined sitting and talking with her, and wondered what might follow.

He sipped his coffee and pretended to study the bulletin board. Paige got her order and smiled broadly at him as she walked back to her table. Jonah might skip that meeting. Then he remembered he'd promised to meet Manny there. He smiled and waved comically at Oliver, then went out the door.

• • •

Bill took Angela to an expensive restaurant on the waterfront. They studied the menu, then ordered. Angela seemed preoccupied.

"I'm so worried about Angelica," she said. "Lupita has been getting letters and phone calls from the school." She picked up her water glass and took a sip.

Angela told Bill she'd run into her niece at the mall a few days ago. "She was walking with three older boys wearing those thick bandanas"—she put her hand to her forehead—"so low they almost covered their eyes. When she saw me, she barely nodded, like she didn't want to let her friends know I was her tia."

Bill struggled with competing impulses. He felt empathy for Angela and wanted to help her. But he also felt rising irritation. He'd lived through this nightmare, and in Al-Anon, he'd learned that there was not much a parent or aunt could do once their loved one started burrowing into an addiction rathole. He'd worked hard to detach from Kenny's problems and attend to his own well-being. And now, another addict was turning this date into a family therapy session—and stirring up Bill's sadness about his son. Damned addicts, he thought: They make everything about them, even when they're not in the room.

"You might just have to detach from her emotionally," he said. He could see Angela didn't understand. Then he surprised himself by asking, "Have you heard of the Serenity Prayer?"

"No. How does that go?"

"God, grant me the serenity to accept the things I cannot change, the courage to change the things I can, and the wisdom to know the difference."

Angela slowly turned her water glass and looked down at the table. "I've never heard that," she said softly. "I pray for Angelica all the time. I pray for her to realize how much she's hurting her mother and her brothers. I pray for her to change."

Bill took a deep breath and grasped Angela's hand. "With this prayer, we're praying for ourselves. I know that sounds selfish, but it helps us—helps me remember that even though I'm powerless over my son's addiction, I can do things to make myself feel better with it all. And I can stop doing things like me and my ex used to do to enable his addiction."

The server came with their food. Bill was pleased with his steak, and Angela told him her fish was perfect.

When they finished, Angela got out her phone and scrolled through movie listings. But Bill said, "I have another idea for the rest of the evening."

Angela put her phone down and looked up, obviously intrigued. "De veras? Should I guess?"

"I think you'll like it," Bill said mischievously. "If you don't, we can go to a movie."

On the sidewalk, she threaded her arm through his. They walked past his car, and she asked, "Are we walking all the way?"

"It's not far," he said.

In a couple of blocks, they turned on Fifth Street. Bill led her to a glass door that announced *Eureka Dance Academy*. She laughed. "We're going dancing? What kind of dancing?"

"Cumbia."

•   •   •

At home in his cabin, Jonah called up mental images of Paige. He was back at the café, sitting with her and Oliver, making faces that delighted the boy. Paige gazed at him with adoration. When Oliver began to doze off, she invited him to her apartment.

"It's right around the corner," she said, with a smile that told Jonah what was coming.

She gathered up Oliver and they left, walking close together on the sidewalk. At her apartment, she put the sleeping boy down on his bed, and they began making out in the hallway. Then, she took him to her bed.

Jonah was hard as a lodgepole as he grabbed his lubricant. He imagined Paige on top, moaning and grinding, her breasts swinging with the rhythm of their bodies, his left hand full of her plump ass.

•   •   •

Bill had practiced at home with YouTube videos, so he felt modestly competent with the basic cumbia step pattern: back with the left foot, then the right, repeat. And he liked the music, with its propulsive steady beat. But leading Angela through the turn the teacher demonstrated didn't come easily. His first stumbling attempts left him thinking this had been a bad idea. Then the teacher gave him some corrections.

"Signal your turn a little sooner. And don't raise her arm so high, just above her head."

When he led Angela through the turn successfully, it felt wonderful.

"Nice," the teacher said. "I think you've done this before."

"She has," said Bill, nodding at Angela. "First time for me, except for practicing with YouTube."

"Well, you're doing great."

"He is," said Angela, smiling.

The teacher showed another turn and made everyone dance with different partners. Matched with an Asian woman younger than his daughter, Bill felt intimidated. But after a few stumbles, he managed to lead her through the new turn. He looked around to see how other dancers were faring. A young Latino man seemed to dance like a pro, swinging his hips to the beat and leading his partner elegantly through the assigned moves and more.

The teacher put on a cumbia hit that made Bill and everyone move their hips and legs. Bill walked toward Angela, but the smooth-dancing young man had taken her hand before he reached her. Bill partnered with an older white woman, glancing enviously at Angela, who danced gracefully with the experienced lead.

The music changed, and Angela came to him and took his hands with a smile. Her forehead glistened, and Bill noticed how much he liked the smell of her breath.

On their walk back to his truck, she held his arm again—tighter this time. They got in the cab, and he was about to ask if she wanted to go somewhere for dessert when she slid over, put her hand on his thigh and tilted her face up. He put his arm around her and kissed her.

They kissed for a few minutes. Then Angela grasped his left hand and put it on her breast. Bill was thrilled but also aware they were parked on a downtown street. He pulled her into a hug and put his chin on her head.

Bill wanted to take her home and make love with her. But he also knew that sex would change their relationship—maybe more than he was ready for after just three dates. "You're really important to me, and I like this," he said. "But I think we ought to wait to do anything, you know, more intimate."

He felt her nod her head. "Estoy de acuerdo, cariño."

Chapter 16

"She was unbelievably hot, and she seemed to be really into me," Jonah told David as they drove to work. "Wish I'd asked for her phone number."

David glanced at Jonah and smiled. "Yeah, you might have found yourself in pussy heaven. Long as you didn't mind becoming a daddy."

Jonah laughed. "Yeah, I know what you mean. But how many chances like that does a guy get?"

"Too many, in my experience," said David. "If I make love with a woman I'm not in love with, right after I come, I want to get the fuck out of there."

Jonah winced. He knew what David meant. He thought of a girl from high school—Sheila? Sharon? Jonah had noticed her flirting with him in math class, and he did his best—which wasn't very good—to talk to her after class. She had nice tits, and that was all Jonah needed to follow her when she suggested they go to a make-out spot just off campus. They started kissing, then she unzipped his jeans and gave him his first hand job.

The next day, she looked at him eagerly, hoping—he saw in her eyes—that he would ask her out or pay her some attention. But Jonah gave her just a quick half-smile, and when class ended, he walked out the door without further contact. Later, she pretended not to care, but he could tell she'd been hurt.

At the house, Jonah followed David into the dusty interior. "Let's start with that crown molding you cut yesterday," David said.

"It's all out back, rough cut to the dimensions you gave me."

They walked onto the back deck, where David stopped short and pointed at the boards stacked on sawhorses. "You mean you just left it outside without covering it?"

Jonah stammered, "Well, yeah. I ..."

"That's MDF," David barked. "When it gets wet, it swells up and is basically useless." He grabbed a piece and ran his hand along the edge. "You see? Some of this can be salvaged, but most of it's trash."

"Uh, I didn't know," said Jonah, his cheeks burning.

"Yeah, and you didn't ask either," snarled David. "Remember what I said? When in doubt, ask. Don't assume you know shit 'cause you don't know shit. This is like a hundred dollars worth of ruined materials, plus another trip to the lumber yard and a couple hours wasted. Fuck!"

"I can go to the lumber yard, and you can dock my pay for the damage."

David threw the ruined board on the ground. "You know what, man? Take the rest of the day off. I don't want you around while I clean up your mess."

Mortified, Jonah mumbled, "Okay, man, sorry," and left.

On his walk to the bus stop, Jonah passed a grocery store and thought about buying a six-pack. Then he'd walk to the Plaza to find some friends or travelers. He'd share his beer; they'd share their weed. But then he touched his phone in his pocket and had a better idea: he'd text Buzzy, buy that six-pack, and take it up to their campsite. The forest would be draped in mist. Buzzy would break out his stash, and Jonah would ease into the blissful fog of oblivion.

As Jonah romanced these fantasies, he was also aware of what he'd lose if he gave in to them. He'd worked his ass off to stay clean for nearly a month. He'd cut himself off from friends, attended a hundred meetings, and started working the steps. And he'd promised his mother he'd stay clean.

The bus came, and Jonah got on, grateful that the spell had broken. Watching the wind stir whitecaps on the bay, he felt angry at David, who should have told Jonah to cover the molding in Arcata's wet climate. It was flat-out wrong, Jonah thought, for David to rip him a new one and send him home.

As the bus crossed a tidal slough and approached Eureka, Jonah thought about how to use this unexpected day off. At the top of his list was attending Serenity Seekers, the noon meeting he'd gone to regularly before starting work.

Jonah arrived home two-and-a-half hours before the meeting. He needed a distraction, so he opened a porn magazine. But the images weren't enough to stimulate him. He thought about Paige, but he'd jacked off to fantasies of her all weekend. So, he put on his beat-up running shoes and headed out the door. After about fifteen minutes, endorphins elevated his mood. The sting from David's outburst went away, and he even felt compassion for David, who was under growing pressure to finish the remodel.

•   •   •

"Look who's back!" said Biker Bob, extending his wrinkled hand to Jonah and squinting through his cigarette smoke. "Ya' stayin' sober?"

"You bet. Twenty-seven days now."

"Yeah, baby!" Bob said cheerfully, smacking Jonah on the shoulder.

As he walked to a seat, Jonah was greeted and hugged by several other members. The meeting started with volunteers reading the usual texts. Jonah gave the words part of his attention while looking around the room. His gaze landed on an attractive woman he hadn't seen before. She had reddish brown hair and—like Paige—nice curves but was tall and athletic. Her eyes were closed as she listened to the reading, so Jonah let his gaze linger. Then her eyes popped open, and she caught him staring at her. He looked away, but not before he saw her bemused smile.

The secretary introduced the speaker, Beth. Jonah had heard her share at meetings before and liked how she talked about her recovery. So, he settled back, expecting an inspirational talk. But Beth shocked him by talking about sex.

"By the time I was 14," she said, "I realized that boys and even men were attracted to me. I craved attention, so I used my sexuality to get it. That worked too good," she said, her breath coming quickly.

"At fifteen, I was gang raped, set up by a guy I thought liked me." A wave of gasps and sighs swept the room. Beth started crying.

"It's okay, sweetie," said a woman sitting up front.

"We love you, Beth," said another.

Beth blinked through the tears and smiled bravely. "Thanks," she said. "This is painful to talk about, even though it happened almost twenty years ago. But I need to get it out, to release the power this secret has held over me."

Beth described how the rape drove her to use drugs and drink to escape her feelings. "I made a total drunken mess of my life all through my twenties," she said. "My recovery started with my second DUI. The judge suspended my license and made me go to an outpatient program. I hated that program, except for the guest speakers from AA. They inspired me to come here."

As Beth talked about the Third Step, Jonah felt a growing kinship. "My faith in God died when I was raped," Beth said. "When it was happening, I prayed to God to make it stop. Then afterward, I prayed that the bastards would get in trouble. Instead, they got away with it."

Beth sat up straighter. "So, when I got into recovery and heard you all talking about God, I almost left. I didn't want anything to do with your damned sadistic God." She paused then, and Jonah could sense the tension in the room. Most people in AA loved and revered their Christian God.

"But I stayed because my sponsor told me I could fire my old God and hire a new one. I had no clue how to do that—until I started listening to other non-believers in this program. People talked about a Great Spirit or 'Good Orderly Direction.' One of us even picked Betty White as her higher power!"

Jonah grinned as he remembered Manny's story.

"It took a long time, but eventually, I found my higher power." Beth smiled brightly. "I call it the power of love. The power of love is always there ... or here," she said, touching her heart. "The more I focus on it, the more it grows." She looked around the room quietly, then concluded. "That's all I've got for today. Thank you."

Members burst into applause and hooted with appreciation.

After the meeting, Jonah stood with others who were mobbing Beth. When he got to talk to her, she reached up to hug him. "You keep coming, Jonah," she said. "I see the light of recovery in your eyes, and it looks good. And you look good, too! Gimme another hug, and make it count."

When they pulled apart, he said, "Your 'power of love' sounds perfect for me. I could never believe in a Big-Daddy-God in the sky or all that mystical stuff that comes with Christianity."

"Whatever works for you, Jonah," Beth said, holding his gaze. "That's the great thing about this program. There could be a hundred people saying the Serenity Prayer in a meeting, and everyone has something different in mind when they say, 'God.'" Then she took both Jonah's hands. "Let's try it now, with 'power of love.'"

"Power of Love," they said together, "grant me the serenity to accept the things I cannot change, the courage to change the things I can, and the wisdom to know the difference."

Jonah felt a pleasant energy roll up his spine. "Wow," he said, still holding Beth's hands. "That really works."

She squeezed his hands. "So, work it!"

"Okay!" returned Jonah.

Then Beth hugged the woman that Jonah had noticed earlier. When they let go, Beth looked at Jonah and said, "Have you met Monica?"

•   •   •

That night, Jonah attended his regular AA meeting at Eureka's old Methodist church. When he walked in, he saw David talking to Biker Bob. He steered clear of the men and made his way into the hall, took a seat, and exchanged greetings with a few people. Then he felt a hand on his shoulder. David.

"Sorry, mate, to go off on you like that. I should remember that you've only been at this for a few weeks."

Jonah stood, and they hugged. "It's cool, bro," said Jonah. "I'd still like to reimburse you for the materials and work a few hours free."

David waved his hand. "Nah. Shit happens. Let's get back at it tomorrow, first thing."

"I'll be ready."

Chapter 17

Bill awoke Christmas morning in a home with no strings of lights, no presents, nor any tree to put them under. It was his first Christmas without Cheri and yet another holiday with no word from Kenny, and he hoped simply to get through the day without being buried in grief. Angela had invited him for coffee with her family, but he'd declined. "I just need to be alone," he'd said on the phone. "Not sure I can explain." They made a date for the coming week.

Bill knew he'd go nuts without something to do, so after breakfast, he went to his shop. From a drawer on the workbench, he pulled three ceramic sharpening stones and a plastic tub. He filled the tub with water from a garden spigot, then submersed the stones. Next, he gathered all his hand planes on the workbench and took apart the largest one.

His phone rang. It was John from Al-Anon. "Bill, just calling to make sure I'll see you at the meeting."

"Think I'm going to skip it," Bill said, bracing for a lecture about the importance of fellowship. John was Bill's sponsor now, which entitled him to give advice.

"Well, whatever you think," John said. "It'd be great to see you, and you know we're having that ice cream social after."

"Just not into it." Bill feared the meeting would leave him feeling gutted. After they hung up, Bill got back to his sharpening project. He picked up the iron from the large hand plane and its cutting edge—no nicks, so it didn't need grinding.

Thinking about grinding metal, Bill remembered the Dodge Charger he and Kenny had worked on for months with the McDevitt boys and their dad. He thought about how that project had ended so abruptly—or at least his and Kenny's parts in it. It was a Saturday morning, and they'd made plans to go to work on the car. Bill was gathering tools in the shop when Kenny came in and told him he wasn't coming.

"Look, we told them we'd be there," Bill said sternly. "A man is only as good as his word." Kenny was about fourteen, almost as tall as Bill. With his eyes, he told his father to fuck off. Bill said something like, "You bail on your friends, you bail on yourself." But Kenny was already out the door.

Bill knew he was sliding into the familiar sinkhole of self-blame and shame. Should he have been harder on Kenny? Tried to force him to go? Or would that just have made things more tense between them?

To test the plane iron, he placed its edge lightly on the back of his forearm and shaved off a tiny patch of hair, neat as a razor. He admitted to himself that this tool didn't need sharpening, nor did the others. He'd hoped this job would occupy an hour of this dismal Christmas, but he wasn't going to do something that didn't need doing. He re-assembled the plane and put it away, took the stones from the tub, set them to dry, and dumped the water outside. Back in the house, he put on his jacket and hat and started walking to the meeting.

•   •   •

Jonah stood with Biker Bob and Manny outside a big church hall, enduring their tobacco smoke as he debated whether to go inside and join the crowd of sober alcoholics were partying on carbs and caffeine.

"Kid, you look as nervous as a cat in a room full of rocking chairs," said Manny. "What's up?"

Jonah pushed his hands deeper into his pants pockets and shrugged. "Just nervous, I guess. Never been to a party where I wasn't getting high or drunk."

"Just pile your plate with food and take a seat with someone you like. Everything will take care of itself. You watch."

Then Monica and Beth walked up. "You boys coming inside?" asked Beth.

"Soon as I finish this pipe," said Manny.

"Jonah?" asked Beth, with Monica smiling by her side. He smiled back, nodded, and walked in with them.

After stacking their plates with food and filling their coffee mugs, they found seats together and started to eat. The event celebrated the end of a marathon day of meetings, an "Alcathon" hosted by AA to fortify members who might otherwise relapse during the holiday. A man and woman were setting up microphones and stools on a stage.

"I guess there's going to be music," said Jonah.

"Yeah, that's Margie and Ben," said Monica. "They're terrific. They play lots of feel-good songs from way back, like the Beatles and Peter, Paul and Mary."

"Cool. My mom used to play those tunes all the time when we were kids."

"Well, feel free to sing along," said Monica. "I know I will."

Ben strapped on his guitar, tapped the microphone, and said, "We're going to start with a tune that's gotten a bad rap as a stoner tune." That got everyone's attention. "But it's really about the magic of childhood and how that time passes too quickly, and kids grow up so fast."

After an instrumental intro, the singers launched into Puff the Magic Dragon. Jonah, Beth, and Monica sang along.

When the singers took a break, Beth looked at her phone. Monica asked Jonah, "What do you do for work?"

"I'm a builder," he said, puffing out his chest comically. Then, laughing, he added, "Well, more like an apprentice. You know David, with the thick accent?"

"Yeah. What a character."

"He's my boss. It's only been two weeks, but I've learned a ton working with him. And we even had our first fight." Jonah didn't know why he'd brought that up, but having introduced the topic, he plowed on. "He chewed me out bad and sent me home after I ruined some materials."

"Ouch," said Monica. "What happened then?"

"It wasn't that big a deal. We made up." Seeing a question in Monica's eyes, he defended David: "He's under a lot of stress because we're behind schedule. And he's got another client that wants him to start yesterday. So, any delays kind of freak him out."

Beth looked up from her phone and said, "Wow, that sounds like a lot to deal with. How much time does he have?"

"Sober? Like maybe five months."

"That's not much time," said Beth. "I hope he can manage all that pressure. He's got a sponsor, right?"

"Manny. Same as me."

Beth laughed. "Well, you two couldn't have picked a better one."

"Unless you're me," Monica said, tapping Beth's forearm affectionately.

Beth's phone lit up again. "Man, this guy just won't let up."

"What's going on?" asked Monica.

"This guy I used to date." Beth shook her head at the phone. "He just won't stop texting me." She looked up, and Jonah could see she was worried.

"Is there anything I can do?" he asked.

"I don't think so. But thanks," she replied. "I might have to change my number." Beth stood up and said, "Excuse me. I'm going to talk to Manny and Karen about this."

Monica and Jonah sat quietly. When their eyes met, Jonah could see she was worried. "I guess being in recovery doesn't mean the drama is over," he said.

"That's for sure," replied Monica.

The singers started again, and Jonah looked at the stage, grateful for a reason to take his puppy-eyed gaze off Monica before he weirded her out. Then, after a minute, he asked her, "What do you do for work?"

"I'm a case supervisor at an agency that matches adult volunteers with foster kids."

"Wow," said Jonah. "That sounds super-important. You like it?"

Monica took a deep breath and picked up her coffee cup. "I do. It's rewarding and important but very stressful at times. Right now, I've got one case that is breaking my heart—just thinking about it makes me want to go outside for a smoke." Then she added, "Thank God I quit the cancer sticks about a year ago."

"Good for you. Do you want to talk about what's going on with that kid?"

Monica looked around the room. She sipped her coffee, then leaned toward Jonah. "Basically, this really damaged sweet boy is getting screwed by his sick family—and by the system."

"How old is he?"

"I can't say—confidentiality." She put down her cup and looked at Jonah. "I see the worst of the worst in my job. A parent has to really mess up badly before the county takes their kid away. You can shoot up in front of your kids, dress them in dirty clothes, feed them cornflakes and candy—and still keep them. To lose your kids, you've got to beat them or seriously endanger them. Those are the kids we try to help."

"Sounds intense."

"It's super intense. I wish I could share more with my friends. It's so hard not being able to talk about what's happening with anyone besides my boss and co-workers."

They sat in silence for a while. Then Jonah said, "I went through some tough times as a kid—not as bad as the kids you work with."

"Yeah, like what?" asked Monica.

"My dad drank and acted crazy. My mom got pissed at him and acted even crazier. Eventually, my father ..."

"Your father what?"

"He died while driving drunk."

Monica leaned toward Jonah. "That's serious, Jonah. When you're ready, like after you've got more stable recovery, you should probably dig into that with a counselor who knows about trauma."

Jonah nodded and hoped she'd keep talking. "I was lucky," she said. "My parents drank some, and they could have done better here and there, but I felt loved and safe in my home. That's why I got into this work, to give back, to help kids who weren't as lucky as me, kids who got the nightmare parents."

"Are they really bad parents, or is it society, capitalism, the isolated way we live?" asked Jonah. "I mean, if we were all living in villages, like in the old days, wouldn't there be grandparents and other elders around to help out and support the parents who were messing up?"

Monica peered into space. "I used to think about that when I was in college. I took anthropology and watched films about communes in Israel and such. But now I just focus on things like figuring out how to convince a judge to leave this kid with his foster parents, who know how to handle him, rather than move him back with his whacked-out relatives."

Monica was close to tears and wiped her eyes with her napkin. Then she smiled and said, "Now promise me you'll never repeat any of that, or I'll have to kill you."

Chapter 18

After Bill told Angela about his dizzy spell in the tree, she convinced him to get over his reticence and seek medical advice—and since she had the day off, she insisted on driving him.

"Shall I come in with you?" she asked after parking.

"No, that's okay," he said. "I'll text you when I'm about done." He leaned over to kiss her cheek, then got out.

Sitting in the redwood-paneled waiting room, Bill felt grateful for Angela's caring—had Cheri been like that? Yes, Bill thought. He picked up a magazine to keep himself from thinking more about Cheri when a medical assistant opened the inside door and said, "Mr. Collins? We're ready for you now."

In an exam room, she took his vitals. Then Doctor Carrigan, a short, stout man with a round bearded face, bounded in. He smiled broadly, stuck out his hand and said, "How are you, Bill?"

"Okay, Doc. You?"

"Good, good." The doctor glanced at his clipboard, then back at Bill. "So, some problems with dizziness?"

"Yeah. And at the worst possible time—seventy feet up a tree with only a few straps and ropes between me and the great beyond."

"Scary," said the doctor sympathetically. "Let's check you out."

The doctor poked and prodded, tapped and listened. When he was done, he sat down and said, "Bill, I can't find anything wrong. BP is good. Heartbeat strong and regular. We'll do some blood tests to see if you've got an iron deficiency or something, but unless you've gone vegan since your last exam, I doubt we'll find anything."

"So, what do you think happened?"

The doctor leaned forward, his forearms on his thighs, and looked over his glasses at Bill. "It's part of aging, Bill. Our balance declines with the years. You heard about Brian McDonald?"

Bill nodded and made a mental note to visit his old friend, who'd fallen from a ladder while cleaning his gutters. "I could tell you about other male patients, some younger than you, who've had the same kind of accidents, losing their balance while high up on a ladder or a roof," the doctor said. "We like to think we'll always be young." He paused. "You still doing yoga?"

"Twice a week."

"Well, keep it up. Maybe work in a third class every week. And practice those one-legged balance postures as much as possible. But it's probably going to happen again." The doctor looked out the window at the redwood and alder trees that bordered the parking lot. "You ever think about doing something else?"

Bill growled, "What the hell am I supposed to do at my age, Doc? Work at CVS for 12 bucks an hour? I got a mortgage, truck payments, health insurance."

"I know, I know," said the doctor calmly. "Just be careful."

Angela picked him up a few minutes after he texted her. When he told her what the doctor said, she replied, "No, no, no. You're not that old. You're strong, and you have all these skills that people need. You just have to be more careful, mi amor. If it happens again, come down and let your partner take over, like last time." He wondered if she believed it or only said it to make him feel better.

"Do you have any plans for the afternoon?" she asked.

Bill was intrigued by something in her voice. "No. You want to do something?"

"How about we go to your place for a cup of tea?"

"Well, sure," Bill said, getting nervous and excited. This would be her first visit.

As soon as Bill opened the door for her, Angela began complimenting his home. "Oh, it's so beautiful," she said.

"Thanks." He looked with new appreciation at his handmade coffee table, the Navajo blanket on the couch, the paintings on the walls. He led her toward the kitchen, but she stopped to stare at a painting of three figures drawn in red triangles and rectangles. They looked human and animal, and they were in a boat on a choppy sea under a full yellow sun and a crescent moon.

"Ay, Dios mio!" she exclaimed. "This is … increíble."

"It is a great painting, isn't it," Bill said, gazing at it with her. "I got it from my dad when he passed. He bought it from a local Karuk artist back when the guy was just starting out. Now he's famous around the world."

Angela then noticed Bill's handmade end tables. "Where did you get these?"

"Made them."

"No! Son magníficos!"

"I guess I've gotten pretty good with woodworking."

"Do you have a workshop? Can I see it?"

"Sure."

After he made tea, they took their mugs to the shop. Bill reached up to a shelf, pulled down a rectangle of redwood, and then sat on a stool to show it to her. The wood's surface rippled like windblown sand, with a blond stripe on one side contrasting beautifully with the plank's deep reddish brown. Angela smiled as she ran her hand across it. "So smooth," she said. "And those lines and colors."

"It's curly redwood," said Bill. "No one knows exactly why some trees get like this, but when I find some, I save it." He gestured at his rafters. "Got a few dozen good pieces waiting for the right projects."

"I've never seen anything like this," she said, running her hand across the surface. She locked her eyes on his, and he put the wood aside. Her mouth was soft, her breath delicious. She stroked his cheek and held his shoulder while he held her by the waist. Then she pulled away and said, "Let's go to your bedroom."

Bill's heart slammed as he led her by the hand into the house and down the hall. They sat on the bed and kissed. After a few minutes, she unbuttoned her shirt and lay back on a pillow while he took off his shirt. He caressed her breasts, and she moaned with her eyes closed then reached for his belt.

After his pants were off, she pushed his head toward her breast. Then she asked, "Do you have a condom, mi amor?"

Bill smiled, then leaned on his elbow to reach into the nightstand drawer. He tore off the wrapping, and she helped him put it on. She lay back and guided him inside her. As he started moving, she responded vigorously, grasping his butt, and swinging her hips against his. He tried to hold off, but he came. "Sorry. It's been a long time," he said. "Would you like me to touch you or something?"

She hugged him and said, "No, no. I'm good."

Bill felt deep comfort and well-being as Angela rested her head on his shoulder and touched his chest. They were still for a while before Angela moved her hand to his penis. He responded, and after he put on another condom, she got on top. They found their rhythm. She climaxed, and he let himself come.

It was almost dark when they got up. She told him to shower first. Then he looked in the fridge and thought about dinner. Angela came into the kitchen wrapped in a towel, and Bill wanted to take her to bed again. "I don't have much for dinner," he said. "You want to go out somewhere?"

"How about if we go get something quick downtown, then go to the arts night together?"

Bill envisioned strolling arm-in-arm with Angela around Old Town Eureka on the one night of the month when the sidewalks were busy with people. They would undoubtedly run into friends and bring their relationship into the open.

"Great idea!" he said, then he hugged her, smelling his Costco shampoo in her damp hair.

After stopping at a pizza joint on Second Street, they held their foil-wrapped slices and walked through the crowds to the boardwalk. They found an empty bench, sat, and began eating.

It was a warm night for winter, and the wind made music with the rigging of boats in the marina. The sun had just set, and the harbor glittered under a spiral of pink clouds that rose from the peninsula on the other side of the bay. Closer in was Indian Island, lit only with a few lights.

Angela pointed to the dark silhouettes of spruce trees on the island. "Those shapes remind me of your painting," she said.

"Could be," said Bill. "That artist works with traditional designs, like ones they use for baskets." An image came to Bill— an Indian woman looking out at that island on a night just like this and feeling inspired to weave spruce-shaped triangles into her next basket.

He thought about the massacre of the Wiyot people by white settlers and wondered if Angela knew the tragic story. He was about to ask her when he saw a familiar young man walking by with a woman.

Jonah recognized him, smiled broadly, and came over. "Hey, Bill. It's Jonah; remember me from our road trip right before Thanksgiving?"

Bill stood, feeling happy to see Jonah. He'd grown fond of him on their road trip and had thought about him afterward. "Of course, I remember you, Jonah." They shook hands and introduced their friends.

Then Monica said, "We're heading to the Gazebo for the open-mike concert. You want to join us?"

Bill and Angela looked at each other and said "yes" in the same instant, which cracked them all up. "Sounds like it's unanimous," said Jonah.

They walked in pairs, Monica and Angela in front. Bill asked Jonah, "So, what are you up to?"

Jonah chuckled. "Oh man, so much. Clean and sober for one thing; a little over five weeks now."

"That's great news. Where you living?"

"South end of Eureka in a cabin. My landlords are big time into AA, and they're giving me a good deal on rent."

"Sounds good. Lots of bears out there, huh?"

"We always lock up the trash."

They arrived at an open square packed with people standing around an elevated gazebo where a woman was tuning her ukulele. Bill noticed a familiar couple in the crowd: King and his wife, Jean. He tried to think of a reason to take Angela somewhere else. But before he could open his mouth, Angela and Monica stood beside the couple.

As Bill walked up to Angela, King noticed him, grinned, and stuck out his hand. Bill introduced everyone and watched King's face light up as he took in the unusual foursome. "You folks having a good time?" he asked, looking at Monica and Angela.

"We're having a great time," said Monica. Then she said to Jean, "You look familiar. Aren't you on our fundraising committee?"

Jean smiled. "I thought you looked familiar, too. Yes, I am. That's my favorite charity."

"And she volunteers for all of them," said King.

While Monica and Jean talked, Bill saw King's grin widen. "How do you all know each other?" King asked. Angela and Jonah looked at Bill.

"Jonah and I met through mutual friends," he said. "And ... uh, Angela and I are dating."

"Well, congratulations." King looked at Angela. "And my condolences to you, ma'am. I wish you luck civilizing this old Sasquatch."

"Well, somebody has to do it, right?"

Bill relaxed and laughed with the others.

The performer began singing in a plaintive drone. Bill looked at Angela, who tilted her head to suggest they move on. Then King said, "This isn't our cup of tea. You folks want to wander up to the next block and see what we see?"

Everyone nodded assent, and as Bill fell in with the group, he admired how the old rodeo pro even knew how to wrangle people.

As they neared Third Street, Bill heard chanting. Behind him, a group came up the sidewalk, carrying signs and yelling about CalTrans logging.

·   ·   ·

When Jonah heard the chanting, he turned and saw about twenty protesters walking toward them. "Look who's come out to play," said King. "Johnny Pinecone and his merry band of protesters."

Jonah feared Bill would echo King's scorn. But after they glanced at each other, Bill kept quiet. King looked at Bill, then at Jonah and Monica. "Of course, I respect their First Amendment rights," he said sarcastically.

They stood aside to let the protesters pass. But one sign-carrying activists recognized King. He stopped and said loudly, "Hey, you're that guy who's always speaking up for clearcuts at the public hearings." He started chanting: "Shame on you! Shame on you!" The others soon joined him.

Jonah felt alarmed that things had gotten so tense. But King seemed unruffled. He started chanting and bouncing on his heels: "Shame on me! Shame on me!" The tension evaporated, and the instigator—a thin young man with his face painted like a raccoon—said, "We'll see you at the next hearing."

"Count on it," said King, holding out his fist for a bump, which the young man did not return.

As the protesters moved along, Jonah saw Buzzy. They slapped their palms and hugged. "Dude, where you been?" Buzzy said. "And why aren't you on the streets with us?"

Before Jonah could answer, he noticed Buzzy recognize King and Bill and grasp that Jonah was with them. His friend shook his head. "Man, what has happened to you?" He walked on.

As the protesters crossed Third Street, an empty logging truck approached the crosswalk. It slowed down and honked several times, then sped up and drove through the group of protesters. People scattered, and some fell on the street.

Jonah ran to the scene. He quickly ascertained that the people who fell had not been hit by the truck but stumbled as they moved out of its way. No one was hurt badly. He thought about calling 9-1-1 but noticed several people had their phones out.

Monica, Bill, and Angela came up to him. "Looks like no one is hurt," Jonah said. "I'm going to stay until the police show up and offer to be a witness since I saw the whole thing."

"I'm damned glad no one was hurt," said Bill. "Gotta say, though, I can understand why that driver is so pissed. Don't approve of what he did, but these folks are trying to take food out of his kids' mouths."

"But that trucker just tried to run them over," Jonah said, shocked that Bill would defend the driver. He looked to Monica in exasperation, who motioned with her hand for him to calm down. Jonah felt gut-punched.

A couple of minutes later, a female officer arrived. She took out a notepad and pen. Jonah walked up to her and said, "I saw the whole thing, and I'd like to give a statement."

"Me too," said Bill, standing beside him.

•   •   •

Jonah sat in the passenger seat while Monica drove. His thoughts had turned from the night's events to what might happen next. He and Monica had become friends after the Christmas Alcathon, and when he asked her to go to the arts night, she'd readily agreed. Now she was talking with excitement about what had happened and how much she enjoyed meeting Bill, Angela, King, and Jean.

"Did you see how he handled those protesters?" she said. "I mean, I probably agree with them more than him, but I admire someone who can turn around an attack like that."

"Yeah, I'll give him that," said Jonah.

"And I liked meeting Bill and Angela. He's the guy you told me about, right? Gave you a ride down to the Bay Area?"

"Yeah, that's him."

"Very cool." Monica pulled up in front of Manny and Karen's place. "Well, let's talk soon," she said, twisting to hug him.

When they pulled apart, he looked at her and said, "Can I kiss you?"

She looked down at the steering wheel. "I like you, Jonah. But I just want to be friends."

Chapter 19

Kenny swept the broom across the worn floorboards. From the large windows facing south and west, morning sunlight filtered through the haze over Eureka and warmed the dining area of the rooming house. To sweep under the table, Kenny maneuvered the broom around the feet of two men who sat drinking coffee and eating day-old donuts. "Don't mind me," he joked.

"Do you have to do this now?" one asked sarcastically.

"Yeah, can't you see we're in the middle of charging up our blood sugar?" said the other, using his fingers to rake colored sprinkles from his beard.

Kenny chuckled and continued sweeping while the men talked about a hunting trip. "We stalked that buck all day, up and down the hills out Yager Creek."

"Private land?"

"Yeah, my dad knew the owners."

The story continued, but Kenny became absorbed in his own hunting story. He'd been about twelve when his dad took him deer hunting for the first time. Before dawn, they drove to a parking area in Freshwater Valley between Arcata and Eureka. With other dads and their boys, they drove in a caravan into the hills east of the bay. They parked and hiked up a logging road until they came to an open prairie.

"Time to practice," said one dad.

It was Kenny's first time shooting his father's .300 Magnum Winchester. He was already nervous, and as he prepared to shoot at a log fifty yards off, another boy taunted him. "Don't be scared, Kenny. She won't bite." Kenny tried to brace the rifle firmly on his pack, but when he pulled the trigger, the recoil jerked the gun up, and he missed the log. He tried a couple more shots, then gave up.

The group spent a long day tromping up and down canyons and waiting behind rocks and trees. One boy got his first buck. Kenny didn't even shoot. He remembered how ashamed he felt and how he yearned for his father's comfort. But on the drive home, his dad had said nothing.

After finishing his chores, Kenny walked down the building's rickety outdoor stairs to the street. With mounting dread, he walked east and approached the Humboldt County courthouse. This would be Kenny's first voluntary visit to the place he'd been required to go as an accused thief, trespasser, and drug possessor. He'd promised his friend George—on trial for assault—that he'd show up and support him.

Kenny went through the glass doors and the metal detectors. He took the stairs to the second floor and entered a busy hallway with benches full of people who looked anxious or bored. Lawyers in suits hovered with briefcases, chatting briefly with one client before moving to the next.

George stood outside a courtroom door. A large man of about thirty, he wore a dress shirt and tie for the occasion. "You look like the usual suspect," Kenny joked as they shook hands.

"But I'm not—not this time. I really didn't do what they busted me for." He said this like he doubted Kenny—or anyone— would believe him.

Kenny knew the feeling. They'd both been habitual criminals for years, and it was tough to shake that reputation in a small town. "I believed you when you first told me," Kenny said emphatically. George nodded his thanks.

George had already spent a few weeks in county jail. And as Kenny and every other NA member in town had heard him say many times, his jail time had turned into a blessing because he kicked meth in there. Once released, he'd jumped into the recovery fellowships and found a room at a sober house. But this case still hung over him.

"Do I have time to get a cuppa coffee upstairs?" Kenny asked.

George pulled out his phone. "Better if you stayed. The judge could show up any minute."

"No problem," said Kenny.

He looked up and down the corridor, recognizing a few faces but no one he knew well. Then a sheriff's deputy walked by, glanced at Kenny, and said with a smile, "Kenny Collins, right?" Kenny froze in fear. Despite the deputy's apparent goodwill, he couldn't imagine an interaction with a cop turning out well.

"I'm Steve, Steve Johnson, a friend of your dad's." The cop stuck out his hand. "Say, uh, you're looking a lot better than the last time I saw you."

Now Kenny remembered where he knew the deputy from. He'd busted Kenny for shoplifting a couple of years back. "Okay, yeah, I remember when you took me in," Kenny said. "What was that, two, three years ago?"

Steve shrugged. "Something like that. So how you doing now?"

"I'm doing great. Clean and sober, about a month and a half. Living at the recovery ranch over there on Fourth Street."

"Good place," said Steve. Then he looked at Kenny thoughtfully. "Hey, let me show you something, okay?"

Kenny shrugged and said, "Sure."

Steve opened a folder and pulled out two mug shots. They showed the two men Kenny had turned in for attempting to gang-rape the girls in Devil's Playground. "When you were out on the streets, did you ever come across these two?"

Kenny pretended to study the photos. "They look kinda familiar, but I don't think I know them. Why?"

"We busted them for attempted rape but had to let them go for lack of evidence. Pretty sure they did it—and other assaults all over the county. That's why we're helping EPD with the investigation." He pulled a card from his shirt pocket and handed it to Kenny. "If you see them or you remember anything about their activities, where they hang out and stuff, would you give me a call?"

As Kenny took the card, a bailiff announced, "Courtroom three open."

"Gotta go," said George.

Steve said, "Well, anyway, congratulations on staying clean and sober. That's not easy. I'll bet your dad is proud."

Kenny hoped the shame on his face wasn't obvious to the deputy as he said goodbye. He entered the courtroom behind George.

Chapter 20

Manny pulled the minivan to the curb in front of Monica's house on a quiet street in southeast Eureka. Jonah's pulse pounded when she came out the door and walked toward the van. He got out and held the door. "You want the front seat?"

"How gallant of you, sir." She hugged him and got in. Jonah opened the sliding door and sat in a second-row seat. Monica leaned across to hug Manny. "Good to see you."

"Good to be seen," Manny replied. "Now, where does Beth live?"

"We're meeting her at The Hamilton," Monica said.

Manny nodded and put the van in gear. Monica looked at Jonah. "How's Jonah?"

"Really good. Really good," he said, trying to appear calm. "Learning a ton on the job with David. Staying sober."

"How long now?"

"One month, one week and three days," he said proudly.

"Way to go," Monica said, reaching back to bump his fist.

The sun was setting as they approached The Hamilton, an old elementary school that had been renovated into a community center. The playground bubbled with kids—even though it was a brisk winter evening. They played a game in a circle, and two adults played with them—one was Beth.

Beth waved when she saw the van. She gave every kid a high five, then jogged over to the van and got in the back seat. After hugging Jonah and touching Manny and Monica on their shoulders, Beth said, "I just love volunteering there."

The center was bringing new hope and life to Eureka's mostly poor westside, she said. "When me and other neighbors first started working on it, a lot of people doubted we could do it. It's still a work in progress, but it's coming together. Local families love it," Beth said, her eyes glowing.

"Some of our foster kids and their advocates go there for playdates," Monica told Beth. "We're even considering renting one of your rooms as a space for family visits."

"That'd be so awesome," said Beth.

Manny said, "I gotta admit, I was one of the skeptics. I doubted you could do it. I mean, that school had been closed for six or seven years, just sitting there with more broken windows every year. Plus, this neighborhood ..." Manny trailed off.

Beth sighed. "Yeah, we've got more than our share of junkies and criminals, that's for sure. But there's a lot more of us who really care about the community."

"It shows," said Manny.

"It was a Power of Love thing," said Beth, smiling at Jonah. "Love for our neighbors got us started and kept us going."

"Mark 12," said Manny. "Love your neighbor as yourself."

"Amen," said Beth.

They left the city and crossed a small valley with gently leaning barns and a creek meandering through pastures. Jonah let the beauty fill him up, and he thought about how much he'd come to like Eureka: the AA meetings, the funky old town, friendly people, the waterfront, and now Beth talking about The Hamilton rising on the power of love. It was all so different from what he had thought.

Tonight, they were driving to another town with an even worse reputation among his Arcata activist friends—Fortuna, the center of Humboldt County's timber, ranching, and dairy industries. But there were AA meetings in Fortuna, and the four were headed there on what Manny called a field trip. "At least a couple times a year, we need to go to meetings in different communities," he'd told Jonah. "So we don't get bored shitless hearing our own stories over and over."

When Jonah got out of the van in a church parking lot, he smelled the comforting scent of wood fires. Then he noticed several big mud-splattered pickups. One had a bumper sticker showing a semi-automatic rifle and the slogan, "I don't call 9-1-1." Another truck displayed a cartoon character urinating with the caption, "Piss on liberals."

Inside the church hall, the ambiance felt familiar to Jonah: plastic tables and metal chairs, the hum of conversation, and the smell of cheap coffee. Manny went to talk to a friend while Jonah stood with Monica and Beth, feeling awkward. An older woman approached and said, "You must be our guest speakers."

"That's us," said Beth.

"What?" asked Jonah, panicking. "Guest speakers?"

"Manny didn't tell you?" Monica asked with a teasing smile. "He probably figured you wouldn't come."

"He was right about that." Jonah tried to think of a way out. He could go for a walk. But he didn't know the town at all. Maybe he'd sit in the back and refuse to speak.

Manny waved them up to the front table. "What the hell, man," he whispered before taking a seat. "I don't know what to say."

"Just keep it real. And short," said Manny, giving Jonah an "I-believe-in-you" smile.

The meeting began with the usual prayers, readings, and announcements. Jonah was too nervous to pay attention, worried about what he would say, and busily sizing up what appeared to be a tough crowd for him to speak to. Those old guys sitting in the back row hated environmentalists; he could just tell. The two men wearing Carhartt jackets and camo caps had probably killed a thousand trees this week. The woman in front, with a big cross on her chest, was a dogmatic, self-righteous Christian.

Manny spoke first. Jonah had heard his tales often, so he wasn't expecting anything new. But this time, his sponsor seemed to be performing, not sharing, trying to entertain the group with stories of his hobo life. And he was succeeding at making people laugh.

• • •

Bill collapsed on his couch, picked up the TV remote, and found a college basketball game. He didn't care what teams were playing. He just wanted a distraction from the pain.

When Angela had suggested spending an afternoon with her nephews, Bill jumped at the opportunity to be with her and bond with the boys. They met at a big park in the center of Eureka, and Bill was instantly charmed by Rico, with his thick black glasses and serious expression, and Nesto, with a lopsided haircut.

When Angela introduced them, Rico looked at the ground, and Nesto hid his face behind a soccer ball. Before she could apologize for her nephews' shyness, Bill looked at her and said, "It's great to see you, Angela. Let's sit down on the bench so you can tell me about your week."

After getting a nod from Angela, the boys sprinted onto the field, dribbling and passing the ball. Angela hugged Bill tightly, and they sat down.

"Cute boys," Bill said. "Eight years old?"

"Yes. And I can't believe it," Angela said, putting her hand to her forehead. "They're so full of energy ... and so moody."

"They get along?"

"About half the time. The other half, they want to kill each other. Rico even asked his mother the other day, 'What would happen if I pushed Nesto under the school bus?'"

As if on cue, Rico screamed, "Stop, Pendejo! Stop!"

Nesto had the ball under his arm as he sprinted away from his brother, grinning like an evil clown. "He's so slow he'll never catch me," he said to Bill. Then he asked, "You want to play, Mister?"

"Mister Bill," corrected Angela, looking hopefully at Bill.

Bill hadn't played soccer since Kenny was that age, but he felt trapped. "Sure," he said. "What should the teams be?"

"Me and Tia against you and Nesto," said Rico.

They used pinecones and soda cans to mark the goals and agreed to out-of-bounds lines. Bill huddled with Nesto. "What do you think partner?"

"I think you should play goalie."

"You got it."

Bill was surprised at Angela's agility and skills, and soon a deft strike from her right foot sailed by him. "Goal!" she and Rico shouted, slapping palms.

On the next play, Nesto passed the ball to Bill. Bill jogged downfield, but Rico pecked the ball from between his feet and made a quick point through the undefended goal.

Nesto and Bill huddled again. "Maybe you should just stick with goalie," Nesto said in a voice that reminded Bill of his junior high coach. Bill agreed.

For the next half hour, he crouched, squatted, bent from the waist, and did things with his hips, thighs, and knees that he hadn't thought possible. Angela and Rico gleefully scored six points to Nesto and Bill's two.

Finally, Bill called time. "I gotta rest for a while." As soon as his butt hit the bench, pain radiated from his lower back.

•   •   •

On the ride home, Jonah and Monica sat in back. Jonah was about to ask Monica about her work when she asked him, "How did you feel about your share?"

Jonah was surprised at the question. "Pretty good, I guess. Never done that before, you know, spoken to a big group of strangers like that."

Monica was quiet for a moment, then said, "I wonder why you brought up the logging stuff?"

Jonah had told the group how his mission to save trees brought him to Humboldt. "It just seemed like a natural thing to say," he replied, feeling defensive. "I mean, it's true and a part of my story."

"But there are so many other parts to your story, Jonah. And you know AA tries to stay non-controversial." Monica spoke with confidence—and gentleness, and Jonah understood she was taking a risk to give him some strong feedback. "I've never heard you talk about logging or environmental issues in our meetings. So why bring it up there?"

Jonah felt embarrassment grip the back of his neck. Monica was right. He'd brought up logging because he knew loggers and other people there supported the timber industry.

"Oh my God!" said Beth from the front seat. "That's my ex, right there in front of my house!"

Jonah saw a man leaning against a chain-link fence. "Don't slow down, Manny," Beth said, turning her face away and sinking in her seat.

"You want to call the cops?" he asked.

"I don't know," replied Beth. Monica had put her hand on Beth's shoulder, and Beth clung to it. "I keep thinking about a restraining order, but I haven't got one yet."

Questions whirled through Jonah's mind. Had the creep threatened or hurt Beth, or was he just stalking her so far? Would he be brave enough to confront the guy if they went back and he was still there?

A few blocks away, Manny pulled over. "I think you ought to call the cops," he said. "They'll tell the bastard they got a call about a suspicious person loitering, and they'll make him move on. Maybe he'll guess it was you, but either way, they'll run him off."

"And you definitely need to get that restraining order," said Monica from the back seat.

Chapter 21

On a bright, windy Saturday afternoon, Jonah got off the Arcata bus and walked uphill. Soon, he was on the main forest road, chilled by the damp but happy to see the thick tree canopy overhead.

Since the protest in Old Town Eureka, Jonah had wanted badly to clear the air with Buzzy, to see Owl and a few other friends, and to walk again under these trees. With nearly two months clean and sober, he thought he was ready. Manny agreed but advised Jonah to include an AA meeting in his plan for the day.

Jonah let his gaze roam from the forest canopy down into the ravines carpeted with ferns. He savored the smells of damp ground and composting duff. As he started up a familiar hill, he sprinted to the crest and skipped down the other side.

When he approached his old campsite, he looked around to be sure the road was clear before climbing up the bank. Then he noticed a group of people just ahead. They were listening to a speaker—Mike Doyle from the environmental center.

Jonah walked up to the group and felt elated to see Fawn, Buzzy, and Owl. His stomach tightened when he recognized Alder. Fawn looked tired, but she still fascinated him. He wondered whether she was single. Then he noticed she held Alder's hand.

Doyle was pointing to some trees. "This forest has some of the oldest and tallest second-growth redwoods anywhere on the planet," he said. "The primary old-growth forest here was logged over a hundred years ago, and the city has been managing the forest to re-create old-growth characteristics."

"Then why are you logging the forest?" Alder shouted.

Logging the community forest? Was that what Doyle was talking about? Jonah was incredulous.

•   •   •

Bill was on his second cup of decaf. "La café es... muy buena," he said to Pamela, who sat in a chair opposite him.

She smiled and responded, "Gracias, Bill. Estoy feliz de escuchar eso. I'm glad to hear that."

Angela, who sat beside Bill on the couch, touched his knee and said, "Pero se dice' el café es bueno.' Café is masculine."

Bill shook his head in mock frustration. "Even when you gals are drinking it?" The sisters laughed. "Ai, ai, ai, this Spanish is so confusing."

"But you're doing great," said Pamela, standing up. "Mas café Bill?"

"Porque no?" He drank off what was left in his cup and handed it to her. Angela followed Pamela to the kitchen and asked Bill, "Otra galleta?"

"Another chicken?" he replied. The sisters laughed again at his bilingual wordplay, and he was pleased. He looked at his watch—almost eleven. When Angela had asked him over for coffee at Pamela's, he wondered if the older sister wanted to quiz him about his intentions and finances. But so far, it was all convivial fun.

Angela's phone rang. She looked at it and said, "I'm sorry. It's an important call I have to take." To Pamela, she said, "Es mi abogado," then retreated to the next room.

"Avocado?" Bill asked Pamela.

"Abogado. Lawyer," said Pamela seriously. "It's about her visa."

Pamela sat down and said to Bill conversationally, "Angela says you sometimes have to climb as high as a hundred feet up a tree."

Trying to sound modest, Bill said, "Yeah, sometimes. Though usually just fifty or sixty feet."

She placed her hand on her chest. "I could never do that. I'm afraid to go up a ladder."

Bill nodded and said, "I'm always a little scared. But I've been at it so long, I'm mostly used to it." He did not mention his recent episode of vertigo.

"Does it pay well?"

Bill felt a chill. Was the interview beginning? "It pays real good by the hour, but the hours vary. Some months I put in forty or fifty hours. Others, maybe just a couple days. I still work on commercial logging crews," he added. "That doesn't pay as much by the hour, but you generally work ten hours a day for a week or more, depending on the job. 'Course, that season's over for the winter now."

"I see." Pamela frowned. "Do you think you'll keep doing it until you retire?"

Before he could stop himself, Bill said harshly, "Do you want to see my tax return, too?" Seeing Pamela's shocked expression, he said. "Sorry, I know you're just looking out for your sister."

Angela came back into the room, obviously upset. "What happened?" Bill asked.

She shook her head and sat down. "Just my visa problems."

•   •   •

"You can bullshit all you want about age classes and old-growth characteristics," Alder yelled. "But you're still planning to slaughter trees!"

"Yeah," Buzzy echoed. "Just leave the forest alone, and it will do fine on its own."

Jonah had been trying to follow what Doyle was saying about the logging plan devised by the city's forest committee. But it still seemed just plain wrong. Even though they would do selective logging, not clearcutting—why do it here?

Owl spoke up. "Mike's got a lot more to show us," he said, sounding reasonable. "How about if we continue the tour and hold our judgments until the end."

Jonah agreed, but Alder said harshly, "You fuckin' sellout!" Then to Doyle, he said, "I've seen enough of your plan." He grabbed Fawn's hand, and they walked away. Buzzy followed, and Jonah almost went after them. But he glanced at Doyle and Owl and saw them looking at him. He stayed with the group.

Owl came over to hug Jonah. "So, I haven't seen you around for a while."

As they followed Doyle and the group up the road, Jonah was glad for the chance to explain his absence. "I had to get the heck out of Arcata to … um, get my weed addiction under control."

Owl raised his eyebrows. "For real?"

Jonah thought Owl was mocking him at first, but the look on his freckled face appeared earnest. "Yeah, very real. I'm a pot addict and an alcoholic. I've been living in Eureka, renting a cabin from a couple of AA members, and going to meetings. Haven't smoked or drank for almost two months."

"Good for you, bro," said Owl, raising his palm.

Jonah high-fived Owl, relishing his approval. "It's hard, but it feels terrific. I was wasting my life getting high so much."

Doyle stopped next to a tight stand of seven or eight redwoods. When everyone had come close, he opened his hand toward the trees and said, "See how these trees are so close together, growing in a circle? These are all stems that sprouted from one old-growth tree cut down in the early 1900s."

Jonah knew about stump sprouting. Where was Doyle going with this?

"In a minute, I'll show you which we're going to have the loggers cut and why," Doyle continued. "But first, it's important to remember that when you log a redwood, you don't kill the tree. Instead, it will live, basically, forever, sending up new sprouts that grow into multiple trees—like these. That's why the redwood's Latin name is Sequoia sempervirens, always living."

Doyle was over fifty and weighed at least two-fifty, but he climbed gracefully down the steep hill. He pointed out stripes of orange spray paint on two of the trees. "So why did we pick these two to cut? You might think, at first, those are big trees—a lot bigger than the skinny thirty- or forty-year-olds you'd cut if you were doing industrial logging. But that's because they're so old, at least a hundred years, maybe a hundred-twenty-five."

Doyle brought his palms close together. "But look how close together they are. For optimal growth—which we want to encourage—this group needs some thinning." He pointed at the base of one spray-painted tree. "This one is growing out the side of the original stump, so it's weak and will most likely fall in a storm one day."

He pointed up into the canopy. "As for this other one, if you look carefully up there, you'll see its upper branches are shading several shorter trees. When we cut down this one"—he pointed again at the doomed tree—"the others will be able to grow faster with more sun."

"By removing these two, the rest of this group will have more room to grow. And that's what we want—big trees to get bigger.

And while we're helping the forest recover, we'll earn some revenue to support trail and road maintenance."

• • •

It only took three pulls for Bill to start his lawnmower, and he was gratified to hear the old engine purr smoothly.

As rectangles of mown grass grew under his feet, he thought about Angela. She hadn't told him the details of her visa problems, and he hadn't pressed the subject. But it must be serious, or she wouldn't be so upset.

Bill admired Angela. She had the grit and self-possession to escape her bad relationship and build a life in Eureka. And he respected how much her family meant to her. She'd told him she wanted to meet Denise and Aaron, and she seemed confident that Bill would continue becoming close with her family.

Bill was okay with that, although he worried about being drawn into a lot of family drama. There was the addict niece—where was her father, he wondered? And did Lupita's twin boys have the same father? Angela had told him that Pamela's husband—the father of her two nieces visiting Mexico City—worked as a vineyard supervisor down in Napa.

Bill liked both sisters. Pamela's questions about his finances had made him defensive, but still, he respected her concern for her younger sister's future. Like other Mexicans Bill had known, the Garcias seemed more traditional and family oriented than most of his American-born friends.

Bill remembered two Mexican men he'd met on a logging crew about twenty years ago, Lazaro and Hector. Bill was already seated in the van when they got in. They shook hands and said their names, then they chatted with each other in Spanish. Bill assumed Lazaro was Hector's dad.

Lazaro leaned forward and asked Bill, with a thick accent, "You work for this boss before?"

Bill nodded. "Sure. Lots of times. You?"

"First time," he said, "My nephew and I from Mexico. Guanajuato. You ever bean?"

Bill chuckled. "Can't say that I have. Is it nice?"

Both men smiled, and Hector said, "Oh yes. Beautiful. Tranquilo."

"Your family still down there?"

"Yes," said Lazaro, the elder. "Children. Parents. My wife." Then, the men lapsed into silence. Bill surmised they were thinking of their distant families and homes.

Bill's lawnmower coughed and whined. He cut the engine, turned it on its side, and cleared the wet grass. Then he pulled the cord and resumed mowing.

That job with Hector and Lazaro lasted about ten days. On the last day, Lazaro invited Bill to a barbecue. "Bring your family," he said. Bill accepted.

Cheri was reluctant to go when she learned the party was on the westside of Eureka, in a neighborhood known for drugs and crime. But Bill felt honor-bound to attend, and Cheri eventually agreed.

When they arrived at the apartment complex, Bill was surprised to see a crowd of about twenty people. Guys stood around a smoking grill, holding beers and laughing. Women sat on plastic chairs and talked. And kids played soccer on the patchy grass.

Lazaro greeted them warmly. He called out to one of the soccer players, who sprinted over and got Denise and Kenny to join the game. A young woman took the potato salad from Cheri and found a place for it on the buffet table. They sat in lawn chairs, ate spicy food, and drank beer. Kenny and Denise bolted down their food, then resumed playing with the Mexican kids.

Most of the conversation was in Spanish, but Lazaro or Hector usually hovered near Bill and Cheri to translate as well as they could. Bill learned that Lazaro was not Hector's father but his uncle. Back home in Guanajuato, neither man could earn a decent living, so they made the journey to Humboldt County to find work. Lazaro left behind his wife and five children; Hector, his parents and siblings. Both men sent money regularly— enough for their families to build better houses, eat better food, and send the kids to school.

The other guests also came from south of the border, Bill learned. The men worked in logging, construction, or landscaping; the women as motel cleaners, waitresses, or manicurists.

Bill admired how Lazaro, Hector, and their friends had created a community far from home. He wanted to ask how often they visited their families, but he sensed that would take the conversation onto painful ground.

Bill turned the mower over to clean the grass clippings from the underside. Then he wheeled it to the shed that was attached to his shop. He got out his electric weed whacker and long extension cord and began trimming the edges of his lawn.

•   •   •

Jonah whistled as he approached the campsite. Then he said, "Buzzy, you there?" Hearing no response, he looked under the tarp and saw someone else's gear in his place. Anger flashed through him—what the fuck was someone else's gear doing in his spot? Then he laughed at his reaction. It was only right for his friend to share the space after he didn't return from Thanksgiving break and didn't call or text.

He backed out and walked up the hill toward Bella. He was about to hug her when he saw a stripe of orange spray paint on her trunk. He looked around in a panic and saw two of her companions had been marked with the same color.

•   •   •

Bill was cooking pork chops and broccoli when his phone rang. It was his logger buddy Eric. "Hey, old-timer," he said. "Just calling to see if you want to go surf fishing up by Klamath next weekend. Maybe invite Jim for some eeling."

"Hell yeah," said Bill. "Still early for perch, but it'll be good to get out there."

"Sounds good. I'll call Jim and see if he's up for it."

"Any work lined up?"

"Not much. You?"

"Kinda slow right now."

"How's your Latina girlfriend? And when do I get to meet her?"

Bill didn't know how to respond. He wanted to share his joy at how their relationship was blossoming—and his worries about Angela's visa problems. But it was a crapshoot opening up to Eric—he might manifest real interest or resort to the usual stoic teasing. "She's doing okay. Really busy. I don't get to see her more than once a week or so."

"Well, that ain't bad. You'll tell me if she has any younger sisters visiting, right?"

"Yeah, right," he said with mild sarcasm. "Hey, my dinner's about done, so ...."

"Okay, I'll let you know what Jim says."

• • •

In shock over learning that Bella would be cut down, Jonah's instincts led him to plaza, his need to process the shocking news trumping his fears of meeting friends who'd tempt him to get high. Buzzy, Alder, and Fawn were there, deep in conversation with other young men and women. "Gonna shut those motherfuckers down," he heard Alder say.

Buzzy saw Jonah and smiled. They hugged. "So, what'd you think of that bullshit Doyle was tryin' to sell up there?" Buzzy asked.

On his walk down from the forest, Jonah had been thinking hard about the situation. He believed in selective logging. Doyle's explanations made sense. But then he'd seen Bella marked for slaughter.

"Tell you the truth, I'm not sure," said Jonah.

Fawn grimaced. "What do you mean, Jonah? How can you accept that they're going to kill trees in the people's forest?"

"Well, it's not clearcutting, which is what I—what we—think is really bad. It's selective logging, which we say we support."

Fawn looked hurt. Alder said, "Well, they can fucking do their selective logging somewhere else, not in our forest."

"Damn right," said Buzzy. Some of those listening murmured agreement, but Jonah noticed a few who seemed undecided.

Then Owl walked up. "Come to preach at us about the city's great plan to destroy trees?" taunted Alder.

Owl remained calm. "No, just wondering what Jonah thought—since the rest of you bailed before Doyle got a chance to show how their logging system works."

"He's a sellout, just like you," Alder spit.

"Like I was saying," Jonah said. "I'm not sure. What Doyle showed us made a lot of sense. Like how they select a few trees in a group for logging so the others can grow better. I just wish they weren't going to cut down Bella."

"They marked Bella?" asked Buzzy with shock. "And you're still not sure?"

Jonah could only shrug and look at the ground. Buzzy shook his head and turned away.

Jonah wandered off and walked uphill to the Wildflower Market. He bought a sandwich and sat at a table on the market's back porch, hoping he wouldn't run into anyone he knew. He was upset over Bella. And yet he could also see the situation from Doyle's point of view.

Looking out the window, Jonah saw the lights coming on in downtown Arcata. Humboldt Bay glowed silver in the twilight. When he'd first come up to Humboldt, charged with a passion for protecting old-growth forests, he'd been a half-assed activist because of his addictions. He'd thought that once he got free from cannabis and alcohol, he would take a stronger stand for Mother Earth. Until now, that would have meant doing anything to save Bella from the chainsaws.

But it seemed the environmentalist community was divided over logging in the community forest. Or perhaps it was just a few zealots who were outraged that chainsaws would take down any of their beloved trees.

After finishing his sandwich, he walked to the AA meeting just down the hill.

When he entered and saw Monica, his heart sang. She stood to hug him.

"What a crazy day," he said after they sat down. "Found out the city is going to cut down my favorite redwood tree."

"Oh no."

'But the weirdest thing is, it might be okay. I was on this tour with Doyle from the environmental center. What he said about their selective logging plans was pretty reasonable."

From the front table, a woman said loudly, "Hi, I'm Sally, an alcoholic."

Jonah and Monica repeated, "Hi, Sally." Jonah looked around for Manny but didn't see him.

Another member read from the AA Big Book: "Rarely have we seen a person fail who has thoroughly followed our path ..." Then a commotion by the door interrupted the meeting.

Jonah heard panicked voices: "Oh no!"—"My God, no!"—"It can't be!"

Jonah stood with everyone and looked at the knot of people near the door. He saw Manny walk slowly to the front, his face pale, his eyes sunken. "My friends," he said. "It's my painful duty to let you know that our beloved Beth C. has died. She was murdered."

Chapter 22

At Tony's Café, they were so subdued that the waitress asked them what was wrong. Monica told her, and she sucked in her breath. "Oh no, that's terrible."

Karen rubbed Manny's back. Jonah felt Monica's hand on his. "Yeah," Monica said. "It is just awful."

"Well, coffee's on me tonight," said the waitress. "In honor of Beth."

"I just can't believe it," Monica said, shaking her head and dropping a tear on the table. "I can't believe we saw this fucking ex-boyfriend just a couple weeks ago, stalking her out front of her place."

"I wish she'd gotten that restraining order," said Manny, his face sunk in his hands.

Biker Bob came to the table, his face etched with pain. "Well, don't this beat all," he said. "Our Beth taken away just like that. At least they got the son-of-a-bitch. Hope he gets the damned chair."

When the group broke up, Monica offered Jonah a ride home. They got in her Subaru and she said, "You want to sit and talk a bit?"

"Sure, absolutely."

"I just can't believe she's gone," said Monica. She put her forearm on the steering wheel, rested her forehead on it, and cried softly. Jonah placed his hand on her upper back. "I think about the light in her eyes," said Monica, sitting up. "The love she radiated. I felt such a strong connection to her like she really knew me and loved me."

She pulled him into a hug. He felt her tears on his cheek, then he felt her kiss him just above his jaw. He kissed her temple. They drew their faces together, their lips met, and she opened her mouth as he stroked her neck. A car engine started in the next parking space. They moved apart before coming back together, foreheads touching.

"Want to come over to my place?" she asked.

"Yes, very much."

Inside Monica's apartment, they grabbed each other and kissed deeply. Then Monica pulled away and led him to a couch. "We need to have the STD conversation," she said. "I got tested after I broke up with my ex, and I haven't been with anyone since."

"I'm clean as far as I know," Jonah said. "Haven't had sex with anyone for about five months. I haven't been tested, but I don't have any sores."

"Okay then," she said, leaning in to kiss him. "We're safe for oral sex, and I've got some condoms. I want to take a shower first. You want to join me?"

"Fuck yeah."

Monica took off her bra, and Jonah gazed in awe at her breasts. She danced out of her pants and rolled her belly and hips seductively. When he stripped, his penis sprang up, eager and pulsing.

In the shower, he caressed her breasts, and she stroked his cock. Then, he came on her thigh. "Sorry," he said, mortified.

"Don't worry about it," she said, grabbing the soap. "I'm sure there's more where that came from."

They toweled off, and she led him to her bedroom.

Afterward, they snuggled under the covers. "I think Beth would be happy for us," Monica said wistfully.

"Definitely."

In the morning, they made love again. "Wow," Jonah said in the breathy afterglow. "That was amazing."

"Really amazing."

Monica made him a cheese omelet with whole-grain toast, apple slices, and plain yogurt.

"This is just great," said Jonah gratefully.

"Glad you like it."

It was a Sunday, and Jonah hoped to spend the day with her. But she had other plans. "I'm supervising volunteers to do the annual cleaning at our playspace. Then I'm meeting some friends for lunch." She smiled coyly and added, "Besides, I think it's good to take it slow at the beginning of a relationship. Let's give each other some space, get together in a few days."

Jonah was disappointed, but the word "relationship" glowed like neon in his mind. She offered to drive him home, but it was a pleasant morning, so he decided to walk. They kissed while standing by her car, and she waved and grinned through the window as she drove off.

•   •   •

Beth's memorial was held on a rainy Saturday afternoon at the white-steepled Methodist Church. Jonah sat with Monica near the front. He looked at the large photo of Beth by the altar and thought that without her help, he might not have found his higher power.

The female pastor spoke briefly; then, people lined up at the microphone. Jonah was awed to hear how much Beth had given to so many. Neighbors described her as a dedicated and hardworking volunteer at the Hamilton. One young woman whom Jonah knew from meetings said Beth saved her life. "I was literally going to kill myself before she became my sponsor."

Another said she and Beth talked every day. "She helped me keep my head above water when I was drowning."

When the ceremony ended, Jonah felt emotionally exhausted and deeply connected to this community brought together by grief.

They lined up for the buffet in the room next to the sanctuary, then found seats next to big Jerry Watson. A rare black man in Humboldt County AA, he was someone Jonah liked and admired for his honesty and humor. With him was a man named Kenny, a little older than Jonah, husky, with a neatly trimmed beard.

They talked about Beth. "What a dear, sweet person she was," said Jerry, his eyes moist.

Monica nodded. "The best."

"Can't believe she's gone," said Jonah.

"Wish I'd known her better," said Kenny.

They ate silently for a minute, then Monica said, "This one time, I was feeling just totally fucked up. I mean hopeless. I can't even describe it now or tell you what caused it. But when I tried to talk to people about it, they would try to cheer me up with some AA pep talk, like 'God never gives you more than you can handle.' Such bullshit."

Jonah glanced at Jerry. He was such a stalwart cheerleader for AA, that Jonah thought he might react negatively to Monica's cynicism. But Jonah saw only compassion in his eyes. "She wasn't my sponsor then, but I ran into her at a meeting and asked to talk." Monica wiped her nose with her napkin. "We sat on a couch, and she listened and asked a few questions. Then she shook her head and said, 'We're so fucked up, aren't we?' It was exactly what I needed to hear. I wasn't alone in my darkness."

"That's cool," said Kenny. "She just let you be you and feel what you were feeling."

"Yeah," said Monica.

To Jonah's relief, their conversation moved on to other topics. Kenny talked about his job working graveyard at a gas station and convenience store. "I spend half the time serving customers and the other half trying to watch for shoplifters, mostly addicts like I used to be."

"Used to be?" Jerry queried sternly.

"I mean, I mean, uh, active addicts like I used to be," Kenny rejoined, turning red. Jonah sympathized at Kenny's embarrassment for mistakenly discounting a cherished twelve-step principle—that addicts never graduated, never fully recovered, but were always recovering.

Jerry nodded his approval. Then he asked, "How do you like this tri-tip?"

"Darn good," said Jonah.

"Terrific," said Monica. "Didn't you notice the green salad and veggies, though?" Monica teased, pointing at Jerry's plate, which featured only meat and potato salad. "You know, you can't live on meat and potatoes alone."

"Oh, I know, darlin'," Jerry said, leaning toward Monica. "After I make short work of this, I'll be sure and get two big pieces of carrot cake." The big man patted his belly. "After all, better plump than drunk."

•   •   •

Jonah sat in the passenger seat as David drove north under clear skies. They passed McKinleyville; then the highway dropped toward a long, empty beach. Offshore, long ribbons of white surf rolled in and crashed on the sand. Farther north, a rocky wooded headland leaped from the azure water; beyond that, pale mountain silhouettes rode the horizon.

"Damn, this is incredible," said Jonah, who had never traveled north of the Humboldt Bay area.

"Just getting started, mate. This part of the coast is truly amazing."

After passing the long beach, the road went uphill through a dark corridor of conifers. Soon, they were back along the sea, crossing a big lagoon where two windsurfers flashed across the choppy surface.

"Wow," was all Jonah could say. Then he yawned.

David asked, "Big night with Ms. M?"

"Big night finishing my fourth step. Gotta read it to Manny for that fifth step soon."

"Good for you, mate." David held his fist up for a bump. "I did my fifth step with Manny a couple weeks ago. Felt like taking a big dump after being constipated for like—ever."

Jonah chuckled, but David's update on his step work surprised him. "What about the third step?"

"I battled and wrestled with that shit for months until Manny referred me to that appendix in the back of the book, Spiritual Experience. You read it?"

"Nah. I Couldn't get through that We Agnostics chapter."

David smiled and shook his head. "Yeah, me too. Fucking arrogant Christians telling us agnostics that we're some kind of nihilistic fools." He looked squarely at Jonah before looking back at the road.

"But you should check out that appendix, man. There's one phrase I memorized: 'An unsuspected inner resource.' Some AA old-timers back in the thirties didn't believe in a great mythical man in the sky. They knew that what we need is inside us." David touched his chest with an open palm. "It's our genuine original nature that got lost and fucked up in our addiction. That's my 'unsuspected inner resource.'"

"I like that," said Jonah. "That's really what my 'power of love' is."

At the next lagoon, they stopped and walked along the shore. Fog hovered over the water while the early morning sun shone through trees.

"Meditate for a few?" asked David.

"Sure, why not."

They sat cross-legged on the gravel. David pulled out his phone. "Twenty minutes?"

"That's long for me," said Jonah. "How about 15?" David nodded and set the timer.

The minutes dragged by as Jonah thought about the past and fantasized about his future, mostly with Monica. Then, David said, "Want to try something?"

Jonah glanced and saw David staring at the water. "Okay."

"Keep your eyes open and focus on what you see, not just the center of your vision but everything, out to the periphery." After a pause, David continued: "And tune into what you hear—from the cars on the highway to the surf. But don't name what you're seeing and hearing. Just see. Just hear." Then David was quiet.

For a few seconds, Jonah felt a blissful sense of being one with the nature around him. Then, like a puppy, his mind dragged him into fantasies about learning to surf and thoughts of where he could find a used surfboard.

After the timer sounded, they returned to the car and continued north. Jonah was looking at the passing forest when David asked, "You think it's going to work out with you and Monica?"

Jonah felt his chest being squeezed. "I sure hope so."

"Do you think much about dating strategy?" David asked.

"Huh?"

"Have you thought about playing it cool, like not putting your heart all in so early in the relationship?" When Jonah didn't reply, David went on. "Sometimes a guy will fall so hard and fast for a woman that it can feel stifling to her if she's still checking the guy out."

"Oh, man, I haven't even thought about that," said Jonah nervously. "I guess I'm just trusting that, you know, love will have its way."

In the national park, a herd of elk grazed by the road, so they got out and took photos with their phones. Then they followed the narrow two-lane highway into a dense old-growth forest along a creek. They crossed the Klamath Bridge just after ten AM.

Full of spring rain, the river had flooded the bright green alders and willows on its banks. Jonah looked upriver, where the valley narrowed before disappearing into the mountains. "Dang," said Jonah. "So beautiful."

They passed sheds and storefronts that advertised "salmon jerky" and "jet boat rides"—all closed for the winter. Then David turned west. After a few miles of winding road, they stopped at a viewpoint over the ocean. The roaring surf and barking sea lions delighted Jonah, but he couldn't spot the river as he looked down at the broad estuary and narrow beach.

"Where does the river come out?" Jonah asked.

David pointed at the foot of the bluff they stood on, and Jonah spotted a blue ribbon melting into the deep green ocean. "That's where we're headed," David said with a grin. They piled back in the Subaru, and in twenty minutes, they arrived at a dirt parking lot south of the river.

The path to the beach went through a complex of low wooden structures with slanted roofs and porthole-shaped windows. "What is this?" asked Jonah, astonished. "Who built these?"

"They're Yurok Indian buildings, mostly ceremonial, I think."

Jonah crouched near a round door and knelt to enter. "I don't think we ought to go in," said David. "It might be okay, but we should get permission first, you know. We wouldn't just walk into a church or a mosque without an invitation, right?" Jonah agreed.

As they approached the shore, the surf roared more loudly. They emerged from a thicket of willows and blueberries onto a deserted beach. "Race 'ya!" David yelled and took off running for the water. Jonah sprinted after him.

At the shore, David asked, "Up for a swim?"

"Are you fuckin' kidding me? That water is like fifty degrees."

"I'm not going to take a bath in it, just get wet."

"I think I'll settle for wading."

Jonah took off his shoes while David stripped. "C'mon, man. It'll give you something to brag about to Monica tonight."

Jonah hesitated, then said, "What the fuck." He stripped and followed David. When the water immersed Jonah's feet, his instincts screamed for retreat. David grabbed his forearm. "Let's get it over with, mate!"

They walked deeper into the surf. Jonah wailed as a wave submerged his genitals. A bigger wave approached. They turned their backs and dropped into it. Jonah screamed when he surfaced and slapped David's palm. Then, they turned to dive under the next wave.

Jonah jumped around on the shore to warm up, then dressed quickly. David pointed north to the smoke drifting from a fire. Two fishermen waded in the shallows, and another stood knee deep, holding a curved stick over his shoulder.

"Let's go," said David. "Maybe they'll share their fire."

As they got closer, Jonah recognized Bill and his buddy Eric. "Hey Bill," he said, when he got close enough to be heard over the surf.

"So, it was you trying to scare the fish away," Bill said, with a mocking tone. They shook hands, and Bill added. "Gotta say, though—takes balls to get into that water without a wetsuit."

"Speaking of balls, mate, ours are about to freeze off," said David. "Mind if we warm up by the fire."

Eric said, "Help yourself. Plenty of driftwood around, so build it up good and hot. We'll be wanting to warm up soon too."

The two men built a strong blaze, and soon Bill, Eric, and the other man came up to share the warmth. After introductions, the man named Jim asked Jonah, "Haven't we met?"

"Yeah, yeah," said Jonah. "Before Thanksgiving. You were hitching up to Hoopa."

Jim smiled and shook his head. "And drunk off my ass. But that was my last day drinking."

"Way to go," said David. "We're both sober, too."

"No shit! And how do you know this old-timer?" Jim said, tilting his head toward Bill. Then he grinned widely. "Oh, wait." Looking at Bill, he said, "This must be the guy you told me about. Your first and only hippie friend."

"That's him," said Bill.

"And he's my first redneck friend," said Jonah.

"And now you got a redskin friend," said Jim.

"Thought we weren't allowed to say that anymore," said Eric.

Jim hauled back his fist at Eric. "Don't you try it, homie." The men cracked up.

After they settled in around the fire, Jonah asked Jim, "What were you fishing for out there?"

"Eels," said Jim.

"You mean like leeches?" said Jonah, disgusted.

Jim mimicked a public television narrator, "Also known as the Pacific Lamprey, this ancient sea creature feeds by attaching itself to a larger fish and consuming its blood." Then, in his normal voice, he added, "And we Indians freeze our asses off trying to get one of those bloodsuckers to put on the dinner table."

"It's about more than food, though, right?" prompted Bill.

"Got that right." Jim settled back on his elbow. "I wasn't but seven or eight when my dad started teaching me to eel with a little hook and pieces of garden hose in the backyard. My older brothers and cousins had all got at least one eel by then, and I wanted to catch up.

"The first time he brought me out here was just before sunset on a cold winter's day. We'd left the house without eating dinner, and pretty soon, I started whining about being cold and hungry. Then he told me, 'Son, we're not going to eat unless we catch an eel.'

"We were the only ones out here." Jim looked at the shore. "We stood right there in the waves, looking and looking for a damned eel. My feet and legs were numb inside my waders, and I could barely hold my flashlight and spear."

Jonah picture a young Indian boy shivering in the surf, the fog drifting across the beach. "After an hour, we finally took a break and built a fire to warm up," Jim said. "I felt sure he'd break out some smoked salmon or something. But no. Instead, he fed me some wisdom about our people: 'Son,' he said, 'our people are just hanging on. Half the kids grow up to be addicts or mentally ill or criminals. Do you know why that is?'"

Jim paused for several seconds, and Jonah could tell that he took this story seriously. "I knew what he was talking about. I'd already seen it in my own family: aunties, uncles, and cousins who'd become addicts, got locked up, couldn't keep a job. But I didn't know why. So, he says, 'We ended up like this because we lost our culture, our way of life, the way of life that sustained our grandparents, and great grandparents and ancestors going all the way back.'

"He said how it didn't do any good to blame our troubles on the white man—even though they were to blame. 'Now it's up to you and your brothers and sisters and cousins to rebuild what was lost.' And he said that meant learning to catch and cook and eat these eels. We had to carry on that tradition because it was part of getting back what we had lost."

Jim grasped a handful of sand and let it pour slowly from his hand. "That's what he said. I remember it like it was yesterday."

After a moment, Jonah asked. "Did you get an eel that night?"

"No. Not even after another half-hour in the water. But my dad broke out some sandwiches for the ride home. He wanted me to feel what my ancestors felt, to really get it."

Eric spoke up. "Well, we don't have any eels or even hot dogs to cook on this fire, so how about if we head on over to that burger joint in Klamath?" The men agreed. After packing up their gear, they made for the parking lot. On the way through the

Yurok compound, Jonah wanted to ask Jim about the buildings, but Jim was in his truck before he got the chance.

They ordered at the counter and occupied two tables in the small dining area. Jonah asked Jim, "So what else did your dad teach you?"

"He tried to teach me to speak some Yurok. Never took though. All I can remember is cheguen for salmon and k'ween for eel."

Eric leaned toward Jim. "Surprised you don't remember how to say 'ugly dumbass.' Figured your aunties would have made you memorize that one."

Jim rejoined, "Yeah, I hear your name means 'dog fucker' in Norwegian."

Eric flicked his hand at the weak comeback. Then David said, "I got to know some Maoris in New Zealand and did some eeling with them."

"Cool," said Jim. "What was that like?"

"They timed it to the phases of the moon," David said. "It was really complex, and I didn't learn their system. But I remember they'd never eel on the full moon because the eels were inactive then."

"The moon, huh?" said Bill. "Makes sense since she controls the tides." Jonah was surprised to hear Bill call the moon "she."

David responded, "I think they held off because the light from the full moon made it so that the prey could see the eels more easily. The eels took that one day off from hunting—and so did the eelers."

"You ever eat an eel?" asked Jim.

David made a face. "Yeah. Can't say I liked it all that much. Really oily."

"Gotta know how to cook 'em," said Jim.

Their food arrived, and the men dug in. The burger and fries were okay, but the company was the best relish Jonah could want. He felt a sense of belonging. Jim's story touched him and made him want to learn more about American Indians on the North Coast.

When he finished eating, he got up to use the bathroom. Before sitting back down, he went to the server and paid the check for the entire table with a generous tip.

After a few minutes, Bill said, "Well, it's about time we settle up and head on." He gestured to the server. "Can we have the check?"

She pointed at Jonah and said, "Your friend took care of it."

The men thanked him. David joked, "I must be paying you too much."

Eric fingered the fish-stained sleeve of his jacket and said, "Now that you're making bank, bet you can spare twenty bucks for me to go to the laundromat, huh?" Jonah and Bill cracked up. Jonah considered explaining the joke to Jim and David, who looked curious; but the moment passed.

On the drive home, Jonah mused over the day: his deep talks with David, dipping in the frigid ocean, hearing Jim's story around the fire, and the men's approval when he paid the check. Beguiled by it all, he got out his phone and composed a long text to Monica.

Chapter 23

Jonah was rolling out vapor barrier on the bedroom floor when he heard the homeowner come into the house. "How's it going?" she asked David, who was on his knees replacing a dry-rotted strip of oak flooring in the living room.

Jonah knew the question wasn't just a casual greeting. They were behind schedule, and David's anxiety had been mounting. He'd snapped at Jonah over a half-dozen little things—like putting six or eight nails in a piece of molding where only two were needed. David would quickly apologize, but Jonah worried about how his friend was coping with the stress.

"A little behind schedule," David said, pronouncing it SHED-jewel. "But not too bad. We should be done in two, maybe three weeks."

"Sure hope so," she said, looking at Jonah who'd come in to join the conversation. Then, scraping her foot on the dusty floor, she added, "Didn't expect it to be so messy."

Jonah felt defensive, but David seemed unruffled. "We don't tidy up until the end of the day, but we could do it a couple times a day if you'd like," he said mildly.

"No need, but thanks anyway." She shifted her posture and asked, "Could you come outside with me for a sec? I want to ask you about this big tree." They followed her through the living room, into the kitchen and out to the backyard.

"That redwood," she said, pointing to a tree towering over the southeast corner. "I used to love it, but it's putting more of my garden in the shade every year. And my neighbors are worried one of those huge limbs will drop on their garage in a storm. Do you happen to know a good tree professional who could take it down safely and not charge me an arm and a leg?"

"We could ask around," David said.

Jonah said, "I bet Bill could do it."

•   •   •

Bill opened the glass door to the Starbucks and savored the smell of fresh coffee. The barista looked up and said, "Good morning, Bill. The usual?"

"You got it, Mike."

A young woman at the counter took his money and said, "Looks like it's a nice day out there."

"Yep," said Bill. "Still need more rain, though."

She frowned. "If you say so." Then, smiling, she said, "Mike will have your double decaf Americano up in a second. Have a good day."

"You too."

Bill got his coffee and picked up a copy of the Redwood Weekly. On the cover was a story about the cannabis industry.

Bill had never worked in that business, but he knew growers—mostly kids Kenny's age who bought new pickups every other year—and some ranchers and homesteaders his age who kept a lower profile. That industry had been the silent partner in Humboldt County's economy for a couple of decades.

But the growers knew that full legalization—which would eviscerate their profit margin—was on the horizon, so they'd been expanding like crazy to get what they could, and they were drying up streams and even stealing water from rural schools and homeowners.

According to the story, the county was trying to induce growers to get permits and licenses and be more environmentally responsible with water. Good luck with that, Bill thought. He couldn't imagine a bunch of outlaw growers showing up at the county courthouse to ask for permits.

Then, his phone rang, and he saw a number he didn't recognize. "Hello?"

"Hey Bill, it's Jonah."

"Hey, Jonah." He was surprised and happy to hear from him. "How you doin'?"

"Good man. How about you?"

"Okay. What's up?"

"I'm calling about a tree job." Jonah provided the details, but Bill had trouble paying attention.

"So, what do you think?" asked Jonah.

"Why don't you text me her number, and I'll set up a time to take a look," said Bill.

As Bill walked home, he felt ashamed and confused. Since his dizzy spell just before Christmas, he'd been contacted about tree work by several homeowners. He'd given some bids but had put off scheduling any jobs because he was scared to climb.

When he got home, his mood lifted as he thought about the day ahead. First, he would take Angela on a walking tour of Eureka's Victorians. Then they'd visit the Draft Horse Millworks and Museum, where Bill's friends Phil and Victoria Nadelbaum, would give them a private tour—all that before eleven AM, when Angela had to go to work. Then, Bill would pick up sandwiches to share with the Nadelbaums before coming home to work in his shop on a couple of pieces he had in mind for Angela and Denise.

He had a half-hour to spare before picking up Angela, so he went to his shop and sorted through curly redwood planks. He'd put two aside when he felt his phone buzz. It was Cheri, his ex-wife. He took a deep breath and answered as calmly as he could. "Hi, Cheri. What's up?"

"I've heard from Kenny," she said. "He's sober more than a month now." Bill felt a surge of joy followed by crushing doubt. Kenny had proclaimed himself clean and sober so many times before relapsing. Before Bill could ask Cheri how she knew for sure, she said, "I know you don't believe it, but it's true. He's really clean and sober."

Bill sat down on his stool. "Oh, I hope you're right, Cheri. What's he up to? Where's he living?"

"He needs money for a deposit on an apartment and clothes and stuff. I was hoping you could come up with fifteen-hundred dollars."

Bill didn't have $1500 to spare. And if he did, he wouldn't give Kenny that much unless he was sure his son's recovery was stable. And he thought that if Kenny wanted money, he should man up and call Bill himself.

"I don't know," he said. "Things have been tight."

"Well, how much do you think you can come up with?"

"Maybe seven or eight hundred for now. I've got a lot of bills." Bill didn't like how whiny he sounded. As if to compensate, he said forcefully, "But I think he should call me himself if he wants money."

Cheri was quiet for a beat. "Is this what you learn at those meetings? Don't give your only son anything unless he comes groveling? This is the kind of shit that made me leave you." She hung up.

Bill almost threw his phone at the wall. His mind raced. Was Kenny really off drugs? If so, would he stay clean? Why is he scared to call me? He considered calling Cheri back or texting her to get Kenny's number. But it was Kenny's move.

Bill was too agitated to continue puttering, so he grabbed his hat and jacket and walked outside. He turned west and walked down a steep hill into the gulch where Eureka High's athletic field lay in the shadow of redwood and spruce trees. A couple dozen students were running track, and Bill recognized the gym teacher. He pulled his hat down, quickened his pace, and thought about when Denise used to practice soccer here. On Saturday mornings, he and Kenny would drive by, wave and honk to embarrass her on their way to the drag strip or the McDevitts to work on that Dodge.

As he walked up the other side of the gulch, Bill remembered family barbecues at Petey's place and trips to the river in the summer. Those had seemed like the good old days.

At the top of the hill, he sat on the high school's entrance steps and tried to collect himself. In his despair, he realized he'd be lousy company, so he texted the Nadelbaums and Angela to cancel. Then he remembered there was an Al-Anon meeting this morning.

Back home, he moped away the hour before the meeting, then drove to the church. Walking into the hall, Bill scanned the faces and nodded at a few people he knew, but he couldn't manage a smile. Then, he was surprised to see Jim, his logging partner, seated in a back corner. When Jim saw Bill, he grinned shyly. Bill sat down next to him, and they shook hands. "Didn't expect to run into you here, partner," Bill said quietly.

"Decided it was time," Jim said. "Since I got sober, it's been harder to ignore all the addicts in my family. My AA sponsor told me I ought to try this program to learn how to deal with them."

The meeting started, and Bill felt calmed by the familiar rituals. But Bill could not stay present during the sharing time and follow what people said. Instead, he tried to visualize Kenny somewhere in Eureka, maybe in an AA or NA meeting. Could it be true?

When the Serenity Prayer ended the meeting, Jim asked Bill to go out for coffee. "Sure," Bill said. "Just let me go chat with this fellow a minute. Meet you outside."

Bill made his way across the room to John, his sponsor. John opened his arms when Bill approached. "How's Bill this morning?"

"Not too good. My ex called and told me Kenny is sober." Bill knew that John—whose son was an addict—would understand that Bill couldn't trust the news. "She asked me for money so he could get an apartment, clothes and stuff."

John nodded and looked at Bill with interest. Bill continued. "I don't know what to do. I wish he'd contacted me himself, but maybe he's scared of me or something. And I'm wondering if I should get his number from her and contact him. Or wait until he's ready to get in touch with me." His words had a pleading sound that Bill detested.

John smiled sadly, grasped Bill's shoulder, and said, "We just don't know what the hell to do, do we?" Somehow, that was what Bill needed to hear.

•   •   •

At a busy café across from the hospital, Jim told Bill why he'd decided to try Al-Anon. His brother was an addict who sponged off their mom and dad, and his favorite male cousin had gone off the rails doing meth. And his auntie was killing herself with prescription opioids. "And to cope with all that crap, my mom and dad are drinking more than ever."

Bill wanted to feel compassion for Jim, but he was impatient and frustrated. Jim's troubles reminded him of his powerlessness to help Kenny. When Jim finally took a breath, Bill told him: "You've just got to detach from them. Addicts will always suck you into their drama and drag you down."

Jim leaned back and opened his eyes wide. "I don't know what you even mean by that, dude. I can't turn my back on my family. No matter how bad they get, they're still family. Would you cut Kenny off like that?"

Bill shook his head. "You're right, man. I guess the advice is 'detach with love,' but to tell you the damn truth, I don't know how to do that with Kenny."

Jim nodded. "Okay. Well, when you figure it out, let me know. I could use some of that with my crazy family." They sat quietly for a moment, then Jim asked, "Any tree jobs coming up?"

Bill leaned on his elbows and looked out at the street. "Tell you the truth, I've got a few lined up, but I'm just not sure I'm up for it after, you know, nearly falling out of that redwood down at King's place."

Jim smiled confidently. "I know you're worried about your balance, but you can still climb, man. And when you're not up for it, I can do the high work. You ain't too old to do the ground work." Jim mimed grasping a rope. "Just need to work on your timing. It'll come back to you."

Bill looked at his young friend and thought about when he was Jim's age. Back then, an older man's limitations were a complete mystery to him—just like Bill's were now to Jim. But Bill was buoyed by Jim's confidence. "Maybe you're right. Sure got to do something. Too poor to retire."

•　　•　　•

It was pot roast night at the Eureka Elks Lodge. Bill didn't feel like socializing, but he was hungry and didn't want to shop or cook. He arrived as the meal service started, and after filling his plate, he walked through the hall, nodding at a few people he recognized, grateful that no one offered him a seat. He sat alone at the edge of the hall.

Just after he'd taken a few bites, Deputy Steve walked up to his table, accompanied by a younger man. "Hey Bill," said Steve. "You saving these seats for anyone?"

"You," said Bill.

They shook hands. "You remember my son Freddy?

"Of course," Bill lied. "It's been a while. What're you up to?"

"Police academy at College of the Redwoods," said the strongly built young man, whose crewcut looked brand new.

"Good for you. We need more good cops like your dad."

Steve said, "He'll probably have to hire on in one of the cities first, down in the Bay Area, or maybe Redding, before he can get on up here."

"Nothing wrong with that," said Bill. "Big world out there."

Then Eric walked up. "Got room for another bull elk?"

"It's a free country," said Bill sarcastically. Then he added, "Good to see you. How're you keeping?"

"Can't complain. You?"

"Nothing wrong with me except my age."

When Eric heard Freddy was training to be a cop, he said, "Better than being a logger."

"I've done some logging," Freddy said. "With my uncle. Damned hard, but I liked it. Paid great. Figured that industry was on its way out, though."

Bill was the first to break the silence. "We're down but not out," he said. "This recession has hammered the lumber market. And before that, a lot of jobs had been eliminated by automation—in the mills and the woods. And, of course, the crazy regulations haven't helped. But people still need lumber."

"And business is picking up," said Eric. "The economy is coming back, home construction is starting up again, at least in the rich parts of the Bay Area. But the damned protesters hate to see us doing well. So, they're back sitting in trees, locking themselves to gates."

"And accusing us of being violent when we move them out," said Steve. "Like we're supposed to let them take over a public street or private land because they can't get their way legally."

"You hear about Ernie Miller's kid, Sammy?" Eric asked. "Used to work for me. Now he's up on felony charges because some protesters jumped out in front of his truck last month."

With all the calmness he could muster, Bill said, "I was there, Eric. Saw the whole thing. It wasn't like that. He drove right through a bunch of people in the crosswalk. Just lucky the son-of-a-bitch didn't kill or hurt someone really bad."

Eric clenched his fist on the table. "Not the way I heard it," he said.

"Bill's right," said Steve. "In fact, the kid was loaded—and dealing. EPD found meth and more than a grand in cash in the cab. And he wasn't even licensed to drive that truck. It belonged to his dad. DA is throwing the book at him: attempted vehicular manslaughter, possession with intent to distribute, not to mention the DUI."

"Can't imagine what it's like for his dad," Steve added. Then, looking at Bill, he said, "Hey, by the way, buddy, I saw Kenny at the courthouse a while back. Man, what a change. You must be so happy to see him straightened out like that."

"Uh, yeah, yeah, right." So, Kenny really was sober. Bill's joy at hearing this confirmed was tainted by the shame he felt for being excluded from his son's life.

"Say hi to him for me," said Eric. "And for Christ's sake, bring him around sometime so we can show him some sympathy for having such a hard-ass dad."

Bill grinned and fake-chuckled. Soon after, he excused himself and took off.

•   •   •

"Spare any change, brah?" The man looked about sixty. He sat cross-legged on cardboard and smoked a cigarette under a store awning.

"Nah, sorry man," said Jonah, smiling tightly and striding on.

Jonah had more than a hundred dollars in his pocket and about eight hundred hidden in his cabin. He'd been working off his monthly rent to save money so he could take off in the summer for Oregon and Washington—and maybe even British

Columbia to see the old-growth forests and help stop the corporations from clearcutting them.

But his savings goals didn't keep him from spending money on good coffee. And with an hour to spare before the evening meeting, he headed for his favorite café in Eureka's Old Town.

After waiting in line, he took his two-shot Americano to a table, opened his paperback copy of the AA Big Book and looked up the Spiritual Experience appendix David had mentioned. Before he read the first sentence, he noticed two young men enter the café with backpacks, grubby clothes, and dirty hair. After they got their coffees, they came straight to his table.

"Hey, bro," said a tall guy with glasses. "Remember us? From Santa Rosa, a few days before Thanksgiving?"

With a surge of pleasure, Jonah remembered them from his night under the bridge in Santa Rosa.

"Fuck yeah." He stood, and they hugged. "How are you, dudes?"

"Good," said the tall one, taking a seat. "Headed north."

"No shit? Where 'bouts?"

"Eugene," said the other man, shorter with wispy sideburns and sunburned cheeks. "The town so friendly you can call it by its first name. Buddy of ours has a big indoor grow up there. Needs help."

"We worked there last year," said the first man. "You should come on up if you need a job."

Jonah felt like he had teleported back into a past life—a life that seemed positively ancient, even though he'd only left it a few months ago. "No thanks. I got a good job here, and I'm trying to stay away from the pot industry."

"Sure, sure, I get that," said the first man. "Our friend is way cool, though, and his operation is totally legit. He's got permits and contracts with a bunch of dispensaries." He reached into his jacket pocket and pulled out a small Ziplock bag. "And the quality is off the hook. Want to take our coffees outside and sample some?"

The café went quiet and dark. The gnarled green bud pulsed in Jonah's vision. His heart pounded, and his hearing became more acute. Suddenly, he wanted to get loaded like he wanted to guzzle a glass of water after a week in the desert. And here were two friendly acquaintances, and wouldn't it be rude to refuse their kind offer. He could get back on the recovery train tomorrow. It had been more than two months, after all.

Jonah gripped his seat and rocked unconsciously. His acquaintances looked at one another, confused by his silence. Then, Jonah thought to look at his phone. "I don't have time, fellas," he said. "Gotta go." He left without shaking their hands.

As soon as Jonah got outside, he dialed Monica. To her voicemail, he said, "Hey, it's me. Can you give me a call? I could use some support."

Next, he tried Manny, who answered. "I'm proud of you, kid. Those are the moments that make your recovery."

"Oh, Manny, if I'd gone into the alley and smoked up with those guys ... I don't even want to think about it."

"Well, you ought to think about it. Make a whole movie about it in your head, with every little detail as clear as if you were Stephen fucking Spielberg. Then play that video the next time you feel tempted."

"Okay," said Jonah, although he didn't quite grasp what Manny meant.

"You going to the meeting?"

"Shit yeah," Jonah said. "I may go to the later one too, Eastside Survivors. Either way, I'll see you at Sobriety Society, six sharp."

"I love you, kid."

"Love you too, Manny."

Pedaling the three miles to the meeting, Jonah thought about what would have happened if he'd gone to the alley with the two men.

After hitting the pipe, he'd feel a glorious release from worry and a heady rush of pleasure. Then, he would treat his friends to some high-quality ale that they'd drink discretely by the railroad tracks along the bay. At the end of the night, unable to return to Karen and Manny's, he would find a cheap motel or try to get a bed at the mission.

The next morning, he'd wake up hungover and desperate to stay clean, but he would repeat the same pathetic routine, telling himself it was just one more day and that he'd get back into the program tomorrow. It might take days, weeks, or even months before he'd commit himself to recovery again. In the meantime, he'd do the same shit over and over—avoiding his sober friends, feeling remorseful and desperate, and doing more weed and beer to numb those feelings.

Jonah laughed out loud as he realized he was doing just what Manny had suggested, visualizing the horror movie of what a relapse would be like.

Chapter 24

Bill sat in his kitchen looking through index cards that detailed the clients he'd recently given bids to. He was about to call the client on the first card when his phone rang with an unknown caller. "Hello?"

"Uh, hi, Dad."

Bill's breath caught in his chest. He couldn't speak.

"Dad?"

"Hi, Kenny. Sorry, you took me by surprise. How are you, son?"

"I'm good, Dad. You?"

Bill let out a long sigh as he struggled to contain his feelings. "I... I'm, I'm okay. I'm okay. Happy to hear from you. It has been a while."

"Yeah, yeah, I know. Sorry about that. You must've been worried. I know Mom was."

Bill thought "worried" didn't begin to describe how he'd been feeling. "Where are you?"

"I'm on Broadway, walking to the mall. Then going to a meeting after."

Bill could jump in his truck and drive over there. In ten minutes, he could see his son, hug him, and look him in the eyes. They could go for coffee or take a walk in the mall. He'd buy him a sweatshirt or something. They'd talk like old times—or more accurately, they'd talk like they'd never talked before. Bill was about to head out to meet Kenny when a caution warning told him not to push too hard, to take it slow.

"Where are you living?" he asked.

"Sober house downtown."

It didn't seem real. "How long have you been clean?"

Kenny paused before saying, "About two months."

Bill could hear the anger rise unbidden in his voice as he said, "You sure waited long enough to call me."

Kenny sighed deeply and said, "I know, Dad. I'm sorry. I should have called earlier. It was just that I wanted to be sure I was really going to make it this time rather than let you down like all those times before."

Bill felt his gut relax.

"I was sorry to hear about you and Mom breaking up."

"Yeah, me too, although I think it's for the best."

"That's what she said, too."

That stung. But Bill stuffed his reaction and said, "Speaking of your mother, she called to tell me you needed some money. I'm a little short, but I could give you seven or eight hundred now and probably another five hundred next month."

There was silence. Then Kenny said, "That's weird. I never asked her for money. Fact is, I'm working graveyard at a gas station and paying my rent and other bills."

"Wow, that's great. I wonder why she told me you needed money."

"No fucking clue." Kenny sounded angry.

Bill felt defensive for his ex. "Maybe she figured you'd want to get out of that recovery house and rent your own place."

"Well, whatever. I don't need any money from you guys."

Kenny's response grated. Bill had offered money even though he was nearly broke. And now his son was getting pissy. "All right then, son," he said with an edge. "Sounds like you're all set."

"What is that supposed to mean?"

"It means what it means," said Bill, although he did not know what he'd meant.

"Whatever," said Kenny. "I gotta go." He hung up.

• • •

Kenny had been counting on his dad to give him a chance to prove his recovery was for real. His mother had told him Bill was going to Al-Anon, and the news made Kenny hopeful. He'd envisioned his dad coming to one of his AA or NA meetings, and Kenny might attend an Al-Anon meeting with Bill.

But his father had hardly expressed any happiness about his sobriety before getting bent out of shape over money issues. Kenny stood and watched cars and trucks zoom past him. The drivers were all in a hurry, indifferent to his pain. Then he peered into the woods that separated Broadway from the bay and visualized the paths leading to Devil's Playground.

Kenny remembered the tent he used to live in, and how wet and cold he'd been on rainy nights. But there had been good times, too—a wild and free life without all the responsibilities and emotional hassles of sobriety.

Summoned by the crushing disappointment of that phone call, Kenny's addiction had taken control. It told him that freedom, joy, and comfort were only a needle or a snort away. He looked at his phone and thought about calling Jerry. But there was no power behind that notion. The addict was in charge. Kenny turned west to find the nearest path into the woods.

• • •

Bill decided to drive to the Del Norte Street Pier to get some air, and on the way, he'd pass Broadway, where Kenny said he was walking. Maybe if the two set eyes on each other, Bill thought, something would break loose.

He knew he'd fucked up the conversation by failing to show Kenny how much he loved him and wanted to see him.

Kenny had not called for money but to connect—for the first time. And then, with a few careless words and a defensive tone, Bill chased him away.

As Bill drove toward the bay, he was so immersed in thoughts of his son that he barely noticed the clouds getting thicker and the wind picking up. Waiting at the light to cross Broadway, he looked up and down the sidewalks and thought about cruising the busy street in search of his son, but that didn't feel right. When the light changed, he drove straight.

•   •   •

Kenny soon found a campsite on a path behind a tire shop: two tents planted in a clearing between willow and alder trees. A man who looked about fifty was sitting on a five-gallon bucket, talking to a woman who sat inside her tent.

When the man noticed Kenny walking into the clearing, he stopped talking and looked at a spot about a foot below Kenny's eyes. "Hey," said Kenny. "I'm looking to get well. Anybody here selling?"

The man laughed, spat on the ground, and said to the woman in the tent, "Like I was saying, nothing wrong with this place that a little pest control wouldn't fix." The woman chuckled. Kenny turned and walked away, thinking he'd have to play it cooler next time.

After a few minutes, he saw a larger hamlet with four or five tents. Two guys sat on milk crates and passed a joint. As he approached the men, Kenny watched his footing on the rough trail—and he realized that his good shoes, shaved face, recent haircut, and clean clothes advertised that he was employed and housed and a fat target for a rip-off. But Kenny had gone beyond caution or prudence. He called out, "Hey, fellas," and walked toward the men.

•   •   •

The sky had gone dark over the pier, and the wind tossed the bay into whitecaps. Bill grabbed his cap to keep it from flying away while he watched people fishing or crabbing. Some leaned against the railing; others sat in camp chairs. Bill perched his forearms on the scarred wooden railing and looked at the gray-green water popping and bouncing in the wind. Then he heard a man say, "That you, Mr. Collins?"

It was Charlie, Petey's son. "Hey, Charlie," Bill said.

"Thought that was you."

They shook hands. "Any luck?" asked Bill.

Charlie pointed to a line that dangled from the railing. "A decent-sized ling cod."

"Not bad."

"Gotta hit it when the tide's turning."

Bill nodded, leaned his hip against the railing and looked out at the bay. "From the looks of that sky, though, you're not going to have much longer to try your luck."

"Yeah," said Charlie. Then gesturing to his bicycle. "You wouldn't be able to give me a ride home again, would ya?"

Bill thought for a moment. "Sure."

•   •   •

Kenny didn't recognize either man. The tall and wiry one wore an Oakland Raiders hoodie that couldn't hide his sunken cheeks and missing teeth; the other, short and overweight, wore camo pants and a filthy Carhartt jacket. They ignored Kenny.

"Looking to score," Kenny said.

Neither man responded.

"Crystal," said Kenny. "If you're selling, I'm buying. Or maybe you know someone...."

The wiry one looked at him and said, "We can help you, but it might take a while."

Kenny looked around as if he were considering going somewhere else. Then it started to rain, and the wind whipped raindrops against his cheek. "How long, you think?"

"How much you spendin'?" asked the other man.

Kenny couldn't stop himself from feeling his wallet in his right front pocket. He had about a hundred-fifty in cash, enough to get the three of them high and leave Kenny with meth for a few days. But the dealers who retailed meth in Devil's Playground usually didn't have that much on them, since their customers could only put together ten or twenty bucks at a time.

Before Kenny answered, another man came into the camp. He was Kenny's age with a shaved head and prison tattoos on his neck. Kenny recognized him, and from the way he looked at Kenny, the guy recognized him, too. He was one of the two men Kenny reported to the cops.

•   •   •

Bill and Charlie loaded Charlie's bike and gear into the truck and took off. As they crossed the bridge over the bay, Bill said, "I visited your dad right after I saw you—on the day before Thanksgiving."

Charlie looked at Bill. "How was he?"

"Not too good," Bill said. "I stayed about an hour, tellin' him stories from the old days. He smiled and nodded, but it didn't seem like he remembered anything I talked about. I don't know if he even knew who I was."

Charlie's shoulders hunched up. "Yeah, that's what it was like last time my brother and me went down there."

"How long's it been since you've seen him?"

"I don't know. Maybe four months," said Charlie. "It just makes me too sad. And I figure if he doesn't know me, what's the point."

Bill nodded. He understood. The man who had been Bill's mentor and friend wasn't there anymore. As sad as that made Bill, Charlie must have felt it much worse. But Bill couldn't stand the thought of Petey being down there all alone, with no visitors. "I know what you mean, but how about if you and I go down there sometime? I mean, he's completely alone now."

Charlie gazed out at the dark clouds. When he looked back at Bill, his face was wet. "Ah, thanks anyway, but I don't think so. It's just too hard. Got enough to cope with just keeping my own self together."

Bill nodded.

The wind had died down, but the rain had built up to a steady patter, not a downpour but enough to send a stream of twigs and duff under Bill's tires as he turned left at the end of the bridge. Out here on the peninsula, he thought, they get the worst of the storms.

•   •   •

"Where you been, man?" asked the man with neck tattoos, grinning at Kenny with fake bonhomie.

"Here and there," said Kenny, stalling. He knew his hasty exit from the camp two months earlier had been noticed—especially by this fellow and his partner, whose plans had been interrupted by cops and handcuffs.

"You know each other?" asked the wiry one.

"Yeah, we do," said Neck Tattoo, moving closer to Kenny. "Kenny, right?"

Kenny nodded and took his hands out of his pockets, prepared to swing or run. Then he heard a woman giggle in one of the tents.

"What's that?" he asked anxiously.

"What?" asked the wiry one.

"You're awful jumpy," said Neck Tattoo. "Maybe you ought to sit down for a bit."

Kenny smiled and began to sit on a milk crate. When he was in a crouch, he sprang up and sprinted for the trail. Neck Tattoo was right behind him. "You're dead, motherfucker!"

Kenny ran like a deer. He dodged through four lanes of traffic on Broadway, then ran south on the narrow sidewalk before turning uphill. He didn't look behind him until he'd run all the way to the Winco shopping plaza. Neck Tattoo was not in sight. Kenny rested his hands on his knees and gasped for air. After catching his breath, he started walking quickly toward Jerry's trailer.

When Jerry opened the door and saw Kenny's state, he asked sternly, "You relapse?"

"No, no," Kenny said earnestly. "But I need to talk."

Jerry pulled the door open and stepped back. When Kenny was inside, his sponsor gave him a bear hug, ignoring Kenny's wet clothes. "Have a seat. You want a cup of coffee?"

While Jerry made coffee, Kenny spilled the story: how his pain at his dad's rejection led him to crave oblivion, and how he instantly became powerless over his obsession with crank. "I came this close to fucking everything up," said Kenny, holding out his thumb and forefinger.

"And close to being dead or in the hospital. Unfortunately, you're probably going to see that guy again. Better think about talking to the cops."

"I wish the cops had kept those guys locked up after I snitched on 'em."

"Maybe it's better this way," Jerry said.

"The fuck!? How?"

Jerry handed Kenny his coffee. "Maybe God put this incident in your life to wake you up, to help you see how close you were to a relapse. Like I said, you may not believe in God, but it sure looks like God believes in you."

"Yeah, but not enough to make my dad love me."

Jerry looked over his glasses at Kenny. "Did I ever tell you about my kids?"

A half-hour later, Kenny left, feeling a little better after Jerry described how long it had taken him to mend his damaged relationships with his two adult children. Kenny walked to his rooming house and took a nap. He woke up in time for the evening meeting. And after the meeting, he walked to the gas station to start his shift, grateful that his job was on the other side of town from Devil's Playground.

Chapter 25

The rain fell in sheets and dark clouds marched slowly across the sky. Bill looked out his front window and tried to imagine Kenny in a sober house.

It was a little after six AM, so Kenny might be getting home from his graveyard shift now. Bill considered driving to one of the large sober houses. He'd park in front and wait until Kenny approached the door. Then, he'd get out and call Kenny's name, and when Kenny saw Bill, he'd understand that his father had come looking for him. They'd hug and make a new start.

Or Bill could get up early tomorrow and make a pre-dawn tour of gas stations. Meeting Kenny when he was behind the register or cleaning a restroom would be awkward. But it would show him what Bill had not been able to say over the phone—that he wasn't going to give up on their relationship.

Thinking of Kenny, Bill's eyes were drawn to some family photos on the wall. One showed Aaron and Denise in front of their house in Santa Rosa. Another pictured the whole family up at the river when Denise and Kenny were about nine and seven. And there was a recent photo of Aaron—holding the wooden toy truck Bill had given him. Next to that was an old photo of Kenny, about the same age as Aaron was now, clasping a football to his chest and looking serious.

Like other grandparents he knew, Bill was kinder and more loving to Aaron than he'd been to Kenny—the result of experience and the freedom from primary parenting responsibilities. He could be more playful and relaxed than he'd been while raising his children.

But as Bill looked at the photos, he saw a fresh indictment of how badly he'd screwed things up, not only yesterday, when his edgy tone had led Kenny to hang up, but over Kenny's entire childhood. He said aloud, "You fucked it all up."

But before the last syllable had left his mouth, scenes from the past played through Bill's mind like a movie on ultra-high speed: Kenny taking his first steps on a sunny morning in the park; Kenny at eleven or twelve refusing to do his homework; Kenny sneaking off with his friends to get high; Kenny throwing his hard hat into the trees and storming off the job.

Suddenly and viscerally, Bill understood something that had been just an abstract idea until then. Even if he had been the best father in history, Kenny could have become an addict anyway. Addiction is a disease, not a result of bad parenting.

A sob came up Bill's throat, a moan of deep grief over his son's fate and forgiveness for himself. He felt both deeply sad and unreasonably happy. And he knew what he would do with the rest of his morning.

•   •   •

Monica parked next to a one-story office building, and Jonah followed her to the side door. She unlocked it, and they walked through cubicles and down a hallway into a large open room with windows that looked out on a playground, soggy with puddles.

Monica showed Jonah the coffeemaker and supplies in the kitchen, then went into the main room and began setting out boxes of toys and games.

He got the coffee going then hovered near her in the big room while she sorted through files. She looked up and smiled briefly.

"Sorry, but I've just got to concentrate on this, or I'll lose my place."

"I got the coffee going."

"I can smell it. Thanks."

Seeing Monica hard at work, knowing how much responsibility she took for the kids whose cases she oversaw, Jonah felt a wave of admiration. He moved to her side, caressed her upper back, and said, "I admire you so much."

She laughed nervously. "Okay, mister. Thanks." She looked up from her paperwork. "Now, would you just leave me alone for a few minutes? I'll come up with something for you to do when I finish this."

Deflated, Jonah drifted away and plopped down on a black beanbag chair. He picked up a toy truck and rolled it absently up and down his thigh while reading wall posters. "Advocates give voice to foster children." "Today's going to be a great day!" "Every child needs someone to believe in them."

He thought about what it meant to believe in someone, to know that someone believed in you. Had his parents believed in him? Did his father believe in anything? Not in God, that's for sure.

Jonah remembered a time in his young life when he wanted to believe in God. He was about nine and had started absorbing ideas of God and Jesus from Christmas carols and TV shows. He'd imagined Jesus as a brave young superhero and God as a kindly old wizard.

One summer afternoon, when he played at his friend Joey's house, Joey started talking about Jesus. "He loves me, and he loves you. He and his Father God watch out for everyone on earth, especially kids."

Jonah wanted to believe there was magic in the world, and he loved what Joey said: that God and Jesus were watching out for and caring about him. But a few days later, his dad called him to the backyard for "a little chat." Nothing like this had ever happened, and Jonah was nervous and intrigued.

"Your mother tells me you've been asking about God," his father began. Jonah nodded eagerly.

Then, his father told him that God did not exist. "People invented God to explain things they couldn't understand, like floods and earthquakes. The God of the Christians is no more real than the old Greek gods like Zeus and Apollo," said his father. "We're atheists in this family, Jonah. My father was an atheist, and so am I, and so is your mother. We don't need those old myths because we have science, logic, and common sense."

Jonah felt sad, but he kept that to himself because he saw and understood his father's pride in being an atheist.

Monica picked up a phone call. After listening for a few seconds, she inhaled sharply. "You've got to be kidding me," she said, alarmed. She listened some more. "Can we get the judge to intervene? She knows how good those foster parents are for him."

Jonah had moved to sit across from Monica in a kid-sized chair. He heard a panicked female voice on the other end of the line. She glanced briefly at Jonah, then looked away. "Well, let's brainstorm on this when you get here. There's got to be something we can do.

"Goddamn it," she said when the call was over. "Shit. Fucking hell."

"What happened?" he asked.

"Goddamn it," she repeated, standing up and walking across the room to stare out the window. "I can't say much, but this very damaged kid we placed with some terrific foster parents just got yanked last night and placed in a group home." She folded her arms. "Because of some political bullshit. Next, he'll probably go back to his nutty aunt who hasn't a clue how to parent him."

Jonah searched for words to comfort her. All he could think of was offering a hug. She accepted his embrace but pushed him away quickly. "I know you want to help, but I just need to contain my emotions and get ready for all these advocates and kids who will start showing up in a half-hour. I need you to leave now."

•   •   •

After lighting the stove, Bill picked through his stash of curly redwood until he found a piece that seemed about the right size. He studied the grain, then sketched lightly on the board with a pencil.

A half-hour later, when the stove had finally begun to drive off the chill, Bill stopped, examined the pencil marks he'd made and visualized how he'd cut the piece, what tools he'd use to round its edges, how much sanding he'd do, and what finish he'd use.

He hadn't done much by his usual standards: no cutting, planing, or drilling. But he wanted to take this project slowly and allow the swirling grain patterns in the curly redwood to guide him. He looked at his watch. Angela would arrive soon, so he closed the stove damper, tidied the shop and left.

The day had lightened and there was blue sky in the east and thin rays of sun filtered through the clouds. And there was a waning crescent moon, with its round side pointing at the sun. Bill felt warm energy rising from his belly and he laughed with joy.

•   •   •

Walking home, Jonah mulled over what had happened. He understood Monica's need to be alone to digest the bad news and get ready for her event, but he still missed her. He tried to think of a way to spend the night with her, but he knew that trying to weasel into her bed tonight—after she'd told him she had other plans—would be a mistake.

Jonah got out his phone and pushed David's number. He wanted to ask him about what he'd called dating strategy. When David didn't pick up, Jonah texted him.

Maybe he'd look up "dating strategy" on Manny and Karen's computer. He'd never given much thought to dating, much less any strategy for it. In high school, he was too shy to ask girls out. He'd had some hook-ups in the Bay Area, and he'd fallen into two short-term relationships since coming to Humboldt.

Elaine was an activist traveling to the Bay Area from Portland. They met at a party at Owl's apartment. First, they made out on the balcony; then they did it in Owl's bedroom— using the condoms she'd packed for such occasions.

She had broad shoulders, small breasts, and ripped abs from competitive swimming in college. Jonah wasn't strongly attracted to her, but he enjoyed sex with her several more times before she moved along.

A few months later, he met Jeronica on the pot farm, where they both worked as rookie trimmers. A striking beauty with dark brown hair, she fascinated Jonah from the first moment he saw her. She liked him, too, and their attraction was so obvious that one of the grandmas on the crew teased them about it. "You two can use my tent anytime," she said over a table piled with bud and baggies. "Just clean up after yourselves."

On a clear night, they held hands and walked up the road to a ridge about a half-mile away. They sat and watched the stars and made out. She told him she wanted to sleep with him but didn't want to go all the way. He was disappointed at first, but soon found their oral sex and mutual masturbation so pleasurable that he didn't miss intercourse.

Like the rest of the crew, they got stoned every evening. While partaking rendered Jonah incapable of meaningful conversation, Jeronica stayed lucid and in touch with her feelings when stoned. Jonah intuited that she wanted more than sex from him during their evenings together—some emotional connection that he, in his stupor, couldn't give her.

Jonah hoped she would come to Arcata with him after the season wrapped up. But she was headed for San Luis Obispo, where an organic farm had promised training, lodging, and meals in exchange for work. Jonah was committed to staying in Humboldt and fighting to save the forests.

On a blazing hot October day, they hitched together to the crossroads town of Redway. And when the moment to part came, Jonah changed his mind.

"Let me come with you." He held her hands as they stood in the dusty parking lot of a general store. "I want to be with you."

She stood on her toes and kissed him on the cheek. "No, Jonah. You've got your path. I've got mine. Text or call me sometime. And if you come south, I'd love to see you."

Jonah returned to Arcata and processed his grief in a haze of pot smoke. In a week or so, he was over Jeronica and fantasizing about other women in the activist scene.

With Monica, Jonah experienced great sex and an emotional intimacy that was as deep as it was unprecedented for him. Jonah envisioned moving in with her and planning their future together. Like that Depeche Mode song, he just couldn't get enough.

He stopped walking, pulled out his phone, composed a love message, and then pressed send—without a second thought for dating strategy.

• • •

When Angela arrived, she hugged Bill tightly. He savored the smell of her hair, her warmth, her softness, and the caring he saw in her face. He made her some tea and himself a decaf coffee, and they sat on the couch, their thighs touching. Then, he told her what had happened between Kenny and him the day before.

When he finished, she reached to hug him. "I'm sorry, Bill. That sounds really painful."

"It was. It is," he said. "But I also have this strange feeling that things are going to work out, that somehow we'll reconnect." He shook his head at how odd this sounded, yet it felt real. "I had this, this … experience earlier today."

"Experience?"

"It's hard to describe, maybe impossible." Bill looked at the photos of his son and grandson and took a deep breath. "It was like I felt the worst I've ever felt about Kenny, and at the same time, I had this feeling that I'd been forgiven. And this confidence that I would get a fresh start with him."

Angela held his hand and looked at him intently. "That sounds magnifico. And I think it's true."

They sat in comfortable silence, until she said, "Do you remember, on our first date, what you asked me about why I was interested in you?"

"Uh, yes." Bill's face flushed, and his heart sped up.

She moved away from his side so she could look at him directly. "In our first phone calls, I could tell you were a good man just by how you listened to me and didn't talk about yourself all the time, and how you talked about your daughter and grandson." Angela paused, then said, "And the more we talked, I understood that you were, I don't know how to call it—working on yourself—trying to change—trying become a better man."

"Yeah. Okay."

"So, I saw you were a good man who was not satisfied with himself, who was working on getting better, on being a better person, a better dad. That's why I'm interested in you."

Bill chuckled. "That and my awesome cumbia dancing, huh?"

She snuggled back by his side. "That, too, como no."

Chapter 26

Jonah woke to the alarm on his phone. He threw off the covers, stepped into his sandals and walked through the wet grass to pee. Back inside, he wanted to crawl under the comforter, but he pushed himself through some yoga postures, dressed, grabbed his backpack, and went into the house. After eating breakfast and packing a lunch, he hopped on his bike and rode to the bus stop.

The bus was ten minutes late, so when Jonah got off in Arcata, he ran the eight blocks to the house. David insisted on starting promptly.

But David's Subaru wasn't parked in front. Jonah went inside and texted him, "Where you at?" And then, looking at the text thread, he noticed David hadn't responded to several messages. That wasn't unusual since he'd started seeing a new girlfriend. Jonah hadn't met her yet, but David—obviously smitten—talked about her a lot.

Jonah started working where he'd left off, sanding window trim. After thirty minutes, he checked his phone: no response. So, he called David and got voicemail. Now Jonah became gravely concerned. David had never been late. He thought about calling Manny but didn't want to worry him needlessly.

After another hour, Jonah ran out of tasks he could do independently, so after texting David to let him know he was taking off, he packed up his gear and walked to the bus stop.

At home, Jonah ran into Manny in the kitchen. "You seen David?" he asked. "He didn't show up at work." Before Manny spoke, Jonah saw the sadness disfiguring his wrinkled face. Jonah opened his arms, and they hugged.

Manny said, "Damned alcoholics will break your heart every time."

Over coffee, Manny told Jonah how he'd learned David had slipped off the wagon. "When he didn't show up for our usual meeting last night, I called. He picked up, and the minute I heard his voice, I knew." Manny frowned. "He knew I knew, and that was that. I just said, 'Call me when you're ready to get well.'"

Manny asked Jonah, "Did you see any signs this was coming?"

"Nothing. Yeah, he was stressed with the remodeling job and had another customer breathing down his neck. But it seemed like he was working a strong program, going to meetings, talking with you. He even figured out what his higher power was."

At the noon meeting, it was apparent that other members had heard about David's relapse—and those who hadn't were soon made aware. Some people cried, some were stoic, and others were impassioned with the recovery gospel. "This disease will kill you!" thundered Biker Bob. "It's like the Terminator. It can't be reasoned with or bargained with, and it doesn't give up hunting you until you're dead!"

Manny took a softer tone. "God loves David, and so do I, and I know most of you do, too." When the meeting ended, the group dedicated its closing prayer to David and other suffering alcoholics who'd relapsed or hadn't yet found recovery.

•　　•　　•

Jonah sliced tomatoes and cucumbers for a salad while Karen braised pork chops and microwaved potatoes. Manny was watching Wheel of Fortune, and Jonah was glad to hear him yell at the TV. "Never a dull moment. C'mon, you can solve that."

At the dinner table, Manny said, "Biker Bob said he ran into David at the store tonight. Said he looked terrible and smelled like a barroom."

"Damn," replied Jonah.

"All we can do is pray for him," said Karen, reaching her hands to take Manny's and Jonah's.

"Jesus, we know you have the whole world to look after, but if you can shed some of your love light on our brother David who is wandering astray, please help him," she said with her eyes closed. "He's a good man who suffers from a disease. We know you forgive his sins, and you see his goodness. We ask your blessings on him and on us all, in your name, Amen."

•   •   •

Eureka sparkled under a bright sun and clear blue skies, but Bill sat at his kitchen table, ignoring the splendor outside as he worried about why he hadn't heard from Angela for a day and a half.

Between their dates, they'd been texting or talking by phone every day. Until yesterday. Bill picked up his phone and typed, "Can we talk? getting worried." Then he deleted it. Maybe she needed some time to herself—although that didn't sound like Angela.

He considered driving by her apartment to see if her car was there—but that would be like stalking. He couldn't think of any mutual friends he could call except one of her sisters. Looking at his watch, he saw it was ten-thirty. Pamela's restaurant was only a mile away and opened at eleven.

He hadn't seen Pamela since the morning he snapped at her for asking questions about his financial status. He'd apologized but wondered if his reaction still stung. Bill figured he'd deal with that if it came up. He stuck his phone in his pocket, grabbed his hat and jacket, and started walking to the restaurant.

Bill arrived just after it opened. A server showed him to a table. When he saw Pamela coming out of the kitchen, his heart sped up—she looked like Angela. She smiled and said, "Hi, Bill. It's good to see you." She shook his hand, sat opposite him, and asked, "Has Angela been in touch with you since she left?"

"Left? Where'd she go?"

Pamela sat back and brushed the skin below her eye with a finger. Bill braced for the worst. "She flew to Mexico City to help take care of our mom, who had a sudden heart attack."

"Oh my," said Bill. He leaned back against the booth cushion and felt the tension drain from his shoulders. "Is she all right, your mom?"

"Looks like she's going to be okay. But Angela will stay for a while to help her and make sure that she and our dad have whatever they need."

Customers had lined up by the door, so Pamela had to go. But before she got up, she said, "If you don't have Skype already, you should get it. That's the easiest way for you two to talk. You can message each other first and set up a time." Bill nodded. He'd heard of Skype, but worried whether he could manage using it.

Bill's food came, and he ate hungrily. He was almost done when Pamela returned to his table. "I'm sure Angela will contact you soon," she said. "I know she's very fond of you."

•   •   •

The next morning, Jonah called the homeowner. "What do you mean you can't get in touch with him?" she asked anxiously. "Was he kidnapped or something? Got in an accident?"

"I can't really say." Jonah wanted to be transparent but felt it would be wrong to disclose to David's client that he was an alcoholic.

"You can't say?" She sounded frantic. Then she slowed down and asked, "Did he relapse? Is that it?" Her tone shifted to compassion. "I knew he was in recovery when I hired him. He told me all about it, and I have relatives in the program."

Jonah told her it was true.

"Oh, that's terrible."

"It still doesn't seem real," said Jonah.

"He was such, I mean, he is such a good guy and so talented. This disease is crazy."

"You're right."

"Do you think you could finish the job yourself?"

He fantasized about it for a second, then said, "No. I've learned a lot, but I'm still just a helper."

"Okay. I'll start looking around. It shouldn't be too hard to get another contractor in this recession but finding one who can start right away and finish it before my tenants are scheduled to move in will be tough."

Jonah said he'd ask around, and she promised to mention him if her next contractor needed a helper. Before she hung up, she asked, "Hey, do you have the number for that tree guy? He called me and said he'd come over and do a bid, but I haven't heard from him since. And I lost his number."

"Sure." Jonah gave her Bill's number.

•   •   •

Sitting at his computer after dinner, Bill found the website where he could download Skype. But the instructions for setting up an account and creating a handle baffled him. So, he called his daughter Denise for help.

Aaron picked up and screamed, "Grandpa! Are you coming to visit?"

"Next month, kiddo," he said, his heart soaring. "How was your day at school? Did you make any more pictures?"

Aaron told Bill that his class made banana bread. "I got to mush the bananas," he said, sounding as excited as if he'd gone to Disneyland. "It was so fun." After another minute of chatting, Aaron put his mother on the phone.

"Hi, dear. I was hoping you could help me get Skype going on my computer."

"Sure," said Denise. "Who you Skyping with?"

"Angela. I got Skype but don't know how to set it up."

"Sure, I can walk you through it. Is she out of town?" Denise had been lobbying Bill to bring Angela on his next visit.

"Out of the country. Had to go to Mexico to take care of her mom for a while. She had a heart attack."

"Oh, wow," said Denise. "I hope her mom's okay."

"I hear she is." Bill didn't want to get into the details. "Anyway, what do I do?" With Denise's help, Bill created his account, made a test call, and even found Angela's Skype handle. "Hola mi Amor," he typed in the message window. "Pamela told me about your mom. Want to Skype sometime tonight?"

•   •   •

Jonah's heart pounded as he bicycled to Monica's apartment. When she opened the door and smiled, he melted with love and burned with lust. They hugged, and she asked, "Do you want a cup of tea?"

As they waited for the tea, he told her about David. "Oh my God, that's just awful. This disease. I'm still amazed at how powerful it is."

When they sat with their tea, she asked more about David: Had he been working a solid program? Going to meetings? Did he have a higher power?

Jonah answered yes while resenting David for intruding on his romantic evening. To change the subject, he asked Monica about the event on Saturday with advocates and foster kids. As she told him about it, he had trouble following because he wanted so badly to caress her. But he knew she wouldn't be in the mood yet. So, he rallied his attention and asked about the dramatic phone call she'd received before he left.

"Oh Jonah, I wish I hadn't blurted out what that was about," she said, looking down at her teacup. "I'm supposed to be—no, I've got to be totally confidential with any information about foster kids." She looked at him and continued. "Let's just say that the system can be brutal. Sometimes kids get chewed up by it, and that's the most heartbreaking thing about my job."

She moved closer to him, and they kissed. Jonah was thrilled to hear her moan with pleasure as he glided his hand around her breast. She kissed his cheek and ear, then lavished his neck with gentle bites.

After they'd made love, Jonah asked if he could spend the night. She hugged him and said, "Not on a work night." He drifted off anyway and was jolted awake as she shook him. "Time to get up, Jonah."

When they said goodbye at the door, he touched her through her bathrobe and got hard. She noticed. "Okay, Casanova. On your way. Ride safely."

Chapter 27

As Bill and Jim drove to Arcata to check out a tree job, Bill struggled to contain his feelings. He was stoked about his date to Skype with Angela tonight and worried about when he'd see her next. But he didn't want to mention this to Jim—whom he hadn't told about Angela because of his hostile attitude toward people he called "illegal aliens" or worse. He wondered if Jim had heard about Angela through mutual friends.

While Bill kept a lid on his emotions, Jim gave full-throated expression to his happiness at completing three months sober. "Man, it's like a whole new world out here," he said, opening his hands toward the windshield. "Didn't know what I was missing."

"I'm proud of you. It's not easy."

As they turned off the highway, Jim stuck his head out the window and yelled, "I love my sobriety!"

Bill felt mildly embarrassed and very happy for Jim. Drinking had been his great weakness and the source of growing problems. Jim had always shown up on time for work and worked a full day, no matter how hungover. But as quitting time approached, he would check his watch frequently. And the minute the day was done, he'd race off to a bar or liquor store.

"You remember we're going to the river to meet Uncle Jackie after, right?" Jim asked.

"Yes, although I don't really understand what we'll be doing."

"Like I told you: collecting materials for the sweat lodge." Then, Jim added with a grin, "The men's recovery sweat lodge, which I expect you to come to one of these days."

"We'll see." Bill pretended nonchalance but he was intrigued by the idea, especially if Jackie oversaw whatever happened inside.

The homeowner met them and led them around back. Jim and Bill sized up the tree. "Looks like we'll need a chipper," said Jim.

"And an extra guy," said Bill. "Should be able to get it done in a day," he told the homeowner. "Maybe a day and a half."

"A day, easy," Jim said with a chuckle.

Bill added the numbers in his head. "You're looking at $1800 to two grand," he told her. "And that doesn't include hauling away the stem."

"The stem?" she asked.

Bill explained that after limbing, topping, and falling the tree, there would still be a thirty-to-forty-foot stem—the tree's trunk, shorn of limbs—in her yard. "You could get someone with a mini-mill to come and turn it into boards," he offered. "They'd share the lumber with you or pay you something."

"Or you could hold a chainsaw carving contest," Jim said with a wry grin. "Or maybe get some Indians to come make a canoe with it."

Bill could see she didn't get Jim's attempt at humor. "We'd do it for you, but it's not our skill set, and we don't have the equipment."

She frowned. "Okay. I'll figure out what to do with the stem. When can you take the tree down? My neighbors are getting more and more nervous about those big limbs."

"How about Monday?" asked Bill. "It'll take a few days to line up the chipper and another guy."

"Fine," she said.

"And do you think you could pay cash?" he asked her. "That makes it easier for me to pay the guys and the rental shop."

"Sure. By the way, my contractor went … uh, he had to take a break. So, if you know any builders looking for work, please give them my number."

"Sure," Bill said. "Jonah still working for you?"

"He wants to, but he doesn't have the skills to do the work on his own."

They said goodbye and went to Bill's truck. As Bill started the engine, Jim said, "Since Jonah's out of work, how about calling him for this job?"

"Good idea." He handed Jim his phone. "Then call Humboldt Rentals to see if we can get a chipper and chip truck for Monday."

When Jonah answered, Jim said, "Hey, this is Jim, your Indian friend."

Bill heard Jonah's voice on the speaker. "Oh, hey. What's up?" He sounded sad or tired. Bill hoped he hadn't relapsed.

"Me and Bill got a custom tree job from that client you were working for in Arcata. You want to help us out Monday?" Before Jonah answered, Jim turned to Bill and asked, "What are you paying?"

"Twenty an hour. Hundred-fifty minimum if it's a short day—which I doubt it will be."

"You hear that?" Jim asked.

"Yeah. Good money. What would I be doing?"

"Hauling slash to the chipper and a bit of everything else. Might even let you run a chainsaw."

"My dream come true." Bill was relieved to hear Jonah's sarcasm. "Yeah, I'll do it."

"Cool. We'll pick you up Monday, seven sharp."

Bill followed Jim's directions to the northern edge of Arcata. After they parked, Jim grabbed a duffel bag from the back, then led Bill through a dense grove of alder and willow—bare and gray, but with buds thickening on the branches. Bill could hear the Mad River get louder as they approached.

When they emerged from the trees and saw the river, Bill recognized Jackie standing on the bank, hand-sawing a branch off an alder tree. "Uncle Jackie," yelled Jim. Jackie stopped, waved, and walked toward them.

"My friend," he said, extending his hand to Bill. "So glad you could make it."

"Me too."

"How are you?"

"Not too good, partner. Missing my son. You remember me talking about Kenny in meetings?"

"Course I remember."

"He's finally clean and sober. He even called me, but we couldn't, you know, connect."

Jackie nodded and said calmly, "It'll happen, Bill. Addiction does so much damage to families, and it takes a long time to repair. But it'll happen."

"Damn sure hope so. So, what are we doing here? Jim said something about materials for a sweat lodge."

Jackie explained that they were gathering willow and alder limbs, an inch or two thick, to build the frame for a sweat lodge. "We do it with reverence for the Great Spirit, knowing that these are His trees," Jackie said. "We need live branches, but we don't take more than one or two from any tree."

Jackie gestured for them to join hands, and he led a prayer. Then Jim handed Bill a pruning saw.

Bill would typically do a job like this, thinking only about how to get the limbs cut and loaded into Jackie's truck as quickly as possible. But now he worked slowly and meditatively. He felt a little bit like he was a part of the trees—and even the rocks, the sand, and the water.

When Bill saw Angela's face on the screen, he reached out to touch her. She noticed and laughed. "I know, Bill. I want to hug you too."

"That your parents' house?" he asked.

"Yes," she said quietly. "I'd forgotten how small it is. Just a two-bedroom apartment. I sleep here on the couch." She held the laptop camera to show him.

"Yeah, looks tight. How's your mom doing?"

"She's doing great. She and my dad want to meet you. Is that okay?"

"Right now?" Bill reached up to straighten his hair and wished he'd put on a dress shirt. "Uh, sure."

She carried the laptop into the kitchen, and Bill saw a couple that looked just a little older than him. Angela's father had a broad, strong face with a thick mustache, and wore a blue sailing cap. Angela's mother looked like her daughter—same captivating smile—but older and with red curly hair.

"Bill, I'd like you to meet my mother, Fernanda, and my father, Rico. Mami, Papi, quisiera presentar mi novio, Bill."

"Hola, Bill. Mucho gusto conocerle," said Angela's mom.

"Mucho gusto," managed Bill.

"No habla mucho español," Angela told her parents.

"Tell your mother I'm glad she's feeling better."

"Dice que esta alegre que sientas mejor, Mami."

Fernanda smiled broadly. "Gracias, Bill. Muy amable."

Two teen girls bounded into the kitchen, talking loudly. "Tranquilo," Angela's father told them. "Angela habla con su novio estadounidense."

The girls smiled and waved at Bill. "Hola señor," said the taller one. "Angela nos ha dicho mucho de usted."

Angela translated shyly. "They say hi, and I've told them a lot about you."

"Just the good stuff, I hope."

"There's nothing else to tell," she said with a smile. Angela told her family to bid Bill goodnight, then took the laptop back to the living room. She asked Bill about his work. He told her about the tree job with Jim and how he'd hired Jonah. "You remember when we met him and his friend at the Eureka arts night?"

"How could I forget that night?" exclaimed Angela.

He asked more about her mother's condition. Angela said she had fully recovered. Then he asked his most important question: "So when are you coming back?"

Angela looked stricken. "I've been trying to figure out how to tell you, Bill. I don't know when I can come back or even if I can."

"What do you mean?"

She sighed. "You remember what I told you about how I entered the United States on a tourist visa? How the plan was to get a green card with my fiancé—I mean my ex?"

"Yes, of course."

"That's still my situation. I could get another tourist visa. But that takes a lot of money and other stuff, and even then, I would become illegal again once the visa ran out."

Bill felt miserable. "Well, Angela, I sure hope you can come back soon. Is there something I can do to help?"

"Let's just take it one day at a time for now," she said. "I miss you."

"I really miss you, too." They made a date to talk in a few days.

After Angela's image disappeared from the screen, Bill sat stunned with disappointment. Then he opened his web browser and entered "flights to Mexico City" in the search bar.

Chapter 28

Monica had invited Jonah to come over, and since it was Friday, he expected to spend the night—and that meant sex tonight and probably in the morning. To show her how happy he was with their relationship, he stopped at a market to buy some flowers. Then he rode one-handed to her apartment, gripping the bouquet under his left arm.

After locking his bike, he leaped up the stairs. She opened the door and smiled. They hugged, and she took the flowers to her kitchen, but the bouquet did not seem to delight her as he'd expected. Instead, as she cut off the stems, she gave him only a brief, tight smile. Then she put the flowers in a vase with water and put on the kettle for tea.

As they waited for the tea, she leaned back against the kitchen counter and asked him what he had been up to.

"Mostly lots of meetings, since I'm not working with David anymore." Then, thinking it would impress her, he added, "And I started on my fourth step."

She smiled warmly. "I know that will be good for you."

Then she was quiet, and he groped for something else to say. He moved toward her, seeking a hug, which she returned. Their tea was ready, and they sat down. And by then, Jonah knew that something was wrong.

"Jonah, I feel so awful." She hunched forward and looked from his face to the floor. "I want to embrace you now and take you to bed." She paused, then looked directly at him. "But the truth is that even though I like you and love you, I'm not in love with you."

Jonah couldn't believe what he was hearing. Yet he knew what it meant. Sadness drenched him. "Oh shit."

"I'm so sorry," Monica said. "I'm sad, too, Jonah." She had tears in her eyes. "I hope we can be friends. I like you, and I think you're a wonderful man. I know you'll make some woman very happy."

"Yeah." He stood up. He grabbed his bike helmet and moved to the door.

She stood up and reached out her arms. "A hug?"

The hug felt dry and lifeless. Jonah walked to his bike and began riding home—only no place felt like home now.

In the morning, Jonah looked at porn magazines. He felt no arousal; instead, he felt sorry for the women posing nude—and sorry for himself. Jonah had built a world of hopes around Monica. Enthralled by her beauty, drawn to her strength and openness, he'd told her things about his childhood that he'd never told anyone. And it all had happened so easily—like they were meant to be.

He wanted to call David and tell him he'd been right—he should have taken things more slowly. But Jonah knew he couldn't have managed that. She had swept him away, like in a movie romance.

As he thought about making love with her, he got hard. He reached for his lubricant and recalled one of their peak sexual moments. He came, and then, after wiping up, he curled into a ball.

A loud knock woke him. "C'mon, Jonah," Manny yelled. "Time to get up and go to the meeting."

"Not up for it, Manny."

"Bullshit," Manny said sternly. "You're coming." He opened the door and spoke more softly. "Look, I heard what happened."

"What? How?"

"Monica called someone, and that someone called Karen, and she let me know. Now get up. You're coming to the meeting." Manny backed out the door. "Coffee's on. We're leaving in fifteen."

They arrived at the church after a car ride in which Manny was mercifully silent. Jonah left Manny outside with the smokers and made his way to a seat, where he stared hard at a stain on the carpet. After the usual readings and announcements, the secretary introduced the chairperson for the meeting. It was Kenny, whom Jonah had met at Beth's memorial.

"Hi, my name is Kenny, and I'm an alcoholic-addict," he said.

"Hi, Kenny," said Jonah with the rest—except for Jerry, who shouted from the front row, "You damned sure are!" Kenny grinned and hung his head comically, and Jonah understood that this was a joke between the two that had started after the memorial when Kenny said he "used to be" an addict.

"Today," said Kenny, "I can appreciate some good-natured teasing from an older man." He nodded at Jerry.

"Who you calling *older*?" demanded Jerry, raising his palms and contorting his face.

When the wave of laughter ebbed, Kenny continued. "I could never relate to my dad like that." Kenny described growing up with a father whose approval he always craved but never received. "My dad was tough as nails. He didn't beat us up or anything like that. But he was constantly dissatisfied with me, judging me."

"He wanted me to be like him, but I wasn't like him." Kenny's face flushed. "I didn't like logging or working on cars. I wanted to play sax in a jazz band or something like that. He wanted me to get up early on weekends and go hunting or fishing. I wanted to lounge on the couch and read a sci-fi novel."

"But he was my dad," Kenny continued. "So I tried to go along with what he wanted until I was about thirteen or fourteen when I discovered weed and alcohol." Kenny told the group how he soon graduated to harder drugs. "I dropped out of high school, and pretty soon, I was living in the homeless camps around town, scrounging and panhandling and stealing to get what I needed."

After a pause and a deep inhale, Kenny said, "I don't know exactly how I got here." Jamming his index finger on the table, he said, "But it's a frickin' miracle that I'm three months clean and sober."

The group erupted with applause. "You go, Kenny!"—"Attaway!"—"Keep coming back!"

After the closing prayer, Jonah sat down to think. He realized with a shock that Kenny was probably Bill's son. Right name, right age, and Bill fit Kenny's description. In the short time Jonah had known Bill, he'd felt the sting of his judgment and anger. But he'd also seen a caring and vulnerable side of Bill. And he knew how much Bill missed his son. He wondered what he could do to bring them together.

Chapter 29

From the window, Jonah saw Bill's pickup roll to the curb. He hustled outside, climbed into the passenger seat, and was surprised to see Jim behind the wheel. "Hey, Jim. Where's Bill?"

"Driving the chip truck and chipper we rented." Putting the truck in gear, Jim accelerated quickly. "How you been, man?"

Jonah had planned to keep his breakup to himself, but Jim's friendly vibe prompted him to tell the truth. "Kind of shitty, actually. Girlfriend just dumped me."

"Aw, man!" Jim looked at Jonah sympathetically. "That sucks."

"Yeah. She's an awesome person, but it's not meant to be, I guess."

"Plenty of fish in the sea," said Jim. "Especially for a young sober buck like you."

"Fuck that." Jonah smiled to let Jim know he appreciated the thought. "Not ready. I should follow my sponsor's advice and wait until I get a year."

"Yeah, right. Nature will have her way, and you'll be boning some young babe before spring equinox."

"What about you, man?" Jonah shot back, eager to shift the lens from his love life. "Any dating?"

Jim looked out the window. "Nah, man," he said somberly. "I ain't ready. After twenty years of rippin' and runnin', it'll be a while 'fore I'm civilized enough to even ask a lady out for coffee."

"I get it," said Jonah, although Jim's gutter-drunk experiences were mostly a mystery to him. "Why don't you tell me what we'll be doing on this job?"

"Pretty standard. Taking down a yard redwood. Lots of limbs to cut and lower first, then we'll top it, then chunk it, then fall it."

"Chunk it?"

"You'll see." Jim gunned the truck through a yellow light and said forcefully, "I hope you packed your A-game. Bill and me, we're old-school lumberjacks. We work hard, we don't fuck around, and we'll expect you to do the same."

"Glad I brought my large thermos of coffee," Jonah said.

When they arrived at the house, Bill stood by a white truck with a yellow chipper attached. After a quick greeting, the men unloaded the pickup: bins and buckets of ropes and harnesses, slings and carabiners, helmets and spike boots. Jonah had seen gear like that when Alder packed his backpack for their madcap mission. He glanced at Bill and again thought about confessing his role in that caper. Not today.

As Jim showed Jonah how to run the chipper, he pulled aside the rubber flaps that hung over the mouth of the in-feed table and pointed at a metal drum. "See that? That drum and all the reamers and whatnot behind it are why this thing will shred a twelve-inch log in a second." He snapped his finger. "Just imagine what it could do to you."

"Good way to get rid of a body."

Jim didn't laugh. "Yeah, and a good way to get yourself killed. Or lose a hand or an arm."

They returned to the backyard, where Jonah watched Bill move smoothly up the tree with a chainsaw and other gear dangling from his waist. When he reached the first limbs, he and Jim rigged more ropes. Then Bill fired up the saw, and in a few seconds, a heavy limb descended slowly, controlled, Jonah saw, by Jim, who worked a device at the base of the tree.

When Jim had untied the limb, he gestured for Jonah to haul it to the chipper. It was so heavy that Jonah could barely move it. Jim saw this, motioned Jonah aside, fired up a small chainsaw, and quickly cut the limb in two. Jonah fumbled with the limb before he figured out how to grip it and drag it efficiently. Jim followed him out to the street.

As instructed, Jonah let the machine warm up before activating the drum. Then, as he wrestled the limb onto the in-feed table, Jim hit the red idle switch. "Like I said," he yelled over the engine, "you always feed 'em from the side. Push it straight in like you were gonna do, and you could get snagged and hauled in."

Jonah nodded, and Jim engaged the drum. Jonah stood to the side and heaved the limb into the chipper—which jerked it from his grip so fast his right wrist got roughly scraped. The chipper sounded like a hailstorm on a tin roof as it gobbled the limb and spewed chips into the truck bed.

An hour later, Jonah was covered in pitch and sawdust and scratched like he'd been playing in a blackberry bramble. He sat down to rest and watched Bill and Jim set up some new rigging. The lower part of the tree had been shorn of branches, and Jonah noticed the sunlight falling on the homeowner's garden beds.

Jim stood holding a rope that angled down from Bill's position in the tree. "Ready," he yelled. And after a quick burst of sawdust from Bill's saw, a limb hurtled down the rope toward Jim. He settled it on the ground just before it smacked into him.

"This is the zipline," Jim told him as he freed the limb. "We'll lower the rest of the limbs like this until we get to the top."

When Bill stopped to maneuver higher, Jonah pointed to the zipline. "Is that dangerous?"

"Only if you don't let go of the rope," said Jim with a laugh. "You want to try?"

Jonah wanted to rest more, but he wasn't going to wimp out. "Sure."

"You've got to brace yourself good 'cause even those skinny limbs are heavy as lead," Jim instructed. "You drop the rope too soon, you'll have farther to drag it to the chipper." He gestured at the redwood's dense canopy. "With forty or fifty more limbs, that'll add up. But if you hang on too long, you could get hurt."

Jim handed Jonah the rope, then he grabbed a limb and started hauling it to the street. From the tree canopy, Bill looked down at him. Jonah bobbed his head to show he was ready. Within seconds, a limb came hurtling down the line toward him, its weight and momentum nearly pulling him off his feet. He panicked and let go, then had to run halfway across the yard to free the zipline. He returned to his position and saw Bill signal again. Jonah gripped the rope harder and squatted lower. This time, he dropped the limb closer to where he stood.

After forty-five minutes, Jonah trembled with exhaustion. He was about to ask Jim to take over when Bill hollered, "Lunch time."

They spread out on the grass. Jonah lay flat on his back with his eyes closed. Bill and Jim ate without speaking for a few minutes. Then Jim asked Bill, "You going to the logging show?"

"Wouldn't miss it," Bill said. "You?"

"Dunno. Last year I drank way too much beer. Might skip it this year."

"Logging show?" asked Jonah, propping himself up on his elbow and opening his lunch.

"North Coast Logging Expo," Jim said. "Happens every year, either up here or down in Ukiah."

"What's the 'show' part?" asked Jonah.

"Chainsaw carving. Log rolling. Ax throwing. You name it. You ought to go."

"Doubt it," said Jonah. "Unless I was going to protest clearcutting."

Bill ignored the comment, while Jim deadpanned, "You're dead to me, punk."

Jonah went into the house to pee. The half-done remodel job made him miss David.

When he sat back down with the men, Jim asked him, "What happened to David, anyway?"

"Relapsed."

"Yeah, I know. But any idea how or why?"

"No fuckin' clue," said Jonah. "Seemed like everything was going good for him, then—BAM—he's just gone."

"This fucking disease," said Jim. "That's why I go to so many damned meetings and hang out with boring, sober white motherfuckers like you all the time."

Then Jim looked at Bill. "I heard you tell Jackie that Kenny is sober."

Bill nodded but said nothing.

Jim persisted. "What meetings does he go to? I don't think I've seen him, but it has been so long I might not recognize him."

Bill was quiet for a few seconds, then said, "To tell you the truth, I don't know what meetings he goes to or if he goes to AA or NA or what. Haven't seen him. I just talked to him on the phone. Once."

Jonah wanted to blurt out what he suspected: that the Kenny he knew from AA was Bill's Kenny. But this didn't seem like the right time.

"I know for sure he's sober, though—or at least he was. My buddy, Steve, the sheriff's deputy, saw him and talked to him about a month ago. Said he looked good."

"He'll come around, man," said Jim. "Probably embarrassed after scaring the crap out of you and your ex for all those years—wants to be sure he's gonna stay sober for good this time."

"Could be," said Bill. He looked at his watch. "Another five and we're back at it."

Jim wiped his hands on a paper towel and said, "You guys check out the gal we're working for? She's fine. Kind of old for me." Looking at Bill, he added, "She might be interested in an old-timer like you, though."

"I think she's gay," said Jonah, and he wondered whether Bill had told Jim he was dating Angela.

• • •

Bill and Jim looked up at the tree. "What do you think?"

Jim turned his face to the northwest, then looked back at the tree. "With a light wind like this, the top will fall right where we want it with a nice clean Humboldt cut."

"Yep, I think you're right. You want to do it?"

Jim looked surprised, and a huge smile opened on his dirty, sweat-streaked face. "Hell yeah!"

"Good, 'cause I felt a little unsteady before lunch." Bill was making that up—partly. He felt deep fatigue, but that didn't seem like a good enough reason to switch roles with Jim. "Then you can just stay up there and start cutting the chunks."

As Jim geared up, Bill helped Jonah haul limbs to the chipper. When they returned to the backyard, Jim was halfway up the tree. "What's he going to do now?" asked Jonah.

"Top it."

"What's that?"

"Just watch."

Starting about ten feet from the top, Jim made a straight cut from the front. Then, under that, he made another cut angled toward the first at forty-five degrees. A little wedge of wood fell to the ground. After moving to the back of the tree, Jim made another cut, killed the saw, steadied himself and pushed. The Christmas-tree-shaped top tilted, then broke off clean. After it hit the ground, Bill and Jonah cheered. "Damn, that was amazing," said Jonah.

"A true artist," said a female voice behind Bill. He turned and saw his client standing on her deck.

"Glad you could see the show," Bill said to her.

"Me too!"

Bill grabbed a small chainsaw and waved for Jonah to follow him. At the tree's base, he cut branches from the top and told Jonah to spread them on the grass. In a few minutes, a landing zone was ready. They moved away, and Jonah watched Jim cut a foot-long chunk from the top. He pushed it, and the piece fell hard and bounced off the lawn. Bill told Jonah to roll it away so Jim could drop another.

After they'd collected a half dozen chunks, Bill said, "You use the splitting maul to bust them up into pieces small enough to go in the chipper."

"Seems like a waste," said Jonah. "Can't we do something with these?"

Bill suppressed his impatience. "Redwood doesn't make good firewood, and those rounds will split as they dry. Guaranteed. But you're welcome to take some if you can fit 'em in the truck."

After Jim had chunked the tree down to about thirty feet, Bill signaled for him to descend. Before coming down, Jim secured one long rope to the top of the bare stem.

Bill and Jonah spread more slash. Then Bill picked up his thirty-six-inch chainsaw from the lawn. As he lugged it toward the tree, Jim said, "Can I do it?" Jim must have noticed how worn out he looked. Gratefully, Bill handed him the saw.

After about ten minutes, Jim had finished two cuts that left a massive wedge in the trunk. He waved Jonah over, and they used pry bars to wrestle the wedge free. As it slipped from the tree, Jonah leapt away to avoid injury. Bill saw this near miss, and fear flashed through his chest. Then anger. He was about to bark at Jonah, but something on the young man's face—panic, relief, vulnerability—prompted him to say instead, "Glad you got fast reflexes." Then he added, "Wouldn't want to quit early to take you to the hospital."

Jonah nodded agreement.

As Jim moved to the back of the tree, Bill handed Jonah the rope that dangled from the top. He pointed to the far end of the yard and said, "Chances are this won't be needed, but take it up there and put some tension on it. Then, when I signal, pull for all you're worth."

· · ·

With sawdust spraying from the saw, Jonah could only see Jim's blurred figure behind the tree. Then Jim cut the saw and backed away. "Here it comes!" Bill yelled. Jonah felt the rope give way. He pulled fast but only got slack. The ground shook as the tree landed and bounced on the slash. After a tiny interval of silence, the three men whooped and hollered.

Bill and Jim cleaned up while Jonah hauled slash and the split rounds to the chipper. He set aside one large round to take home. The homeowner paid Bill cash—adding two hundred as thanks for getting the job done so quickly. Bill handed Jonah two hundred-dollar bills. "Wasn't quite eight hours, but you worked your ass off."

Jim volunteered to dump the chips at the compost yard and return the chipper. Bill offered Jonah a ride home, but he said he'd like to go with Jim. "I'd like to see this compost operation."

"You killed it, dude," said Jim as they pulled away from the curb. "First day on the job, and you did great."

"Feel like I got run over by a truck."

Jim laughed. "Couple of ibuprofen and a good night's sleep, you'll be wanting more of this."

Jonah kept his doubts to himself. As they pulled off the highway, Jim said, "So I'm curious. Since you're a tree-hugger and all, what did you think of that job?"

Jonah thought for a moment before answering. "Well, I can see why that redwood had to come down. Too dangerous. And it kept the yard in shadow half the day. She's probably already digging a new garden bed."

"And she'll probably come here for the compost." Jim pointed to a dusty parking lot where a beat-up sign said Western Landscaping and Compost. They parked and unhooked the chipper, then drove around mounds of tree limbs, piles of brown compost, and fluffy heaps of mulch until they reached the chip area. Jim backed the truck toward a pile of chips, and they got out. After showing Jonah how to engage the hydraulic lift, Jim got in the cab and backed closer to the pile. At Jim's signal, Jonah lifted the bed and watched most of the chips slide out.

"Okay, bring it down halfway," Jim said. Then he pulled a few feet forward. "Now lift her all the way." The rest of the load slid out.

"That's it," yelled Jonah. After the bed was lowered, he hopped back in the passenger seat.

On the highway, Jim nodded at the forest to the east. "You hear about them dumb-ass protesters getting busted?"

Jonah steadied himself and took a deep breath, "No. What happened?"

"They took exception to the tiny bit of logging the city's doing up there, so they went up and poured hydraulic fluid down the exhaust pipes of a loader and a skidder. Did about a hundred grand in damage. Cops found them on the plaza later the same day."

"How'd they ID them?"

"Caught 'em on video with a motion camera." Jim shook his head. "Dudes are going to do some time. Insurance covered the damage, but that's some serious monkey-wrenching."

Chapter 30

Twenty minutes of yoga and 400 milligrams of ibuprofen attenuated Jonah's pain enough so that he could ride his bike to the noon meeting.

As soon as he walked in, he spotted Monica at the coffee counter. He tried to avoid her, walking quickly toward a seat. But she noticed him, smiled, and approached. He was tempted to scorn her, but he still liked her and loved her. Then this line from a movie he'd seen with his mother came to him. *"Of all the gin joints in all the towns…"*

"Casablanca," she said, opening her arms for a hug. "Only this time, there's no gin."

"And the coffee sucks," Jonah said, and they laughed together. It felt blissful—and at the same time, cut him deeply. If only, he thought.

She pointed to a scratch on his face. "What happened?"

"A job, bringing down an old redwood."

Monica looked at him with disbelief. "My buddy Jonah slaughtering a tree?"

"Gonna buy a dirt bike next, go tear up some backcountry," he joked. "Seriously, though, that tree needed to go. Now her garden gets twice as much sun, and the neighbors don't have to worry about big limbs crushing their garage in a storm."

She looked impressed. "Maybe a new career for you?"

"I liked it more than I thought I would—and the money was great."

•   •   •

As Bill walked from his truck to the fairgrounds, the whistle of a steam locomotive stoked his excitement. He had been going to the logging show since he was a kid, and he looked forward to seeing old friends and new equipment, log-rolling and ax-cutting contests—and his favorite part of the logging show, the "shoot-out" contest between mini-mill companies to see whose rig could turn out boards the quickest.

He walked to the main exhibit area and checked out the feller-bunchers and harvester-processors. They looked like alien battle robots from the *War of the Worlds* movie—and machines like them had been killing jobs in the woods for years. But Bill had to admit that with one skilled operator doing the work of three of four guys on the ground, the machines had kept a few loggers from getting maimed or killed.

Then Bill ambled to the informal heart of the logging show, a place by the beer truck where loggers and timberland owners, foresters and consultants, truck drivers and equipment sellers stood around boasting, complaining, teasing, and bullshitting— all the while exchanging news, rumors, and market intel.

Bill joined a small circle with King, Eric, and a couple of other guys. "You still taking them yogurt classes, Bill?" asked King. "I'll bet you see a lotta great ass in there."

"You can only imagine," Bill said, regretting the words as he spoke them.

"Do tell?" asked King. "I hear the young ones like to do it with old guys—fulfill those daddy fantasies."

Bill cursed himself for steering the conversation here. As far as he knew, King and his other friends would never exploit a woman for sex. But their minds and mouths still followed the old high-school game trails. "Not sure about that," was the best rejoinder he could muster. Then, gratefully, he remembered that he hadn't talked to King about what happened at the recent arts night.

"Quite the evening we had last month."

"Protester versus truck," said King. "Good thing nobody got hurt."

Eric looked away.

"Guy like that, don't know how he ever got behind the wheel of a logging truck," said Bill.

"Yep," agreed King. "And he played right into the enviros' hands. Made great headlines for their newsletters: 'Logger tries to kill protesters!' Helped them raise more money from their rich backers down in the Bay Area."

"You sure handled those protesters nicely when they started chanting at you."

"Oh, yeah? What happened?" asked Eric.

"Just played along with them."

Bill explained, "One of them recognized King and got everyone chanting 'shame on you,' or some shit. King here just chanted right along, like it was his idea. Took the wind right out of their sails."

"Wish I could do the same with the legislature. You guys hear the latest?"

Bill tuned out as King began describing how legislators from the cities and suburbs were—once again—trying to regulate the industry into extinction. In the past, Bill would have gotten worked up with King and the others, pissing and moaning over the latest outrages from Sacramento. Now, he put the news into the category of "things I cannot change."

He nodded his goodbyes and wandered back downhill to where the mini-mill shoot-out was about to start. Then he saw Phil Nadelbaum sitting on a stool, smoking his pipe, and watching students who were operating antique, human-powered cutting machines for a small crowd.

An old friend from the logging business, Phil and his wife ran the Draft Horse Millworks and Museum, which included an alternative school for teenagers—including Kenny, for a brief time.

"Bill!" shouted Phil when he saw him. He stood, and they grasped each other's calloused hands. "Good to see you. What are you up to?"

"Just checking out the show." Bill had to restrain himself from telling Phil that he'd recommended him, fruitlessly, as the keynote speaker for this year's show. Bill had known it was a long shot, and as expected, the committee picked a politician. "I didn't expect to see you here," Bill said, gesturing at the students hunched over machines and the people watching. "Nice crowd you've drawn."

Phil nodded with satisfaction. As they watched, Bill paid particular attention to a heavy girl with long black hair and tattooed arms cutting small wooden objects with a scroll saw she operated with her foot. Phil must have noticed Bill looking at her. "One of our best students." Then he called to the girl, "Janie, your hair."

She smiled, stopped the machine, pulled a hair tie from her pocket, and wrapped her long hair behind her head. "When she first came in, she was so shy she wouldn't look at anyone. She just sat in a corner with her cap pulled down to her nose. Now she's ready to run for class president."

"It's amazing what you and Val do with these kids."

"Most just need some good old-fashioned praise and encouragement." He leaned toward Bill. "My secret method is the same with all of them. I tell them they're naturals at whatever they're trying to learn. Of course, they're not, but that puts the wind in their sails and gets them to keep at something long enough to get good at it."

Bill nodded, thinking that this was not something he'd ever done with his kids.

"Any word from Kenny?" asked Phil.

Bill rubbed his forehead. "Well, he's sober, so I hear. But I haven't seen him. Only talked to him once since he got off the drugs—and that conversation didn't go well."

"It's good he's sober," Phil said emphatically, knocking ashes from his pipe. He looked thoughtful, then added, "I can still remember how much he loved making pots."

"Pots, huh?"

"He didn't stay with us long," mused Phil. "How old was he when he started running wild, getting loaded all the time?"

"About fourteen or fifteen."

"I hear that when someone gets off drugs and booze, it's like they pick up where they left off, I mean developmentally, or whatever."

"Yeah?"

"Yeah. So, Kenny might be twenty-four or twenty-six, chronologically speaking. But inside, he's still just a kid." Then, after a pause, Phil added. "So, you give him my best when you see him—and I know you'll see him. And remember, that kid is an all-star, a natural-born talent."

"At what?"

"At whatever the hell he wants to try."

•   •   •

After weeks of labor on his fourth step, Jonah told Manny he was ready to take his fifth step—the Rubicon of twelve-step recovery, where members reveal their "searching and fearless" personal inventories to their sponsors.

Manny had a special place for that. As they drove north along the coast, Jonah reminisced about his road trip with David. He'd heard nothing from him despite sending an occasional text and leaving a few voicemails.

Manny turned inland, and they drove up a steep, bumpy road on the north side of Redwood Creek Valley. Jonah was so anxious he barely noticed the coastal panorama that opened wider as they drove higher.

They sat at a picnic table. Manny recited a prayer, then nodded that he was ready.

Jonah opened his notebook and began reading about how he'd acted selfishly, disrespecting teachers and coaches in high school, and ignoring his mother's needs and his little brother's mental health challenges. He detailed how his addiction led him to stay aloof from friends and screw up his prospects for jobs, college, and even his environmental activism.

That was all prelude, however.

"You want to take a break? Go for a walk?" asked Manny, who must have sensed Jonah's mounting anxiety. Jonah wanted to close the book, get in the car, drive home, and pretend the last pages were blank. But he knew he needed to get this off his chest.

He was fifteen at the time, and Django was eleven. They were home alone, watching TV, when his mother called, breathless with panic. "Jonah, your father just called me from his friend's house. He's drunk, and he demanded I go pick him up. I told him I couldn't get him for a while because I just got to Mama's place. He said he'd take a cab home, drive the other car to a bar, and get even more drunk."

Jonah had never heard his mom sound so scared. She asked him to hide the keys to their second car. Jonah promised he would. He hung up and started looking for the keys.

Then a friend knocked on the door. "Hey, bro. Want to share some of this dank bud I just got?" Jonah figured he'd get a quick buzz, then return and hide the keys.

But he got so high that he forgot about his promise. When he returned home, the car was gone, and his mother was insane with distress. His father had driven off in the other car before she got home—with Django. Jonah knew his mother could tell he was stoned. She didn't berate him for once, but the profound disappointment he saw in her eyes flayed him more painfully than any scolding could have.

A police car arrived. Django bolted out of the car's back door, ran to his mother, hugged her, and cried like a baby. The officer told Jonah and his mother that her husband had died in a car accident. Django hadn't been hurt because he wore his seat belt.

Jonah looked up from the notebook. Through his tears, he saw Manny was also crying. Manny put his hand on his shoulder. "Thank you, Jonah, for honoring me with your truth."

Jonah was in a trance. He heard the birds singing for the first time since sitting down and felt the wind on his cheek.

On the drive home, Manny told Jonah it wasn't his responsibility to control his alcoholic father. "I guess I know that's true. But if I'd found those keys instead of getting stoned, my dad might be alive today. Django wouldn't have gone through that horror show. Maybe my dad would have gotten sober. Maybe I could call him right now and tell him I love him." Jonah choked up thinking about this. "Maybe he and my mom would have stayed together."

Manny nodded his understanding. "We'll never know. The only thing you can do now, as I see it, is stay sober and live like the man you were meant to be before your life got twisted and torn apart by addiction."

When they got home, Jonah hugged Manny and then retreated to his cabin. He called his mother. "Mom, I'm just calling to say I love you," he said to her voicemail. He texted Django, "L'il bro! Thinking of you with lots of love."

Chapter 31

Kenny seemed to be at every meeting Jonah attended over the next two weeks. He was certain now that he was Bill's son. When he asked Manny for advice about what to do, he counseled Jonah to let things take their natural course. But that didn't sit right with Jonah. He knew Bill was suffering, and he knew he could do something about it.

After the noon meeting broke up, Jonah saw Jim and Kenny talking. He walked up, and Jim told him, "Kenny here was just telling me about this weird character he knows from his job at the Texaco down on Fourth Street."

Jonah looked at Kenny. "This guy comes in once a week or so at about six-thirty when things are still quiet. He dresses like a logger." Kenny put a hand on the front of his shirt. "Denim vest, suspenders, a cap with 'Stihl' or whatever on it. He gets his coffee and stands around and talks to me about logging. I don't mind. Helps the time pass." Kenny gestured at the air with his coffee cup.

"But after a while, it seemed kinda strange. I mean, logging is all the dude ever talks about. No sports, no girls, no bitching about the weather." Kenny mimicked a high-pitched voice. "'You're out in the woods all day, getting paid to do what you'd do for free.' Once, he showed me an ad in a trade magazine for a used loader. 'Two hundred and forty grand and you'd have your pick of logging contracts,' he says, or something like that."

"Okay," said Jonah. "So, he likes logging. What's weird about that?"

Kenny chuckled, looked down at his coffee, then back at Jonah and Jim. "The guy is a bookkeeper. Probably never used a chainsaw in his life."

"How'd you figure that out?" asked Jim.

"I just asked him a few questions, like what logging outfits he'd worked for. He didn't pretend or anything, just told me right out—he'd never worked in logging."

The men laughed. "Well, he sounds harmless," said Jonah.

"Maybe your dad and me should charge him to come watch us," said Jim.

Kenny's face tightened. "I didn't know you worked with my dad," he said quietly.

"I know your dad, too," said Jonah. "In fact, I worked with him and Jim a couple weeks back. Hardest day's work of my life. But good pay."

Kenny looked like he wanted to punch Jonah. "Me and my dad don't get along."

Jim said, "I imagine he ain't the easiest guy to have for a dad. Old-school hard-ass."

Then Kenny's sponsor, Jerry, walked up.

"Good to see you, Jerry," bellowed Jim, reaching out to hug the big man.

"Good to be seen!" responded Jerry.

"Let me get some of that," said Jonah, opening his arms to embrace Jerry.

"Anytime, Jonah." Jerry held him tight. "It's always good to see you."

Then he asked Kenny, "You ready?"

"Ready as I'll ever be," said Kenny. Looking somberly at Jonah and Jim, he added, "Fifth step time."

"Good going," said Jonah. "Just did mine."

As soon as Kenny and Jerry were out of earshot, Jim asked Jonah, "So what the hell are we going to do?"

•   •   •

Bill had been talking with Angela for forty-five minutes and wanted nothing more than to remain at the kitchen table with her on his laptop screen. She wore a tight black top, teal earrings, and a purple and white bandana over her hair. "So, what are you going to do for the next few days?"

"Ai, mi amor. I can't believe how much there is to do here. Cooking, cleaning, shopping, watching my nieces after school. I don't know how my parents do it on their own."

"Nothing fun planned?"

"Oh, it's all fun, Guillermo. I have coffee with my mom every day, and we just talk and talk." She paused and looked down. "Of course, I miss you, and Pamela and Lupita, Angelica and the twins. I wish so much I could travel back and forth. If only I hadn't trusted that pendejo."

"Couldn't your sisters sponsor you to get a green card?" Bill had been doing some research.

"I could try that," she said. "But since I overstayed my tourist visa by, like, years, I'm worried that if I apply for a green card, that will show up, and I'll get on some kind of lista negra and never be able to come back."

They knew she needed money for her immigration lawyer, but neither had the necessary cash. Bill wondered if her sisters would help her financially, but it wasn't his place to ask.

Behind Angela, a commotion started—her nieces. "I should probably go. I love you, Bill."

"I love you, Angela." They said goodbye with a promise to Skype again in a few days.

Bill looked at his phone and thought about who he could talk to—someone who'd show sympathy, but also ask him tough questions and help him think through the situation.

"Hiya Bill!" said John, Bill's Al-Anon sponsor. "Good to hear from you."

Bill had told John about Angela's involuntary hiatus in Mexico City, and it only took a minute to update him.

"My, that sounds very difficult," John said.

Hearing John's sympathetic voice brought Bill's sadness closer to the surface. "Yeah, I miss her like crazy."

"Well, let me ask you this, Bill. Do you want to marry her?"

Bill's heart shouted yes, but he told John of his reservations. "I'm not sure. Maybe. We've only been dating a couple months. I figured that kind of decision should wait, like, at least a year."

"Of course, that's prudent thinking. How about going to Mexico to visit her?"

"Yeah, she has invited me, and I can swing it with a credit card. Still..." he trailed off.

"I know, Bill. I wish I could help you with the big picture, but this is totally outside my experience. Have you thought about calling an immigration lawyer?"

"Angela has a lawyer, but this kind of thing can cost as much as ten grand." Before he ended the call, Bill promised John he'd see him at the Saturday morning meeting.

Chapter 32

As he was getting ready for bed, Bill got a call from Jim. "Me and Jonah are goin' fishing for perch tomorrow about dusk out at Mad River Beach, campfire after. You want to join us?"

"Yeah, sure," said Bill without hesitation. "Still early in the season, but I heard the perch are running good." Bill knew that dusk would be perfect, and he'd enjoy being on the beach with Jim and Jonah.

"Great. Can you drive? Pick me up about five?"

"Sure. What are you going to use for bait?"

"Night crawlers. Already got some, plenty to share."

"Great. I'll bring some squid from my freezer."

In the morning, a heavy mist wrapped Bill's neighborhood. He hunkered down on the couch with a steaming cup of decaf and a movie on his laptop. The action-adventure flick distracted him from thinking about Angela or Kenny until it was time for his morning meeting.

He drove to the church and parked, then walked inside, greeting John and others. As soon as he'd taken a seat, the secretary, a woman about his age, came over and asked, "Bill, would you chair today's meeting? The person I had scheduled can't make it."

After months attending Al-Anon, Bill had yet to chair a meeting. He felt intimidated at being in the spotlight. But turning her down didn't seem right. "Sure." He followed her to the front and sat in the speaker's chair.

While the usual opening texts were read, Bill tried to think of an Al-Anon topic to focus on. But when the secretary introduced him, his mind was still blank. Bill looked down at his hands, then raised his eyes. "The truth is, I don't know what the heck to say," he began. "I wish I could tell you about my serenity and how I'm using the Al-Anon tools to feel better about myself, but I'm so torn up right now about my son—and my girlfriend—that I'm just a mess, a big mess."

"It's okay, Bill," said one member. "We love you," encouraged another.

Bill smiled and breathed into his belly. "Thanks. Most of you know what brought me here. My son got hooked on meth, and I wanted to get help for him—you know—get the parents' manual that would tell me what to say to get him to stop killing himself." Several people chuckled.

"At first, I was royally pissed off when some of you told me that Al-Anon wasn't about that." He moved his gaze around the room. "And when you told me the program was for me, I didn't have a clue what you were talking about. But I kept coming and eventually learned to focus on myself, my needs, my well-being. But most of the time, I still don't know what the hell I need or how to give it to myself."

Bill leaned back and looked at the ceiling. "The truth is that I screwed up as a dad."

As if warding off objections, he raised his hands. "I know, I know. There's no such thing as a perfect parent. Addiction is a disease that can affect anyone. I know these things are true. It's not my fault Kenny became an addict. But it seems like if I want him in my life, which I do, now that he's sober, I have to change. I have to become almost a different person—a different dad, anyway. And I don't know how to do that."

• • •

After an early dinner, Bill put his fishing gear in the back of his truck and drove to Jim's house. Jim's nephew Denny answered the door. "Hello, Mr. Collins. Jim's about ready. You want to come in?"

"Sure, Denny." Bill moved his hand to tousle the boy's head but stopped just in time. The kid wasn't seven anymore. "And it's Bill, Denny, not Mister Collins."

His face reddening, Denny said, "Okay, uh, Bill."

Sitting on a leather couch, Bill asked, "What have you been up to, Denny? Looking forward to baseball season?"

Denny shook his head and laughed. "No, Mister Bill. I'm more into skateboarding."

"Oh, down at Cooper Gulch, the new skatepark?"

He nodded.

"I live right near there. I'll look for you next time."

Jim came in dressed for a cold night. "Looks like you're ready for the mountains, partner," said Bill. "Thought we were going to the beach?"

"Fuck off," he said, then punched Denny softly on the shoulder. "Oh, sorry, Denny."

"The fuck do I care?" said the boy, causing Bill and Jim to crack up. Denny kept his face straight, which made them laugh even harder.

When the two men were in Bill's truck, Bill started the conversation he'd been putting off. "I've got something to tell you. Should have told you sooner."

"Okay. Shoot."

"I met a gal a while back, online. And we got together almost two months ago."

Jim's grin spread wide. "No shit! Aren't you the quiet one to keep it to yourself all this time. King and Eric know?"

Bill glanced at Jim. "Yeah. A few other friends, too. The truth is, Jim, I haven't told you because she's an immigrant from Mexico."

Jim was quiet for a second. "Man, I got nothing against immigrants, just the ones that come here illegally."

"Well, Angela isn't legal—or she wasn't. Right now, she's stuck in Mexico City. Had to go down for a family emergency, and she can't come back 'cause she doesn't have a green card."

"Oh man. That sucks." They were on Highway 101, and Bill could see from the bay's calm surface that the wind had died down. Beyond the bay, the sun hung a few degrees above the horizon, high clouds getting pinker by the minute. Bill told Jim Angela's story: entering on a tourist visa with her ex, fleeing Fresno, and moving to Eureka to work for her sisters.

"Man, I feel for you. This don't change my opinions, but I sure hope she can work it out and get back here. You thinking about marrying this girl?"

Bill smiled. "Thinking about it. I really love her. But first, I'm going down there. Next week, in fact. Meet her parents, see what Mexico City is like."

•   •   •

Jonah had borrowed Manny's minivan for the drive to the beach. After parking on Fourth Street in front of Kenny's rooming house, he ran up the narrow outdoor stairs and walked in. A few steps down the dark corridor, he came to a large kitchen and dining room where a heavy man with a bald freckled head was washing dishes.

"You must be Jonah," he said. "Kenny's expecting you. Have a seat."

The dining area was warm and bright with late afternoon sun. "This is a gorgeous spot to be on a day like this."

"Yes, it is," said the man. "By the way, I'm Roger."

"Good to meet you. Are you the cook?"

"Chief cook, dishwasher, and general manager, at your service."

"How does this place work, anyway," Jonah asked.

"It works real good," said Roger with a mischievous smile.

"I mean, who gets to live here, what do they pay, and stuff like that."

"It's four-twenty-five a month for a shared room, and they get one big meal every day about four o'clock. That's what I'm cleaning up from right now.

"They pass a drug test to get in and get tested regularly. Right now, we're at about twenty, but we've had as many as thirty. It goes up and down. Last week we kicked two people out for bad tests. That's hard to do. But fortunately, most of our guys stay clean and sober."

Kenny entered with his backpack over his shoulder. "Like this one here," said Roger.

"One what?" asked Kenny.

Taking his hands out of the sink, Roger snapped a wet finger, shuffled his feet, and sang, *"One for the money, two for the show, three to get ready, and ..."* He put up his hand for Kenny to slap. "One who's gonna make it, that's what."

Jonah and Kenny bid Roger goodbye and went down to the street. In the van, Kenny asked, "So what are we doing again?"

"Mad River Beach. Perch fishing and campfire with Jim. He's bringing extra gear for us. We just gotta stop and buy licenses."

"Works for me."

At the license counter, they were shocked at the twelve-dollar price for one day. "Man, we better catch a lot of fish," said Kenny.

Back on the road, Kenny asked Jonah about his program. "Going good. Did my fifth step with Manny a week ago, telling him all my deep, dark secrets. Fuckin' hard. But totally worth it. How about you?"

"Yeah, I did mine." Kenny wiped his brow comically. "Jerry'd given me like five pages of questions for my fourth-step inventory. 'How have I been selfish? Self-centered? Dishonest?'"

Jonah laughed. "I think Manny used the same one with me: 'Why do I hold onto resentments?' 'What lies do I tell myself?'"

"What kind of marriage did your parents have?" added Kenny. "How old were you when you first masturbated?"

Jonah laughed so hard he almost missed the Arcata exit. "Sounds like you got the advanced version."

"That shit is hard," said Kenny. "But it seems to work. And I don't really have a choice. I know what's waiting for me out there if I don't stay clean. I still get tempted. Almost relapsed a few weeks ago."

"Yeah, me too."

"This disease is a motherfucker," Kenny said. "Fuckin' Terminator."

"You knew David, right?" Jonah asked. "I mean, you know him?"

"Met him a few times. Heard he relapsed."

"Yep. Sucks."

They drove an old pot-holed road through the flat bottomland west of Arcata, passing green pastures, gray barns, and brightly painted farmhouses. Then they glimpsed the Mad River, wide and full as it approached the sea.

"They say it's gonna be a good year for the salmon," said Kenny.

From the parking lot, they walked with their gear through the dunes until Jonah found the landmark that Jim mentioned—a giant stump wedged into the sand above the high-water line. They dug a pit and gathered driftwood for the fire. As the sun touched the horizon, Jonah saw Bill and Jim approaching.

When Kenny saw them, he demanded, "What the fuck is this, man?!"

"It's time you and him made it up. That's why Jim and I arranged this."

"Who the fuck gave you the right." Kenny grabbed his backpack and walked away down the beach.

Jonah followed him. "C'mon, man, at least give it a chance."

•   •   •

Bill recognized Kenny and felt a surge of joy. His son must have set this up with Jim and Jonah. Good for you, Kenny—he thought. But then he saw Kenny stalking away, yelling.

"Wait here," said Jim, then he jogged toward Jonah and Kenny. Through the roar of the surf, Bill could hear, "Not ready … toxic parent." Bill's heart froze as he realized this meeting was not Kenny's idea and that his son did not want to reconnect with him. He turned and walked toward the parking lot.

Then Jonah came running up beside him. "Hold on, Bill."

"Look," said Bill. "I know you and Jim meant well. But it's obvious he's not ready."

"Don't give up yet," Jonah pleaded. "Kenny needs you, Bill. He needs his father."

"He seems to be doin' okay without me, staying sober, working. Got friends like you looking out for him."

Jonah shook his head. "No. He needs you, Bill. He needs you to clear out whatever's in the way of you being his dad."

Bill remembered what Jonah had told him about his own father being a drunk and dying in a car accident. In a flash, he realized something that had been staring him in the face for months: he and Jonah were on two sides of the same family tragedy. Bill lost Kenny to drugs when his son was about the same age as Jonah was when he lost his father. Bill looked toward Kenny and Jim. They were sitting down, and Jim was lighting the fire. He patted Jonah on the back. "Okay. I'll give it a try."

Kenny stood as Bill approached the fire, and Bill let his tears come. As they embraced, Bill felt his son's chest heaving with his. He put his hands on the back of Kenny's head and caressed him like he was a little boy.

"I'm sorry, Kenny."

"Me too, Dad."

They sat down around the fire, both still crying. Bill breathed deeply to steady himself and looked from Kenny to the other two men, who were also holding back tears.

For a few moments, no one said anything. Finally, Bill broke the silence. "The McDevitt brothers are still racing that '69 Charger."

"The Orange Monster," Kenny said with disgust. "Man, that project ruined my whole summer. And you never let me drive it."

Bill couldn't tell if his son was teasing or angry. "You were fourteen," he said, sounding edgier than he'd intended.

"You could have at least taken me out to the mill parking lot on a Sunday to drive it."

Bill shrugged and looked at the fire. Then Jim said, "Was there anything you liked about that project, Kenny?"

Kenny threw a twig in the fire and smirked. "All right, Mr. Counselor. Since you asked, yeah. Me and the McDevitts got stoned together out behind their garage while our dads drank beer and watched sports in the house."

Bill chuckled.

"What's so funny?" demanded Kenny.

"We knew what you were doing. We just figured that if we gave you shit for it, you'd go somewhere else, maybe get into real trouble."

Now Kenny laughed. "What else did you know about my secret life in teenage wasteland?"

"More than I wanted to," said Bill, and they all laughed.

Jim had brought food, cooking gear, and water. They grilled hot dogs and roasted marshmallows while the new crescent moon brightened above the horizon. Bill looked at his son across the flames. In Al-Anon, they counseled "detachment with love." But Bill hadn't figured out how to do that. Instead, he'd built a wall around his love for Kenny. That seemed like the only way he could cope. But tonight, the wall had come down, and Bill's love for Kenny felt as fresh and strong and joyous as the day Kenny was born.

Kenny, Jonah, and Jim were trading stories about their recovery when Kenny mentioned that he'd nearly relapsed a few weeks ago. "It was like I was high before I'd even used. Five minutes earlier, I was feeling solid and confident in my recovery. Then— 'BAM!' I was back in DP looking to score."

•   •   •

"What led up to it?" Bill asked.

Kenny did not want to admit to his father that their painful phone conversation had triggered his cravings for meth. "Tough to say. "Tough to say." Kenny shook his head and moved back from the fire, which blazed up with a log that Jim tossed on. "Might just have been that things were going so good."

Jim interjected: "Yeah, I know what you mean. My sponsor said the other day that when things get good for an addict, that's when we really gotta pile on the meetings and the step work." Jim ran the edge of his hand down the midline of his scalp. "It's like our minds are these eight-lane superhighways, and they only take us to one damn exit, the road to hell. To stay sober, we got to cut a new path right across that highway, and that's fucking tough."

"The three of us"—he pointed at Jonah, Kenny, and himself— we've all made this little itty-bitty start. It's like we pulled over to the shoulder, opened the car door, and put our foot out. But that traffic is speeding by, ready to suck us back in a heartbeat."

"Damn, Shakespeare. Way to work the metaphor," said Jonah with a grin.

"Meta-what?" asked Jim, then he chuckled, "Just kidding. I went to community college. May go back and get my master's in addiction studies."

"You're already way ahead of the class," said Kenny.

"Think they give extra credit to an Indian who gets sober? You know we got it in our genes."

"Definitely," said Kenny. "And I'll probably get some extra cred for my Irish heritage, right Dad?"

Bill ignored this and asked Kenny, "Are you sure it wasn't just after we talked that you almost had that relapse? I know I was pretty torn up after that—first time I talk to you in almost a year, and we get in a fight."

Kenny looked at Bill and let out a long sigh. "You got me, Dad. That is what happened." In the silence, Kenny listened to the fire crackling and the surf breaking over his shoulder. No one said anything for a while—the silence felt strangely comfortable.

Through the fire, Kenny could see Bill looking at him. He saw love and fear and hope in his father's eyes. "I'm sorry, Dad," he said, choking up. "I'm so sorry. I can't imagine how you and Mom felt. And Denise and Aaron." Kenny saw his dad get up and walk over to him. He stood and they hugged. "I love you, Dad."

"I love you, son. And I'm sorry, too. I know I wasn't the best dad in the world."

Kenny let go and held Bill at arm's length. "You did the best you could, Dad. I'm an addict. Who knows why or how it happened, but that's just what I am. You could've been the best dad ever, and I still would've done what I done."

They sat back down next to each other on the same side of the fire.

"Ain't that a nice moon," said Jim.

•   •   •

The four men silently watched the moon dissolve into the line of fog. Then Jim asked, "Anyone want more marshmallows."

"Damn straight," said Kenny.

"Yep," added Jonah.

"Just one more," said Bill.

As Bill poised his marshmallow above the coals, Kenny said, "I remember when you first taught me how to do this."

"Out at the lake?"

"Yeah. Those were some good times."

"I remember you got a job at the boathouse that one summer. You were what, thirteen? Fourteen?"

"Thirteen. That was the summer I started smoking weed."

Bill ignored that and said, "As I recall, you did good at that job. Didn't you even learn how to tune up an outboard motor?"

"Yeah," Kenny said with pride. "My supervisor taught me."

"You ever think about going to auto mechanic school at CR?" asked Bill. "After three or four semesters, you could get your ASE certification, probably start at twenty bucks an hour."

Kenny scowled. "Listen, Dad. I don't know what I'm going to do for a career, but it's not going to be wrenching or logging or working in a mill or selling firearms or any of the other jobs you think I should do. I spent too many years as a kid feeling bad about myself because I couldn't live up to your expectations."

"Okay, okay," said Jim. "Take a couple breaths, Kenny. Your dad didn't mean no harm. He's just looking out for you, in his way."

Bill felt sad yet grateful for Kenny's reaction. His son pointed to an insight that had been taking shape for Bill—the realization that he felt compelled to interfere in his kids' lives because he thought that's what a good parent did. But advising and interfering was a misguided strategy, he'd realized, to manage his fear and powerlessness over what might happen to them.

Yet, when Bill spoke, he cringed at how defensive he sounded. "Well, excuse me for being interested in what you do for a living. You just keep working graveyard at the gas station." Bill wanted to stab himself with his marshmallow stick.

Before Kenny could respond, Jonah said, "You know, my mom does that same thing. Last time I saw her, she had a whole career track worked out for me, something involving shiny shoes and a tie. Pissed me off. But once I calmed down, I could see where she was coming from." Jonah looked at Kenny. "And I think your dad has the same interest. He just wants you to be financially secure and okay. Isn't that right, Bill?"

Grateful to Jonah, Bill said, "Yes, that's right." Then he said to Kenny, "I'm sorry, son. I get what you're saying. You've got to—you get to—make your own choices."

Kenny still seemed roiled, but he was calm enough to say, "Okay, Dad. Thanks for that."

●   ●   ●

Kenny regretted eating so many marshmallows. On top of the emotional swings, the sugar made him more jittery. "You got another hot dog?" he asked Jim. Jim nodded and handed Kenny a skewer and a dog. As Kenny positioned it over some coals, the silence around the fire grew uncomfortable until finally Jim started telling what sounded like a joke.

"You guys hear about the Yurok, the Hoopa, and the Karuk council leaders who got together with the farmers upstream on the Klamath and finally agreed on how to share the water?"

"No," said Jonah.

"Neither did I," said Jim, chuckling.

"I don't get it," said Kenny.

"It's an inside joke," explained Bill. "Supposed to be funny because it will never happen in real life."

"Don't give up your day job," Kenny told Jim.

"What day job? I only work for fun with this old-timer here." He pointed to Bill.

"You got a strange idea of fun, partner," said Jonah. "It took me half a bottle of 'profen to recover from that beating I took with you guys, taking down that yard redwood."

As Jim and Jonah bantered, Kenny's thoughts went back to his one logging job, working for his dad and his dad's friend Petey. He'd only lasted a few hours before his dad made him so angry, he walked off the job. Kenny had written about that moment in his fourth-step inventory. And when he'd told Jerry about it, his sponsor looked at him with a depth of feeling that almost scared Kenny.

Jerry had explained that the incident—when a log fell from the yarder cable and almost killed Kenny—reminded Jerry of how his own father had treated him. "He was always getting angry, telling me I wasn't doing things right around the house and the yard," Jerry said.

"I resented him like the devil. But when I finally stayed sober long enough to do my own inventory, like you're doing now, I understood how much he cared about me. That was the best way he knew how to show it, by trying to toughen me up and get me ready for the world."

Kenny looked at Bill and felt himself wrestling between resentment and compassion. He knew Jerry was right. And Jonah, too. Bill gave Kenny the advice he thought would help him because he cared about him. But it still pissed him off.

·   ·   ·

A half-hour later, they packed up and headed to their cars. In the parking lot, Bill asked Kenny if he could drive him home. Kenny said yes with a smile.

On the way to the rooming house, they talked haltingly about Kenny's recovery and his plans. "My sponsor says not to make any big decisions for the first year. I figure I'll keep working at the Texaco, take on more shifts over the summer. And this fall, I plan to take at least one course at CR."

"They've got a great woodshop and construction program over there," said Bill. "Plumbing, electrical, carpentry, they teach it all."

"I was thinking about music theory," said Kenny. "Or maybe art history."

Bill mentally scrolled through options for a supportive response. "Oh, okay. Yeah. Whatever you want."

Glancing at Kenny, Bill saw his son's Cheshire Cat grin. "Just messing with you, Dad. I'll take something more practical." Bill enjoyed the sound of Kenny's laughter blending with his. It had been a long time.

Chapter 33

On his first morning in Mexico, Bill lay awake, listening to Angela breathe. The house and the streets outside were quiet. He wished he'd brought a paperback.

When he heard activity in the kitchen, he got up. And after using the bathroom, he met Angela's father, Rico, drinking coffee and reading a newspaper at the kitchen table. "Buenos Dias," he said warmly.

"Buenos Dias." Bill smiled and searched his brain for a Spanish phrase that would fit the occasion. He had nothing, but Rico gestured to the coffee pot. Bill nodded. "Descafeinado, por favor," and Rico made him a cup of instant Nescafé.

They sat and drank coffee, exchanging awkward smiles. Then, all at once, the rest of the family came into the kitchen. Angela greeted Bill with a kiss, causing the nieces to giggle raucously. For the next thirty minutes, the kitchen buzzed with cooking and eating, smartphone-gazing and chatting. Bill couldn't understand much, but he enjoyed the atmosphere.

After everyone else had left, Angela gestured toward the bedroom with a smile.

An hour later, they emerged onto the quiet street in front of the Garcias' home. They soon reached a busy main boulevard where six lanes of cars, buses, and trucks hurtled by, and the sidewalk was crowded with people walking briskly. Bill felt disoriented. Angela held his hand as they crossed on the green light.

After walking a few blocks, they were in an elegant and quiet commercial neighborhood. Bill saw the charm and beauty that Angela had spoken: brightly painted buildings from the 1920s and 30s, wide sidewalks shaded by jacaranda and ash trees, and people strolling or sitting at cafés.

They sat at a sidewalk café, and after ordering, Angela asked him, "What do you think of Mexico City so far?"

"Well, it's different from any place I've ever been, that's for sure." He looked around. "It seems to change from block to block. This part here is really nice." He looked up at the trees. "Bet these jacarandas are pretty when they flower."

"Oh, yes." Angela beamed. "I wish you could stay a couple more weeks to see them in bloom."

Bill grinned shyly. "And I wish you could come back in time to see the rhodies bloom in Eureka. They're almost as beautiful as you."

Angela smiled and reached for his hand. "Thank you, Guillermo. I wish I could come back for the rhodies, too. But mostly I wish I could come back for you."

Bill caressed her hand, and they kept their eyes locked. Then Angela said, "Now that you're here, there's so much I want to show you: La Alameda, El Centro, el Palacio de Bellas Artes, el Museo de Antropologia, the floating gardens of Xochimilco, maybe the pyramids. It's too bad we've only got five days. I could keep you busy for a month."

"Floating gardens?"

"Oh, yes. The floating gardens are ..." Angela stopped. "You know what? I won't tell you anything about them. And don't look them up online. We'll just go. I want you to be surprised."

•　•　•

From his window seat on the Greyhound bus, Jonah watched the woods, rivers and mountains roll by. South of Garberville, the deciduous trees were starting to shed their wintry gray and green up. Farther south, the oaks and bay laurels danced in the wind, already outfitted with spring foliage.

Despite the beauty, Jonah was anxious. After losing his job with David, he'd called dozens of contractors. Those who answered their phones said they were full up. He'd called Bill to ask about more tree jobs, but Bill had nothing that he and Jim couldn't handle. He'd applied at stores, restaurants, and coffee shops, but the Humboldt County economy was still on life support two years into the recession.

He'd tightened his budget and worked off his March rent. But to buy food and other essentials, like this bus ticket, he was depleting his savings.

He'd already decided to postpone his trip north and focus on building a stable life in the Humboldt Bay Area. But Manny and Karen's deadline was coming fast, and Jonah didn't want to live outdoors again after four months sleeping in a watertight cabin and taking showers regularly.

He was also worried about what lay ahead in San José, his mother's judgments and Django's mood swings.

Jonah had learned some new methods—tools, they called them in AA—to manage his anxiety. So, as the bus approached San Francisco, he repeated the Serenity Prayer to himself, substituting "Power of Love" for "God" and "Mom and Django" for "Things I cannot change."

Jonah emerged from the bus station onto Market Street and spotted his mother's white Camry. He got in and leaned across to hug her.

On the drive to San José, she told him that Django had started a job with a fencing company. "We know his boss from church. They're busy, thank God. I guess people can still afford fences."

She gave Jonah a meaningful look, and added, "The best thing is the boss knows how to handle your brother's mood swings."

When they arrived home, Jonah noticed a new redwood fence bordering the yard. "Wow, nice fence."

"Yes, I finally replaced that wreck that your father built," she said. "Got a good deal from your brother's company."

She made them tea, and just as they sat at the kitchen table, Django bounded in. "Big bro!" he shouted, clasping Jonah. "How's it going up in Eh-oo-REH-kah?" When Jonah just looked puzzled, Django explained he was learning Spanish on the job. "I told them where you lived, and that's how they pronounce it."

As their mom made dinner, Django beckoned Jonah to follow him outside. "Come check out the fence we built."

Seeing the fence up close, Jonah admired its fine details and elegant design. With great enthusiasm, Django described the entire building process, from staking out the lines to sanding the curved top rails that floated between posts.

"Remember that fence we built with Dad?" he asked Jonah.

"How could I forget?"

"We had to tear down the last of it before putting this up."

"I'm surprised it lasted that long," said Jonah.

"Remember how he insisted we use rocks around the posts, no concrete?"

"And that made it impossible to get the posts plumb. It was fun, though, working with Dad, I mean."

"Yeah. Dad knew how to make work fun."

Jonah was about to bring up their father's death when he heard their mother call them to dinner.

In the morning, Jonah went for a run. Then he showered and joined his mom in the kitchen for breakfast. Django was still in bed. "I'll wake him at eight-thirty if he's not up." Jonah could see she was becoming anxious. "Service is at nine-thirty, and I like to get there early."

After breakfast, Jonah was cleaning the kitchen when he heard his mother down the hall, "But Sweetie, it's almost time for church." Django mumbled something that Jonah couldn't make out.

She came into the kitchen looking bereft. "He's not getting up. He's crashed after playing video games all night again. This still happens every couple weeks."

Jonah went to Django's door and cracked it open. "Hey, bro. Are you getting up for the church service?"

"Nah, man," Django mumbled. "I can't make it."

"It sounds like Mom is counting on you to go with her."

"You go," he said without emotion.

Wearing one of Django's dress shirts, Jonah walked with his mother from the parking lot to the entrance of a modern beige building with a large white cross on its roof.

In the sanctuary, a band was warming up and the pews were almost full. Old people smiled down at children, teen girls in dresses chatted gayly, and boys wearing neckties exchanged words while holding their arms crossed. The congregation's diversity struck Jonah—more black, brown, and Asian faces than he was used to seeing in Humboldt County.

As his mother led Jonah to a seat, he stepped carefully by an elderly white couple. After they sat, she introduced him. "This is my son, Jonah."

The man held Jonah's hand for a couple of seconds. "It's good to see you here, Jonah. We've been praying for you." In shock, Jonah realized his mother must have asked them to pray for him. Had she asked everyone in the church?

The band began a song, and Jonah stood with everyone else. He kept quiet at first, but as he grasped the meaning of the lyrics, he joined in.

"Draw the circle wide, draw it wider still, no one stands alone, standing side by side, draw the circle wide."

Scriptures were read, more songs were sung, and spirits were rising—but Jonah felt at first unsettled and then distressed by the heavy Christian dogma, Almighty this and Satan that. He considered leaving, but he knew that would mortify his mother.

The pastor took the pulpit, and a hush fell over the pews. Jonah gripped the front edge of his bench and imagined walking on a beach in Humboldt County. "How can we take Jesus's teachings to live more as he lived?" the pastor began. He paused and swept his gaze across the sanctuary. "In Mark 12, He is asked, 'Of all the commandments, which is the most important?'"

Mark 12, Jonah thought. Hadn't Manny mentioned that verse?

"He said the most important was to love God with all your heart and soul, all your mind and strength. And then He went on to say the second most important commandment was to 'Love your neighbor as yourself.'" Jonah relaxed slightly and looked up at the pastor.

"He did not say, love your neighbor 'as you love yourself,' but 'as yourself.' Do you see the difference?"

"As yourself means there's no difference between people. I am you, and you are me." Now, the pastor came down from the pulpit and stood between the pews.

"Words like that have been used in love songs, some that we wouldn't consider very Godly. But when we look at our children or spouse or our parents or our boyfriend or girlfriend, I think we feel what those songwriters are talking about. There's a sense of union, of oneness. When my child or my grandchild is threatened, I am threatened. When my wife or my mother are celebrating, I am celebrating."

Jonah glanced at his mother, and she smiled briefly in return before looking back at the pastor.

"Jesus tells us that we must extend that sense of oneness to our neighbors." The pastor placed his hands together and was quiet for a second. "And Jesus was a nomad, right? So, everyone was his neighbor." The pastor paused again to let that sink in. "Jesus' message is to treat everyone like a neighbor and every neighbor as ourselves."

Wrapping up his sermon, the pastor said, "Now, please stand if you're able to join me in the Servant Song." Jonah and his mother stood.

"Will you let me be your servant, Let me be as Christ to you. Pray that I may have the grace to let you be my servant, too."

Swept up in the spirit, Jonah sang heartily.

"We are pilgrims on a journey, we are travelers on the road. We are here to help each other, walk the mile and bear the load.

"I will hold the Christ-light for you, in the nighttime of your fear. I will hold my hand out to you; speak the peace you long to hear.

"I will weep when you are weeping, when you laugh, I'll laugh with you. I will share your joy and sorrow till we've seen this journey through."

Jonah had taken his mother's hand, and as the song concluded, he drew her into a hug. "I'm sorry, Mom," he cried. "I'm sorry I killed Dad."

His mother pulled away, grasped Jonah's forearms, and looked at him intently. "Oh, Jonah." Her voice quivered. "Jonah, Jonah, Jonah. You did not kill your father. Your father got blind drunk and killed himself, and he nearly killed your little brother." She held his gaze a moment longer, then hugged him tightly.

Jonah felt a hand patting his back. He looked around and saw it was the old man, his eyes misty, nodding with approval. He looked back at his mother, still holding his arm, her eyes moist.

This was the power of love, Jonah thought, enormously relieved that he'd finally shared his secret shame with his mother. He was elated by the sense of oneness that the singing and the sermon evoked for him, and he felt humbly bemused over playing the reluctant prodigal for a church full of devout Christians.

•   •   •

The trip to Xochimilco began with a six-block walk to the metro station and Angela's instructions on how to pronounce the name of the place. "The 'X' is pronounced like an 'S.'"

"So-chee-MIL-koh," he said.

"Perfecto!" Bill savored her approval.

At the metro, they waited a few minutes on the platform before a train swept in. Squeezing on with scores of others, they grasped the same metal pole. Bill tightened his grip as the train moved out. "You doing okay?" Angela asked him.

"Just fine, my love." He reached his free hand to take hers.

Despite the crowds and chaos, Mexico City was growing on Bill. In the evenings, he'd walked with Angela and her family through plazas and parks filled with families and friends who so obviously enjoyed being together.

At the anthropological museum, Bill was astonished by the tools and artwork of Mexico's indigenous tribes—and the pyramids and temples the Aztecs and Mayans had designed to track the solar system and built to last for centuries.

Before Bill had met Angela, he'd gotten to know Mexican men on logging jobs, but he'd never asked much about the places they came from. He'd assumed they were all from rural villages, leaving behind a burro and a dusty cornfield along with the families they supported with their American paychecks. Over a few days in Mexico City, Bill had learned that Mexico was much more diverse and complex than he'd thought.

With Angela translating, her parents had told him how their parents migrated from farming communities in nearby Puebla and Michoacán to afford their children the chance to go to college. Rico and Fernanda had worked and saved for years until they could open their own pharmacy. And yet, even with their busy careers, they kept strong ties to the states their parents came from. "Yo soy Michoacano," Rico had said to Bill when they sat around the dining table after a meal. Bill had understood the words—and the pride.

Taller than anyone on the subway car, Bill could see many other passengers. His eyes rested on a young man about Kenny's age who tapped his phone screen. The man looked up and saw Bill looking at him, and before Bill could look away, he smiled warmly, and Bill responded with a big grin.

"What are you smiling at?" Angela asked.

"Just a young guy who smiled at me," he said.

"You're such a softie." Angela nestled her shoulder into his chest.

"That's me."

After getting off at the Xochimilco station, they hailed a cab and Angela told the driver which embarcadero to go to.

At the dock, several dozen flat-bottomed boats were moored so closely that their gunwales rubbed and squeaked as they rode the ripples. Each had a papier-mâché archway that announced its name in bright colors: "Fernanda" "Linda Veronica" "Diosa del Amor."

Several men approached Angela and Bill, saying, "Half day cruise, twenty dollar." "Gira de tres horas, seiscientos pesos para dos." Angela ignored them.

"First, we have to decide whether we want our own trajinera or a colectivo boat that we share with others."

"What do you think?"

"A colectivo. Cheaper, plus it's more fun to be in a group."

Bill nodded in agreement, and Angela chose the trajinera named Diosa del Amor. "It means Goddess of Love, so it's perfect for us." Bill held her hand and followed her under the archway to sit in a chair that faced a long table. They exchanged greetings with the family opposite —a young mother and father with three small children.

Soon the seats were filled, and the strong-armed remero—who never smiled, Bill had noticed—used a long pole to push the boat away from the dock and into a colorful floating traffic jam. Bill became alarmed by how close the other trajineras came. But he relaxed when another boat glanced off theirs with no damage.

Across the table, a boy about four and his two older sisters took turns glancing shyly at Bill. When he played peek-a-boo with the boy—sliding his palm up and down in front of his eyes—the child became so excited that his parents, with good nature, told him to calm down.

Angela talked with the parents, and Bill could make out a few words. He heard the dad say "güero"—WHERE-oh—which Bill knew meant "white person." Then Angela nodded toward Bill. "Es mi güero viejo."

Bill saw the parents try to contain their mirth and avoid looking at Bill, but the children became drunk with laughter.

"What did I miss?"

After Angela calmed her laughter, she said, "Okay, Bill. You know what güero means. And viejo means old—like you'll be in another ten years or so."

"Yeah, right." He enjoyed her embarrassment. "Go on."

"Pues, viejo also means, like, 'old man,' you know, he's my old man, my lover."

"Oh, I get it—so you said, 'He's my old white man,' or something like that."

Angela began laughing again, as did the parents and the three kids, who'd watched their exchange as if it were a delicate negotiation. Bill looked at the family, nodded to Angela and deadpanned, "Es mi vieja Mexicana." And then they all laughed so hysterically it infected the other passengers, and even the stern-faced remero grinned.

They ate lunch served from a floating restaurant. When a mariachi band latched onto the side of the boat, the children stood up and danced.

They stopped at a nursery and bought some plants for Angela's parents. Bill was impressed to learn the nursery was built on a chinampa, one of the floating gardens that had enabled the Aztecs to feed their growing population.

On the metro ride home, Bill was grateful they found seats since he knew it would be a long ride. But as he put his arm around Angela's shoulders, he saw that she'd crossed her arms tightly around her chest and was staring at the floor. "What's up, mi amor?" he asked. "You look kind of down."

She looked up at him, then back at the subway floor. "It was those kids, Bill."

When she didn't continue, he asked, "The kids?"

She took his hand and leaned into him. "When I was in my twenties, I got pregnant ... and had an abortion." She looked up at his face. "Abortions are illegal in Mexico, so I had to see someone who wasn't a doctor. And something went wrong." She looked back at the floor. "I bled a lot. Then I was okay, but I became ... I couldn't have children after that."

She was silent for a moment. "And I couldn't talk about it to anyone because I'd get in trouble. Not even my parents. They still don't know."

Bill felt a wave of compassion for Angela. He put both arms around her and hugged her tight. He thought back to their first conversations on the phone, when he'd told her about his kids, and she'd mentioned her nieces and nephews. He wondered then what her own story was—why hadn't she, who loved her sisters' children so abundantly and grew up in Mexico's Catholic family-centered culture, had her own kids. He'd never brought up the topic, assuming that—given their ages—having kids was off the table.

"So, I'll never have my own kids," she said, with deep sadness.

Was she regretting the past, Bill wondered—a family she wanted to have but never did? Did she think Bill might have expected to have children with her?

"I have all the kids I'm ever going to have, plus my grandson," he said gently. "Maybe there will be another grandkid or two or three with Kenny or Denise someday." He put his hand on her face. "And you've got those two nephews and your three nieces. So, let's spoil all those kids as well as we can for as long as we can."

She folded herself under his shoulder. "That sounds really good, mi viejo."

•   •   •

Jonah and his mother went to a Starbucks after the service. When they were settled with their drinks, she said, "Give me your hand Jonah." She gripped his hand hard. "I can't believe ... I mean, I'm so glad you told me you blamed yourself for your father's death."

Her gaze was so intense that Jonah looked away. Studying the baristas, confident and efficient in their steamy domain, he wondered how Django had held down a job in one of these places.

Then he looked back at her. "You told me to hide the keys. Instead, I went out to get stoned with a friend. When I came back, he was dead. It was my fault, Mom. It was."

Now she began to cry. "Jonah, your father, by that point, was killing himself with booze. He'd lost his license for drunk driving—yet he still got in that car, drunk off his butt, with your little brother, and drove into a telephone pole." She looked away now. "It was a mercy he didn't kill Django or anyone else."

They were quiet for a minute. Then his mother said, "I know how you feel, though, blaming yourself. I used to blame myself—sometimes, I still do—for not leaving him sooner. I mean, what was I thinking? If I'd gotten out a year or two before he died, you and your brother wouldn't have had to experience the worst of your father." She looked out at the passing cars. "Who knows, it might have shocked him into getting sober."

"We'll never know." Jonah realized with a shock that they shared the same trauma and guilt. He saw it in her eyes and knew she saw it in his. Jonah felt his tears falling.

Chapter 34

In the back room of the Arcata Environmental Center, an open window let in the warm spring air and the thumping bass from the bar next door. Jonah listened to a woman with long gray hair and gold-rimmed glasses. "Fish and Game should be doing more to rein them in. They can cite the growers for their illegal dams and animal traps. And if they're harming an endangered or threatened species, they can arrest them and charge them with felonies."

"The game wardens indeed have law enforcement powers, but these growers aren't deer poachers or people fishing without a license," responded Doyle, the bear-shaped man who ran the center. "They're armed criminals with the networks to see a Fish and Game truck coming miles away. It's outlaw country out there, and a few wardens with handguns can't do much about that."

Jonah thought about the grower he'd worked for last summer. The man was friendly but tough, overseeing the trim crew carefully. Sometimes he wore a handgun in a holster strapped to his thigh, and Jonah assumed he had more firepower available to defend his assets and cash from thieves.

"It's not just up in the hills," said a fit-looking man about sixty. "There are a half-dozen grows in my neighborhood here in Arcata. I can't open my windows without smelling that crap. And they're running fans and gigawatt grow lights all the time, wasting energy like a goddamned fleet of V8 Hummers."

Jonah had been surprised over the winter to hear from Bill and then Doyle—people on opposite sides of the timber controversies—about the environmental damage being done by weed farms. Since then, he'd heard and read more about growers draining creeks in the fall when salmon needed water to spawn. Their lethal traps were killing fishers and other mammals. And their pesticides were polluting creeks and doing untold damage to harmless forest creatures.

As a former patron and worker in that industry, Jonah felt some responsibility for helping solve this mess. So, when Doyle had invited him to this meeting, he agreed to attend.

"What about a public awareness campaign?" asked a woman who wore blue medical scrubs under her jacket. "Or some certification for responsible growers? We pay more for organic produce because it has less environmental impacts than conventional produce. Maybe we can get the cannabis dispensaries and recreational consumers to demand something like that from their suppliers."

Jonah knew there were still mom-and-pop growers out there—people who donated to the local schools and spent their earnings in the community. Maybe the woman's idea about organic certification would appeal to them. But a Gold Rush mentality had changed the pot industry dramatically. Established growers and newcomers were racing to expand and get their profits before the inevitable legalization of recreational pot in California.

Jonah was struck by how complicated the situation was and how elusive good strategies were. The movement's direct-action methods would not work, he knew. For one thing, the young activists who'd used their bodies to blockade logging roads would never mount that kind of effort against the growers who supplied their beloved cannabis—and employed them in the harvest season. And even if some were willing, they'd be risking a lot more than a night in jail if they tried locking themselves to a grower's gate.

•   •   •

Bill met Kenny at the door of his rooming house. "You ready?"

"Ready as I'll ever be."

It was only four blocks to the police station, but Bill had to battle his instincts the whole way to hold back from giving Kenny advice. He used a method that he'd heard about in Al-Anon: visualizing his mouth shut with duct tape.

At the thick glass window, the dispatcher asked them to wait. Then Deputy Steve came out with a Eureka Police officer. They all shook hands, and Kenny followed the two cops back into the station.

A half-hour later, Kenny came out looking calmer than when he went in. "How'd it go?" Bill asked, holding the street door for him.

"Good, I think. I just told them everything I knew. What I saw happen in DP, the first time those girls came around and what I heard the guys talking about doing to them."

"Did you mention running into that scumbag later?"

"I did," said Kenny. "They asked if I'd testify in court against him and his partner. I said I would. They also wanted to know anything that could help find them."

They stopped talking as they crossed busy Fifth Street. When they were on other side, Bill asked, "So, did you have any info about where they might be?"

"I told them a few places where they might be hiding out, you know, down in the gulches and along parts of the waterfront. But they seemed to know all those spots."

"Sure hope they catch 'em."

"Me too. Don't want them on the loose to fuck with some other women...or trying to jump me if they catch me alone somewhere."

Bill shuddered. Then Kenny added, "I doubt that'll happen, though because I'm not ever going to go hanging around with people who think a needle is the stairway to heaven."

Both men chuckled at this, and Bill patted Kenny on the shoulder. "No, son, you're not." Then he reached into his pocket and pulled out the heart he'd made for Kenny from curly old-growth redwood. He wanted to say something appropriate for the occasion, but all he came up with was, "Here. I made you this."

It was about three inches around, elegantly shaped, sanded smooth, and polished to a rich finish. Kenny held it in his hand before meeting Bill's eyes. The two men hugged and cried together while cars and trucks rumbled by.

•   •   •

Jonah was breathing hard when he reached the grassy meadow at the edge of Arcata's community forest. The park was churning with activity: children running and laughing on the playground, teenagers playing kickball on the field, college students throwing frisbees, and travelers lounging on blankets.

Jonah crossed the meadow and took the main trail uphill. The forest was cool and quiet enough to hear crows talking in the canopy. He followed another path down a ravine, crossed the creek on a plank bridge, and switch-backed up the other side until he hit the main road.

When he approached his old campsite, Jonah stopped and listened to make sure no one was nearby. The road was clear, so he stepped carefully up the bank, placing his feet between the ferns. Soon, he came to the spot where he expected to see the familiar brown tarp. It was gone.

Owl had told Jonah that Buzzy got arrested with Alder for vandalizing the logging equipment. Then, either the cops must have found and cleared out the campsite, or maybe Buzzy had sent a friend to get his gear.

Jonah felt sad looking at the vacant campsite. This had been his home where he'd spent evenings with Buzzy and friends, sheltered from the rain, getting high, talking about how to save Mother Earth.

He walked farther up the ravine to Bella, the orange mark still on her trunk. He leaned against her and stroked her shaggy bark with both hands. After a moment, he stepped back and looked up at her canopy. Stepping farther back, he examined her little family. He'd long ago noticed that they'd all sprouted from the same old-growth stump—but now he could also see how removing Bella and two of her sisters would give the rest of the brood more sunlight and room to grow.

Jonah had accepted the logic behind the plan that called for logging Bella and two of her sisters. But it still didn't feel good. Jonah loved this huge tree, and even if the same organism continued living, the Bella he knew would be gone.

Jonah put his palms together in front of his chest and looked again up into Bella's canopy as it swayed majestically with the wind. "Bella, may you always live here in the forest," he improvised. "And may you also become something new after you're cut down. May you become sustainable shelter for the two-leggeds."

When he arrived back at the meadow, he found a patch of mostly dry grass. He lay down, put his hands behind his head, and tried to empty his mind, to let the drifting clouds fill him up. He focused on sounds, too—children laughing, wind brushing the trees, birds singing.

Jonah thought about the people who'd filled his life with camaraderie and connection in the last few months: Karen and Manny, Bill and Kenny, Jim. David. Monica. Beth. He thought about other AA members: stern Biker Bob and funny, sentimental Jerry Watson. He thought about a newcomer, a man a little older than himself who'd arrived at his first meeting wearing a tan canvas jacket covered in fish scales. He stood awkwardly with his coffee, so Jonah approached and stuck out his hand. They only chatted for a minute, but Jonah could tell that the man felt a little more comfortable after they'd talked.

Connecting with people authentically was new for Jonah—a dimension of life he'd longed for but could not articulate, even to himself, before joining the program. And he longed for more— even more of what he'd felt in church with his mother.

Those Christians had strange beliefs, but they'd anointed his mother and brother with acceptance and kindness. And Jonah's experience on that one Sunday opened his heart, led him to confess his patricidal guilt to his mother, and to receive her complete forgiveness. The confessions they'd shared after had opened the door to a more honest and intimate relationship than he'd thought possible with his mother.

Chapter 35

The church parking lot was full, so Manny parked on the street. "You run on ahead," he said. "Let the committee know you're here."

Jonah trotted by a dozen people. Some recognized him and wished him good luck. He held his breath as he passed the smokers, then walked into the church hall and nearly puked with nervousness. The monthly Humboldt County Intergroup meeting had drawn more than a hundred people—AA and Al-Anon members—and he would soon have to stand in front of them all and speak.

"There he is!" said Jerry Watson, chair of the organizing committee. They hugged, and Jerry asked, "You ready?"

"Ready as I'll ever be."

Jonah sat in the front row. The meeting started with the usual greetings and readings, but Jonah was too nervous to pay attention. So, he was surprised when Jerry announced from the podium, "And now it's my pleasure to introduce our first speaker for tonight, Jonah."

At the podium, Jonah felt a fresh wave of nausea as he took in all the faces focused on him. Fortunately, his first words were easy. "Hi, everyone. I'm Jonah, an alcoholic/addict." As the group responded, Jonah focused on his notes. "Breathe," he'd written at the top.

He described his childhood, growing up with an alcoholic father and a mother intent on controlling that alcoholic. "There were good times, too." Jonah's face and neck became warm as he talked about Saturday morning nature trips with his father and brother. "But I always knew that more fighting and more drama was coming. By the time I was fourteen, I was desperate to escape from my family and how I felt. I found that escape in alcohol and marijuana."

He recalled squandering opportunities for friendship, learning, and meaningful work. "And I didn't see any of that at the time. I just thought I was having fun.

"Worst of all, I was only half alive. I knew something big was missing from my life, but I didn't know what. And I couldn't imagine living without getting high."

Jonah had learned to leave his political views at the door in AA, so he said only that it was his desire to be closer to nature that led him to Humboldt County. "I thought Mother Earth would fix me. But the geographic cure didn't work because I brought myself with me." He heard wry chuckles of recognition.

He described his impromptu flight from Arcata—"Where everyone I knew used and drank"—his ride with Bill, as well as his near-miraculous encounter with Manny who introduced him to AA and, with his wife Karen, gave him a safe, sober place to live.

Jonah devoted his final minutes to the phases of his recovery: conceiving of a higher power, coping with heartbreak, doing a personal inventory, and revealing his secrets to his sponsor. And he talked about the continuing journey he saw ahead. "I'm just beginning to understand the impact my father's drinking had on me as a kid."

He wrapped up by saying, "Thank you all. Thank you, Humboldt AA, for allowing me to find what I was always looking for." The applause lasted until Jonah resumed his seat.

After several other speakers, the meeting ended. Jonah received hugs and blessings, and then the crowd thinned out, and the committee members started putting away chairs. Jonah stood with Bill, Jim, Manny, and Kenny.

"Really nice job, Jonah," said Bill.

"Yeah, except you forgot to mention me," smirked Jim.

"Or me," said Kenny.

Jonah searched his mind for a snappy retort, but he found only gratitude. "You've all been really important to me. We've been through a lot together." He was quiet for a moment. "Especially losing Beth. And David."

"Beth is dearly missed, and I pray David comes back soon," said Manny. "But I celebrate the recovery I see right here"—he spread his arms wide—"especially you and Kenny and Jim." Manny looked at each man, his eyes glistening. "You're all miracles, and you give me hope."

Jim asked, "So everybody on for Tuesday night?"

"I don't think I'm going to make it," said Manny, shaking his head. "Too old."

"Dude, my uncle is older than you." Jim patted Manny on the shoulder. "Besides, you don't have to do all four rounds. Just do one or two, then sit by the fire and watch the stars come out."

"Maybe another time."

"Okay, brother," Jim replied. "The rest of you are still on, right?"

"Can't weasel out now," said Bill. Jonah and Kenny agreed.

"Wear your bathing trunks under your pants 'cause there's no place to change," Jim said. "Bring a couple towels and water. Lots of water."

•　•　•

Bill tried to nap, but he was too keyed up. Looking at his phone, he saw it was only five-thirty. The sun wouldn't set for two hours—and that's when the event would start, according to Jim.

"You can do it," Angela had said when they Skyped earlier. "Just sleep in the next morning."

"You're right, mi Cielo," he replied, omitting the observation that for him, sleeping in meant getting up at six instead of five-fifteen. "I'll be okay." Before they hung up, he promised her a full report.

He ate a light dinner, then headed out for his walk. Since returning from Mexico City, Bill had upped his daily average mileage to five. He took a path through some woods down into Cooper Gulch. Emerging from the trees, he saw kids swooping and gliding at the skateboard park. He walked over to watch with his cap pulled down against the low sun.

Among the boys and young men, Bill noticed a girl waiting her turn to skate down the steep side of a bowl. She was about to launch when a boy tried to cut her off. She muscled past him, swooped to the bottom, then up the other side, leaped into the air, grabbed her board, turned, and glided back down. Bill clapped for her. No one seemed to notice, and he didn't care.

Bill walked west and took a path up to 11th Street. When he reached J Street, he decided to walk to the waterfront, then follow the bay back through Old Town.

When he got to the Old Town boardwalk, he leaned on the railing to rest and watch some kids rowing a pencil-thin racing shell. They moved gracefully—but their red, sweaty faces showed how hard they were working to skim across the water.

When Bill got home, he checked his smartphone: 5.7 miles. And he still felt strong. He grabbed his pack, got in his truck, and headed for Jonah's place.

"How the hell are you?" he asked, shaking Jonah's hand.

"Great, Bill. You?"

"Just terrific," said Bill. "How's school?"

"It's fucking awesome. Not like working for David—or you—but really good."

As Bill knew, Jonah had accepted his mother's financial help, stopped looking for a job, and enrolled in College of the Redwoods' construction program. Bill had helped Jonah convince the head teacher—a friend of Bill's since junior high—to let him start mid-semester based on prior experience.

"Whatcha learning?"

"Rough carpentry mostly. Foundations, floor joists, framing. Some of it's stuff I learned with David, but it's mostly new."

"Good for you. By the time you graduate, this recession will be over, and you'll get a good job."

Then Jonah stammered, "Listen, man. There's something I've got to tell you."

"I'm listening."

"It's pretty embarrassing." Jonah took a deep breath and continued. "Before I met you, I went out with a couple other guys to try to stop a logging job. We thought it was old growth, but we were wrong. And we arrived too late 'cause the logging was all done."

As Jonah's silence lingered, Bill's gut tensed. "Okay. Go on."

"Well, once we learned the trees were all down, this one friend—well, not a friend exactly—he cut the hydraulic lines on one of the machines. I tried to stop him, but I was too late. Then they—well, I'm pretty sure it was you, Bill, and maybe Eric. You guys arrived, and someone chased us down the hill."

They had exited the highway and were driving through the farm country between Arcata and the ocean. Both men were silent for a moment. Then Bill started laughing. After a second, Jonah joined in.

"Don't that beat all," Bill said. "Good thing Eric didn't catch you. You might not have lived to tell me this story."

"I guess you're right. Anyway, it was stupid, and I've felt bad about it since then."

Bill nodded. "Yeah, I get that." Then he added, "I think we ought to keep this between you and me. If Eric finds out, even now, after he's gotten to know you a bit, it could get ugly."

"Understood."

After another moment, Bill said, "I appreciate you telling me. Let's talk it over more another time."

"Sounds good."

Bill slowed the truck and pulled into the driveway of a two-story farmhouse and parked. In the corner of the backyard, he saw a blazing fire next to a low dome covered with tarps. As he and Jonah approached, Bill recognized Jackie. They hugged, then Bill introduced Jonah.

"I've known Jackie since I was a kid in Blue Lake. He's Jim's uncle and the leader of this whole shindig." Then he asked Jackie, "What exactly are we going to do?"

"It's a traditional purification ritual. I could say more but that would take away the mystery." He winked. "Don't worry, though. I'll make sure you know what you need to know when the time comes."

Jim and Kenny arrived, and Bill hugged his son and his friend. Then other men arrived, and soon, about fifteen men stood around bantering while Jackie and his assistants worked at the lodge. Kenny stood with Bill, watching the massive fire.

"You ever done anything like this before?" Kenny asked.

"Me? Are you kidding? Never."

"Me neither," said Kenny, pointing at the rocks that glowed orange under a pile of flaming logs. "Those rocks look damned hot."

"So, how was Mexico City?" asked Jim.

"It was really different, especially for a country boy like me. But nice. And fun. And Angela's parents were great."

"How's Angela?" asked Jonah.

Bill thought for a second before replying. "She's doing good. But she really wants to come back. Misses her sisters and her niece and nephews, and me too—she says."

Jim grinned at Kenny and Jonah. "Hard to believe, huh?" Then looking at Bill, he said, "Of course, she misses you, dude."

"So, what are you going to do?" asked Kenny.

"Going to ask her to marry me." Bill looked shyly at his son and his two friends. "It may sound crazy, but I really love her and can't imagine not, you know, having her in my life. I don't know how we'll sort everything out with immigration, but from what I read online, it can be done."

"Good for you, Bill!" Jonah said.

"She sounds like a great gal," said Jim. "I look forward to meeting her."

"You're assuming she's going to say yes—and that I can get her back here."

"Of course, she'll say yes," said Jim brightly. "Don't know about the other part."

"If that doesn't work, do you think you'd move down there?" asked Kenny.

"No. It's so busy and crowded. And I'd have to learn to habla Español a lot better." Bill paused and looked at his son. "Plus, I'd miss you too much." Kenny smiled and looked down.

There was a buzz of activity around the lodge. "Time to get ready," Jim said. He led them to a big poly tarp on the ground. They stripped to their swim trunks, then everyone formed a circle around the fire. Bill draped his towel over his shoulders and shivered. He felt vulnerable, like it was his first day of gym class in junior high, lining up for the mandatory showers.

Jackie got everyone's attention. "To enter the lodge, you get down on your knees. Bow your head and say a prayer of your choice. Then move to your left, staying clear of the hole in the middle. Crawl all the way around and fill up the space. Should be room for all of us to sit in one row.

"We'll do four rounds," he continued, "and the heat will get stronger with each round. You can leave between rounds—or you can leave at any time, just by saying a special phrase: 'Open the door!'"

When everyone stopped laughing, Jackie looked at Bill. "Bill, would you come up and stand behind me at the front of the line?" Then he pointed to Jim, "And Jim, you stand behind Bill." Bill was tempted to joke about getting senior privileges, but something told him this wasn't the time.

Jackie went to the lodge door, kneeled, bowed, and whispered some words into the earth that Bill couldn't make out. When it was Bill's turn, he said simply, "Thank you."

In the dark interior, Bill crawled behind Jackie. When Jackie stopped, Bill sat beside him on his towel, holding his shins awkwardly with his forearms. Then, when everyone but the two fire tenders had come inside, Jackie called for the first rock.

Through the low door came a pitchfork bearing a glowing volcanic rock. Jim used a pair of antlers to slip it off the pitchfork and into the center pit. Bill heard men murmur the word "grandfather," and he realized they were talking about the rock.

After six more hot rocks had been placed, the door was closed, and Bill began to sweat. Jackie asked everyone to state how they intended to purify themselves this night.

"I want to become the good man I know is inside me," said the first to speak. "I want to let go of the asshole that shows up when I get scared or hurt so I can be a better father to my kids and a better husband to my wife." Bill understood.

Some men mentioned God, and some used Indian phrases Bill didn't understand. But they all seemed to be in the same boat, pulling hard to steer their lives away from addictions and bad habits and toward recovery and love.

When it was Bill's turn, he said, "I'm just so grateful to be here with my son and my good friends."

"We've all lived on the dark side," said Jackie. "We've all done things we're ashamed of, things we wish we could do over."

"That's right!" "Amen!"

"Let this lodge tonight be a turning point for you, pointing you toward the path you need to walk to align your will and your lives with the Great Spirit." He threw a ladle of water on the rocks, then another. Then he started a song, and others joined in.

Bill felt overwhelmed by the heat. He turned to look for a gap in the tarp where he might find fresh air. Then Jim leaned over to him. "Put your face down to the ground if you have trouble breathing." Bill adjusted his posture to kneel and pushed his face into the grass. He inhaled cool air and felt instant relief.

When the door was opened and the night air streamed in, Bill considered leaving. But before he knew it, the seventh rock was in, and the door was closed for the second round.

Jackie asked Jim to open the round in his own way. Bill heard Jim suck in a sharp breath. He thought about what it must be like for these two friends—the uncle, a legendary sobriety champion, and his newly sober nephew—to share this healing experience.

As Jim led a Christian prayer that was popular in AA, Bill looked at Kenny on the other side of the lodge. His son was healthy, sober, and making good choices. And they were here together.

Then Jim began the song Amazing Grace. As Bill joined for the chorus, he felt he really had been blind but now could see, had been lost but now was found.

Bill made it through the second round. And the third. As Jackie had warned, the last round was the most intense, with the heat of seven fresh rocks piled on top of those already in the pit. But Bill stuck it out, plunging his face into the grass when he couldn't take the heat and steam.

When the door opened, Jackie gestured for Bill to leave before him. As he crawled through the opening, one of Jackie's assistants held out a hand and helped Bill steady himself as he stood up. Bill nodded his thanks and stepped away. Jim came out next, then two other men, and then Jonah and Kenny.

It was Kenny who said, "Look at that moon, Dad!"

The clouds had parted to reveal the full moon in the western sky. Bill said a silent "Thank you." Kenny stood on Bill's right and put his strong, sweaty arm over his shoulders. Then Jonah came close on his left, and Bill grasped him by the shoulder. He looked from one to the other, their faces shining with sweat and joy in the moonlight.

Jim brought over a water hose. "You ready to get doused?" he asked them.

"Bring it!" shouted Kenny. "Yes!" said Jonah. Jim sprayed them, and it felt to Bill like bathing in a waterfall.

Jim handed the hose to another man who sprayed him. Then, looking at Bill standing with Kenny and Jonah, holding onto each other, he joked, "You guys should get a room."

"And you should get your ass over here," said Bill, gesturing for his friend to join them.

Jim came up to Bill. They put their heads together, and Jim kissed Bill on the cheek.

Then they opened their little circle to face the moon.

Gratitude

Creating this novel took more than ten years and the support of dozens of people.

I first wrote the story of Jonah and Bill in 2013 as a forty-minute film. I shared it with Carla Baku, Ben Bettenhausen, Paul DeMark, Will Guilfoyle, Ian Strope, and a few others, receiving encouragement and suggestions—and a pointed question from Ben, a video producer: *how did I expect to produce a film with no money and little experience?* His question helped me decide to write a novel instead.

From 2014 through 2019, John Daniel, Aaron Gottschalk, Tim Graham, Jonathan Kraker Tom Leskiw, Sharon Levy, Dave Mohrmann, Ricardo Page, Fhyre Phoenix, Janine Volkmar, Nancy Wheeler, and members of the Now Novel online writers' community read and responded to my early chapters.

In 2020, the pandemic wrote me a prescription to sit at my desk long enough to finish my first draft—which I turned over to Mary Carroll Moore (her latest, *A Woman's Guide to Search and Rescue*). After rewriting with Mary's guidance, I sent the revised draft to friends who'd agreed to be beta readers. Aaron Clegg, Elizabeth Conner (my ex-wife), Mike Hess, Ellen Ingraham, Patrick Oliver, Michael Richter, Birgit Semsrott (my wife), and Rondal Snodgrass gave me robust kudos and smart suggestions, with Aaron, Birgit, and Elizabeth providing detailed page-by-page notes.

My next draft, completed in spring 2022, was much improved but needed a professional critique. Rachel Eve Moulton (her latest, *The Insatiable Volt Sisters*) guided me in developing and refining most of what you've just read.

With a finished manuscript, I still needed an agent or publisher. Alyssa Jarrett (her latest, *Love Apptually*) and Cam

Torrens (his latest, *Scorched*) helped me write the query letter, summary, and other text that gained the team's attention at Black Rose Writing.

I was also greatly helped by people I interviewed, officially and casually, to create the worlds of Bill, Jonah, and Kenny. I consulted online sources extensively, most notably the archives of North Coast Journal, where reporting by Heidi Walters was especially helpful. And the empathic, embedded journalism of Humboldt native Linda Stansberry inspired me to render our county faithfully, with its rich culture and traumatic conflicts, its rugged beauty and rough edges.

My own memories, notes, and stories (published and unpublished) as a writer and recovering addict in Humboldt County provided the bulk of my background material. From my journalist's perspective, two men on opposite sides of the timber controversies (both deceased) taught me a lot and modeled courtesy and respect for their ideological opponents: Tim McKay of the Northcoast Environmental Center and Bill Boak of Boak Logging.

Two other men, also deceased, deserve special mention. Maury Scanlon and Eugene Wilson embodied the selfless compassion and playful wisdom that helped me and many other addicts and alcoholics make our recovery stick.

I also wish to thank the members of Humboldt County recovery fellowships who drove me to meetings, listened to my atheistic objections to the "higher power" notion, applauded when I achieved thirty, sixty or ninety days, and told me to "keep coming back" after my relapses. Without you, my life would be a mere shadow, and this book would not exist.

About the Author

Jim Hight had written for dozens of newspapers and magazines in Los Angeles and Boston before he moved to rural Humboldt County, California, in 1996 as the staff writer for North Coast Journal. The city boy was intrigued and fascinated by his new subjects—loggers and forest defenders, fishermen and scientists, ranchers and dairy farmers, small-town mayors and tribal leaders, county sheriffs and cannabis growers. His writing delighted readers, and he won an environmental and agricultural reporting award from the California Newspaper Publishers Association.

But Hight had moved to cannabis-friendly Humboldt at the worst time for his recovery from marijuana addiction—and the best time for this novel, as things would turn out.

Note from Jim Hight

If you enjoyed *Moon Over Humboldt*, please leave a review online—anywhere you are able. Even if it's just a sentence or two. It would make all the difference and would be very much appreciated.

Thanks!
Jim Hight